Holy Flame Trilogy, Book 1:
The Call To Duty

C.J. Peterson

Texas Sisters Press, LLC

ISBN: 978-1-952041-21-1

Published by Texas Sisters Press, LLC. Lufkin, TX U.S.A.

The characters and events in this book are fictitious. Any similarity to real persons, living or dead, is coincidental and not intended by the author.

Texas Sisters Press, LLC.
2020

Second Edition

This book is dedicated to my loving husband and dear family who love and support me. You all mean more to me than you will ever know. Thank you! I love you!

It is also, dedicated to those brave men and women of the military, along with the firefighters/paramedics and the police officers who work night and day to keep us safe. Thank you!

A portion of the proceeds of this series will go to Airborne Angel Cadets of Texas – a non-profit group of hardworking volunteers who send care packages to our soldiers overseas. You can find them at: http://www.airborneangelcadets.com

To learn more about C.J. Peterson, you can find her online at: http://cjpetersonwrites.com/

'While the stories are fiction, the journey is real!'

C.J. Peterson
<u>**Summary**</u>

Courageous. Strong. Brave. Fearless. Heroic. Valiant. These synonyms are often used to describe firefighters/paramedics, police officers, and military personnel. They face danger and lay their lives on the line each time they leave for work. But what is going on in their lives? What are their struggles?

Casey Carter is a newbie to the firefighting family of Engine Company 15. Not only does she have to prove herself as a probationary firefighter, but she also has to battle misconceptions of females within her newly chosen profession. As situations begin to arise, can she count on the firefighter brotherhood to have her back? Will she be able to pass the tests placed before her, or are there aspects of her life she was not even aware existed?

Often there are two realms in play. There is the physical realm – what is right before you; and there is the spiritual realm – what is unseen. Each can directly affect you, whether you believe they are there or not. Can Casey overcome them? Can she keep them in balance when she is not exactly sure what she is fighting? Can a group of men help her to see what cannot be readily seen, to hear what cannot be readily heard, and to be able to overcome what she never knew existed? Will they be able to show Casey her true Call To Duty?

Ephesians 6:12-13: [12] For we wrestle not against flesh and blood, but against principalities, against powers, against the rulers of the darkness of this world, against spiritual wickedness in high places. [13] Wherefore take unto you the whole armour of God, that ye may be able to withstand in the evil day, and having done all, to stand.

Table of Contents

Summary 5

Table of Contents 6

Chapter 1: Four Alarm Night 7

Chapter 2: The Lake 41

Chapter 3: Late Night Run 51

Chapter 4: Skeletons 73

Chapter 5: Welcome Back 93

Chapter 6: Real Life Visual Picture 103

Chapter 7: A Lesson in Trust 127

Chapter 8: Fallen Brothers 151

Chapter 9: Jumpin' Jack Carter............................161

Chapter 10: Let the Games Begin..........................181

Chapter 11: A Shift Change..................................211

Chapter 12: Jack, Signing-Off 233

Chapter 13: Picking Up the Pieces........................249

Chapter 14: Blindsided 261

Chapter 15: Overload..299

Chapter 16: Reality 309

Chapter 17: Duel Mindset....................................333

Chapter 1

Four Alarm Night

Casey Carter and her partner, Tommy McCormick, entered the room where Brennon Hanson and Jack Callan used the ceiling hook to pull down the plaster from overhead. The fire started in the chimney before heading into the attic, so the firefighters had to make sure the insulation was not smoldering or it could ignite, causing another fire.

"What are you two doing in here?" Callan asked. He jammed the pole into the ceiling. His six-foot-three frame allowed him to reach the higher points on scene, which is the reason LT sent him and the six-foot-four Hanson to the upstairs rooms after the firefighters got the fire under control.

"LT said to clear this room and we're done," Tommy said. The group took their masks off when the fire was extinguished. While they kept them handy, they were not needed. "Carter, we'll hit the walls together so you can see what I'm looking for."

"Sounds good." Casey agreed. Casey was new to Engine Company Fifteen so she felt she had a lot to prove. While she was not the first woman in the company, she was the oldest female and a rookie at thirty-five, so she was grateful for the opportunity. Initially, Chief was hesitant to hire her but she won him over during the interview with her strength of character, persistence, and fortitude.

Hearing her voice, Brennon Hanson spun around toward her. He admired her beauty and brains. However, since they were on the same shift, she was not going to be an option for him. That didn't stop him from admiring her assets though.

"Hanson!" Jack shouted as the ceiling buckled where Brennon pulled on it.

Casey looked up to see a portion of the ceiling cascade above Tommy's head. She shoved Tommy out of the way. As they hit the ground, a chunk of sheetrock dragged down her shoulder. She groaned, knowing it would probably leave a mark.

From where he was standing, all LT could see was ash and dust shooting threw the attic into the air. "What happened?" LT demanded from where he stood by the engines.

When the sheetrock, plaster, and insulation rained down on them, it made the air thick and hard to breathe. Tommy coughed up some of the ash as he reached for his radio. "Ceiling collapsed."

"Everyone okay?"

Tommy saw movement from the other three through the rubble. He wiped the soot from his eyes as he said, "We're mobile."

"I'm sending Barnes and Katz up there to check things out."

Callan waved to clear the air in front of his face as he grabbed his radio. He climbed over the debris to Brennon and saw him moving around. "No need. We're fine, LT," Callan said into the radio. Then he turned his head away so he would not be heard over the open channel and growled at Brennon, "You'd better pray everyone is okay."

"It was an accident. It happens," Brennon said in his defense as a nervous anger flashed across his face and adrenaline coursed through his body.

"You weren't paying attention," Jack snapped, much to Casey and Tommy's surprise. Jack tended to deal with his feelings through humor. "Someone's going to get hurt!"

Brennon snatched his pole from the rubble. He pawed his way through the debris, leaving the threesome stunned that he would abandon them without finishing his job.

"You two okay?" Jack asked Casey and Tommy in concern. When everything came down, he saw the main part of the ceiling fall toward them.

Casey helped Tommy off the ground. "Yes."

"Katz will have to look at my shoulder later, but otherwise, I'm okay." Tommy brushed himself off before he searched for his pole. "Thanks, Carter."

Casey pulled his pole from the debris to her right and handed it to him. "No problem." Inside, she smiled proudly. Tommy hadn't handed out too many compliments over the past month while working with him.

After ten more minutes in the room, the three of them headed outside. "Clear," Jack said to LT, handing Casey his hook to put away. "Hanson was out of line."

"What happened?"

"He caused the accident and then left us in there," Jack glared at Brennon, who watched him from where he was rolling one of the drained attack lines.

"Talk to me," LT said. He enjoyed his job, but not the conflicts that arose. While the job often put him under a lot of duress, he would not have it any other way. He loved the camaraderie with the other firefighters. The adrenaline rush he got during the fires would be hard to replace.

As Casey rolled the hose, she glanced around at the men of her crew. While they were cleaning up the scene, she saw them sharing stories. There was no doubt in her mind that some were embellished as they used their hands to tell the story. That's when she saw him. Brennon's actions disgusted her. You never leave a man behind. She shook her head when she saw Vinnie Barnes slap him on his shoulder and handed him an ice-cold water bottle.

After she and Will Weston heaved the hose onto the back of the engine, Will wiped the sweat off his face with a grin, and said, "This job has its share of excitement."

Casey sighed. "It does."

"What happened?"

"Hanson wasn't paying attention and the ceiling came down on us."

"That's not the first time. He's going to get someone hurt." Will scowled at Brennon. "Come on, let's get the rest of this hose up so we can get back to the station."

In the trucks and on the way back to the firehouse, Casey felt the wound pulse underneath her turnout gear. The anxiety replaced the adrenaline that churned within her as she hoped her clothing would cover the wound so no one would see it. Her biggest concern was that the guys she had come to admire over the last month would think she might not be able to handle the job.

Once back at the station, Will Weston hung his turnout gear in his locker and sighed. "Now *that* was a good one!"

The overpowering smell of smoke mixed with sweat clung to every firefighter. It took Casey a couple of weeks to get used to the stench it generated without gagging, but she handled it in stride now. She had to convince herself that it was normal until she became immune to it.

The soiled trucks sat in the engine bays coated with a layer of soot and ash. They would have to wait until after lunch for a cleaning. After a hearty workout from a structure fire, sustenance was the first thing on everyone's mind.

"Yeah, when I woke up this morning, I thought to myself, *Self, it looks like a great day for a fire*," Tony Patrone, who everyone called 'LT', said as he hung his coat on the hook of his doorless cabinet. Not only was he the lieutenant, but he was also the supervisor of 'A' shift, Casey's shift.

"You okay, McCormick?" Vinnie Barnes rested his big Italian hand on Tommy's shoulder. "I heard you took a nasty blow from that slab of ceiling."

"Yeah. It wouldn't have happened had *Hanson* been paying attention instead of drooling over Carter." Tommy playfully smacked Casey's arm before looking down the line toward Hanson. "Watch this."

Hanson's cabinet was down the wall near the other end, away from Casey and Tommy. "Who said I was looking at her anyway?" Hanson's voice was sharp as his face reddened. "There was a fire. Why would I pay attention to some chick when I could get burned?"

"Some *chick*?" Casey raised an eyebrow, leaning back, glaring at Hanson.

His face flushed as he shook his head. "I give."

Casey sighed, as she saw several firefighters light cigarettes. "Didn't you inhale enough smoke?"

"It's how we relax." Rob Katz defended himself.

"Besides, I get enough grief from my wife, don't be a nag too," Marty Nelson grumbled.

"Just saying." She stuffed her gloves in the sleeve of her jacket. "You guys have families to think about."

"At least we know she cares," Scott Kendall pointed out.

"Well, wouldn't go that far," Casey said in jest. "I am just saying that our jobs are rough enough. Our families have enough on their minds without worrying about you purposely putting yourself in line for lung cancer."

"I know." Marty agreed. "My wife keeps telling me the same thing, but what can I say? It's a vice."

"Might wanna try something a little healthier like lifting weights." Jesse McFadden nudged him.

"No, one muscle man around here is more than enough." Marty shook his head. Then he added, "Braun but no brain, such a shame."

"The lack of brains is awarded to Hanson for this fire," Jesse shot.

"That's enough!" Brennon growled.

"If you can't take the heat, get out of the kitchen," LT said as he walked towards the office. Then he added to Brennon, "I want to see you in Chief's office when you're done."

"About time you got busted," Will snapped. "You're going hurt someone one of these days."

"He already did." Tommy shot him a dirty look. Hanson knew by the look on his face not to comment. Tommy didn't show emotion much, so when he did people paid attention.

"On that note, I need to get a shower," Casey said to Tommy. She left her turnout pants and boots downstairs in the cabinet with the rest of her gear before she slipped her shoes on to head upstairs.

Hanson shook his head. "Carter."

"What?"

"That's not a good thing to say."

"Why not? We just came in from a fire. We are *all* going to take a shower…at least I would *hope* we would all take a shower. If you don't, I'm not cooking for you tonight."

Tommy was tying his. "It's your night, *probie*!" he said sharply. "You don't have a choice. You still have another month of cooking detail."

She smirked. "Yeah, well, doesn't mean I have to make it good." When she went through the doors that led upstairs, she heard them laughing and smiled to herself.

As she went up the stairs, she couldn't help but admire the old structure the station was encased in. Built to last in the nineteen forties, the red brick building had survived a lot of history. The old woodwork and molding around the doors and windows were found throughout the station, along with its many historical artifacts that still adorned the structure. Some of these included the first fire bell made when the house opened in nineteen forty-three, an antique hose reel, and within showcases there were some of the old turnout gear, helmets, and equipment that was used by her predecessors of Engine Company Fifteen. Also, among the historic artifacts was the fire pole from the sleeping quarters. Casey remarked at how exciting it was to see one in the station. Though it was well polished and in good condition, they did not use it. The guys stated that it was there for show and for safety purposes, they did not recommend its use.

Generations of firefighters had gone up through its ranks over the course of the building's seventy-year history, and Casey took pride in being one of them. Tucked in a suburb of Denver, Colorado, its structure had been through many storms, fires, and changes of technology through the lineage. And, even though each generation took pride and cared for the station as best it could, the musty smell of the firehouse still told its old age.

Casey stopped by the sleeping area before she went to the bathroom to clean up. In the sleeping areas, each person had their own room of sorts due to the partitions that cordoned each one off from the others. Since they were on multiple calls through the night, those assigned to the ambulance for the twenty-four-hour shift were in another room adjacent to the main sleeping area. There were four ambulance crewmembers each night, and the remaining crewmembers on the shift filled the engine crews.

Down the hall from the sleeping area were the bathrooms. The men's bathroom was across the hall from a single bathroom that Casey used when she was on shift. It had a shower stall, a sink, mirror, and a toilet. There were two other females on 'B' shift, and one on 'C' shift who used the single bathroom when they were on duty.

Before her shower, she cracked the window open a bit to let out the steam. The smell of spring poured in, counteracting the tang of incinerated wood that permeated the firehouse as the other firefighters ascended the staircase for their showers. The birds had already returned from their southern migration from the winter, serenading the trees to sprout new leaves, propelling the flowers to blossom to their fullest. Casey loved watching the spring flora aggressively grapple its way through the snow, showing the world its tenacity. In addition, when the honeysuckle vine that climbed the station wall commenced its welcome to the season…well, there was no substitution for that efflorescence scent. Spring always gave her a sense of hope. Things were fresh and new, showing the world that while the winter may be desolate and barren, spring was just around the corner, waiting with assurance and promise of marvelous things to come.

After her shower, she dried off, went over to the mirror and wiped the condensation off with the palm of her hand. As she stood there, she touched the new bruises and scrapes that had formed and winced. She knew if she had complained, they might have accused her of being a wimp. On a crew of men in this male-dominated field, she didn't feel comfortable reporting her injury just yet. Working in this environment as a female was tough as it was without adding an injury on the job.

She groaned though, knowing there might be some explaining to do. Sighing, she brushed out her long chestnut-brown hair and then threw it up in a twist with a clip. Then she slipped into a fresh pair of uniform pants, black socks, department-issued t-shirt, and black shoes before shoving her dirty clothes into a bag to take home later. She glanced in the mirror one more time before she headed toward the bedding area to put away her clothes.

By the time she headed toward the dining area to eat lunch, the men from the ambulance crews for the day were already sitting around the table. Benches lined each side of the long wooden table, and a single chair sat on either end. On 'A' shift, the head seats belonged to LT and Katz, the watch commander and second in command of the shift.

Jeff Campo looked up when Casey walked into the kitchen. "Hey, so I hear we're destined to have a horrid dinner."

"Only if someone decides to skip their shower," she clarified, putting her lasagna into the microwave.

Katz leaned back in his seat, his elbows resting on the arms of the chair. "What are you cooking for dinner?"

"Oh, I dunno." She crossed her arms, deep in thought. In reality, she had no idea what she was going to make for dinner. In fun, she decided to keep them guessing.

"That lasagna sure smells good." Johnny Marshall nodded toward the microwave. "Maybe another one of those?"

"Maybe." She placed the garlic bread in the microwave after she pulled out the now fully heated lasagna. While it cooked, she poured the ranch dressing over her salad.

"Seriously, what *is* for dinner?" Callan asked. "Inquiring minds want to know."

After the timer went off from the microwave, she sat down at the corner seat of the table. "You guys don't need to know *everything*." She tore a piece of the bread, glancing at the men around the table. "A girl's gotta have her secrets."

"Come on…please? If you do, maybe we'll take it easy on you during drills," Campo hinted.

"You guys *never* take it easy on me in drills." She rolled her eyes. "It's your duty to make it hard on the rookies."

"Carter, just the person I want to see. The crew is curious as to what's for dinner?" Bryan 'Mac' MacIntyre strolled into the kitchen with his hands in his pockets. Vinnie Barnes came in on his heels.

Snickers came from around the table from the ambulance crews.

"What?" Mac crossed his arms. He did not like being the joke, especially where Casey was concerned. Truth be told, he would run interference with Katz for her because he liked her. He enjoyed having a little pull, especially knowing how Brennon felt about her. He often rubbed Brennon's face in it when she was out of earshot.

"We've already been trying to get it out of her," Johnny pointed out. "She's not budging."

Mac paused for a moment before he placed a hand on the table beside her and asked, "Does the threat of drills make any headway?"

"She says we never take it easy on her during drills anyway." Callan shook his head. "Nice try."

"Well, I *happen* to know drills are the stairs today." Mac leaned down next to Casey so they were eye to eye, resting his elbows on the table. "Wanna give us a clue so we know whether or not to take it easy on you?"

"What if I do?"

"Then...." He gestured for her to go forward.

"Then...*what*?" she pressed, setting her fork down. She was interested to see what arrangement he wanted to propose this time. She and Mac had a mutual give-and-take deal-making relationship. There have been multiple times where he saved her by running interference with Katz from rough drills with his deal-making abilities. Katz often had it in for the rookies and made drills harder on them, but Mac had a unique way of making Katz feel generous when it came to training – if he was *inspired* to do so.

Vinnie chuckled. "She's tough to crack."

"What are you guys doing to my partner now?" Tommy walked in with the remaining crewmembers of 'A' shift. "Need some back up, Casey?"

"Casey?" Brennon raised an eyebrow. "Since when do we go by first names here?"

"She's my partner." He shrugged. "You also took a chunk of that ceiling for me when you shoved me out of the way...didn't you?" He rested his hand on her hurt shoulder.

Heart racing, she asked, "Now, why would you say that?"

"The bruise I see forming right here on the back of your arm. Can I take a look?"

"Ohhh," she groaned, dropping her head onto her hands.

Katz went around behind her. "Let me see. I've already taken a look at McCormick."

She let him pull back her shirtsleeve to look at her shoulder. "Uh, Carter?" He cocked his head to the side, getting a good look at it.

"What?"

"Do you have a tank top in your clothes?"

She turned and looked at him suspiciously. "Yeah...*why*?"

Tommy cringed. "Doesn't that hurt?"

"Some," she reluctantly admitted.

"What's up?" LT came over from the kitchen to take a look. "Um, you are going to have to fill out a medical report on that."

"No, please," she groaned. "It doesn't hurt *that* bad."

"I beg to differ." LT shook his head. "Go get that tank top on so we can see it better."

"Fine," she relented. She knew she could not fight LT. She left the room while everyone else made their lunch or continued to eat.

She quickly changed in the bathroom. While she was in there, she glanced at the injury in the mirror again. She did a double-take, as it had gone from red and a little swollen, to black, blue, and purple in a matter of minutes. She cringed, and then sighed, shaking her head in frustration.

As she walked back out to the kitchen area in her tank top and pants, most of the guys were still eating at the table. Tommy was leaning back on an ice pack and eating his lunch on the couch.

"Wow!" Brendon practically choked on his food. "*That's* a change!"

Vinnie slapped him on the back, shaking his head. "Get a grip, man! Let me give you a piece of advice – try *chewing* your food."

"Come over and sit down, Carter." LT got up from his chair, which was right next to her seat at the end of the table.

Katz brought his EMT bag over and sat it on the counter behind LT. "I just took care of your partner. Now it's your turn."

As she sat down, she longingly glanced at her barely touched lunch. She was sure the lasagna was cold by now, and the salad was probably warm, but she was hungry. She couldn't believe they were making such a fuss over a couple of bruises. She dropped her head into her hands in embarrassment.

"Wow! That ceiling *did* get you, didn't it?" LT said in concern.

"Yeah," she admitted.

"By the way, thanks for looking out for me," Tommy said over his shoulder.

"No problem. I'm sure you would have done the same."

He nodded in agreement. "Any time."

Katz immediately went to work on her shoulder, and then afterward, Casey and Tommy filled-out injury reports to file for worker's compensation. Casey already knew she wasn't going to file the paperwork, though – her shoulder was fine enough to work. Besides, she knew she would have the next forty-eight hours after this shift ended to rest her shoulder. Since they worked twenty-four hours on and forty-eight off, she knew it would be fine by the arrival of her next shift.

After about a half hour of icing her shoulder, Casey got into the cupboards and refrigerator for dinner ideas. Due to their injuries, LT kept both Tommy and Casey from drills for the day. He then sent Tommy, Casey, Mac, Nelson, Vinnie, and Will to the store to get food for dinner. They took one of the engines in case there was a fire call while they were gone. If so, they could just take off from the store.

"Do *I* get to know what's for dinner?" Tommy asked, as he and Casey were walking through the crowded store. He pushed the cart, mainly because he knew this store inside and out. His house was just down the road, and he and his fiancé frequented the aisles at minimum of two to three times per week.

While Casey and Tommy talked, the others were joking around with each other, and picking out other snacks.

"*You* get to pick," Casey said to Tommy.

Surprised, Tommy asked, "You mean you didn't have any plans for dinner?"

"Nope."

"Well then. What are our choices?" He felt a little burst of power not only being able to pick what was for dinner, but also in knowing what was for dinner when no one else did.

"Well, do you want Mexican, Italian, or good old-fashioned American?"

"Are there specific meals with those?"

"Not anything in particular. What do you want?"

"What about…hmmm…what about Italian? You know, to make LT happy," he decided.

"Good idea," she agreed. She thought for a moment before she asked, "What about manicotti stuffed with ricotta cheese that's mixed with parsley, hamburger, mozzarella cheese, parmesan cheese, and minced garlic? We'll also have mushrooms stuffed with breading, spices, and crabmeat sautéed in butter. Then we'll finish it off with freshly made garlic and butter bread. And, of course, a salad with tomatoes, green peppers, and carrots, topped off with an olive oil and vinegar dressing, and sprinkled parmesan cheese."

"I *think* you're going to have several offers for marriage if you cook like that and it's good!" He chuckled when she laughed.

Together, the group went through the aisles for the next thirty minutes, picking out some of the dinner items not yet at the station, along with some extras for homemade snacks to re-stock the snack cupboard. When they returned, the others went to drills, while Casey went to work on dinner.

Despite their best efforts to guess what was for dinner by what Casey put in the cart, they were never even close. Casey enjoyed the game and kept them guessing.

Before heading over to watch the news, Tommy gave her a hand in cutting the vegetables. He said something about feeling lazy if he didn't lend a hand somewhere.

At about five-thirty, as the scent of manicotti, stuffed mushrooms, and bread diffused its way throughout the entire fire hall, Casey dispatched Tommy to let LT know it was a thirty-minute countdown until dinner. She purposely sent him early so the men could clean up the area from their drills and still be able to get another shower before sitting down to eat.

On the way through, there were multiple comments on how delicious dinner smelled. Casey just shot back at how horrible they smelled. They shook their heads, laughing, on their way to the showers. Casey enjoyed the lighthearted way the crew interacted with one another. She often imagined it was similar to how a large family would communicate.

By the time everyone finally made it back to the kitchen, Casey had arranged the table with a place setting for each firefighter. There was a salad in a bowl on top of their dinner plate, along with a glass of ice water, and a chilled glass of milk at each of their seats.

"This looks fancy," Jack remarked, spreading his napkin on his lap.

"Do we get to know what's for dinner yet?" Jesse smirked. The food was out of the oven, but covered. While they were able to get a decent whiff of dinner, Casey kept silent on the actual contents.

"*I* know what's for dinner," Tommy bragged.

"How do *you* rate?" Johnny asked, slightly surprised Tommy was able to get information no one else seemed to be able to get out of her.

He crossed his arms with a smug look. "Partnership has its privileges."

Casey had to smile at that one as she brought over the pan containing the stuffed mushrooms. She set it on the potholders in the middle of the table. "There ya go," she said, lifting the foil off the pan.

"*This* is dinner?" Brennon Hanson asked. "You *do* remember we're meat and potatoes kind of guys. We work up an appetite."

"I do." She nodded with a sly smile. "There is crabmeat in those mushrooms."

"Um, while crab *is* a meat, it's not a *meat*-meat, ya know? We're not...there aren't any vegetarians here, probie." Katz glanced at the mushrooms and then back at her with a slightly agitated.

Casey smiled as she sat down. She was trying not to make eye contact with Tommy, who she heard snickering from across the table.

"What's going on?" LT looked from Casey to Tommy and back again. "While this *does* look good, I, uh, have to agree with Katz and Hanson on this one."

"You guys are too easy!" Casey laughed, getting up from the table.

She grabbed another set of potholders and set them on the table. Then she brought over the sliced, fresh-made garlic bread and uncovered it. There were a couple nods of approval, but LT, Katz, and Hanson still looked for more as they sat there with their arms crossed.

"You *really* want to work hard for drills on your next shift, don't you?" Katz threatened.

Casey smiled as she went back to the oven. She uncovered the manicotti before she brought it over, setting it on the table with a smile. "There, is that better?"

"Much!" Hanson grinned.

"We'll know as soon as we taste it if you have been redeemed, but it looks good," Katz said.

"I've had your food. I approve." LT smiled, pleased, as his eyes grazed over the entire meal now before him with a look of pure delight. He inhaled deeply before reaching for the manicotti. He scooped out a piece, pulling on the cheese that was stringing from the pan. He then replaced the spoon back into the dish, and then picked up his fork. All eyes were on him. A nod of approval was required before the commencement of eating.

He cut a bite, studying it for a moment, before he placed it in his mouth. He savored it, allowing the flavor to meld together. He then sipped the ice-cold milk to clear his palate, before taking a bite of the stuffed mushrooms. Finally, he tested the garlic bread.

Not a muscle moved around the table as they awaited the decision.

"Probie, that is perhaps the most…" he paused a moment while Casey took a breath in anticipation, "The most delightful meal I have ever had. Do not ever tell Carol I said that, or I will deny it to my grave."

Casey smiled, pleased. "Thank you, sir."

"Mac, as our resident clergy, would you like to bless this terrific meal?" LT asked.

"Of course," he said. "Father, we thank you for this wonderful meal before us, and ask you to bless the hands that made it. We also thank you for the safety while we were at the fire with only minor injuries. We ask for your continued safety for us, as well as our other firefighters throughout the city as we go about our regular duties. Thank you, Father, for giving us the strength day in and day out to do our job proficiently. Please bless the remainder of this evening. In Jesus's name we pray…"

"Amen," everyone said in unison.

They looked to LT, who said, "Lady and gentlemen." He gestured toward the meal before them.

With that, voices erupted in various conversations around the table, as almost all of the men talked at once about the fire and the drills, while passing the various portions of the meal around the table. Everyone enjoyed dinner, followed by Casey washing all the dishes for over an hour. Being that she had only been there for a month, she was still the probie, the newbie, the rookie, and therefore she got the jobs no one wanted...for at least another month. She had to cook dinner, do all the dishes, mop the floors, help roll the hose on the fire scenes, and usually had to do most of the clean up after the drills were run every time she was on shift.

While she enjoyed her job, she enjoyed her time off even more. She liked the shifts and the variety in the days. The schedule during the day was different every time, and the guys were great to be around as well.

Just as she finished the dishes, there was an ambulance call, which Callan and Marshall took. Outside of the fire, the day had been a slow one. The ambulance crews were usually gone on a continuous basis throughout the day, alternating each call, but today was an exception with only three or four calls. The fire crews for the day had to wash the trucks down at least once a shift and spray the garage floor to keep it clean, which the men promptly did after lunch before they ran the drills.

Since the trucks were clean, they did not have to worry about washing them for the rest of shift, so they enjoyed a movie and popcorn after Casey finished with the dishes. They headed toward their beds at about eleven o'clock, just as Katz and Campo got an ambulance call.

As she lay in bed, she was once again lulled to sleep by the sound of the guys in the room. She knew each of the men on her crew by their snoring or the breathing of their sleep patterns. She slept in the comfort that these brave men surrounded her and went off to dreamland, fondly thinking about each of the men that she now called 'brother.'

*   *   *

The firefighters were peacefully sleeping or resting, when at about three o'clock in the morning there was a sudden, ear-piercing fire bell for a structure fire that woke them with a start. They snapped to attention before springing into their turnout pants and boots. Then they bolted down the stairs toward their lockers and loaded up with their remaining turnout gear, before jumping into the respective vehicles amongst shouts of orders by LT and Katz.

"Carter and McCormick, I want you two to settle back a bit. I don't want your injuries to get worse," LT yelled back to them after he radioed to dispatch that they were responding.

Tommy objected. "LT, come on, we're both fine. We've rested all day."

LT debated in his head for a few moments, before he asked Casey, "Are you okay too?"

"Yes, sir!" She grinned. She didn't want to hang back on scene. To have a fire on your shift is rare, but when there were two – it was a bonus.

He sighed before he finally relented. "All right. Just be careful. Chief is going to have my head for you two getting hurt in the first place. Let's not do it twice in one shift, okay?"

"Deal!" They both smiled, pleased with his decision. As soon as his head was turned, they quietly gave each other a high-five.

"You're okay, right?" Tommy asked directly into her ear so no one else could hear.

Casey nodded. She didn't want anyone to have any idea what he asked her. Then she pointed to him, and he nodded that he was okay as well.

*   *   *

When they pulled up on scene, the fully engulfed three-story warehouse looked like it had been going for a while. The auto-extended fire scene had flames pouring out from every window, even puncturing the roof. The stench of burning rubber, wood, and metal permeated the atmosphere, making it hard to breathe. As the Incident Commander, LT immediately requested a second alarm.

The firefighters jumped down from the vehicles to lay the supply and attack lines, when they suddenly had to dive to the ground as an explosion rocked various parts of the building. Glass and chunks of brick from around the windows sprayed in every direction as the ground rumbled below their feet. Casey looked up, surprised to see the structure still standing.

LT got on the radio and reported what happened. He also asked for dispatch to send a third alarm while the rest of the squad scrambled to get the supply lines hooked up.

"If you thread that line any slower, we can roast marshmallows on the embers," Brennon sarcastically remarked toward Casey.

"Back off, Hanson!" Tommy snapped. "She's *my* trainee."

Brennon shook his head and walked off, while Tommy and Casey continued to hook up the supply lines amidst the flurry of activity around them. By the time they had all of the hose lines laid out, Vinnie stood by at the truck ready to charge the lines.

"Ready?" Vinnie asked. They nodded, and he opened the lines one-by-one until they were all filled with the much-needed water. They watched the water almost immediately fill the flat hose lines, and felt the nozzle jerk slightly, letting them know they were charged and ready.

As they stood in front of the broiling inferno, Tommy said over his shoulder to Casey, "Let's go, probie. We need to put the wet stuff on the red stuff." Casey felt the thrill and rush of adrenaline as they fearlessly headed into the fiery warehouse.

Another engine company pulled up on scene as the other firefighters attacked the warehouse. They took one look at the warehouse and called for more back up, while LT let out a barrage of orders to the new companies as to which direction to head. Mac and his partner, Marty Nelson, went with Casey and Tommy to the front entrance, while a couple other teams targeted the windows, and others operating the deck guns of the two engine companies attempted to pump water directly onto the roof in hopes of containment.

While Casey had been in fires before, they were nothing of this magnitude. Their little band were the first teams in, and what they walked into Casey would never forget. The fire was streaming down the walls like a waterfall, as well as dancing across the ceiling like a flashover (only there wasn't one.) It was as if someone poured gasoline on the walls and ceiling before they lit it up. There were metal containers, shelves, catwalks, and various other pieces of equipment parts knocked over, hanging off the catwalks or from atop stacks within the warehouse from the explosion. The heat was intense, as if they'd walked into a furnace. Fires were hot, but the heat blasted them as they walked through the doorway, shoving them back a step.

Tommy shook his head in disbelief. "Where do we start?" They were drenched in sweat as soon as they were within ten feet of the building.

Scott Kendall and Jesse McFadden came in shortly after they walked in, hauling their attack lines with them in teams of two. "Whoa!" Scott shook his head, the hair on the back of his neck standing on end. No one else said anything for a moment. They were at a loss as even where to begin. The entire building and its contents were ablaze. It was awe-inspiring yet spine tingling. Even in the heat, Casey got chills as the hair on her neck stood on end.

As she surveyed the scene, her eyes suddenly got wide. "What's that in the back?" She pointed toward the back of the building at a storage tank.

"What's going on? Why aren't you guys working?" LT demanded over the radio.

"Sir, there's…." Nelson shook his head, stunned. As a seasoned veteran, he was sure he had never seen anything like this before. The fact that it was this engulfed yet still standing boggled his mind.

Tommy swore before he said, "LT, be advised there is an above-ground storage tank in here."

At that time, a couple teams from the other departments came in, including the Captain from Engine Seventeen. "LT, I don't think there's anything we can do. Even the brick is on fire. We're going to have to let it go and keep the other buildings in the area from going up. That tank could go at any time and we can't get to it to see what it is. Contact hazmat as well."

Henderson confirmed what LT suspected. He knew his team, and since they weren't attacking it with the fierceness they normally did, he had an idea that the magnitude of the situation was critical, but he was hoping his intuition was wrong. He took pride in his team and their record, and knew this would hurt it, but his main concern was for the members of his squad. "Copy that, Henderson. Bail out. Rest of the teams, redirect to the surrounding buildings. Let's prevent any further damage, but make sure you are out of the collapse zone in case it comes down. We're shifting to defensive attack," LT ordered.

Just as they were about to leave, Casey heard a shout from about ten to fifteen feet away. "Did you hear that?" She asked. Everyone stopped and stared at her, which made her feel awkward. She strained to listen again, hoping she was right. That's when they saw a man on fire, screaming, as he stumbled toward them. Casey stared at what was left of the walking flesh, horrified, knowing the immense pain and agony he was in. "Oh my," was all she could squeak out.

She knew they couldn't open the line on him, as the pressure would push him back, so Casey aimed the hose into the air with light pressure so it came down like rain on him, while a couple of other teams ran over to get him. They were having a hard time directing him, as any touch to his body caused immeasurable pain to the man. Tommy stood behind Casey to keep a hold of the hose.

Casey's heart broke for the man at hearing the screams and seeing the agony on his face. She smelled the stench of his burning flesh and hair, and saw portions of his clothing as they hung, along with parts of his skin. There were sections burnt clear to the bone. There were places where his clothing seared to what skin remained on his body. She almost felt it would have done him better had he burned in the fire. Her stomach wretched as he got closer. The miasma atmosphere that surrounded him reeked with the unmistakable scent of death. It was a ghastly reminder of how fragile, yet strong they were as humans.

"Keep it going!" Henderson yelled over the sounds of the inferno. "LT, we have a casualty coming. He has third degree burns on over twenty-five percent of his body and second degree burns to the remainder." He shouted as the man and the teams came closer to the door, bringing Casey back to the reality of the situation.

The pain and agony coming from him almost brought her to tears. The odor in the warehouse was rancid, drenched with the overpowering smell of the chemicals it contained. As the man stumbled closer, the emanation of the foul air magnified tenfold. Casey fought to contain the vomit that threatened to come up.

When the others got near Casey and Tommy, they turned the hose, hitting the wall and doorway they headed toward to keep the path clear. As soon as they were out, Casey and Tommy shut the hose down and dragged it out the door. Then they ran in with a couple other teams to get the remaining hoses clear of the building, leaving the flaming inferno behind them.

Just as they pulled the last hose out, there were several more explosions that sent all six firefighters, including Casey, at least fifteen feet through the air.

The seconds seemed like forever, as the building expelled the firefighters along with the remaining debris it held within the structure. Everything pummeled them when they landed on the ground with a thud. Casey felt the pain jet through her body, but she didn't think anything was broken. She curled up into a ball for protection.

No one on scene could see or hear anything as the deafening roar and blinding light from the explosion engulfed the entire area. The air was thick with ash as the remains of the building blew out for a moment before it sucked itself back in and went up toward the sky. Then it collapsed flat on the ground, shoving its aftermath toward the injured firefighters, entombing them within the rubble. All Casey could do was cover her head, hoping to prevent any further damage to her body than what had already occurred. The ground shook around her.

Two-by-four chunks of building pounded the ground on top of Casey, making a tent of sorts as it landed in an A-frame shape. She hoped the others had the same luck, as the building, the equipment, along with fragments of the metal canisters, catwalks, and anything else left of the warehouse, bombarded the area.

After what seemed like an eternity, everything finally settled around them. The firefighters from two of the companies clawed their way through the dust and debris to get to their comrades, while the remaining firefighters continued to contain the aftermath of the explosion. Furiously, the two companies tossed the refuse aside in order to clear the way.

"McFadden, Kendall, Carter, McCormick, Mac, Nelson – can anyone respond?" LT's voice appealed, a nervous edge breaking through his earlier command state as his heart raced.

She waited a moment to see if others would respond before she said, "This is Carter. I'm okay…for the most part." She continued to move, so her PASS device wouldn't go off just yet. The ear-piercing scream of her Personal Alert Safety System was definitely not high on her list of things she wanted to hear as her head throbbed from getting thrown. She also wanted to hear what she could over the radio to ensure the others were okay before she set hers off.

"Are you injured?" LT asked.

"I was hit by a couple of chunks, but parts of the structure landed in an A-frame over me. I'm fine. I don't know where the others landed though."

"This is Mac, I'm okay. I heard Carter through the rubble. She's not too far from me."

"Good," LT said, relieved to hear from two of them. "What about the others?"

"This is McCormick. I have a concrete pinning my leg. I can't move."

"This is Nelson. I'm under about fifty tons of rubble, but it's all good. I'll just hang while you guys work for a bit, eh?"

"We're working on it," LT nervously responded.

"This is McFadden. I have a huge chunk pinning the bottom half of me. I'm not going anywhere fast," he groaned.

"Kendall?" LT called out. There was nothing in response. "Kendall, are you there?" LT called out a couple moments later.

You always know it is a possibility, but the idea that one of the men she had grown to admire over the last month might be dead terrified her. Her heart raced, and in a panic she attempted to move the chunks of brick above her in hopes of seeing some sign of the rescue efforts. This only resulted in the rain of more debris. Even though she had her mask on, out of instinct she covered her face when it poured in toward her left.

"Don't do that, Carter!" Mac yelled into the radio while coughing.

"What happened?" LT stopped moving. He pressed his earpiece into his ear to hear better.

Casey's heart skipped a beat. She turned toward the left, and asked, "How close to me are you?" For him to have felt that, he had to have been close.

"What happened?" LT demanded.

"She moved some of the debris, and it came in on me," Mac said, still coughing.

Casey frantically dug through the remnants in the direction she guessed Mac to be by what he had said. After a couple of minutes, her fingers punctured through the rubble. She felt something smooth with her gloved fingers. "Is that you?" She tapped his helmet.

"Yes!" he said, excited and relieved at the same time. He reached up and grabbed her hand, giving it a squeeze.

"Are you two together?" LT asked, trying to figure out what was going on. He stopped, while everyone continued to dig around him to listen.

"We're a couple feet from each other," Mac confirmed.

As they carefully pulled away the debris that separated them, she and Mac could hear the others doing their best to clear the remains of the building in order to locate them.

"You two sit tight. We're coming," LT said, while Casey and Mac pulled away the remaining refuse, allowing them to see each other.

Casey reached down and turned on her flashlight to illuminate her little cavern. She didn't let Mac's hand go, except to replace it with her left hand so she could resume digging with her right.

She and Mac dug for several more minutes until they finally broke the wall away that was between them. "Hey gorgeous!" Mac grinned as Casey's flashlight beam hit his face. There was a two-foot space open between them.

Alarmed, she asked, "Where's your mask?"

"My tank ran out."

Casey let his hand go to take her helmet off. She slid her mask off and gave it to him to put over his face, before replacing her helmet.

"I take it you two are now face-to-face?" LT asked.

Casey groaned. The open channel on the radio was great during an emergency, but not if you wanted to keep a personal conversation private.

"You don't think I'd say that to Nelson, do you?" Mac said, trying to set Casey more at ease.

"You cheating on me again, Mac? That's it! Our relationship's over," Nelson said. Casey could hear the smile in his voice.

"I love that guy," Mac said quietly to her as he set the mask down.

She reached over and put it back on him. "No, keep it near your face. I don't know how much is left."

"So, you come here often?" Mac asked a little louder into the radio.

Casey decided to play along. "Na, it's my first time, but I hear this is one of the most explosive places in the area."

"Yeah, it's the bomb."

"Will you guys quit?" McFadden groaned. "It hurts when I laugh!"

"At least you have some entertainment," Casey said.

"That's me," Tommy shouted, as he reached his hand through the rubble.

"We got one!" The firefighters cheered.

Casey smiled in relief. "Good. He's safe."

"No worries, Casey, they'll get to you soon," Tommy said while they pulled him out. "Ow! Easy! Watch the leg!" he snapped.

"Watch it. He can get grumpy," Casey commented.

"*Get* grumpy?" Campo chuckled. The snaps of the straps from the rescue basket had Casey breathing easier knowing he was safe, even if he was cussing up a storm. "He already *is* grumpy. Unfortunately, I have to take him all the way to the hospital."

The four firefighters pulled him through the rubble to the waiting ambulance.

"I'm glad he's okay," Casey whispered to Mac, hoping with all the extra noise the radio wouldn't pick it up.

"Me too. I wish we would at least *hear* from Kendall."

Just then, they heard over the radio, "We found another one."

"It's Kendall. He's unconscious and his helmet is cracked, but he's alive," a guy from one of the other companies said.

"Good," LT said, with the relief evident in his voice as his crewmembers were now all heard from. "Get him outta there and to the hospital."

"Consider it done."

"Good." Casey said. As she lay there, her head began to swim and she felt dizzy so she closed her eyes.

"No, here," Mac said in his normal voice as he put the mask to Casey's face.

"What's wrong?" LT asked.

"Carter's starting to go on me."

"What do you mean?"

"I'm–I'm fine." Casey pushed his hand away, shaking her head to clear it. She felt like she was going to pass out.

"LT, we don't have any air in here except for her air pack. She never got all the way to the surface, and the way the debris fell, it sealed us in, creating a vacuum." He reached over and manually triggered her alarm, before setting his off.

"Hustle up, boys! They probably don't have much time," LT snapped.

"That's me," Jesse said when they broke through to where he was located. "Please be careful, there's a – ahhhhheeeeee!" he screeched. Mac and Casey looked at each other in wide-eyed surprise, as they listened.

"Sorry, mate," one of the firefighters said with an English accent.

He continued to moan and groan in pain, as they removed him from the rubble that fought to keep a hold of him. Everyone heard him swearing at the other firefighters over the radio as it took them several more minutes before they could break him free. Once released from the rubble, they swiftly got him to an ambulance and on his way to the hospital.

"Hey, how about pulling the rest of us outta here?" Nelson grumbled. "This is getting a little old…fast."

"They'll get to ya soon, hold your horses," Mac said.

"At least *you* have company," he shot back. "I'm here in the middle of nowhere by myself."

"You're not pouting are you, Nelson?" Mac asked. Casey couldn't keep her eyes open anymore so she closed them. Mac reached over and touched her neck. While he checked her pulse, he noticed her shallow breathing. He gently tapped her face to get her to wake up. "Carter? Carter, come on, stay with me."

"What's going on in there?" LT asked.

"Quit asking questions and get us outta here!" Mac snapped. "Carter, come on, open your eyes. Here…." He reached over and put the mask on her face. "LT, I can't see her tank because my ankle is trapped. I don't know how much is left." After a moment he added, "Come on, Carter! Work with me here!"

"I'm…." She moved her head and mumbled, "I'm okay."

"We found another one," another firefighter said.

"It's about time!" Nelson grumbled. "I was beginning to wonder if I was going to have to bed-in for the rest of the night."

"Quit...whoa!" Mac took the mask from Casey to get a big gulp of air before replacing it back on her face. "This isn't good. You guys need to get us out of here."

"We're working on it." LT insisted.

"Carter?" Mac asked quietly. She struggled, but could not open her eyes. He moved so his head was closer to hers and rested the mask over both of their faces so they could get what little air remained.

"Hmmm?"

"Can you open those beautiful, green eyes of yours for me?"

"Huh-unh." She shook her head.

"Please?" he rested his gloved hand on the side of her face. "I don't want to have to be the one to tell McCormick he needs a new partner. He likes the one he has. Besides, we have the best cook right now. I don't want to have you replaced by some horrid one."

"I'll be fine," she responded. Her voice was weak, and her body was limp.

Mac took another deep breath of air, before he moved back over to her side of the enclosure, leaving the mask resting on Casey's face. She obviously needed it more than he did at that moment. After another minute, Casey's air tank beeped. It started slowly, and then picked up pace as it emptied, multiplying the volume in the cavity.

"I hear that!" LT said, excited.

"Good, because she's almost out, and I'm on my way there too," Mac said.

Hearing Mac's voice, Casey fought to open her eyes. "Mac?"

"Carter? Is that you?" LT asked.

"Um-hmmm." She slowly nodded. Everything to her seemed to be going in slow motion, as if she were in some time dilation bubble.

She groaned as she heard the alarm on the tank beep faster. The last of the air filled what it could of the small chamber before it abruptly stopped.

"It's coming from over here!" Casey heard one of the firefighters shout through the rubble above them.

There was a flurry of activity above their little cavern for several minutes before the rock, dirt, ash, and rubble debris slowly gave way as the firefighters desperately tried to reach them. While it was only a couple of minutes, it felt like an eternity without air.

When they finally broke-through, Mac raised his hand. "We're right here."

There were shouts and cheers of joy as they excitedly continued to dig. The dust was so thick that it made it even harder to breath. Mac put his mask loosely over his face, before holding Casey's to her face so they wouldn't suffocate.

Casey could see the rescue lights shining down like rays of sunlight on a cloudy day. They cleared the way for Mac first, finally releasing his ankle. As they pulled him out, Casey lay there still unable to move. She felt disconnected from the scene, as if she were watching it on television. She tried to reach toward the hole, but her body would not cooperate.

After they got Mac out, LT dropped into the hole. "Hey, Carter." He took his mask off to put it on her while the others shifted position to release her from her cavern of debris.

"Hmm?" She turned her head toward him. She could see him, but he looked fuzzy. She squinted to see if that would help, but it didn't, so she closed her eyes again.

"Move it!" LT shouted to the other firefighters. She could hear the nervousness in his voice. He was down on one knee with his head poked out of the rubble while he held his mask to Casey's face, giving her a portion of the precious oxygen she needed. He braced himself with his other hand on the rubble of the entrance of the cavern they created.

"LT?"

"What's up?" He ducked his head in to see Casey. He almost didn't hear her; her voice was so weak.

"I need...." She shook her head as a black cloud threatened to overtake her mind.

"I know. We're working on it. Good job!" he said as they finally punctured a hole through to where they could pull her out.

One of the firefighters reached in and touched her helmet. "She's right here," he said to the others. He glanced into the hole to where he could see that her flashlight was still on. "She's free in there. We just need to open it up on this end and slide her out."

"Get an oxygen tank ready. She's going to need it," LT yelled to the ambulance crew. "Carter?" He looked down at her. She wasn't moving. "Carter?" He came down further into the hole and took his glove off. He felt her neck for a pulse. It was slow, but it was there. "Get those rocks outta the way! She's unconscious!" He yelled as he kept his fingers on the ceratoid artery on her neck feeling for her pulse.

It took them a few more minutes to break her free before a couple of the firefighters were able to reach in and pull her out. When she was clear of the hole, they slid her into the waiting rescue basket before they quickly got her to the expecting ambulance. On the way to the hospital, Jeff Campo took off some of her turnout gear so he could get an IV set up.

"Hey, Carter? Can you open your eyes for me?" He waited a minute before he said, "Come on, I don't want to have to be the one to tell McCormick his partner's not awake, he was cranky as it was."

"She awake yet?" Katz asked from the driver's seat.

"No." Campo took her blood pressure, pulse, and temperature. After a couple of minutes, he gently tapped her face again. "Carter, come on. Wake up."

"We're here." Katz pulled into the hospital parking lot, up to emergency.

Campo swore. "She's not awake yet, and her vitals are low."

"Then let's get her in there." Katz ran around and opened the back doors.

Chapter 2

The Lake

While she was in the hospital, Casey had a nightmare. It began with the smell of rancid, burnt flesh, much the same as when the man at the fire scene stumbled by her. Then, it compounded with the pungent sulfuric stench of brimstone on fire. She slowly opened her eyes to find that she was in a cold, rough catacomb structure that weighed heavily in desperation and despair. The chambers were about five feet long and two feet tall. They lined the walls of the cavern, stacked about five or six high depending on the height of the cavern at that point, and she was in the second one up from the ground.

Casey rolled over, and what she saw petrified her. Moving or breathing was the furthest things from her mind as she saw things her mind could not conceive. Fire coated the walls, but it did not consume them. There were hideous creatures walking around that were dark red, almost black in color. They had skin made of scales like a reptile. They had large wings like a bat, talons for nails, and yellowish-green eyes that darted around everywhere, searching for any sign of movement from their prey. They had fangs dripping with saliva as they scoured the scene before them, as if it were a Thanksgiving feast.

There were people walking around with only parts of their clothing still on them, some with chunks of their flesh hung off their bodies. The people walking around were in shock as they wondered around aimlessly and despondent.

She continued to scan the area the scene was almost indescribable. She was not sure she would ever be able to explain it to anyone. About thirty feet away from her was a vast, literal lake of fire. As the fire danced atop of the water, it reminded her of when someone sets a puddle of gasoline on fire. The emanation of brimstone was powerfully potent. It was suffocating to her. It overpowered any other scent, making it even difficult to breathe. Then, just when she thought she had seen it all, she noticed there were people in the lake…and they were alive! All she could do was lay there watching people reach out, grabbing others, pulling them back, deeper into the abyss. The hands had absolutely no flesh on them, yet the people were alive!

She studied the scene for a brief moment, almost mesmerized, when suddenly one of those hideous, reptile-like creatures appeared right in front of her. His tight, leather skin crinkled as he folded his arms, resting them on the side of the catacomb. He leaned down near her face. "Well, hello there," he sneered, drumming his claws on the rock.

She could not form a single thought in her head. Words were not an option. Her heart raced as she stared at him in terror. For the first time in her life she was literally scared stiff.

"Welcome, Mzzzzzz Carter," he hissed through his fangs.

She had to consciously remind herself to breathe as the saliva dripped off his sharp teeth, landing in tiny puddles less than an inch from her face.

He reached his claws out and gouged her arm, digging his claws into her skin. She closed her eyes and a scream finally escaped her mouth...only to open her eyes in the safety of a hospital room.

The nurse ran into the room. "Ms. Carter!" She put an oxygen mask on Casey "Deep breaths," the nurse coaxed. Casey was pale and visibly shaken while she grasped the bed rails, panicked. She was also breathing rapidly and gasping for air, despite the oxygen. "The monitor shows your oxygen is one hundred percent and your heart rate is skyrocketed. I need you to calm down. You're hyperventilating."

Casey looked at the arm the creature clawed, only to see it bandaged. She shook as she stared at her arm in panic. She then startled the nurse when she screamed again.

"Ms. Carter! Casey! Please! Calm down!" The nurse yelled over the screams. "We need to get you calmed down!" She gave up and ran out of the room to get a sedative.

The nurse came back in a couple minutes later and gave Casey Diazepam through her IV. Tommy hobbled in on crutches behind her, shortly followed by Jeff Campo, Will Weston, and Mac (who was also limping). To everyone's surprise, Casey sat there breathing heavily and her face was white as a sheet, and dripped with sweat.

"Take deep breaths," Jeff rested one of his hands on the back of her neck while he held the oxygen masts to her face with the other. "Come on, breathe in...and out. That's it, in...and out. Slow your breathing down."

As the nurse put a sedative into the IV, Will pulled a chair over for Tommy to sit on. At first, the medicine didn't seem to affect her. After about thirty seconds, Casey suddenly felt a rush of warmth over her body, followed by a feeling as if she was floating on water. She shook her head in an attempt to clear it as things around the room blurred together.

"What happened?" Mac sat on the side of the bed down near her feet. He, Tommy, and Jeff were all on the same side of the bed, while the nurse and Will were on the other.

"I was out at the nurse's station," the nurse started, as Casey finally calmed down. "Her heart monitor suddenly took off and I heard her scream bloody murder."

"Well, she's calmed down now." Mac rested his hand on her ankle.

Casey's head slowly went side to side, and she felt the vomit churning in her stomach, threatening to bring up dinner. She was dizzy and nauseous. It almost felt to her that her head was moving without her body.

"She looked at her arm like it was on fire," the nurse continued. She turned on the automatic blood pressure cuff while she went on with her story, "You'd think someone was attacking her. She was screaming so...." she shuddered.

"Would it be okay if we stay in here until she wakes back up? I don't think she should wake up alone again. It doesn't sound like it will be a good wake up," Will pointed out.

"Go ahead," she nodded. After glancing at Casey's blood pressure, satisfied, the nurse left, closing the door behind her.

The guys settled into chairs around the room, while Casey fought for some type of control over her body. She didn't open her eyes though, because when she did the room spun out of control.

Tommy sat to the right side of the bed with his leg propped on another chair. Mac stayed sitting on the corner of the bed, with his leg also propped on the same chair Tommy had his leg on. Meanwhile, Jeff and Will each sat on a chair next to the wall, also on the right side of the bed. They talked quietly amongst themselves while Casey drifted off to sleep.

*   *   *

After several hours, she let out a moan. "Casey?" Tommy struggled to get up from his chair. Jeff and Will went around to the left side of the bed.

Casey stared at her bandaged forearm. "Scissors."

"Did she just ask for scissors?" Will asked.

"Think so," Mac said. He limped out of the room toward the nurse's station.

"Do you want a pair of scissors?" Tommy asked. Casey nodded. "Why do you want scissors?"

"Need to...." Casey shook her hand free and reached over, frantically tugging on the bandage. She needed to know what was under it. She needed to know if the nightmare was real. The sense of panic convulsed within her.

"No, don't." Will rested his hand on the hand she was using to loosen the bandage.

She shook loose of him, tugging on the bandage again.

"Honey, now stop that," the nurse walked in with Mac.

"Need this off!" Casey yanked on the bandage. Tears welled up in her eyes. She was angry and scared at the same time and didn't know what to do with her emotions.

"Stop. Listen to me," the nurse calmly said. When Casey calmed, the nurse explained, "I'll cut that off and let you see it, if you let me clean it and then re-bandage it. Deal?"

Casey nodded.

"Good," the nurse said, relieved. She went out to the nurse's station and returned a couple moments later with a clean bandage, iodine, scissors, and medical tape.

While the nurse was gone, Casey took deep breaths in an attempt to get herself under control. She fought back the tears, not wanting to cry in front of the guys.

The nurse returned. She cut a slice into the bandage on Casey's arm. With each twist of the bandage, Casey's heart rate picked up.

"If you don't stop that, she'll stop unwrapping," Mac warned, glancing at the monitor from his spot at the foot of the bed.

Casey shook her head, not taking her eyes off her arm. Her eyes got wide as the last of the bandages fell to the bed. The terror within surged as the bandages seemed to drop in slow motion. When they hit the bed, she saw was what looked like three claw marks going horizontally across her arm. She stared at it in horror for a few moments, not even breathing.

"Whoa, partner!" Tommy turned her face toward his. "When they pulled you out, they found that some of the debris dug into your arm. Calm down."

Her body trembled in fear while she shook her head in shock. She couldn't hold them in any longer as the tears streamed down her face. *Could it have been real? Could the dream have been true?*

"I'm going to go get...." The nurse gestured over her shoulder toward the door.

"No." Jeff told the nurse, "She'll just wake back up like this again." He gently moved her out of the way and he got down near Casey's face. He rested his hands on the sides of her face so she would focus only on him. "Tell me," he simply said.

When she didn't respond, he brushed the tears off her cheeks, and said again, "Tell me."

She took a moment before she finally responded. "Dream."

"You had a dream?"

She nodded.

"Tell me," he said again.

She shook her head before he demanded that she tell him. She knew she was not going to get out of telling him, so she said, "There was...." She closed her eyes and shuddered. "They looked hideous."

"What did?"

"The creatures!"

"What did they look like?"

"Human bats. They had yellowish-green eyes with slits in them. They also had fangs, and...." She tried to turn away from Jeff, but he turned her face back towards him.

"Tell me."

Shaking her head, she said, "There was a lake of fire. There was fire all over the place! It smelled like brimstone!"

"Brimstone?" Head tilted to the side, Mac asked, "Did you just say lake of fire?"

Casey nodded.

"And these creatures...were they evil-looking and walking around?"

She nodded again.

Frowning, Will asked, "Do you know what she's talking about?"

"Were there people there too?" Mac ignored Will.

Casey nodded again. She couldn't believe Mac seemed to know what was going on.

"Was there screaming and yelling? Were the people actually *in* the lake?" he pressed.

She nodded as her heart rate picked back up again.

"Mac? What's going on?" Jeff demanded, crossing his arms.

"And...." Mac leaned, with his elbow on his knee, almost studying Casey. "Did one of them grab you on your arm?"

She nodded as her emotions rocketed between fear and anxiety.

"Okay," he rested his hand on her leg. "I got it. I know what happened."

Tommy rubbed the back of his neck, anxious. The fact that Mac seemed to know what was going on did not make him comfortable either. "Mind sharing it with the rest of us?"

"Scoot over a sec," he said to Tommy. Tommy switched places so Mac sat on the side of the bed, but up by Casey's head. Mac took both of her hands into his and asked, "Do you trust me?"

She hesitated for a moment before she nodded.

"Then," he said to the others, "if you guys want to stay, you can, but this is going to be a deep conversation that will have prayer involved."

"With you it usually does." Tommy slid into the chair his foot was originally resting on so he could see what was going on. He crossed his arms as he looked up at Mac almost daring him to make him leave. "She's my partner. I'm staying."

Jeff moved his chair over so he was sitting by the top of the bed, opposite Mac, while Will moved his chair over as well. "I'm staying too," Jeff Campo said adamantly. "And I don't mind. Like McCormick said, with you it usually does end up in prayer. We're kind of used to that by now."

Will crossed his arms. "I'm curious to see what's going on. I'm staying."

"You guys seem to have it covered. Call me when you're done so I can re-bandage that," the nurse said on her way out the door.

"What *was* that place?" Casey asked Mac as the others settled.

"Hell."

She gasped. "*What?*"

He reached into the nightstand next to the bed and pulled out the Bible left in the drawer. He let it rest on the side of the bed and he took her hands. "Casey, those creatures you described were demons."

Casey shook her head. "Mac, I...."

He cut her off, "Just bear with me here. The place you described is Hell. In Revelation 20:10," he opened the Bible, "it says that, *'the devil, who deceived them, was cast into the lake of fire and brimstone where the beast and the false prophet are. And they will be tormented day and night forever and ever.'* Now," he looked up at her, "sound familiar?"

She took a deep breath to relax herself before she nodded.

"So, if I'm following your nightmare correctly, one of them clawed your arm?"

She stared at the marks on her arm. She nodded as she rubbed them with her fingers.

"Have you ever been to church?"

"No."

"Well, hmmm…" he thought for a moment. He closed his eyes and prayed aloud. "Father, I don't know where to start. I know this lovely lady is a lady of peace. I know that she, deep down, will someday know You. Please give me the words. Please fill me with the knowledge of what to say and do." He stopped, and with his eyes still closed, he rested one of his hands on her forehead and the other on her stomach. "What Satan had tried to lay claim to, I demand, by the blood of Jesus, that she be set free. I demand that what has a hold of you, releases, in Jesus name. I pray for strength and courage for those angels who are in a fight for your very soul right now." He got louder and his voice stronger as he continued, "I see the chains that bound you begin one by one to have the locks opened. I see them dropping to your feet as you stand firm on Jesus's name. I see the creature trying to keep a hold of you – holding onto your arm with all of its might as you struggle to get free. I see the angel reeling back his fiery sword and swinging forward as he lets out a shout of glory. The sword easily slices through the middle of the creature. The glory that encompassed the sword dissolves the creature on contact." He stopped for a moment as she lay there shaking below his hands with her eyes closed.

More calmly, he continued, "I see you falling to the ground. I see Jesus come up beside you. He wraps a blanket of peace around you. You are wounded, but He will heal you. You are damaged, but not destroyed. You are a daughter of The King. A sister in Christ. He wants to heal those wounds. He wants to bring you back home and let you rest."

Casey felt tingles wash over her body. She was shaking, and her body felt heavy as if there was something holding her down. In that same instant, she also felt peace. That feeling was almost foreign to her. She had not felt it for a long time. In truth, she could not remember when she felt that way. It was a sense of almost freedom. She soaked in it as the peace and the medicine took over her body.

"If you want this, you just need to ask. You just need to ask Jesus, the One who gave His life for you, to come in, take over, and be your King," Mac said. When she didn't answer, he slightly jostled her. Noting her vital signs on the monitor, he knew she was okay, so he leaned down and whispered, "It's okay. We'll be here when you're ready. Don't move until you can."

After several moments of silence, Will finally asked, "Um, what was that?"

As Mac slid down into the chair, Tommy moved his leg to the couch. "That," Mac laid his head back on the chair, and heaved a heavy sigh, "was exhausting."

"Yeah, I see that, but what *was* that?" Will pressed.

"What did you feel?" He glanced at Will out of the corner of his eye.

He shook his head, "It was…I felt…." He shook his head again. "Weird."

Jeff glanced at Mac, and then he looked at Will, "You felt it, didn't you?"

"You too?" Will asked in surprise. Jeff nodded. Then they both turned to Mac, and Will asked again, "What *was* that?"

Mac smiled. "That, gentlemen, was the Holy Spirit."

Chapter 3

Late Night Run

When Casey woke up a couple hours later, the room was dark. The familiar sterile chlorine smell told her she was in the hospital. As she struggled to get her bearings, she heard the clock tick in sync with the beep of her heart monitor.

As she listened, she could decipher a couple different people sleeping in the room near her. By their breathing patterns, she was sure they were Mac, Jesse McFadden, and Brennon Hanson.

Once she got her eyes open, she used the light that came from under the door to make out various objects in the room. She was able to count three bodies in the room with her, so she assumed her guess was right.

She maneuvered her fingers over to the call button and pressed it. A male nurse walked into the room a moment later.

"Hi," he whispered, as he leaned down near her head. "I'm Jake, your nurse for the nightshift. You have a couple friends still in here with you, but they're sleeping so let's try to keep it down for them."

"Am I okay?"

He sat down on the side of the bed. "You tell me. Do you feel dizzy or are you in any pain?"

She did a quick inventory of herself before she said, "No."

"Can I get you to sit up for me?"

"Yeah. Give me a minute."

After struggling for a few moments, she sat up on her own. There was no dizziness or blurred vision. As far as she was concerned, she felt perfectly fine.

"Well?" he asked.

"I'm fine. I'm just hungry."

"Can I get you to stand up on your own?"

"Sure." As she swung herself around the side of the bed to stand up, he helped her keep the IV line from tangling by holding the IV pole. She then pushed herself up by using the bedrail.

"Okay, what if you take a walk with me to the nurse's station? If you can do that without dizziness, I'll not only get you some food, but I will also make sure to let your doc know as soon as he gets in. He'll probably release you this morning if you're successful."

"Good, because I have to get back to work as soon as possible."

"Uh, I don't think so. You're going to need at least a couple days off. You have been unconscious off and on for almost twenty-four hours."

She gasped. "Really?"

"Yeah."

"No wonder I feel the way I do," she remarked. When they got closer to the door, she could feel her head pulsating with each beat of her heart. She stopped for a moment to catch her breath.

"It's okay. Take it slowly." Jake rested his hand on her arm. "Here, hold the pole for balance."

She grasped the pole and took a couple deep breaths before she headed out the door. Due to the brightness of the lights in the hallway, she had to wait a few moments for her eyes to adjust. When they adjusted, she could see a large nurse's station with four hallways jetting off in the north, south, east, and west. Down each corridor, there were twenty rooms. There was one nurse assigned to each corridor.

"Ready?" he rested his hand on the backside of her arm to assist her across the floor.

"Yeah," she said before they slowly made their way toward the nurse's station.

"Well, well, well," one of the female nurses looked up and smiled, "I see she is finally awake. Do her chaperones know she's out here?"

"Not yet," Jake shook his head. "They're still snoring."

"Nothing I'm not used to." Casey waved him off. He glanced at her out of the corner of his eye, before she explained, "I'm a firefighter. I bunk with those guys at the station when I'm on shift. Trust me, I could probably tell you who is who just by the way they snore."

Jake chuckled while the nurse at the station took a closer look at Casey. "Oh! *That's* where I've seen you before! I don't know why I didn't connect…" She shook her head, as she arranged her thoughts. "I'm on loan to this floor from the ER. You're with Engine Fifteen's crew, aren't you?"

Casey looked up at her in surprise. "Yeah."

"Your partner is very cute." She smiled. "His name is.?" she snapped her fingers, struggling to recall his name. "Tommy McCormick, right?"

Casey narrowed her eyes at her."Yeah."

"Is he still in the room?"

"No, he's probably at home with his fiancé." Casey made sure she got the hint Tommy was not available. Despite popular opinion, not all of the firefighters enjoyed getting hit on all of the time. Truth be told, it irritated some of them…and Tommy was one of them. He and Sally got engaged a month ago after dating for over three years. He was more than happy with her and didn't appreciate forward women.

"Really?" She pouted. "I didn't think…you two seemed so close that…" her voice trailed off.

"Yeah, I got to meet her on my third shift at the station. They have had me over for dinner a couple nights too. She is very sweet. When you work as closely as you do with a partner at the station, you are close. In our case, it is like a brother and sister relationship."

"Oh, I see," she nodded in understanding as Casey and Jake finally made it to the nurse's station.

"Are you ready to head back?" Jake asked.

"Yeah. Um, when you get my food, would you do me a big favor?" Casey asked, hopeful.

He leaned on the counter with one arm in amusement. "What's that?"

"I'm *dying* for a soda!"

He laughed as he nodded. "Consider it done."

"Oh! Thank you!"

He put his arm out, so she looped her arm through his. "You're easy to please," he said. "Come on, let's get back to your partners and see if they're hungry as well."

When they got back into the room, he let her go so he could turn on the light over the bed. That way she could better navigate her through the room.

"What the…?" Mac sat up, stunned. Due to the brightness of the light, he only got his eyes partially opened.

"Turn that off!" Jesse snapped as he covered his head with a pillow.

Brennon rubbed his eyes. Seeing the empty bed, he asked, "Where's Carter?"

Standing by the door, Casey stifled her laughter for their sake, despite wanting to crack up. "I'm right here."

"We took a walk. Are you guys hungry?" Jake pulled the covers back for her to get back into bed. "I have to get her some food. Do you guys want something too?"

"Um, why don't *we* go get her some food?" Brennon stood up and stretched. "Nothing personal, but that, um, I don't even think I would dignify it by calling it food – it's more like that stuff you guys try to pass off as food – will probably make her sick. She's a great cook, and that stuff is…well…yeah." He stumbled over his words.

"What about a pizza?" Jesse perked up at the mention of food. "I happen to know there's a great twenty-four-hour pizza place just down the road. We could get a two liter of soda while we're there."

Jake warned, "Keep it light, and I won't have a problem with it. She might throw it up, though. She hasn't had anything in her stomach for quite some time."

"What if you get her a couple pieces of peanut butter toast while we're gone?" Mac suggested. "That way it can settle before we add to it."

"That sounds like a good plan." Jake smiled, satisfied. He turned to Casey as she slipped into bed, and asked, "What do you think?"

"That sounds good. If possible, can I have the toast sooner rather than later?" she asked. "And, maybe a small glass of clear soda? I'm starving!"

"Will do," he said, and left the room to get her something to eat, as she adjusted herself into a better position on the bed.

"What do you want on your pizza?" Jesse asked.

"The standard will work." She shrugged. "Are you sure you guys want to go buy it though? It's…," she glanced at the clock in the room, "…three-forty in the morning."

"I'm *always* up for pizza!" He grinned, as Casey smiled, shaking her head at him.

Mac and Brennon chuckled in amusement. Jesse was famous for ordering pizza in the middle of the night. When he was on shift, he was normally the one up all night with LT for watch. His reasoning was because he did not want to make mistakes when he was responsible for the lives of other people. To Casey this made sense, but she had a different theory. She decided she would make more mistakes if she *didn't* get enough sleep.

Mac sat down on the side of the bed. "Why don't you two go while I keep her company? I think we need to talk."

"Sounds good," Brennon agreed. They grabbed their jackets, talking about a game that was on the TV the previous night while they walked out the door.

"So?" Casey looked up at Mac as the door closed.

"So…what?"

She crossed her arms and raised an eyebrow.

"All right," he said in a chuckle. "I guess I wanted to make sure you were okay. You know, after your nightmare and with the prayer."

"I guess." She shrugged. "I was hoping to forget the nightmare though." She shuddered as it ran through her mind.

"Casey, I know you normally don't go to church. Have you ever gone?"

"No."

He sighed. "Okay, first off, you need to know that Hell is a real place. On the flip side of that, though, Heaven is real too."

She narrowed her eyes at him, "This isn't one of those religious conversations, is it?"

"I think it might be categorized as that." He nodded with a smile. He enjoyed the way she phrased her thoughts. They often brought a smile to his face. "But I'd like to look at it as more of a heart conversation instead."

"What do you mean by that?"

"Heaven and Hell are a matter of the heart."

"Could you clear that up some? That didn't help."

"Casey, who is Jesus to you?"

"I have no idea. I've heard the name before. I guess some people think He's the Son of God or something."

"But who do *you* think He is?"

"I really hadn't thought about it."

"You want to know who He is to me?"

"Sure." She shrugged. She really didn't care one way or the other, but it was important to him so she would oblige.

"He is the Son of *The* King. He is the One who came from one of the richest Kingdoms ever, to show others, including me, exactly what it is to have a little taste of Heaven. He came, performed many miracles: healing the sick, raising people from the dead, casting out demons, giving the blind sight, allowing the deaf to hear, the lame to walk. He did it all! Most importantly, though, He gave His life for me through a death by crucifixion. He was beaten, ridiculed, slashed, and even nailed to a cross by His hands and feet. He did it for the whole world, but if it was only for me, He still would have done it. You see, it's much the same of how we lay our lives on the line every day to help others even though we know there is a possibility we might die. Jesus Christ came, knowing there wasn't going to be a *possibility* of His death, but an *absolute certainty* of His death…and He did it anyway."

"Why?" Casey asked. While she may not admit it to him yet, what he said intrigued her.

"A long time ago, when the world began, God created man. He created Adam and Eve. When He did, He was pleased and proud of His creation, until Satan stepped in and mucked it all up. You see, God told Adam he could eat from any fruit in the Garden of Eden, except from the tree of Knowledge of Good and Evil. Of course, Satan took that and ran with it. He manipulated Eve into taking a bite of the fruit, which in turn opened her eyes to the good and evil that surrounded her. She turned around and gave it to Adam, who did the same. When they ate the fruit, they disobeyed God. The sin it brought into the world broke communication between God and man. They hid themselves from Him because they were ashamed. They were naked. Well, when God found out what they did, He not only kicked them out of the Garden, placing Angels with fiery swords at the entrance so no one could enter again, but He also cursed them. Man would have to work for his food, and women would have pain during childbirth from that day forward. That wasn't the worst of it though, God and man would have troubles from that point on. During all of this and many years later, Jesus enjoyed His place in Heaven right beside God, the Father, but They were still concerned. You see, while man was in trouble, it also troubled Them. They didn't want to see man hurting so badly, and Satan wasn't helping either! He was having a hay-day down here by making messes all over the place. So, the Father and Jesus got together and made a plan. They decided Jesus would come to Earth and be a living sacrifice, shedding His own blood to bring man back into the Family of God."

Casey nodded, engrossed in the story by this point.

"You see, back in Biblical times, to atone for sin you had to shed blood. Not the blood of just any animal either, it had to be a perfect animal. The lamb had to be without spot or blemish – the cream of the crop, so to speak."

"I see. So, in following your story, Jesus was –"

"Jesus was perfect," Mac cut her off, "even when He was here on Earth. Because He was without sin, without spot or blemish, He was the only One who could make the sacrifice."

"Wait a minute." She put her hand up to stop him when she realized the direction of the story. "Are you saying that due to the sin of Adam and Eve, and consequently the rest of the human race afterward, Jesus had to come here and *literally* shed His blood?" Her jaw dropped.

"Exactly. In John 3:16 and 17, it says, '*For God so loved the world that He gave His only begotten Son, that whoever believes in Him should not perish but have everlasting life. For God did not send His Son into the world to condemn the world, but that the world through Him might be saved.*' And, in Romans 6:23, it says, '*For the wages of sin is death, but the gift of God is eternal life in Christ Jesus our Lord.*' You see, that gift was His only Son, Jesus. He didn't come here spouting about revenge and destruction. He came here to save us from an eternal death."

"So, He died on the cross and shed His blood…right?"

"Right."

"So, He's dead, right?"

"Wrong."

"But you just said…."

"I did," he smiled. "It also says," he took the Bible back out of the drawer and opened it to Matthew. "It says in Matthew 28 – now you might want to sit back for this one, it's going to be long, but worth it – in Matthew, chapter 28, '*Now after the Sabbath, as the first day of the week began to dawn, Mary Magdalene and the other Mary came to see the tomb. And behold, there was a great earthquake; for an angel of the Lord descended from heaven, and came and rolled back the stone from the door, and sat on it. His countenance was like lightning, and his clothing as white as snow. And the guards shook for fear of him, and became like dead men.*

But the angel answered and said to the women, 'Do not be afraid, for I know that you seek Jesus who was crucified. He is not here; for He is risen, as He said. Come, see the place where the Lord lay. And go quickly and tell His disciples that He is risen from the dead, and indeed He is going before you in Galilee; there you will see Him. Behold, I have told you.' So, they went out quickly from the tomb with fear and great joy, and ran to bring His disciples word. And as they went to tell His disciples, behold, Jesus met them, saying, 'Rejoice!' So, they came and held Him by the feet and worshiped Him. Then Jesus said to them, 'Do not be afraid. Go and tell My brethren to go to Galilee, and there they will see Me.' Now while they were going, behold, some of the guard came into the city and reported to the chief priests all the things that had happened. When they had assembled with the elders and consulted together, they gave a large sum of money to the soldiers, saying, 'Tell them, 'His disciples came at night and stole Him away while we slept.' And if this comes to the governor's ears, we will appease him and make you secure.' So, they took the money and did as they were instructed; and this saying is commonly reported among the Jews until this day."

"Who says the second part isn't true? What if his disciples moved the body?" Casey asked, skeptical.

"Almost done…bear with me here," he smiled, pleased she was so into the story. "It goes on in verse sixteen to say, '*Then the eleven disciples went away into Galilee, to the mountain which Jesus had appointed for them. When they saw Him, they worshiped Him, but some doubted. And Jesus came and spoke to them, saying, 'All authority has been given to Me in heaven, and on earth. Go therefore and make disciples of all the nations, baptizing them in the name of the Father and of the Son and of the Holy Spirit, teaching them to observe all things that I have commanded you; and lo, I am with you always, even to the end of the age.' Amen.*'" He looked up at her with a smile. "You see, He *did* die, but He rose again, and is even still with us now."

"How is that possible?"

"He left the Holy Spirit to guide and direct us."

"But –"

"Here's your toast and soda," Jake cut her off, coming in with the tray. He moved the tray stand so it was in front of Casey as Mac stood up. "All right, you eat that, giving it about ten to fifteen minutes to settle before eating pizza and drinking soda, and you should be good to go. Can I take some vitals before I go?"

She nodded. "Sure."

He took her temperature, blood pressure, and pulse. When he finished, he noted the results before leaving, satisfied.

Casey ate her toast while Mac's words floating through her mind. With everything he told her, it was a lot to process.

Mac sat a little further down the bed so he was on the other side of the tray, and asked, "So, what do you think?"

"I *think* this is all new to me." She shook her head. "I've never heard this before."

"But what do you think about it."

"Wild," she admitted. "It seems…I don't know." She mulled in her mind his words for a few more minutes. There were some aspects she was not clear on. "I think I followed it all. But, how do you get from Jesus dying on the cross and being raised from the dead, to being 'saved'?" She made quotes with her hands. "And what exactly does that mean? Saved from what?"

"This is the best way to explain it. In Matthew 16:24-28, it says," he opened the Bible and read, "'*Then Jesus said to His disciples, 'If anyone desires to come after Me, let him deny himself, and take up his cross, and follow Me. For whoever desires to save his life will lose it, but whoever loses his life for My sake, will find it. For what profit is it to a man if he gains the whole world, and loses his own soul? Or what will a man give in exchange for his soul? For the Son of Man will come in the glory of His Father with*"

His angels, and then He will reward each according to his works. Assuredly I say to you, there are some standing here who shall not taste death till they see the Son of Man coming in His kingdom.'" He looked back up at her. "You see, you have to be willing to give everything for Him. He doesn't just want you on Sundays or the bare minimum. He has given His all, His life included, to set you free. All He asks for in return is the same thing. He wants you to give your all for Him."

She struggled to follow his line of thought."How do I do that?"

"Well," he flipped through the Bible, showing her where he was reading, "In Acts 16:30, they asked Paul and Silas the same question. *'And he brought them out and said, 'Sirs, what must I do to be saved?'* Verse thirty-one is your answer. *'So, they said, 'Believe on the Lord Jesus Christ, and you will be saved, you and your household.'* See, it's easy. All you have to do is believe on the name of Jesus, and you will be saved. All He asks is for you to give Him your all. In Revelation 1:8, it says, *'I am the Alpha and the Omega, the Beginning and the End,' says the Lord, 'who is, and who was, and who is to come, the Almighty.'* He's never going to leave you. He always is, always was, and always will be. Your partner may fail you. Your family may fail you. Your friends may even fail you. Jesus will *never* fail you, though. Here's an example. In the warehouse fire you thought you were alone in that little area until you found out I was close, right?"

"Right."

"Well, I knew I was *never* alone."

"Huh?"

"Even though I originally didn't know you were that close, I knew Jesus was right there with me, and I was praying and talking to Him." He paused for a moment to think through his words before he continued, "When you found me, you were relieved, right?"

"Right."

"You weren't going to let me go, even to dig through the rubble to get to me, right?"

"Right."

"Well, my walk with Christ is a lot like that. I won't let His hand go, even though I may be in the middle of a cave-in. His hand, to me, means freedom. It means friendship. He is my all. He is my Savior. Does this make sense?"

"Actually, it does, but I want to know more." She considered his words for several moments, before she looked up at him and asked, "When you were praying with me earlier…what happened?"

"What do you mean 'what happened?'"

"I felt something. I couldn't move. My body felt heavy, but I felt peace at the same time."

"Casey, there is a struggle right now for your soul. There is a battle within you, which was probably the heaviness you felt. God wants you to be free though. He wants you to feel peace. He wants you to have the confidence of knowing that He is battling for you every day, every hour, every minute. He wants you to know that His angels are willing to fight those demons for you. All you have to do is ask. He will free you from those bonds, from those creatures who are trying to take hold of your life. This may be an unseen battle to our eyes, but it is a battle for your very soul."

She looked at him dumbfounded. Just as she was about to say something, Jesse and Brennon came back in. "No, really," Brennon said as Jesse was laughing. "I kid you not! It really happened!"

"That's too funny!" Jesse chuckled, shaking his head. "Anyone want pizza?" he asked, smoothly replacing the pizza box, for the tray the nurse set down. "Complete with…ta-ta-daaa!" He grabbed the two-liter of soda from Brennon and set it next to the pizza box. Brennon gave everyone a cup for soda that he snuck from the snack room of the floor.

Casey grinned in delight. "Mmm! Smells wonderful!"

The group took several moments to enjoy the pizza and soda, while Brennon shared his funny story. Casey was laughing so hard by the end that her stomach hurt. By the time the pizza and soda were gone, there were several funny stories shared. After a while, Casey felt sleepy from being full and laughing so hard. She did not want the fun to stop though. She enjoyed her time with the guys.

"So," Jake came in after an hour or so, while they were still chatting, "How are you feeling?"

"Tired," Casey admitted, "but good."

"How's your head?"

"Fine. Why?"

"A lot of times people wake up from situations like this with a headache at the very least. You're not dizzy, no blurred vision, no headache?"

"No, not really," she said.

Furrowing his brow, he asked, "What do you mean by 'not really'?"

"No, I do not have any dizziness, blurred vision, or a headache."

"Good. Can I get you to take another walk for me while your partners get settled?"

"Sounds good." She nodded. She needed to stretch. She got up, and together she and Jake headed back out to the nurse's station.

"Okay, how do *you* rate?" There was another nurse behind the counter.

"What do you mean?" Casey asked the nurse, confused.

"Well, ya got three good-looking men in the room *with* you who even think highly enough of you to go out for pizza at three-thirty in the morning, just so you don't have to endure hospital food...*and* you get *him* as a nurse," she said as she winked at Jake.

"Well, the three in the room are just looking out for their stomachs."

"Huh?"

"I'm the cook at the station for the moment," Casey explained.

The nurse smiled as they continued their journey across the floor. "Ohhh, I see."

"Well, looks like that pizza and soda did you some good." Jake smiled, pleased, when they finally reached the nurse's station. "You've perked right up."

"Does that mean I get to go home later?"

"I would think so, but I'm not your doctor. We'll see when he gets in."

"Oh, all right, if I have to," she said in a sigh.

"Is she pouting again?" Mac asked, leaning on the doorway, while Jesse and Brennon leaned on the wall. All three of them watched her progress.

Casey playfully glared at him.

"I think her gentlemen friends want her back," the female nurse pointed out.

"Awww, man," he mimicked her. "If I have to."

"You have to," the nurse responded with a smirk.

"Seriously, how is it that you've had no less than three men in that room with you since you've been here?" he asked as they walked back. "Are any of them a significant other?"

"No." She blushed. "I don't have a significant other right now."

"Not for lack of us trying," Brennon pointed out. "I know of at least three dates that were set up for her."

"I can't help it if things came up," she defended herself. In reality, she was relieved things came up. She didn't like blind dates. The idea of going out with someone she didn't know scared her. For the first one, she had to work due to a call off at the station. On the second, she got the flu. Then, for the third one, her cousin got into a car accident and she had to go to the hospital to be with her.

"What would happen if we set you up again?" Brennon asked, crossing his arms.

"Oh, I'm sure *something*'ll come up. I'm not one who likes blind dates anyway," she admitted, knowing they would keep pushing the issue if she wasn't honest with them. "I like to know who I'm going out with."

"What if it's with one of us?" Jesse asked out of curiosity. He had a girlfriend, so Casey was comfortable in him asking that question.

"I don't think so." She shook her head. "That could cause an uncomfortable situation at work." She walked into the room, closely followed by the guys.

"Even though it has to be from a different shift?" Jesse pressed.

She shook her head. "I don't know."

"You know, in this line of work it's hard for females to find boyfriends or husbands," Brennon pointed out.

"Yeah, I know. However, the way I look at it, if I am lucky enough to find the one who I'm supposed to be with, it isn't going to matter what I do for an occupation. It should only matter what's in my heart and personality."

"In ya go," Jake said, helping her back into bed. "If you want to talk or take a nap until Dr. Benton comes in, you're welcome to. It will be at least five more hours until he even gets to the hospital, so you'll be here at least that long."

"Thanks." Casey straightened her covers as she got in a comfortable position. "Does your last statement mean I have your stamp of approval?"

After he checked her blood pressure and pulse, he finally said, "Yes." Then he stuck a thermometer in her mouth. "Don't talk. I need your temp."

"Oh, so *that's* how we get her to shut up." Jesse smiled at her. She knew it was in jest, but she shot him a dirty look anyway.

"Nah, she's okay. Now, we might try that with Martin or Patterson, but two minutes isn't anywhere *near* long enough for either of them." Brennon rolled his eyes, as the other guys laughed. Bobbi Jo Martin and Zoey Patterson were the two girls from 'B' shift. Jessie Martes was the girl from 'C' shift.

"I don't know about that." Jesse thoughtfully rubbed his chin. "Martes might beat them all, hands down."

Casey felt she needed to defend the girls of the station, so when Jake pulled the thermometer out of her mouth she said, "I happen to know there are a quite a few guys who have bigger mouths than the girls."

"Oh yeah?" Mac challenged. "Who?"

"Vega, Miller, Getz, Zohn, Hawke, and Kelley from 'B' shift to name a few." She shuddered, "That shift is *loud*!"

Mac chuckled. "That it is."

"Then, there's Kirby, Richards, Briggs, and Watkins from 'C' shift," Casey continued.

"Too true," Jesse agreed.

"I'm glad we have who we do on our shift," Brennon said in a sigh. "I don't think I could handle the volume on the other shifts. Ours has a good balance."

"I wouldn't want to trade the women out either." Jesse shook his head. "I'm *positive* we have the best cook on our shift."

An idea suddenly occurred to Casey of a way to get out of some of the chores around the station. "I'll make you guys a deal," she proposed, thinking on how to best word the arrangement. "You guys talk to everyone on shift and if they agree, I will cook *all* the dinners from now on if *you guys* cover the other cleaning details – excluding the ones we all have to regularly do anyway."

Jesse mulled it over in his mind. "Hmm."

"That might work." Brennon considered it. "Let us pitch it to the guys later when we go in."

"Can we do that?" Mac asked.

Brennon shrugged. "If LT approves it, I don't see why not."

"One way to find out. Speaking of work, what time is Dr. Benton coming in this morning?" Casey asked Jake. She didn't want to be in the hospital any longer than she had to.

"He usually comes in sometime between seven and nine in the morning," Jake said, finishing his notes in her chart.

"Great!" She smiled, pleased. "I want to work tomorrow."

"I don't think he will let you go into work tomorrow knowing you will be working twenty-four-hours." Mac shook his head. "You were unconscious for quite some time."

"*Straight*?" Jake looked at Casey, wide-eyed.

"I'm used to it," she pointed out. "It's no big deal. I'm fine."

"I don't think you're fine enough to work for twenty-four-hours straight." He shook his head. "You're going to need *at least* a couple days off before returning to work. I'd say when your shift swings around next time you should be good to go."

She put her chin on her hand, upset. "This stinks!"

"That's what happens when you're buried under three tons of rubble," Mac said.

"What are *you* so happy about? You're limping. Do you seriously think Chief is going to let you on a truck?" she shot at him.

"Nope. I've already talked to Chief about it, and I'm on the ambulance. I can lift fine. I just have a limp. Now, your partner is going to be off for a while, and Kendall is finally conscious as of this afternoon, but he'll still be in here for a bit. Nelson's fine, but McFadden is…."

"I'm fine," Jesse rolled his eyes. "I just got a little crunched in the middle."

Mac shook his head. "Your legs are both scraped up pretty badly. I think he'll make you wait another shift and then check."

"I'm fine for the ambulance," he pointed out. "Give me a few days, and I'll be back on track. If they didn't drag me out from under those piles, I would have *been* fine."

"The fact that no one was killed is amazing," Jake said. "Three tons of rubble? Was it really that much?"

"It was a three-story warehouse," Casey explained. "I'm surprised the only thing damaged on me is my arm."

"Are you sure there wasn't any brain damage with the lack of oxygen?" Brennon asked, shoving his hands in his pockets while he leaned against the wall.

She narrowed her eyes at him, making a fist. "Come here and I'll prove it to you!"

Jake laughed as he said, "I'm pretty sure she's fine."

"I'm going to work tomorrow too," Casey said adamantly. "Nothing on me is hurt. I can even work the truck."

"We'll see." Jake shook his head, smiling as he left the room.

"Nice guy," Brennon pointed out after Jake left the room.

"Don't get any ideas." Casey crossed her arms. "You guys are worse than my aunt and uncle!"

"Your aunt and uncle?" Lines formed between Mac's eyebrows. "Usually it's the parents who are pushing for that."

"They died in an airplane accident when I was eight. They were going on a business trip for my dad's company when the plane went down. I had to live with my aunt and uncle for a little while after that, so they think it is their obligation to marry me off."

"Do you have any brothers or sisters?" Brennon rested in a chair next to the bed.

"Yeah, I have an older brother, Jack. He's about five years older than me."

"What does he do?"

"He's in the Air Force on some Special Ops team. I don't get to see him that often. He keeps saying he's going to retire, but at forty I would think he would have already done that by now."

"A lifer, eh?" Mac nodded in understanding. "My cousin is doing that. It's almost an addiction for them."

"Yeah." Casey rolled her eyes. "An adrenaline addiction."

"So, what made you start a career as a firefighter at thirty-five?" Brennon asked. "What were you before that?"

"A landscape photographer. I was also in school for the paramedic portion, doing a little at a time. Once I got a taste of that adrenaline rush by working on the ambulance and volunteering at the station, it was just...." She sighed, shaking her head. "Yeah, now I know why Jack won't leave. It seems like a family curse."

"What did your parents do?" Jesse asked.

"My dad was a stunt man, and my mom was an investigative reporter."

"Geez!" Mac chuckled. "You guys were *destined* to be adrenaline junkies!"

"Yeah, but you should get my brother and I together. When we are, let's just say there were times my cousins left the table in tears from laughing so hard."

"Oh, I'm sure! You've got a good sense of humor," Jesse said. "I can't imagine there being two of you."

"Oh yeah! It's fun."

"Well, speaking of fun," Mac sat down on his chair, "we get to have some of our own tomorrow, and it's been a long night. I'm going to take a nap for now."

Brennon nodded, leaning back in his chair, crossing his ankles. "Sounds like a plan."

"I agree," Jesse said, getting comfortable in another chair.

"You guys ready?" Casey asked after a couple moments of them settling in. They said they were, so she reached up and turned off the light over the bed, and they drifted off to sleep.

Chapter 4

Skeletons

It only took Dr. Benton a few minutes of giving Casey a mini physical, along with talking to her, for him to release her. Despite her pleas, he gave her a note to go back to work in two days – meaning the shift after the next day. She used the time to catch up on her neglected housework, as well as make some phone calls and return e-mails to her aunt, uncle, and brother.

She paced herself through Saturday, hoping to stretch what she had to do through the weekend. Then on Saturday night, she got a call from Mac, asking her if she wanted to go to church with him in the morning. Since their next day back to work was on Monday, she told him she would go. She warned him since she had never been to church a day in her life that it would be an uncomfortable situation for her, but she was curious.

*   *   *

The next morning, he came by the house at about ten o'clock to pick her up. "So," he took a quick inventory of the room, pleasantly surprised, "this is what your place looks like."

Her apartment was natural in its decorative style. She had a couple potted palms on either side of the white canvas couch behind the end tables. There was also a white canvas chair on either end of the couch.

On the main window, there were two panels of sheer white curtains, two light green on either side of the white, and two hunter green on either side of the light green, allowing the light to come in without letting people see in at the same time.

The square coffee table, dining room table and chairs, and end tables were made of oak. On the kitchen table, there was a plain, white, canvas table runner. As a centerpiece, there was a medium-sized, Chinese Elm bonsai tree.

The knickknacks on the oak bookshelves were from the various countries she and her brother travelled to with their jobs, along with some family photos and books. On the walls throughout the apartment were landscape photos in frames. The frames were about a foot-and-a-half tall and two-and-a-half feet wide in various geometric patterns.

The sheer curtain panels on the kitchen window were similar to the ones on the living room window, only they were half as long, landing about four inches below the windowsill. On one of the counters in the kitchen were several cookbooks. On another counter were a couple different types of oils and a spice rack.

The dishes in the dish drainer were thick, white, square dishes, and the glasses were a transparent light green. The napkins and placemats on the kitchen table were a light green to match the glasses with grapevine napkin rings. And, in keeping with the theme of the house, the appliances were all white.

As Mac took a quick tour, she nervously glanced at the air freshener to make sure it was still full. The dispensers would spray a burst of vanilla every fifteen minutes. They were located in all three rooms, set to go off so one sprayed every five minutes. She wanted to make sure her home always smelled sweet.

"Nice." He nodded in approval. "Very comfortable. Did you take those photos on the walls?"

"Yep." She smiled, picking up her purse from the counter. She was dressed in black dress pants with black flat sandals. She also had on a white tank top, covered by a thick, white, short sleeve, lace shirt. Her black purse was small with a long strap that went diagonally across her front, landing her purse on her hip. Under normal circumstances, she didn't carry a purse. However, for those occasions where one was warranted, she had a couple of the same style but in different colors.

"You're very good!" Mac remarked, still admiring the photos.

"Yeah, that's what my agent said. She wasn't happy when I changed careers."

"I have to ask you," he shook his head, dumfounded, "why *did* you change? I would imagine your job was quite relaxing. Why would you change it for a hectic, often dangerous job?"

"It *was* relaxing," she agreed, "but it doesn't beat what we do now. Besides, I can free-lance on my days off if I want to go back."

"You should. I couldn't take photos like these if my life depended on it."

"Thanks." Her face flushed in embarrassment. "I have always liked to take photos, so it was natural for me to go into photography."

"Well, you have talent." He stared at the photos in amazement. He had to commend her skill with the camera because she had a good eye. He wouldn't admit it to anyone though how much she intrigued him. He knew she knew her way around a fire scene. He knew she was a great a cook as well. He also enjoyed her playful banter at the station with the guys, and knew she had an excellent sense of humor. He needed to know if it was solely admiration for her as a person, or possibly something else. After a couple minutes, he glanced at his watch. "You about ready?"

"Yep."

"I know you're nervous, but I'm proud of you for coming." He rested his hand on her shoulder while he escorted her to his recently purchased maroon Chevy Cruz, and opened her passenger side door. He was so excited when he bought it two weeks ago. She smiled, remembering his excitement when he drove it to the station for the first time as she sat down in her seat.

They talked about the car all the way to church. She welcomed the distraction from her nervous state. She was not sure what she was walking into, but what Mac told her in the hospital got her curiosity piqued.

She also noticed while at work, Mac had a strange peace about him. She wanted that. She had a lot of respect for him and the others at the station. While she was nervous, she was also excited to hear more about this Jesus and what He was about. She hoped to find some answers to the questions that plagued her mind over the last couple of days.

*   *   *

When they got to his church, they walked into a stunningly beautiful auditorium. There were padded pews in three sections split by two aisles. The seats were already full of people varying in ages anywhere from newborn babies through the elders of the church. It was a well-balanced congregation. There was not an overabundance of one age group over another.

Lining the two outer walls were stained-glass windows. The sun poured through, casting a dazzling display multicolored light all over the sanctuary.

On the stage in the front of the church were lilies with white bows around the green foil-covered pots. The lilies were also in each of the windowsills, which allowed the fresh scent to infuse its way through the sanctuary. The intermingling of the sights, scents, and sounds gave the church building a sense of peace and calmness.

Up on stage, the worship team ranged from teenagers to middle age. They played a variety of instruments including a drum set surrounded by Plexiglas; a couple guitars – one electric, one acoustic, and one base guitar; a couple keyboards; and an assortment of percussion accompaniments.

While she did not recognize the song, it had a slow, smooth flow to it, adding to the tranquil feeling of worship as the congregation slowly filtered in, filling the remaining open seats.

The people were friendly, and several even introduced themselves to Casey before the service. Mac seemed to know almost everyone they walked by as they went to their seats.

During the singing, the worship team gave traditional songs a contemporary flavor. The harmonious way this church family worshipped, stirred something deep within her that she never felt in her life. This sense of kinship and acceptance was something foreign to her.

Then there was the sermon. While she did not completely understand it all, she got the basic gist of it. The way the pastor spoke made her want to read the Bible more to see what else was in this couple-thousand-year-old book. She was amazed at how the pastor made this antiquated book pertain currently to her life. His message was on temptations. He told the story of David and Bathsheba. He explained that David, even though he fell hard for Bathsheba (to the point of having her husband killed so he could take her as a wife) David still had a reputation of being a 'Man after God's own heart.'

You see, David's kingdom was in the middle of a war, and one night David was looking out over his kingdom and caught sight of Bathsheba taking a bath out on her deck. He had her come to the castle and slept with her, and she ended up getting pregnant from it. To cover it up, he pulled Bathsheba's husband home from the war, hoping he would sleep with her and think *he* was the one who got her pregnant.

Unfortunately for David, it turned out Bathsheba's husband was loyal to him, and refused to sleep with her when he knew the kingdom was at war. Since his plan failed, David had the Captain of his army put Bathsheba's husband, his loyal follower, on the front-line to ensure he would be killed…and he was. After the husband's death, David brought Bathsheba into the castle as his wife. Casey shook her head, not sure who to feel worse for – Bathsheba or her husband.

Long story short, the baby died as a punishment for David and Bathsheba's sin. David repented and fell back into grace with God after a little while.

The pastor then went on to explain exactly what 'grace' meant. He did this by an acrostic. The 'G' stood for 'God's;' 'R' stood for

'Restoration;' 'A' was for 'At;' the 'C' was for 'Christ's;' and the 'E' was for 'Expense.' Altogether, it spelled out 'GRACE': God's Restoration At Christ's Expense.

He then read one of the verses Mac read in the hospital (John 3:16 & 17), before going on to explain exactly what happened surrounding, and during the crucifixion of Jesus. He read the story of The Last Supper, where Jesus told Peter he would deny Jesus three times before the rooster crowed. Peter was of course appalled and swore there was no way he would ever betray Jesus like that. He was one of Jesus's loyal Apostles. To Peter, the thought of betraying Jesus was inconceivable! However, it happened later that morning just as Jesus had said.

Jesus also told Judas he would betray Him, which made Judas angry. He was offended Jesus thought so little of him to accuse him of such an atrocity that he left the supper. As the story goes, Judas sold Jesus out for thirty pieces of silver. Judas felt so distraught after his treachery that he returned the thirty pieces of silver to the chief priests and scribes. He knew he could not live with the duplicity. Out of desperation to make the pain in his heart stop, he hanged himself.

Meanwhile, back to the story of The Last Supper, Jesus and the remaining Apostles finished their meal. (Judas had already left to go to the chief priests and scribes to betray Jesus.) Then, per the request of Jesus, they retired to the Garden of Gethsemane. He wanted to spend a long time in prayer with His Father – The Lord God. While He was praying, the disciples were to stand guard for Him. During the prayer with His Father, Jesus begged God that if there was any other way for the human race to be saved, God would provide the way…but there wasn't.

After a while, the chief priests, scribes, the soldiers, and Judas went to the garden where Judas betrayed Jesus with a kiss. The soldiers went to take Jesus into custody, but the disciples attempted to fight back. Jesus stopped the disciples. He knew He had to go with them, so He went peacefully.

Since Jesus went with the soldiers, Peter followed them to see what would become of his friend and mentor. While he was in the courtyard waiting, he warmed his hands on a fire that some people in the courtyard started.

While he was standing there, several people recognized him. Three times he was accused of being one of Jesus's followers, but he denied it all three times. Just as he denied it the third time, the rooster crowed. As soon as it did, Jesus was ushered through the courtyard and looked directly at Peter, knowing what Peter had done. Peter was devastated. He knew Jesus's prediction came true. He felt sick to his stomach knowing he did exactly what he swore he would never do. He was beside himself and sulked off, distraught.

Through the course of the next day, the soldiers mocked and tortured Jesus. They beat Him within an inch of his life with an instrument called a cat of nine tails. The way pastor described it, it was almost evil! It was a multi-tailed, lead-tipped whip embedded with nails, glass, and bone. Each time the whip made contact, they would drag it off His back, bringing with it, parts of His flesh. His blood coated his body along with the ground around Him. When finished, they placed a purple cloak on Jesus (purple signified royalty back then), along with a crown of three-inch thorns pressed into His head in mocking respect of Him being called King of the Jews. After the blood dried, they ripped the cloak off Jesus's body, re-tearing His flesh. Then they had the audacity to cast lots for the cloak to see who got it!

Casey sat there in awe, feeling horrible for Jesus! He did not do anything to deserve all that was done to Him. She was having a difficult time accepting the concept that Jesus did it willingly for someone else.

Just when she thought it was the end of the story, it got worse. They made Him carry His own cross that was made out of two planks of wood that measured about four-by-six. He had to carry them through the streets the entire way through the town to a hill called Golgotha, where they were going to crucify Him. His injuries were so bad that He could not carry them all the way. After He collapsed, the soldiers finally pulled someone from the crowd to carry it for Him the rest of the way. When they arrived, the soldiers pounded three-inch spikes directly into the hands and feet of Jesus to attach Him firmly to the cross. With each pound of the spike, it ripped through his flesh and bones until they secured Him properly. They also put a sign on the cross, mocking Him by calling Him 'King of the Jews,' as they left the crown of thorns on his head.

When they secured Him, they set the cross in an upright position so He would have to push up with His nailed feet just to breathe. The strain it put on His body was immense.

During this time, two other men on crosses flanked either side of Jesus. One of these men mocked Him, while the other asked for forgiveness from Jesus. Even in the midst of all of His pain and agony, the heart of Jesus broke for the man who asked for forgiveness. With people mocking Him, straining to breathe by pushing up on his nailed feet and bleeding out from his side, Jesus cared so much for that man's soul that He forgave him. He told the man he would have a place in Heaven on that very day. Even with Jesus's last breath, He asked God to 'forgive them, for they know not what they do.'

Casey sat there in awe. She could not believe what this Man went through. Then pastor stunned her even more by saying Jesus did it because He knew people needed Him. He said that Jesus cared so much for those who were His, that He would go through it all over again if He had to…even if it was just for her.

As she sat there, the story went on. He read the section in Matthew 28 Mac also read in the hospital. The pastor explained that Jesus went into the depths of Hell for three days, and then came back, bringing with Him the keys of Heaven.

He not only rose from the dead, but after he rose from the dead, Jesus had the heart to go to Peter, His friend. Jesus made a point to ask Peter *three specific times* if he loved Him, and all three times, Peter said he did, and Jesus forgave him…all three times. When

Casey thought about the significance of it, she realized what Jesus did. Peter denied Jesus three times, and then Jesus forgave him three times, therefore negating Peter's betrayal.

She shook her head at this Man's tenderness. She never heard anything like it until that day. Her life, especially since her parents died, had been in survival mode…every man for himself. She could not believe this Jesus was so selfless. She could not believe what He went through, just so others could share Heaven with God for all eternity.

When the pastor finished his message, he asked if anyone wanted to accept the gift Jesus was offering of salvation from the depths of Hell. Casey *wanted* to believe this was true. She *wanted* to believe someone cared enough for her to go through everything this Man went through for her. There was something deep inside her though, that would not let her leave her seat.

After the service ended in amazing song of worship and prayer, Mac asked if Casey wanted to meet the pastor. She shook her head, still deep in thought from the message.

"What's going on in there?" he asked as they walked out of the church.

"I don't know."

"Is there anything I can answer for you?"

"Well, how do we know the disciples didn't make up that Jesus rose from the dead?" Casey asked. "How do we know what the soldiers said wasn't the truth? I *want* to believe it. I really do! But I just don't know."

They leaned on Mac's car as he opened his Bible to First Corinthians 15:6 and read, "'*After that, He was seen by over five hundred brethren at once, of whom the greater part remain present, but some have fallen asleep.*' It says there were over five hundred witnesses that saw Jesus *after* His death. Casey, I don't know what is going through your mind, but please understand that Jesus just wants you to be free."

"While I want to believe that, I am having a hard time with the concept of believing what all He went through just for me. You have to understand." She shook her head. She wasn't sure if there would be a way for her to explain the complexities of what was going through her mind.

"What if we go out to lunch, and you explain it to me so I can have a better understanding."

"Dutch treat?"

"Yes, if you wish," he conceded.

They went to a local drive-thru restaurant and picked up their food. They took it to a park to eat, instead of staying at the restaurant. They did not want a server to interrupt their conversation.

When they got to the park, they sat down on a blanket from Mac's trunk. He kept an elaborate survival kit in his trunk at all times for emergency purposes.

They ate quietly for several minutes, both lost in their own thoughts. The warm sunshine did its best to distract them as kids played, owners walked their dogs, and people jogged through the park, or took walks around them. They, however, both struggled to come up with the words the other person needed to hear so they could understand each other's point of view.

Mac pulled out his Bible after he finished his meal. He flipped through it for a few moments to find the right verse, before he looked up at her and finally said, "Casey, knowing your past, this is a concept I think *you* of all people will understand. Here, in Romans 8:15 through 18, it says, '*For you did not receive the spirit of bondage again to fear, but you received the Spirit of adoption by whom we cry out, 'Abba Father.' The Spirit Himself bears witness with our spirit that we are children of God, and if children, then heirs – heirs of God and joint heirs with Christ, if indeed we suffer with Him, that we may also be glorified together. For I consider that the sufferings of this present time are not worthy to be compared with the glory which shall be revealed in us.'"* He stopped, setting the Bible down in his lap. "When your parents died, you were granted an inheritance, right?"

"In a way." She nodded. "It was more of a trust fund I received when I turned twenty-five."

"But you got one, right?"

"Right."

"And you were able to indulge in it when you were twenty-five, right?"

"Right." She wasn't sure what direction Mac was going with the conversation.

"And, being an orphan, you can understand the concept of adoption, right?"

"In a way, yeah."

"Okay, then let's take each of these concepts separately. The inheritance concept first," he said, thinking through how to word it. "With your inheritance, you didn't have to wait until you died to get it, did you?"

"No."

"Then by the verses I read in Romans, what is your understanding from them?"

"Well, from *everything* I've heard lately, I think I have it. Jesus is God's Son – the Prince of Heaven."

He nodded. "Yes."

"And, as a Prince of Heaven, He is next in line for the Throne so to speak. But...." she started. He went to cut her off, but she held her hand up to stop him. "*But*, God was, is, and forever will be, so He's not going to die."

"Right." Mac nodded with a smile, pleased she grasped that concept so quickly.

"However, having said that, as a Prince, Jesus still is royalty and is living in the castle with His Father, The King."

"Yes."

"Now, when Jesus came down from Heaven and ultimately died on the cross, even though He rose again, He still gave up His right as the *sole* heir. When He did that, He opened the inheritance to all those who want to accept it, therefore allowing those to live in the castle as well."

Mac grinned, excited. "Exactly."

"But didn't He come just for the Jews? Isn't that why they called Him 'King of the Jews'?"

"Unh-unh." He shook his head. "Well, yes He did, but He ultimately opened it up to everyone. Here, in Romans 10:12, it says, '*For there is no difference between Jew and Gentile – the same Lord is Lord of all and richly blesses all who call on Him.*' You see, it's opened to anyone. They just need to ask. Here, in Matthew 7:7 and 8, it says, '*Ask, and it will be given to you; seek, and you will find; knock, and it will be opened to you. For everyone who asks, receives, and he who seeks, finds, and to him who knocks, it will be opened.*' In John 8:32, it says, '*And you shall know the truth, and the truth shall set you free.*'" He paused a moment before he asked, "Are you free, Casey?"

She looked at him, dumbfounded. That was not a question she was expecting. How did Mac know Casey was struggling with that very thing?

"He *wants* you to be free."

"I want to believe that. I *want* to believe this Jesus guy loves me. I *want* to believe He loved me so much that He went through what He went through, even if it was just for me. I want to believe this whole thing."

"Then what's stopping you?"

"There are things I'm struggling with from my past."

"He doesn't care. We all have our skeletons, Case. Look, one of those men on the cross next to Jesus was a murderer, but Jesus didn't care. He just wanted the man to enjoy paradise."

"You don't understand." Not wanting to make eye contact with him, she nervously played with a blade of grass beside her foot. Her secret was something that only one other person in her life knew.

"Then explain it to me," Mac pleaded.

"It would take too long."

"We have time. It's only one o'clock."

"I don't know if I can." She shook her head. "It's hard."

"Casey, Jesus can use your past to help others. Sometimes He takes us through things so we can assure another person that we understand where they are because we've been there."

"I don't know if you'll understand this."

"Try me."

The tears threatened to overflow from her eyes, but she pushed them back. Shoulders slouched, she shook her head.

"I see the pain." He rested his hand on her arm. "Now help me understand."

"I don't know."

"Case, not everyone has a charmed life. As a matter of fact, I don't know too many who have. Why don't we take turns? I'll start."

Nibbling her nails, she studied him. *Why would he share something personal with her? And if so, was it as deep as her hurt was? Would he possibly make something up just so she would tell him her secret?*

"I was twenty-one, and in college, when I met the most wonderful woman in the world. To me she was everything. She was gorgeous, and one of the sweetest women I knew. She had this stylish, short, spunky-looking, light-brown hair, and these sparkling brown eyes. She was adorable!" He sighed, looking down for a moment before he looked back into her eyes, and continued, "Leah was amazing. She was graceful, kind-hearted, tender, and most importantly a Christian." He paused for a moment of remembrance before going on, "We went boating one summer, about a month before we were to be married, when...." His voice trailed, as he looked back down at the blanket for a moment to collect himself. He took a deep breath before he looked back at her. "We were waterskiing, when I was...I was driving, and she was skiing. I looked forward to see the direction we were headed in, when I suddenly heard her scream. I turned around in time to see her get sucked under the water. Her rope had gotten caught in the motor of the engine, and in her fear, she couldn't let go of the grip she had on the rope." He had a few tears escape from his eyes, as he went on, "It took several months before anyone remotely saw a glimmer of life come back to me." He shook his head. "The pain and agony my soul went through…it made me want to give up right then and there! The blood, the carnage was.…" He sighed, looking up at the sky in hopes of collecting himself. "I was a paramedic and there was absolutely nothing I could do to save the woman I loved. She was my soul mate. With us, it was love at first sight. And in a split second, she was gone," he sniffed. The tears never spilled over, but they rested on the brims of his eyes. "There will never be another woman who can fill the hole that was left in my heart by Leah."

"Wow! I'm sorry, Mac. That's horrible!"

"We all have our pains, Case. We all have things in our lives that break our hearts. Jesus is the healer of our hearts. He is the only one who can piece together those severed slivers, and make your heart whole again."

Casey nervously fiddled with the blade of grass. She knew he wouldn't be able to understand until she confessed.

"What is it?" He searched her eyes for answers. "What is causing you so much pain?"

She shook her head. He quietly waited for her response. She finally took a deep breath in an attempt to control herself, before she looked him square in the eyes and said, "My brother is the only other person on this planet who knows what happened."

"How did you…you mean your other family doesn't even know?"

"No."

"What is it?"

"You have to understand that trust with me is hard." She wasn't sure if she should tell him, but in order for him to understand, she did not feel she had a choice. "I would rather trust you with my life at work, than tell anyone about this."

"Casey," he rested his hand on her arm, "I *will not* tell *anyone*. What you tell me will only be between us. It will be *your* secret to tell."

She sat there for several moments, debating it in her head. This was the biggest secret of her life. However, in order for him to understand the struggle, he needed to know.

"Whatever you decide," he finally said. "If you want me to, I will file it in my head and never mention it again, unless you come to me and ask to talk about it."

"Mac, it's huge."

"Talk to me. I *swear* to you. I make a *vow* to you that I will not say anything."

"If you do, so help me, I will kick your –"

He shook his head. "I won't."

She took a deep breath, before she blurted out, "Somewhere out there is a child of mine."

He waited for a moment, debating in his head whether or not to ask for more. He searched her face for the answers, before he finally shook his head and said, "I'm sorry, I don't understand."

She couldn't control the tears anymore. As a couple of escaped her eyes, she brushed them away. The box in her heart was trying to push open. She was afraid it might spill over if she didn't keep it under control. This was the first time outside of the incident itself that she had the nerve to say it aloud. "When I was thirty years old," she took a deep breath, "I was on assignment in Columbia, when I was attacked and…um…he, um…." Her voice faded as she looked up at him, hoping he could fill in the blank.

"Oh, Casey!" Horror filled his eyes when it registered in his brain what she was doing her best not to say.

"It was totally my fault!" She said, slightly panicked by his reaction. "I wasn't with my guide because he was sick. I should have stayed in the hotel until he felt better, but I thought I would be fine."

"You have to know it was *not* your fault." Mac shook his head. "No man ever has a right to take what is not given to him."

The box of her heart, and the horrors of that day took over. Not making eye contact with him, she pushed through to finish the story. "I didn't report it. I called my brother and he was down there within a couple days to get me. He took an emergency leave-of-absence for two weeks from the military just to come help me." She stopped for a moment to take a breath. "I stayed in my hotel until he got there. When he did, I went into meltdown mode. As soon I saw him, I couldn't help it. I burst into tears." She shook her head as the uncontrollable tears in her eyes spilled over onto her cheeks. "And when he held me, I didn't want him to let me go."

"I can understand that."

"It took me at least a week to get some semblance of my sanity back. We kept it from my aunt and uncle, though. We told them I was spending some of my vacation at his house. They didn't think twice about it." She stopped for a moment. She decided to skip the minute details of the story and gave him the main facts. "When my time of the month came around, and I didn't get it, I figured it was due to the stress of what happened. But when the second month came around with no period, I got suspicious."

He groaned, dropping his head into his hands.

In one quick breath, she added, "Due to the rape, I got pregnant."

His heart broke for her. "Casey, I'm so sorry."

"Jack and I talked about it, and we continued to hide it from my aunt and uncle. When I began to show, we covered it up by saying I was on a long assignment, when in reality I was still at Jack's house. He supported me through it. I could get away with it, because I only had a cell phone since I travelled so much, and my aunt and uncle were used to all the travelling I did."

She took another deep breath in an attempt to gain composure. "Anyway, Jack and I talked. After many days and hours of debate, I decided there was no way I could kill the baby. It wasn't the baby's fault someone raped me. I couldn't keep the baby, though. It would be a continuous reminder of what happened to me every time I looked at it." She took another to line the scattered thoughts in her mind. Then she explained her reasoning. "I couldn't do the baby justice, but I couldn't kill it either. I didn't know what to do."

Mac prayed in his head for clarity of mind and the words Casey needed to hear, but nothing immediately came to mind, so he just sat there, quietly listening.

"Jack and I looked around until we found an adoption agency we felt comfortable with. I kept it a closed adoption though. I didn't want to know where the baby went. It would be too much of a temptation to want to know what happened to it."

He nodded in understanding. "I could see that."

"Well, the day arrived, and I had a little girl. I heard her cry, and could see she was healthy. I was able to hold her for a few moments. I kissed her head and took her tiny hand into mine. Her skin was so soft." She sighed, glancing at her fingers. She remembered how they felt inside her hand.

Rubbing her hands together, she continued with her story, "As I explained to her that her mommy *did* love her, but there was no way I could care for her, she wrapped her fingers around mine. I told her she was going to have parents who would love her and take wonderful care of her. Then I gave her another kiss before they took her away. That was the last time I ever saw or heard about her."

"Casey, I'm sorry," he shook his head.

"Every time I look down at my stomach and see those stretch marks, it's a reminder to me that she's out there somewhere." In control, but with tears flowing, she explained, "Those scars are also a horrible reminder of what happened to me in Columbia. I will never forget that day."

They sat there for a moment in reflective silence before he said, "I can see why trust is so hard for you."

"That's the worst of it, but there are other moments I'm not proud of. My aunt once said I have had more happen to me in my thirty-five years of life than most people would have in several lifetimes."

"I believe it."

"Now you can understand why I'm struggling with the concept that this Jesus guy loves me. Why would He give His life for me? He didn't even know me. While I understand what you have been telling me, it's hard for me to rationalize in my brain as to why He would die for me. To me, it doesn't make sense."

"You do what you feel comfortable with – no more, no less. I'm not going to pressure you in any way. I know you understand it, and I have faith that someday you will be able to accept what Jesus did for you. One day, I have faith that you will want to have a Daddy again…a Daddy who will never leave you. A Daddy who will take the pieces of your broken and tormented heart, and place them all back together again one piece at a time. Until then, I'll be here for you. I will stand by you, even if you just need someone to talk to, or to just sit beside you."

"I appreciate that."

"Casey, I don't think any less of you. I admire you for what you did. Many women in your position would have either had an abortion, or tried to raise the baby themselves, *and* as you said, not be able to give the child justice. I feel bad for what you've been through."

"As you said, we all have our skeletons."

Chapter 5

Welcome Back

Casey slept hard that night. She was sure it was due to finally verbalizing what happened to her so long ago. Vocalizing the visions that haunted her nightmares was a relief. She carried them for so long it was a release to let them out, even if it was just for one night.

The next morning, she got up at six-thirty to take a shower in order to be at work by eight. She slept so hard, she was still not completely awake even by the time she reached the station.

"Hey, Carter." Eden McCullough, from 'C' shift, said. He looked up from the table where he sat, smiling. He was the partner to Captain Marc Adams.

She nodded in acknowledgement."Hey, McCullough."

"Are you okay?"

"Yeah." She shrugged. "I'm just tired."

"Well, it should be an easy day for you. You're on the engine since your partner is temporarily incapacitated." He nodded toward the schedule on the refrigerator.

"Thanks," she mumbled, heading back to the bedrooms to put her clothes next to her bed for the next twenty-four-hours. Afterward, she headed into the conference room for the morning briefing session.

It seemed with Kendall and McCormick gone, the 'A' shift was down by two men. They pulled Christian Hawke from 'B' shift to work with them until Kendall came back. That left 'C' shift with a full crew. 'A' shift would also have Chief Adam Blazedale 'on call' until McCormick came back. The Assistant Chief, Sam Fredrickson, would work with 'B' shift until Kendall came back –

therefore releasing Hawke to go back to his shift. It was a wild swing-around, but everyone knew it was only temporary.

"So, how are you feeling today, McFadden?" Chief asked Jesse after he explained the shift shuffle. Chief was a little over fifty years old, but there was no one else Casey would rather have on a fire scene. His six-foot-four, two-hundred-and-fifty-pound frame intimidated many on scene who did not know he had a funny, tender side. He kept his gray hair short, neat, and clean. He was a firefighter for about thirty years, but refused to retire until he knew he could not safely do the job anymore. To him, safety was the number one priority.

"Oh, it's all good." Jesse smirked, waving him off. "I'm back up to about ninety percent."

"Glad to hear it. What about you, Nelson?"

"I was fine from day one. I'm good."

"Good. Mac?"

"I'm fine."

"Good." He nodded in approval. "Carter?"

Casey jumped, startled. "W-what?"

"Do you need coffee?" Chief chuckled, as some of the guys snickered.

"I don't drink coffee, sir." She blushed. Her pen fell to the ground when she jumped. As she picked it up, she said, "But, thank you." She knew she would never live that one down.

"Remind me after briefing to get you a soda," he said with a smirk. "Besides not being too awake, how are you feeling?"

"Oh, I'm fine. Thank you."

"Good." He nodded, and went on to finish the briefing.

After some general housekeeping announcements, they had an hour of continuous education class. It was on safety on the fire scene. To Casey that was no great surprise due to what happened at the fire the other day.

While they watched the movie/training portion, Chief brought Casey a can of soda. She thanked him as she opened the can, thoroughly enjoying the iciness of the bubbles as they went down her throat – saturating her system with the much-needed caffeine.

After the meeting, they went on to do their chores for the day. "So, Carter, it seems you and I are without partners." Jesse pointed out.

"And…?"

"That doesn't bother you?" He walked backwards in front of her as they walked into the kitchen.

"No. I know Tommy will get back here as soon as he can."

"Well, I don't know if you're aware of it or not, but your partner was usually the one who pleaded on your behalf to the crew regarding your assignments and drills."

"Ah," she smiled mischievously, "but I still have an ace up my sleeve."

"And what, pray tell, would that be?" Will asked as he sat down at the table.

"*I'm* still the cook for at least three more weeks. You guys give me crummy assignments, and I'll do the same favor in return for dinner."

Vinnie shook his head, confused. "But it's *your* dinner too. You'd be punishing yourself in that as well."

"Not necessarily," she knowingly smiled. "When I cook, I snack. I can very easily fill myself enough to last until morning."

"You're a brat, aren't you?" Christian Hawke looked at her in surprise.

"No. I'm just smart," she corrected.

"Well," Chief walked into the kitchen, "I see that soda did you some good."

"It did." She nodded in appreciation. "Thank you, Chief."

"Well, since you're awake, could you come down to the office? We need to talk." Chief rested his hand on her shoulder. She looked at him nervously, as he said, "Don't worry. Let's go."

She went with him, leaving the blanket of silence that enveloped the room at the mention of her having to go talk to the Chief. Chief didn't normally come into the upstairs area, so when he did it generated concern.

When they got to his office, he had her sit across from him at his desk. He pulled her file from the top of the stack. Scanning it for a tense moment, he then looked up at her and said, "It seems you've been here a little over a month, so this is just a little meeting to see how you're doing. Relax, you're not in trouble."

"Thanks," she said in relief, finally breathing.

He crossed his arms in front of him. Sitting back in his seat, he asked, "How do *you* feel your first month has gone?"

"That's a loaded question," she pointed out, "but in all honesty, it's been wild. Every day is different. Every day has its ups and downs. It's a lot of work, but very worthwhile."

"Can I have some examples of that?"

"Well, when I was trapped under the rubble, knowing how much of that building was on top of me, even if at the time I didn't know Mac was near me, I still had the comfort of knowing those guys were giving everything they had to unbury us. I also knew they wouldn't stop until they found each and every single one of us."

"True," he agreed.

"You see, growing up, my brother was my only constant. Here, though, I have a second family. Yeah, I'm a female, and I get teased a lot because of it. I will also admit that it is a lot of work and pressure being a female in a mostly male world, but the end product is worth it."

"Nicely put." He nodded in approval. "So, I take it you are getting along with your crew and partner?"

"Most definitely." She smiled. "Tommy's great! As for the other guys? Every shift we seem to get closer."

"I agree. That's the same thing I heard when I started poking around."

"I *am* concerned with already having to call off one day, though. Speaking of which, here," she handed him the doctor's note from her back pocket. She meant to give it to him before the meeting, but in her sleepy state, she forgot.

"I'd say you had a good excuse." He tucked the paper into her folder. "So, what was going on this morning in briefing? I teased that you didn't look like you were awake, but I think it was more of a deep in thought moment."

"It was," she admitted.

"Do you need to talk?"

"I'm okay." She shook her head. "I was reflecting over everything that has happened over the last several days. I'm fine, though."

"Okay," he nodded. "So, how's your shoulder? I heard you took a hit on the afternoon fire that day as well."

"I did, but I'm fine. It's still a little black and blue, but it'll be okay. How is Tommy doing?"

"He's doing as well as to be expected. He is already going stir-crazy at home, but he won't do me any good here in a cast. He will be out for about eight weeks."

"*Eight weeks*?" Her eyes popped.

"He broke his tibia and his leg is in a cast. If the doctor removes the cast before then, he will be in sooner. With a cast, he can't be on the ambulance *or* the rig, but I'm considering sending him over to the Fire Marshall's office for admin until he's back on his feet."

"I'll bet he'll love that." She felt bad for Tommy. He would go absolutely crazy for eight weeks at home.

"It's better than nothing," he said in a sigh. "Anyway, Kendall's coming back in a couple shifts, which will send Hawke back to 'B' shift. Then I'll be hanging out on your shift until McCormick comes back."

"No more nine-to-five, Monday to Friday for a bit, eh?"

"Well, it depends. When Hawke goes back, I'll probably keep an ear out when your shift is on, and meet you guys on scene if there's a fire. Other than that, I'll just pop in and out."

"How is that going to work in regards to partners if mine is gone for eight weeks, and McFadden's isn't coming back for a couple of shifts?"

"You guys are going to be flipping your partners for the next eight weeks, rotating within the ambulance crews. You are going to work a shift, and then one of the partners in each crew will change out with a new set from another crew. Then the next shift, the two who were on for two shifts will change out for a new set of two."

"Well, that'll shift things around." She looked at him hesitantly, not sure if she liked the idea. She knew she wouldn't have a choice in the matter though.

"Yes, it will. Then, when McCormick comes back, everyone will return to their partners."

"Sounds good." She nodded. Knowing it was only temporary made her feel a little better.

"Now for the review portion."

She smiled nervously. "Uh-oh."

"You are a hard-worker. That's evident in your drills and on scene. You take criticism and direction well. LT is very impressed with you, as well as with your culinary skills." He glanced up at her from his paperwork.

"Yeah, I gathered that." As she sat there, she felt as if he was bracing her for some bad news. The pit in her stomach grew with each passing moment.

"Your attendance is excellent. You even came in for a couple extra shifts when we had a call-off, which attests to your teamwork attitude. Basically," he set the folder down, "as far as your first month, you're doing great. As far as your technical skills, they'll come with time. I'm going to be candid with you. This job *will* challenge you. There will be times when you may have to hang over for one or two days for an out-of-control brushfire, or you will be exhausted from having one ambulance call after another all day only to have a fire call at one o'clock in the morning. There will be times where you will lose a patient and times where you will be able to bring a patient back by resuscitation. There will be days where you and the other teams on your shift will celebrate your hard work at a fire scene. In addition, there will be days where you will mourn together for the loss of a fellow firefighter. This is a hard job, but as you said, it is a worthwhile one. You have started late in your life, but I admire you for it."

"Thank you."

"Having said that, I want you to know that if you keep working hard, continue to do your best, *and* do a great job at it as you have been doing, you should have a good fifteen to twenty years with us."

"Thank you!" She smiled, pleased.

"Good job." He shook her hand. "Keep it up, Carter."

"Thank you, Chief."

"Now, go continue to make Engine Company Fifteen proud."

"Thank you, sir," she said, and then left the office. Remembering the silence when she left the kitchen, she decided to play a trick on the guys. She took a moment to compose herself on the staircase before she continued. She forced the smile off her face and pulled the best somber countenance she could muster.

When she walked into the kitchen, she saw all the guys around the table. They stopped talking as soon as she walked in.

"Well?" Marty asked.

Shoving her hands in her pockets, she looked downcast. Out of the corner of her eye, she saw LT drop his head into his hands in order to hide his facial expression. She saw the glimpse of a smile on his face, but resisted the urge to smile herself.

"What did he say?" Mac asked, concerned.

Visibly upset, Jack asked, "What happened?"

"He sat me down for my one-month review," she said, sitting down at the table, resting her head in her hands. She had to look down because she couldn't keep a straight face while looking at the guys anymore.

"Carter, are you…did he let you go?" Rob's eyes widened, floored.

She took a deep breath before a smile slowly formed on her face. She heard LT burst out in laughter as all the other faces around the room shifted from upset, to confused, to stunned, to utter uncertainty in a matter of seconds.

"Did...?" Johnny stared at her for a moment, before he shook his head, smiling. Unsure, he asked, "Were you playing us?"

Casey grinned, as LT was still smiling. He shook his head as he said, "She got every single one of you."

Rob pointed his finger at her. "You'll get yours at drills."

"Did she really just do that?" Christian asked, amazed. "And here I thought you were this sweet thing, but you're a brat!"

She didn't say anything. She smiled in satisfaction as she went over to look at the list to see what her job was for the day. As everyone slowly dispersed to their chores, they were still laughing about what happened.

LT rested his hand on her shoulder, as he said, "Yep, you fit right in."

"Thanks. You knew I was bluffing, didn't you?"

"Of course. I knew exactly what Blazedale was going to tell you."

"Thanks for the good review by the way. That was very nice."

"No problem. You deserve it. Um, I *did* want to talk to you though."

"Not again." She groaned. "It's only eleven o'clock in the morning, and it's already the second time I've heard those dreadful words."

"It's okay, no worries." He sat down in his chair at the table. "You see, I was approached on Friday with a proposal by a couple of the guys. We pitched it to the rest of the guys on shift, and they agreed to it, so I thought I'd put it by you."

"What would that be?"

"Well, since you're such a great cook, we have a proposition for you."

"Which is?"

"If you cook each time you are on shift, and clean the dishes and your kitchen mess afterwards, the guys will cover all the other maintenance jobs around the station. This doesn't count for the jobs everyone is responsible for each shift, such as your bathroom, your bedding area, and cleaning the truck when we get back from a call."

"I think that's fair," she agreed. Of course it was fair to her. It was exactly what she wanted.

Chapter 6

Real Life Visual Picture

Over the next several weeks, things continued status quo. As far as the partner shift, it turned out to be a blessing in disguise. Casey was able to get to know all the guys in ways she would not have, had the partner shift not occurred. Working with them one-on-one allowed for deep conversations that one didn't get within the regular firehouse setting. She and Mac also had a couple more conversations when they were partners on the ambulance, though none were as deep as they were on the day they were at the park.

Over the course of the last few weeks, Casey went to church with Mac, but the continuous battles of trust still raged within her. She knew her trust issues rooted deep, but she hoped she would be able to overcome them in order to achieve the tranquility she felt when she was in Mac's presence. She knew it was within him, and she wanted it. She also knew trust would be her greatest challenge.

*   *   *

Finally, in mid-July, two months after the warehouse explosion, Tommy was released for full duty. While she was grateful for the time she had with the other firefighters as partners, she was more than ready for Tommy to return. He was too! He came in several times during Casey's shift, mainly for the briefings and classes, so he could keep up with what was going on around the station. He also came around for the continuous education. He didn't want to fall behind in that either. When he wasn't at the station, he worked at the Fire Marshall's office doing administrational work. He frequently mentioned how much torture it was for him to be behind a desk, and that he couldn't wait to be back to full duty.

His first day back was great. It was refreshing to Casey to have him back on shift. She could not believe how much one person's absence changed the personality of the shift.

"Folks," Chief walked upstairs into the kitchen. The living quarters for the station were located above the garage. Casey was working on chicken curry for dinner, while the others worked on their chores for the day.

"What's up, Chief?" Tommy looked up from cleaning the glass doors leading out to the patio.

"First off, welcome back, McCormick. It's nice to see your smiling face back around here."

He grinned. "Thanks, Chief."

"Well, it's that time of year. The Summer Picnic." Chief held up several sheets of paper. One was the announcement and the other three were sign-up sheets. "Since you guys were the last ones with the sign-up sheets last year, you get them first this year," he said, placing them in the middle of the table.

"Is this just an afternoon thing or an all-weekend camping thing like last year?" Jeff asked.

"It starts on Friday morning and ends on Sunday night. Depending on where your shift lands, you will be able to spend one or two nights. Now, this is a family thing, so bring the wives and kids…and boyfriends," he added for Casey's benefit.

"Good! I was hoping he could come," Jesse added his whit to the conversation. Everyone burst out in laughter, knowing he was joking. His girlfriend was a knockout, and they had been steadily dating for over a year.

"Don't forget to sign up to bring something. Oh, and make sure it's on the day you're coming this time," Chief said, looking directly at Callan, who cringed. Tommy later told Casey that Jack messed that up the previous year. This made it difficult for the shift who was camping at the time, because they were missing the meat for their dinner. "Make sure to leave it on the table for the other shifts to sign up as well."

"Thanks, Chief," Rob wiped the TV off as he dusted the living room.

After Chief went back downstairs to his office, the other guys on shift signed in the various slots under the days they were going to be there. Basically, everyone was responsible for their own breakfast and lunch, but the firefighters were to bring something to put together for dinner as a potluck. Chief scheduled it three weeks out, leaving plenty of time to plan.

Casey continued to cook dinner as she wrestled in her mind whether she was going. She and her brother took frequent camping trips when he was home so it would be almost nostalgic for her. As much as she loved camping though, everyone would either bring their families and/or significant others. While the other firefighters would be there, she would be alone.

*   *   *

After the kitchen was clean from dinner, Casey took a run, in order to relax and think. She was only gone for a half-hour when she was on duty, keeping close to the station in the event of a fire call. She also only ran on the days she was on the fire crew since the ambulance calls were frequent.

She would be able to clear her mind on her run when she was out from the chaos of the station. She was single so it was normally quiet around her house. However, when she was at the station the guys were loud, especially if there was a sports event on the television, as there was that day.

When she returned, she waved as she went through to the shower. Some of the guys acknowledged her, but most of them were engrossed in the baseball game on the television.

While she was in the shower, she ran her fingers over the stretch marks on her stomach, remembering the day of delivery. Outside of the conversation Casey had with Mac about eight weeks ago, it had been years since she talked about that day, but the emotional scars were still evident every time she saw the marks on her body.

Casey thought through what Mac said in the park about Jesus wanting to put the pieces of her heart back together. She also considered the surplus of information she gleaned during the church services she attended over the last several weeks with Mac. Despite the fact that everything made sense, she still struggled within herself to trust Jesus.

As she got dressed, the discussions she and Mac had, ran through her head one more time…when she heard the alarm go off for a brushfire.

She tossed her clothes on, and ran her fingers through her hair before she threw it into a ponytail holder. By the time she got to the lockers, the other firefighters had their brushfire turnout gear on. She threw her gear on before she jumped into her assigned engine for the day. LT shifted a crew into the brush rig before the engines took off. The brushfire rig was a tanker truck which carried several apparatuses used specifically for fighting the brushfires.

"Engine Company Fifteen responding," LT said into the radio from his seat in the passenger-side front.

"Copy. Engine Fifteen responding to a brushfire at Roxborough State Park. Time out, twenty-sixteen," the dispatcher responded.

"Now, this is your first brushfire, so stay by me," Tommy said, adjusting his seatbelt while the engine was in motion.

"Engine Seventeen to Dispatch," Captain Henderson's voice came over the radio.

"Go ahead Engine Seventeen."

"You're going to want to send out a conflagration on this one. This looks like it's been going for a while. The wind is high and the fire is about a quarter-mile wide. It has taken out over five-hundred acres already."

"If that thing hits Pike National Forestlands, we're in major trouble." LT remarked to Vinnie regarding Captain Henderson's call.

"Copy that Engine Seventeen, sending out a third and fourth alarm," the dispatcher responded. Dispatch called out Engine Companies Nineteen and Twenty to join the other two companies for more manpower, before sending out the conflagration.

When they pulled up, Tommy passed Casey a water pack and a shovel. The turnout gear for brushfires was much lighter, and there was a different mode of attack used in this type of fire. "Where are we headed, LT?" Tommy asked.

"Check with Henderson. This is his scene," LT said before shouting at the other firefighters from their company as to what gear to pull.

"Yes sir," he nodded. Casey followed Tommy over to Captain Henderson. After the other teams from the station gathered their gear, they checked in with him as well.

Henderson had part of the teams set up a fire-line, since it jumped the one his company made earlier. In the meantime, he sent the rest of them out to go behind the fire, putting out any small fires, or hotspots that could be smoldering and possibly flare back up. Casey and Tommy were in the second group, as they headed out with a couple other teams to put out the hotspots.

*   *   *

They were there for hours. This was going to be one of those fires that would last for days. By the time morning came around, there were over a thousand acres of the four-thousand-acre park consumed by the fire, and containment was at a minimum. There were high winds, tons of trees, and to top it off it was the middle of July – the dry season.

Chief left 'A' shift at the fire, since he called 'B' shift to monitor the station about three o'clock in the morning when he decided it would be a long call. By the time two o'clock that afternoon rolled around, those on scene were exhausted, but determined. They didn't want this fire to win. There were hundreds of firefighters on the ground as well as in the air. They dropped hotshot teams throughout the forestlands, as well as multiple planes dropping slurry in hopes of containment.

The firefighters near Casey were Tommy McCormick, Jeff Campo, Rob Katz, Jack Callan, Johnny Marshall, Vinnie Barnes, and Will Weston. The other teams on duty from her shift were setting up fire lines or putting out hotspots elsewhere. Casey's group had a break at about noon and was not due for another break until around five. During their five o'clock break, they were going to eat dinner and then take naps in tents that were set up. This break would last for eight hours before they would have to go back out to continue the battle. The crews rotated so there were always crews sleeping, eating, fighting the fire, or working in the rescue/medical tent.

Casey's group walked through the forest putting out hotspots. Had this not been a fire scene, this area would have been stunning with its lush green forests and wildlife. Now, however, there were trees burnt and crackling around them, while the ground and taller trees were smoldering. There were various animal carcasses scattered throughout the forestlands. The fire devastated an otherwise gorgeous area. The smell of charred wood was overpowered in some areas by the fauna that were unable to escape. The smells fire generated in its consumption was one portion of the job Casey had a hard time stomaching. The stench was so rancid at times, that she had to force the vomit back down that threatened to spew out.

"We only have a couple more hours, folks," Johnny said at about three o'clock when he glanced at his watch.

Tommy turned toward Casey. "How are you holding up?"

"Me? You're the one who just got your cast off a couple days ago," she pointed out. "How are *you* doing?"

"I'm getting too old for this," Vinnie shook his head. He and Will were about six feet from Casey and Tommy. Vinnie was a full-blooded, six-foot, stocky, Italian – all the way down to his dark brown hair and eyes. He usually had a smile on his forty-year-old face. His heart was just as big as his smile.

"You'll get over it and be right back in the saddle for next shift. You love this too much." Will glanced at him out of the corner of his eye. Will had light-brown hair, medium-brown eyes, and was about thirty-three years old. His six-foot-one slender frame was often misjudged. He was wiry, but he was solid. Unless you knew him, he seemed a bit crass and aloof, but in reality, he had a heart for people. Johnny told Casey that she was of the few who had seen Will cry. He was in the kitchen one day talking to him and Casey was cooking. Will's patient at the time was a six-year-old drowning victim. As he talked to Johnny, he confessed that the hardest part was because it reminded him of his own daughter who was eight, but lived with her mother. Nevertheless, the fact that he took it so hard was what touched Casey's heart.

"You're right." Vinnie beamed in delight. "I wouldn't have it any other way."

"I'm fine." Tommy brought her back to the conversation as he sprayed an area still smoldering. Tommy's approach to the job was to stay disconnected. He often told Casey that in order to survive the harsh parts of this job, he had to separate himself. He joked that the forty-eight-hours off after each shift was a form of detoxification from the stresses of the job.

Casey and Tommy were the closest in age of the teams. The other teams were separated by five to ten years each, whereas they were only a year apart. Tommy was six-foot, blonde-haired, green-eyed, and thirty-six-years-old. When that alarm went off, he went into his zone. However, when he was sitting around the station, or during the times Casey spent with he and Sally off duty, he was a fun-loving, laid-back, life-loving guy.

Casey squirted water on a smoldering log. "Glad to hear it."

"You?"

"I'm doing okay."

"Heads up, folks," Henderson's voice crackled over the radio. "There's a wind shift."

They looked in the direction of the fire, and saw it was less than a quarter mile away.

"Uh, Vinnie?" Casey gaped at the wall of fire. The color drained from her face, as she saw the wind blow in a southerly direction one moment, before it suddenly shifted to northerly the next…heading directly toward them.

"Henderson, this is Barnes," Vinnie shouted into his radio as they ran in the direction of the camp.

"Go ahead."

"We're about three miles out of camp due east with the fire on our ankles!"

"Copy that. Try to get out of there. If you can't, then bunk down in as safe a place as you can, and we will get to you as soon as possible. We have planes dumping slurry, but they are down at the heart. I'll try to get one to hit your area."

"So close, yet so far away," Vinnie said in a sigh. Then he looked over his shoulder one more time and shouted, "Let's move it!"

Casey groaned. "Am I just bad luck, or what?"

"Why?" Will asked.

"First the warehouse, and now this?"

"We'll get out of it. Just pray for another wind shift," Johnny yelled from the other side of Vinnie.

They ran for a half mile before the fire overtook them. "We need to bunk down," Vinnie shouted. He notified Henderson of the situation and their approximate location.

The tiny group scrambled to dig out areas for themselves. Then, they pulled their foil tents from their packs, and tucked under them just as the fire was about to hit. They almost looked like a patch of cocoons.

The tents were made of aluminum foil, woven silica, and fiberglass. They were designed to reflect radiant and convective heat, yet keep in the breathable air so the firefighters wouldn't suffocate. They were created to allow the fire to pass over the firefighters without burning them.

As Casey was under the tent, she thought about the heat of the inferno that was about to engulf them. She hoped the wind would move it swiftly over them, and they would all be fine until it passed.

The hotter it got, the more her mind wandered toward the nightmare she had while in the hospital. With the intensity of the heat, she started to panic. Flashbacks of the nightmare and the fires from that day flashed through her mind.

Then, as they huddled under their individual cocoons, a horrific, shrill scream sliced through any comfort they may have had. Casey jumped. She tightly shut her eyes in fear. The scream was so frightening! There was no way to distinguish which firefighter it was she heard. The nauseating mixture of the roar of the fire, the scream, along with the immense heat and steam, was almost too much for her as it swirled around her. Her mind raced as her body froze.

She took a deep breath and covered her face with the bandana around her neck, while she did her best to survive the blistering heat. In order to keep her mind stable, she thought about each one of the men near her, wondering who it was she heard scream. The yelling only lasted a couple agonizing minutes, but the terror it brought made her blood run cold!

Desperate for some type of distraction, she ran through her head the good things about each of the men there with her. There was Tommy and his smile. She remembered a time of him joking around with LT. He had a refreshing attitude. She thought about Vinnie's broad body, which allowed him to have a boisterous laugh. His laugh echoed around the station. Everyone knew when he was on shift. She thought about Will's slam-dunk at the last basketball game they had while on shift. He was so proud of himself and let out a shout of victory, as those were the final points that allowed his team to win a very tough game. She remembered when Jeff was with her in the hospital, and she had just woken up from the dream. He had both hands on her face, and said 'tell me.' His strength of character and confidence in knowing what he was doing made one feel relaxed around him. She thought about Rob as he barked orders at the others during drills. He made sure they performed them correctly so when they were on a fire scene, they would be safe. The crew had the utmost confidence in him. Then her thoughts wondered toward Johnny's compassion as he sat at the table helping Brennon debrief after a particularly bad call. Johnny's tenderness and empathy made him the most cherished on the shift. And lastly, she thought about Jack as he helped wash the truck one shift after a fire. He took a sponge and chucked it at Scott Kendall, therefore sending the entire shift into a water fight. The guys on her shift had an excellent sense of humor. To the outside world, it may seem uncouth and twisted, and at times a little crass or rude, but it allowed everyone to function and do their jobs. Without the unorthodox sense of humor, the feelings and emotions that come with the profession may become too much.

Casey coughed as the smoke crept its way under the edges of her tent. She adjusted the bandana to a better position, and then sprayed water around the edges she could reach, doing her best not to move the tent too much.

While she waited for the fire to clear, she heard the trees pop, and the roar of the fire slosh all around them. It was as if the fire itself taunted them by dancing around them. The fire knew it consumed one of them, and waited for its chance to claim more victims.

The noise was almost unbearable! Just when she thought she would lose it, she felt the slurry hit her tent, and a few moments later, the fire shifted, and then cleared from of the area.

"Barnes to Henderson," Casey heard Vinnie's voice over the radio. She let out a sigh of relief knowing he was safe. She was not looking forward to finding out who was taken from them.

"Go ahead."

"The fire has cleared us. Please send personnel to assist. We have at least one casualty."

"What's the condition of the casualty?"

"Fatal."

The words hung in the air for several moments before Henderson responded, "Assess the rest of the situation and get back to me as soon as possible. There is a team enroute to your position with a couple rescue baskets and first responder medical supplies."

"Copy that," he responded. Vinnie put his radio back on his belt before he yelled out, "Everyone okay?"

Casey sat up as she slipped the cover off. "I'm fine."

Tommy took his tent off. "Who did we lose?"

"That's what I need to...." Vinnie started, but Will sat up and uncovered himself. "Oh, thank God!" Vinnie sighed in relief.

"I always knew you cared," Will remarked with a smirk. He then looked toward the other cocoons with dread, knowing at least one of them contained a fallen family member.

Jeff uncovered himself. "I'm good."

Rob took his off as well. "Me too."

Everyone turned in the direction of the remaining two firefighters. A charred body rested next to a motionless tent.

"Callan? Marshall?" Vinnie asked, not sure which one was the charred body. He cautiously knelt between them, with Will right behind him. The other firefighters waited anxiously. Casey gulped as she sat there almost afraid to breathe.

As much as Vinnie did not want to lift the cocoon, he knew he had to know. He took a deep breath before he lifted it. As soon as he did, he shook his head and quickly set it back down to cover his fallen friend. The nidorous fumes of the carcasses filled Vinnie's lungs. He swallowed the vomit that filled his mouth at the overpowering stench.

Will covered the charred body with his tent, since the tent that belonged to the body was unusable. Jack and Johnny were the closest to where the frontline hit.

"Which one is which?" Tommy put his head in his hands, felling sick to his stomach.

"Callan was the one whose tent caught. It looks like Marshall died of asphyxiation," Vinnie confirmed. He took his radio off his belt, and said, "Barnes to Henderson and Patrone."

"Go ahead," Henderson said.

"I'm here, go ahead," LT responded.

"Sirs, we have two fatal casualties. The remaining six of the crew are fine."

"Copy that." The discouragement in LT voice was evident.

"Copy. Two fatal casualties, and six able to walk out," Henderson acknowledged.

"Affirmative."

"Stay where you are, assistance should be arriving momentarily."

"Copy that. Thank you. Barnes out," Vinnie said before he replaced the radio back on his belt.

After about fifteen to twenty minutes of complete silence, bordering on tears, Casey said, "I guess Johnny didn't pray hard enough."

Rob's jaw dropped. "What?"

As she dwelt on what occurred, Johnny's words were what stuck in her head. "Right before we ducked under, Johnny said we would get out of it. He said we needed to pray for a wind shift. We got our wind shift, but not soon enough to save them," she pointed out, as she stared at the two cocoons. Thoughts that those bodies could have been any one of them consumed her mind. It could have been her under that tent. She could have died. What was worse was the way her two fellow brothers died. Jack's screams continuously echoed in her mind.

"Casey?" Tommy looked at her in concern.

"Was he a Christian?" Casey asked, dazed.

"Casey?" Tommy asked again.

"Johnny was." Rob nodded. Studying Casey, he struggled to figure out her state of mind.

"A lot of good it did him." Casey stared at the charred body. "He isn't supposed to leave him. Where was He?"

"Where was who?" Vinnie cocked his head to the side, concern and weary written all over his face and body.

"Jesus. Where was He? If He wasn't supposed to leave Johnny, then why didn't He protect him?" She stood up. In a hazy state, she went over to where Jack was, while everyone stared at her.

She picked up the top of the tent, exposing the top half of his body, releasing the odor of the smoldering flesh. As soon as the tang hit her senses, she spun away and threw up. She couldn't contain it. She wiped her mouth from the vomit. Slowly crawling back over to the bodies, her hands trembled. Forcing herself to look at the charred remains, she whispered, "I'm so sorry."

"Casey," Tommy assertively called to her.

Casey reached over to Johnny's tent on the other side of Vinnie.

Vinnie shook his head. "Casey, don't."

She ignored him and lifted the tent anyway. She cocked her head to the side, looking down at Johnny's body. He looked like he was sleeping. It was strange. His face seemed to show pure peace, not the terror that was on Jack's face.

Casey studied the visual picture in front of her as she looked from Jack to Johnny, and back again. The nightmare from the hospital rocketed its way into her mind. When she glanced at Jack, she remembered the people walking around in Hell. However, when she saw Johnny, she thought of the peace he was enjoying in Heaven. The tears slowly rolled down her cheeks.

"Casey!" Tommy snapped.

She was too lost in her own thoughts to hear him as she stared at Johnny. She wanted the peace that was on his face. She did not want the fate that would be awaiting her if she went to the lake of fire. If she died that day, she wanted the confidence of knowing she would be in Heaven. No matter how she died, she knew she could endure anything if she would be able to rest in God the Father's arms when she got there.

She sat down on the ground and lifted Jack's tent again. She glanced from Jack to Johnny. The difference was unmistakably evident. As she looked at them, some of the stories and sermons she heard over the last few weeks began to fall into place like missing puzzle pieces.

Vinnie watched her for a minute before he took her hands and lowered the tents. He kept her hands in his as he shifted so he was kneeling in front of her. "Casey?"

She searched his eyes to see if he had the answers she needed. The tears continued to roll down her cheeks in a steady stream.

"Case?" he asked again.

She couldn't say anything. Eyes glazed, she sat on the ground for a few moments, her body shaking uncontrollable. The reality of what happened finally caught up to her as the adrenaline slowed.

After a minute, Vinnie lifted her chin so he could see into her eyes. "Casey, are you okay?"

"I…yeah." She nodded. She knew what she had to do. "I have to talk to Mac."

"He could be just about anywhere." Vinnie shook his head. "Is there anyone else you can talk to?"

"Mac." She adamantly shook her head. "I need to talk to Mac."

"Case?" Tommy went over, kneeling next to her. He rested his hand on her arm. "We're okay. We made it."

"They didn't." She gestured toward the tents on either side of her. Knowing they were going to have to go through a funeral for both of these brave men slowly sunk in.

As they sat there, several teams ran up to them. LT was among them. "What happened?" he crouched next to Vinnie, while Casey and Tommy sat on the ground next to him.

"It looks like Marshall's tent was on the right, and he...." Vinnie shook his head. He lifted the tent for LT to see.

"Oh my," was all LT said. He turned his face as his stomach churned.

Vinnie lifted the tent, exposing Johnny. "Johnny   was   from asphyxiation."

LT shook his head and sighed. Glancing at the team members, there he stopped at Casey. Her eyes told him she was in shock. "Carter, are you okay?"

"I will be." She nodded. "I need to talk to Mac."

"He's in tent city. You can talk to him when we get back to camp." LT knew she was in shock. He needed to get his crew to safety though, so he did a quick survey of the scene before he shouted instructions. Tent City was the area nicknamed where all the sleeping tents, food tents, and medical tents were located.

LT had the men from the other squad load the bodies into the two rescue baskets, wrapped in the tents that covered them. LT let Tommy, Jeff, Robbie, and Casey carry Johnny's body, while Will, Vinnie, LT, and one of the other guys from the rescue party carried Jack's body. The squad wanted to be the ones to bring their fallen comrades back to camp.

When they arrived at tent city, they were ushered to the medical tent to check out those who made it out alive more thoroughly, while other firefighters loaded Jack and Johnny's bodies into the awaiting coroner's vehicle, which was standing by. The coroner was called in as soon as Henderson was notified of the fatalities. By the time the crew walked the two-and-a-half miles out to the scene, and everyone walked back, the coroner was already at the small tent city.

As a paramedic from another company checked Casey out, she somberly watched the vehicle pull away. Jack's scream would periodically echo through her head, intermixed with visions of their bodies and their faces. Even with the blanket wrapped around her, she shuddered.

Casey looked up when a couple of people walked into the medical tent. One was carrying a camera.

"Oh no. Get out of here!" The medic shouted.

"Run the camera!" the journalist yelled to the cameraman. Then she went over to Casey and shoved a microphone in her face. "Were you there? What did it feel like?"

"Get out!" The medic wrestled with the cameraman in an attempt to get him out of the tent.

"I-I…." Casey shook her head, watching the two wrestling over the camera, before looking back to the reporter in front of her.

"Leave her alone," Tommy warned.

"What can you tell me about the scene?" she asked, jamming the microphone in his face.

Tommy glared at the reporter as he sat there on edge. "Take the hint and back off!"

"Did you know the firemen who died?" The journalist persisted. "What would make experienced firemen make a mistake this critical? How did it happen?"

"That's it!" Tommy jumped up. "Stay away from here! This is a medical tent!" He shoved the journalist out of the tent, and then spun around toward the medic, demanding, "Where are the police?"

"They're near the food tent," He said, before he flung the camera across the tent.

Alarmed, the cameraman shouted, "Th-that's the property of Delta News! You will be charged for any damage to…."

The medic pushed the cameraman out of the tent, before tossing the damaged camera at him. "Leave and don't come back!" The camera cracked and the lenses shattered as it landed between the reporter and the cameraman.

"Watch her," Tommy ordered the medic as he ran out of the tent.

Tommy sent several more firefighters over to protect the tent from the flood of journalists that swarmed the camp on his way to find Henderson. The police were there in a matter of minutes for crowd control. They set a perimeter in order to keep them away from interfering with the firefighters.

"Casey?" Mac came into the medical tent about twenty minutes later with Tommy. "LT said to come find you. Were you in that crew that just…you were, weren't you?" His face registered when he realized what happened. He knelt next to her cot, putting his hands on her arms. "Casey, talk to me."

"She was also attacked by that reporter." Tommy mentioned, as he sat down on the cot next to hers.

"They were…." she shook her head and shuddered. She took a deep breath, and slowly let it out, in an attempt to control her emotions. She knew she could not melt down in front of the other firefighters. She quickly organized her thoughts as best she could. She knew she had to talk to Mac about what happened, but the only question that came out of her mouth was, "Where was Jesus?"

Furrowing his brow, he asked, "What do you mean?"

"When she was on scene, she wanted to know where Jesus was for Johnny," Tommy clarified.

"I looked from Jack to Johnny. The difference between them was…." She shook her head in an attempt to clear it. There were so many images and thoughts trying to push their way through, she couldn't think straight. "Jack wasn't a Christian, and his body was charred almost beyond recognition. Johnny *was* a Christian, and even though he died of asphyxiation, he had this look of peace. It reminded me of the nightmare from the hospital. The heat…." She closed her eyes in remembrance. Taking another breath in an attempt to keep some semblance of composure, she then said, "The roar of the fire…the smell of Jack's flesh burning…the scream…the…." She shuddered.

Mac shook his head. In an endeavor to follow her train of thought, he pleaded, "Case, you're not making a whole lot of sense. I'm trying, but I really need you to help me here."

"Johnny suffocated in his tent, while something happened to Jack's…and he, uh…he was burnt alive," Tommy interpreted for her, as he glanced from Casey to Mac. He knew she was struggling. He wanted to help her, but by what she was saying he knew only Mac could help her.

"Oh my! Are you serious? Wow, guys! I'm so sorry." Mac hung his head. He rested an arm on his knee, while he kept his other hand on Casey's arm. "I hadn't heard the details," he said, shaking his head in disbelief.

The frenzy of police officers and the firefighters clashing with the reporters woke Mac up. LT had come into his tent in the middle of it to get him for Casey. LT told Mac that something happened to Jack and Johnny, but no details. Mac had no idea of the horror that Jack went through and the others lived through. With Casey being a rookie, he prayed for the right words to give her. He could see she was visibly shaken and he did not want to do more damage.

"That could have been me." She searched his eyes, her eyes pleading for him to understand the words she could not form.

Mac sat on the cot beside her. He decided maybe she needed to release what was going on inside her to someone she felt safe with. He and Casey had gotten close over the last several weeks and he cherished the trust she had in him.

"I laid there listening to his screams of pain and agony," she said, as she closed her eyes for a moment. She desperately wanted her body to stop shaking. "I didn't want to die without Jesus! I wanted to talk to Him right there, but I was too scared."

"I know. I'm sorry." Mac gently pulled her toward himself. She rested her head on his shoulder, while he wrapped his arms around her, comforting her.

She cried for several minutes before she finally looked up at him. "When I saw them all I could think was *'where was Jesus?'* Why didn't He protect Johnny? He was a great guy. He was probably the most trusted on our squad. He was a tremendous witness for Jesus! Why would Jesus not protect his own?"

"I don't know. I can't answer that." Mac's heart shattered at the loss of his brothers, but it was breaking in a different way for Casey. He prayed for God to take away her pain. He asked God to give him the words she needed to hear to bring her out of her current state.

Truth be told, he liked her in a romantic way, but had to hold back knowing the station rules. At this point, his love for her friendship was more valuable to him than possibly losing her by wanting more.

"The difference was…it was like I was looking at an analogy of Heaven and Hell right in front of me," she explained.

"It's a good example, but please don't dwell on this. It will suck you in, and you will drown in the nightmare if you continue to stay in it."

"You should have seen Jack's body." She shuddered. "Then Johnny's face was…."

"Casey, you need to focus for me. You're all over the place."

"Mac, it was –"

"I know," he cut her off. "You have to understand that you're in shock. You are even repeating yourself. You need to just relax, eat, and get some sleep."

"No." She shook her head. "I can't sleep. I can still hear it."

"Hear what?"

"Jack's yells were petrifying." Tommy shuddered as it rang through his mind.

"When you guys are ready, you can go eat. Then you guys are on break until one o'clock in the morning," the paramedic said. "That is, unless they get this beast contained."

Mac got up and pulled Casey up with him. "Come on, let's go get some dinner."

Tommy followed them to the food tent. He was not going to let her too far out of his sight until he knew she was okay. He trusted Mac, but Mac did not fully understand what they went through. Only those who were there would be able to understand. He was a seasoned veteran,7 and he was struggling. He could not imagine what Casey was going through.

In the food tent, they had what would be the equivalent of military MRE's (Meals Ready to Eat), along with as much Gatorade as they could drink in order to stay hydrated. Normally in the food tent people were joking around, trying to keep it light, but tonight there was little or no conversation. Everyone in there was exhausted and quickly ate so they could get some sleep.

Casey, Tommy, and the others who were on the crew with them were too consumed with the thoughts of the incident to eat. Mac did his best to encourage them to eat something, but they couldn't stomach any food. Casey would periodically take a bite, but it would just sit in her mouth. She couldn't get the bites small enough to slide down her throat. She would have to gulp it down with Gatorade. She finally gave up eating.

When it was clear they wouldn't be able to eat, Mac, Casey, and Tommy made their way to where the sleeping tents were located. There were six cots per tent. "There is room in our tent for you guys," Mac suggested.

"That will work," Tommy agreed.

"How's she doing?" LT stopped the trio when they got to the tents. He kept an ear out for them, knowing Casey was in the worst emotional shape of the group.

"Still in shock. Give her a couple hours rest and then check back," Mac said, resting his hands on her shoulders as he stood behind her. Tommy stood beside her.

"She's going to be okay though, right?" LT asked.

"LT, *I'm* still even in shock." Tommy shook his head. "Pretty sure everyone who was there is."

"Actually, to different degrees, you are," LT agreed. "I talked to Henderson, and we want you guys to sleep until the morning if you can. I'll check back with you guys at about six or seven in the morning."

"Thanks." Tommy nodded in appreciation. Then he turned to Mac and asked, "You got this?"

"Yeah. Go ahead." Mac nodded. After Tommy went inside, Mac turned to Casey and whispered, "Are you okay?" He knew there were a couple firefighters asleep in the tent and he didn't want to wake them.

She shook her head. "I don't know. What I saw, and what I heard was…." she shuddered again. As much as she tried, she could not get that horrific sound out of her head.

"I know. We need to get some rest, though. That fire is only about thirty-five percent contained. We are probably going to have to continue to fight this beast when we wake up. We need all the strength we can get."

"Before we do, can we pray?"

"We can. Is there something in particular you want to pray about?"

"I want Him."

"Who? Jesus?"

"Yes."

"I'll tell you what. I want you to have a clear head when you do that. I want to have the confidence of knowing that you fully understand what you are doing. So, why don't we talk about it when we get up in the morning?"

She nodded, still in a daze."Okay."

"You need to go to sleep."

She shook her head. "I can't."

They took a walk. While they walked, they prayed for Jack and Johnny's families, for safety for those out fighting the fire at that moment, and for mental stability and clarity for those who were thrown into the middle of the recent situation and survived it.

As they walked, Casey noticed the sunset. The mountains that were normally visible, were blocked. The trees around them were stripped and blackened from the fire. The dirt from the road and the ash from the fire coated the vehicles. What would typically be a gorgeous sunset was marred by the smoke and fire. During the day, the sun looked like a red ball in the sky through the smoke and ash. When it set, it gave off an orange tinge across the sky. The only reason she knew the sun went down was because of the absence of light.

To Casey, the scene looked desperate and desolate. What was once gorgeous, was now destroyed. It would take years to come back. When she mentioned this to Mac, he agreed, but tried to comfort her in reminding her that fire was nature's way of replenishing the forestlands. While it might not seem like it, the forest would recover, and be beautiful once again.

After their walk, they went into the tent. Casey tossed and turned all night long, fighting the visions, sounds, and memories in her mind. She might have gotten about an hour's worth of sleep the entire night.

Chapter 7

A Lesson in Trust

It took a week and a half to contain the twenty-thousand-acre blaze enough for Engine Fifteen's crew to be released. During the battle, they lost four more firefighters from another company. The crew was in the process of setting up a fire line when the fire jumped into the trees and surrounded them before they had a chance to escape. According to those who found them, they died of asphyxiation under their tents. This only reminded Casey of the loss of Jack and Johnny. She and Tommy talked more in-depth about her feelings. He did some training with her on their time off, in order for her to feel more comfortable in the use of the fire-retardant tents.

During that time, the police officers did a terrific job keeping the reporters at bay. They had a camp for the reporters a quarter of a mile from Tent City, giving the firefighters a wide buffer from the insanity. The few brave journalists who attempted to breach the perimeter were promptly caught and given a warning. It disgusted Casey on how they fed on the loss of lives. Between the two accidents, they were chomping at the bit to get some shred of information. From what Chief said, when he visited the scene a couple of times throughout the week and a half, the fire stations back home were having a hard time fighting them off as well. Even after the spokesman made a statement from the Fire Marshall's office, they were relentless in their pursuit for news.

Along with the six lives lost, there were acres upon acres of forestland lost, as well as a couple camping cabins. It was the worst fire the area had seen in years.

Unfortunately, 'B' and 'C' shifts covered the station while 'A' shift was at the fire, and the way the rotation schedule was set up for the year, 'A' shift was on duty the day after they returned. They were exhausted, but there was nothing they could do except hope for an easy shift.

Meanwhile, as soon as LT notified Chief of the loss of the two firefighters, Chief went with Captain Hartley to the families of Jack Callan and Johnny Marshall. It was one of the hardest parts of his job. Trying to bring comfort to a grieving family while he was grieving at the same time was not easy. He felt each one of the firefighters under him was like one of his own family members. He was proud of the group of young men and women in his company. He knew the ramifications of this loss would be felt for months to come.

When he became Chief, the Chief from Engine Company Sixteen congratulated him and then said, "Adam, there will be times where we understand how and why things happen, and there will be times where we simply have to trust that things happened for a reason. When those times come, make sure to understand that those under you are having a harder time with it, and take them under your wing until they can fly again on their own. It is only then that you can process your own feelings. Until then, they are yours to protect and care for."

At the time, Chief did not fully understand the weight of those words, but over the years, he had come to cherish them. He knew his firefighters were going to struggle, and he would do his best to steer them through the rough waters ahead.

With that in mind, he had to work with the City Council to hire two more firefighters. The crew would not be able to function without at least two more. He knew he could never replace Jack and Johnny, but he also understood he had a responsibility to the city to care for those within its borders, giving them the best that Engine Company Fifteen could put forward.

After days of searching, the counsel hired two new firefighters. They were rookies who graduated the previous month. They were highly recommended by their instructor – a close friend of the Chief. They were going to be starting the morning 'A' shift returned. Chief braced himself for the one of the hardest meetings he had to date with 'A' shift.

* * *

"Ladies and gentlemen, this meeting is going to be a long one, with…." Chief shook his head. "There's a lot we have to go over, folks, and I don't know how to categorize it either. First off, thanks to the generosity of the Callan and Marshall families, the funerals for Jack and Johnny were postponed until you folks returned, and will be taking place tomorrow. The calling hours will be tonight, and you *will* be allowed to attend."

Sighs of relief were hear from around the room, while exclamations of surprise were mixed in with the range of emotion felt from those in attendance. They were relieved to be able to attend the funeral, but were surprised Chief would allow them to go to calling hours since they were on shift.

After Chief got them calmed down, he continued, "You can thank 'B' shift for coming in for an hour tonight. You have to return within the hour though, so they can pay their respects as well."

"Yes, sir," came from around the room.

"You will need to go in your dress uniforms, so sometime today stop by and pick them up from home. As far as the funeral tomorrow, while there will be multiple engine companies attending, we will be the lead company. Their caskets will be on the two main rigs, going down the road side-by-side for the half mile between the funeral home and the cemetery. You will need to be here tomorrow morning by ten-thirty to get the rigs ready. The funeral starts at eleven. As you can see, the other shifts have already put up the banners around the station for mourning, along with those on the grills of the rigs. The other crews have also been wearing these black bands on their badges since the day of the accident, and will continue to do so until August 17th, a month after their deaths," he said, handing the bag of bands to LT to pass around later. "Also, due to the severity of the situation, our class for today will be a debriefing session with Tammy Calhoun. She is on the City Council, but she is also a local licensed counselor. She's going to work with us for a couple hours on ways to work through their deaths, as well as ways to continue putting what we do into perspective."

He stopped for a moment to collect his thoughts. Then he sighed, shaking his head. "Guys, I really don't know exactly what to say in a situation like this. Yes, every day we come here we know it's a possibility, but the way those two brave souls left us was...." his voice trailed. Taking a deep breath, he said, "Barnes, Weston, Campo, Katz, McCormick, and Carter, you folks have experienced the worst of this. I give you a lot of credit for even coming in today. In meeting with each of you during some of your breaks this past week, I know you are all still in a bit of shock, and it's going to take a while, but know we are all hurting and stand with you." He was quiet for a couple minutes as he scanned the faces before him.

Lately, Casey had been following Tommy's lead in compartmentalizing the entire situation. Mainly due to lack of sleep, she was able to shove what happened deep down for a while. She knew someday she would have to pull it back up and deal with it, but that moment was not the time. The pain was too fresh for her to look at it objectively.

"Now, on a different note," Chief started, but Tammy Calhoun walked in. "Oh, hello, ma'am." He nodded toward her. "Folks, this is Tammy Calhoun, the wonderful lady we were just discussing. Please have a seat as we finish up." He gestured toward a seat in the front row. She nodded in response as she took the empty seat next to Mac.

"Now, as I was saying, due to the recent unfortunate circumstances, our crew was short two men. While working hand-in-hand with the City Council on this, we were able to weed through the stack of applicants and have two new additions to our crew. Now, I know what you're thinking," he put his hands up to stop the objections that immediately erupted. "But," he continued when it calmed down, "we all know emergencies never take a day off. We all know for each one of us claimed, another has to step up to continue taking care of our fellow citizens. Our job is to protect and to serve. Our job is to care for the injured, to help those who need it, and to take down the beast known to us as fire. This beast tries to claim *whatever* and *whomever* it can. We all have a call to duty, which we have sworn to perform. Now, joining us in this fight are rookies Jay Donaldson and Kim Richter," he nodded toward the two firefighters sitting in the front row that had been silent up to that point. Even now, they obviously felt out of place while the objections rang out around the room. "Now, due to the fact that they *are* rookies, we are going to need to readjust your partners in here so they can be with our experienced fire personnel."

He had to stop the outbursts that erupted again, this time even louder. People jumped up in protest.

After everything that had happened, the idea of partners shifting around was not what they wanted to hear. When one works with a partner, it enables you to know their strengths and weaknesses. This allows the team to work like a well-oiled machine.

"Ladies and gentlemen!" Chief shouted for the third time with not a lot of success. "People!" he yelled, and everyone abruptly went silent. They were not used to hearing Chief yell when he was not on a fire scene. "Sit down, and let me speak! That's an order!" he shouted. It only took a moment for everyone to settle back into their seats. "Thank you. Please be aware that you are not giving our newest family members a good impression of us." He was angry at the behavior of his crew, but understood why they were upset.

Casey raised her hand, praying for God to give her the words to convey what everyone was up at arms about. He nodded toward her to go ahead. All eyes were on her, "Chief, with all due respect, you have to know that we understand the need for our new recruits, but you also have to understand where we're coming from too."

Tammy stood. "If I may?" she asked.

"If you can fix this, go right ahead. The floor's yours," Chief gestured in front of him. He stayed at his podium while she walked to the front of the room.

"Yes, we do understand how you feel," she began. "As a City Council, though, you have to understand that safety is our number one priority."

"Then why didn't you spread the new ones between the other shifts, so all the shifts have one rookie?" Vinnie argued. "We understand the need for safety just as much as anyone. The position you are putting *us* in though, with two new firefighters, along with Carter only two and a half months still new, puts *us* in a *very* bad position. Is there *any* way we can pull two experienced guys from the other shifts and spread the rookies between 'B' and 'C' shifts?"

"No." Chief shook his head. "There are circumstances on the other shifts that won't allow for that."

"Such as?" Vinnie pressed.

"I don't think –"

"Sir, please work with us here," Vinnie cut Chief off. "Help us understand."

"They're going to each be getting a new one within a month as well," Chief explained.

"Why?" Vinnie asked, dumbfounded.

"Tucker from 'B' is retiring and Underwood from 'C' is moving to California."

They sat there speechless for a moment, before Scott Kendall said to the rookies, "Absolutely no offense to you folks, I'm sure you're very competent." Then he turned to Chief, "But, Chief, this is insane! *Three* new rookies on the same shift, compared to only one on each of the others? Come on!"

"You'll work through it," Chief said confidently. "Do you guys trust me?"

Surprised he would even ask, Kendall responded, "You know we do."

Chief looked at each of the faces before him, and said, "Then trust me."

The room was silent for a couple moments. Casey was sure it was a blend of exhaustion, high emotions due to the fire itself, the accident, the idea of losing their partners, combined with the upcoming calling hours and funerals that had them all deep in thought. Emotions were high, and energy was at an all-time low.

"Folks, we're a family," Chief said. "We are all hurting, but we still have a job to do. Help me help you by giving you the people you need. Trust me. The two new firefighters we have in here were very high-ranked in their classes. These two are the cream of the crop. I have the utmost confidence in Donaldson and Richter. All I ask is that you trust me. I've been doing this for quite some time. I *do* know what I'm doing."

"Chief?" Casey raised her hand.

He nodded for her to go on. "Carter."

"We *do* trust you. We even trust the council in this. I think with the emotions of the funerals, and the idea of having to change out our partners, we're just –"

"I understand," he said, cutting her off. "I have taken everything into consideration, though. Folks, there are decisions and choices that as a Chief I don't always enjoy. Each of the teams in front of me is tremendously brilliant, and magnificently proficient at what they do. There is not a single one of you I wouldn't want to respond to a family member of mine in case of an emergency. I just want you guys to take the talent that is before me and share it with Donaldson and Richter. I want them to be of the same quality and caliber as you folks."

No one said a word. Getting a backhanded compliment from him was rare, but getting a direct compliment from him was almost unheard of!

"Now, are you all calmed down enough to hear how the new teams are formed?" Chief asked after another minute of silence. Everyone nodded, giving up the argument. "Okay, here they are. Would you please stand up when your name is called so Donaldson and Richter can see who is who?" The firefighters nodded again. They were done fighting. They knew Chief was right.

"Tony 'LT' Patrone and Vinnie Barnes," Chief started the list.

They stood up and moved near each other while the other firefighters held their breaths, wondering whom their new partner would be. LT was a thirty-nine-year-old, six-foot, full-blooded Italian – a lot like Vinnie. LT, on the other hand, had light brown hair, but still had the dark brown eyes and slightly natural tan skin. He even had a hint of an Italian accent if you listened close enough.

"Jeff Campo and Jay Donaldson."

Jeff stood up and moved over next to Jay. Jay was about twenty-five-years old. He had dark brown hair, blue eyes, and was about six-foot-two. He looked so young. Casey had a hard time believing this would be a good match. There were times Jeff didn't have a lot of patience. She hoped Jay's personality would make up for any shortcomings he would have in the way of his skills until they caught up.

While Jay was young and inexperienced, Jeff was about thirty-eight, and had been in firehouses since he could crawl. His dad was a firefighter, and he was even a volunteer firefighter from the time he was sixteen. He was a full-time, paid firefighter/paramedic since he was twenty-one. Jeff stood about six-foot-three. He had blue eyes, light-brown hair, and while he had a thin frame, he, like Will, was solid muscle.

"Tommy McCormick and Marty Nelson," he said, and Casey gasped.

As Tommy stood up, he squeezed her shoulder before he moved next to Marty, and they sat back down together. Marty was usually happy and full of smiles, but you could tell losing Mac as his partner upset him.

Marty Nelson was thirty years old, and was about six-foot even. He had brown eyes, and medium brown hair. He usually joked around with the best of them, playing practical jokes along the way. Today, however, Casey didn't think anyone was happy.

"Brennon Hanson and Kim Richter," Chief called-out.

"Yes, sir." Thirty-nine-year-old Brennon stood up and moved over to the other side of Kim. Brennon was about six-foot-four, bulky, and had short, black hair and light blue eyes.

Kim, on the other hand, was about five-foot-seven, had long blonde hair and blue eyes. Her figure told that she worked out a lot, and despite her size, could probably hold her own on a fire scene. She was about the same age as Jay.

"Scott Kendall and Rob Katz."

Scott and Rob moved next to each other. Scott was six-foot-five and had dark, curly, brown hair. He was thirty-seven-years-old, with deep, dark, brown eyes. Scott, Casey knew, was going to miss being Jesse's partner – they were known around the station as partners in crime. They loved to gang up on people and were famous for their practical jokes.

Rob Katz, on the flipside of Scott, was a fairly quiet guy but knew his stuff. He was the drill instructor. Usually when one of the firefighters was hurt on shift, he was right there lending a hand. He had a huge servant's heart. Robbie, as they sometimes referred to him, was six-foot-two, with a grayish-red hair mix, brilliant blue eyes, and was about forty-five-years-old.

Will, Mac, Jesse, and Casey had the same thought shoot through their minds, as they waited to see who their new partners were going to be. There was a sense of relief that they would not have to have a rookie, but surprisingly, they were all around the same age. Generally, Chief liked to keep an older firefighter with a younger one. It was obvious he was breaking that rule by the four who remained. Will was thirty-three, Casey was thirty-five, Mac was thirty-seven, and Jesse was thirty-five as well. Casey was not sure what Chief was thinking when he set the teams up.

"Will Weston, you're with Jesse McFadden," Chief said, giving Will and Jesse a chance to move.

People sometimes teased Jesse and Casey that they were twins because they looked so much alike. They both had chestnut-brown hair, green eyes, and were about the same height, five-foot-ten. Jesse, however, had more muscle than Casey, and she was not as athletic as he was either. While she may look thin, Casey was solid. On the other hand, Jesse was burly.

"Last, but certainly not least, Casey Carter and Bryan 'Mac' MacIntyre." Chief announced.

They got up and moved over near each other. Mac was about six-foot even and had dishwater blonde hair and sky-blue eyes. He had a broad chest and was muscular as well. Casey was thrilled to have him as a partner. Outside of Tommy or Jesse, there really was no one else she would rather have as a partner. While she loved all the guys on her shift, and knew there were plusses to each of them, Casey, Mac, Tommy, and Jesse were close to each other.

After the shuffling of the partners, Chief took another half hour for announcements, before Tammy Calhoun got up and worked with them for another two hours. By the time the meeting ended, they were emotionally exhausted and just plain tired.

Unfortunately, they still had a shift to work. While they did their chores, they each took turns taking an ambulance out with their new partners in order to pick up their dress uniforms for the calling hours that night.

When Casey and Mac returned from their run, she headed upstairs to hang her uniform before she cleaned the bathroom.

"Carter?" Kim came into the bathroom about a half hour after she started cleaning.

Casey brushed the hair out of her face, as she looked up from scrubbing the floor. "Yeah, what's up?"

"I wanted to formally introduce myself." Her body language told Casey she felt uncomfortable and out of place. "As the only other female, I just thought…maybe we should...." her voice faded.

"Stick together?" Casey offered.

Kim smiled, instantly relieved. "Yeah."

"Come on in."

"Thanks. So, um, what can you tell me about this crew? What's your brother like?"

Casey raised an eyebrow. "My brother?"

"Yeah. Isn't McFadden your brother?"

"Um, no." She shook her head. Her body was instantly on edge. Casey wondered what *exactly* Kim was fishing for. "I would think our last names would have told you that."

"I just figured you were married. You really aren't brother and sister? You two look a lot alike."

"No." Casey shook her head. She finished the floor area she was working on, periodically glancing up at Kim. "Um, so has Brennon explained what your daily duties are?"

"Yeah. He said you and I are going to be responsible for our bathroom, and I'm responsible for my own bedding area, as well as another area of clean up."

"Yep. We're also responsible to clean the rigs at least once a shift, and the fire rigs again if we get called out on a fire."

"He also said there are drills we have to do to," she said, hopping onto the counter next to the sink.

"Sounds about right."

"*And* he said you were the cook."

"Yeah. Instead of an extra cleaning duty, I get to cook," Casey explained.

"Fair enough."

"It is, mainly because I have to clean the dishes too. Someone else washes down the kitchen itself, but I have to wash the dishes and clean up my cooking mess, so it's fair."

"How is it being a female in a mostly male world?" she asked.

"Well, there are good points and bad points," Casey said, as she got off the floor and brushed her pants off. "A lot of it depends on your personality though. Each of these guys have their strong suits. Think of them as a brother, and they'll look after you as a sister. You have to be on your toes on scene, though. Being that we're on a mostly male crew, you *do* have to prove yourself."

"What do you mean?"

"Not to generalize women by any means, but we have a really bad reputation for being emotional."

"How did…in that meeting…that fire you guys just came from, how did you handle that so well?"

"I didn't, I'm afraid," Casey admitted.

"Not according to the guys who were there. I heard them talking about it later. They were surprised."

"I was in shock. When I heard Jack's scream, it made my blood run cold. I was trapped in the tent with the fire all around us and no way to escape." She looked up at the ceiling in an attempt to keep her emotions under control before she looked back into Kim's eyes. She wanted Kim to get the full impact of what happened. "All I could do was lay there, hoping with everything I had that I wouldn't meet the same fate I just heard. We were trapped. We were at the mercy of the beast. *Never* lose respect for fire," she warned. "It could be the last mistake you'll ever make in your life. It will chew you up and spit you out in a heartbeat." Kim stared at Casey, slightly stunned by the emotion behind her words. "I didn't know who died. All I knew for sure was that there was blistering heat, gusty winds, and a lot of smoke. I knew if I didn't keep myself and the area surrounding me wet, I could very well face the same demon that one of the men I had come to love just faced. You have to understand what we heard." She shuddered. "And then afterward, all you could do was lay there, praying it wasn't your partner. You and your partner are going to become close. Brennon's a great guy, too. Tommy and I were close, and the idea that it could have been him almost made me sick." Casey stopped, struggling to organize her thoughts. "I guess what I'm trying to say is –"

"I get it." Kim nodded in understanding. "And when I go to my first real fire, I'm sure I'll have an even better understanding. While we were in fires at school, they were control burns. The ones from now on are going to be real."

"Coming in on the day you're coming in on, with the funerals…." Casey shook her head. "I don't envy you two. Just file what you are about to see over the next couple of days in your mind and remember it. That way, when you are on a fire scene, you will be more on your toes. You won't want to have to put your family, or your new family here, through that."

She nodded. Casey could tell Kim took her words to heart.

"Anyway, I have to go shopping for dinner if Will and Jesse are back."

"They are. Um, why do you call them by their first names? I thought we were supposed to call everyone by their last names?"

"I can't. Not with everything we go through. Some people do, but I can't. These guys are my family."

*   *   *

Casey was in the kitchen searching for dinner when Chief walked in. "Carter?"

"Yeah?"

"Can you come to the office for a few minutes?"

"Yes, sir." She nodded. After the meeting this morning, she wasn't sure if she wanted to talk to him, but she knew she didn't have a choice.

When she walked into the office, Tammy Calhoun was in there with the Chief. "Have a seat, Carter." Chief gestured toward the empty chair beside Tammy. "After what happened this morning, I wanted to touch base with you. Don't worry, I'm doing it with everyone."

Casey nodded, on edge. "I heard that."

"I think you were among the more outspoken regarding what happened. That's very healthy," Tammy commented.

"I agree," Chief said. "Being a female, that was a heavy concern, but you seem to have a good grip on things – you didn't even cry once."

"Thanks…I think," Casey sad, unsure if it was a compliment.

"Can you tell me how *you* feel about this morning?" Tammy asked.

"Meaning?"

"How do you feel after what all we talked about during debriefing?" she asked.

"I think it's going to be hard. I think there is a lot I'm still going to have to work through. Having said that, I *also* think it's going to take time. I'm pretty sure the funerals will help with closure, but I will never, in my entire life, forget Jack's scream. I was talking to Kim a little bit ago and told her that her and Jay coming in right now, going to the funerals and calling hours, should make them be even more on their toes on fire scenes, so they won't have to put their families, or us, through another funeral. This is a family here. As I was under that tent, I heard that scream. I listened to the roar of the fire and the rushing wind, hoping with everything I had that it would shift soon so no one else would be taken." Casey took a deep breath. "All I could do was fight to survive it. His scream was…there really was no way to know who it was. Not that I don't love each of the other guys on the squad equally, I just hoped with all my heart that it wasn't Tommy, my partner. You get close to your partner, which was also part of our struggle this morning."

"I understand that." Chief nodded. "As close as the partners get, we need to shift them regularly, so you guys can form a bond with someone else. By doing that, it makes the shift stronger."

"I know you know how it works," Casey said. "When you work with someone as close as we do, you know that person inside and out. You know their strengths and weaknesses, and you compensate for them so you work as one."

"I know." He nodded. "And even though you guys are going to take some time to discover that about your new partner, you will find that as well."

"I think it was more of the timing of it, not the concept of it," Casey offered.

"I realize that, but we're not always in control of that."

"I agree."

"This is interesting," Tammy observed.

"What is?" Chief asked.

"While you guys almost seem to be disagreeing, you are on the same page."

"That was what I was trying to tell them this morning." Chief sat back in his seat, crossing his arms in satisfaction. "Carter, you hit it dead-on. Things are going to take time to settle down after this. It is going to get worse before it gets better, though. Having said that, I would like you to look out for Richter, and take her under your wing. You have adjusted amazingly well in this environment, and I think she would benefit from your experience."

Casey nodded in understanding. "Yes, sir."

*   *   *

Casey went back upstairs after her meeting. She was so lost in thought that she almost didn't hear Mac come into the kitchen.

He leaned against the counter. "Hey, Casey, how are you doing?"

"I'm good."

"I've been meaning to talk to you."

"Oh yeah? What about?" Casey turned to him, concerned.

"Do you remember the first night at tent city?"

"Yeah."

"Do you remember what you asked me?"

"I asked you a lot," she said, confused. "Can you be a little more specific?"

"You wanted to pray to Jesus."

"I still do," she said. Then she looked up at him and smiled, as she added, "But not here."

"Do you understand why I didn't let you do it that night?"

"Yes."

"Are you okay with that?"

"Yep."

"Are you okay with the partner switch?"

"Honestly, outside of Tommy or Jesse, you're the only other one I would rather have as a partner."

"Wow," he said, taken aback. "That was sweet."

"Don't go getting all sappy on me." She smirked.

He shook his head, laughing.

*   *   *

About an hour before the 'B' shift crew were to arrive, everyone went to get ready. Being that Casey and Kim now had to share the bathroom, it made them take a little longer than normal, since there was only one shower, one sink, and one toilet, but they managed.

As soon as 'B' shift arrived, they divided and loaded-up into LT, Brennon, and Will's vehicles to head to the funeral home. While Casey had been to quite a few funerals in her life, she was *not* prepared for how hard these funerals were going to be for her.

As expected, Jack's was a closed-casket funeral, but Johnny's was open-casket. Jack's was a little easier since it was closed-casket, but as soon as Casey saw Jack's photo beside the casket, the tears instantly appeared. She refused to let them overflow, though. She dropped her head and blinked her eyes to prevent the tears from forming puddles until they went away. She did her duty and hugged his girlfriend and mother. Then she gave words of condolence to each family member of his, before she and the others headed across the hall toward Johnny's calling hours.

As soon as she saw Johnny, Casey's mind released a cascade of flashbacks. She gasped as she remembered staring at both of their bodies under the tents. She recalled the overwhelming stench Jack's smoldering flesh emitted. The flashbacks evoked the chaotic uneasiness she felt while trapped under the tent, as the smoke seeped under, trying to get to her. Then, Jack's shriek of terror rocketed through her mind…and she froze, wide-eyed and pale. Her heart was beating so hard, it overpowered any other noise around her. All she heard was the pulsating pound of her heart.

Mac nudged her forward. When she didn't move, he asked, "Case?"

"I-I can't." She stared at Johnny's body in the casket, the scream continuously echoing through her mind.

Tommy heard Mac and turned around. "Casey, are you okay? You don't look…um, we need to get you some air, I think." Tommy grabbed Casey's arm.

"Why?" LT turned around, as he was in front of Tommy in line. As soon as he saw her, he ushered the three of them out of the funeral home.

When they were outside in the fresh air, Tommy sat Casey down on a bench. "Take deep breaths. That's it…in…and out…in…and out," he coaxed.

"What happened?" Mac crouched down in front of Casey. "You were fine at Jack's calling hours."

"Seeing him lying there…h-he looked the same as he did on that day." She felt like her head was spinning out of control, while she fought to gain some sense of composure. She slightly rocked on the bench while the thoughts and feeling distressed her mind. It was a feat to have one collective thought.

"Carter, you're pale. Can you tell me more?" LT pressed.

"The flashbacks were so strong. I could even smell Jack's flesh smoldering. I could hear the roar of the wall of fire. I could…." She closed her eyes for a moment and shuddered, before opening her eyes again.

"Are you guys okay?" Jeff poked his head out the door, while Jay looked on from behind him.

"Yeah. We'll be fine," LT said. "Go back in."

"She's not going to pass out, is she?" He asked, getting a good look at Casey. He glanced over his shoulder before he stepped outside. As Jay followed him, he closed the door behind him. "She looks like she's in –"

"She is," LT cut him off. "Give her a few."

Casey resolutely stood. "I'm fine." She took a deep breath. "I'll be fine."

"You know what the definition of 'fine' is?" Tommy asked with a sly smile.

By his facial expression, Casey was not sure if she wanted to know what was going through his mind.

"Fine stands for: freaked out, insecure, neurotic, and emotional."

Casey sighed impatiently. "No, I mean I'm really fine."

Mac crossed his arms as he stood in front of her. "You don't *look* fine."

"I *need* to do my job." Casey knew she had to do her duty and push through like a good little soldier. She knew what was required of her. She had to go pay her respects to Johnny's family and finish her shift. The funerals tomorrow would be a challenge, but she would do what was expected of her.

"You're still pale. Can you sit for a few more minutes?" LT attempted to help her sit back down. Her body language told him she was not ready to go back in yet.

Shaking her head, she said, "Not right now."

"Case, you're stuffing your feelings." Mac pointed out.

"I have to do my job," she insisted, "which right now entails going back in there. Johnny's family deserves the same respect Jack's did. I *have* to do this."

"Okay." LT put his hands up in surrender. "Let's go. Keep an eye on her, Mac."

"Yes, sir," he agreed.

"I'm fine," she said aloud, as the silent battle contended within her.

When they returned to Johnny's side of the funeral parlor, Casey refused to look at the casket. She focused on her duty, and on Johnny's family. She gave his mom and sister a hug, and shook his brother and father's hands. Afterward, she headed out to the vehicles with the others. In order to survive the calling hours, she had to separate from her feelings and shut herself down. She was so intensely focused, that she didn't say a word the entire ride back to the station.

When they returned, Casey quickly changed, before heading into the kitchen to make a snack for the traditional movie time.

"Carter?" Kim cautiously walked in with Jay.

"Hey guys. I'm making popcorn. You two want to pick a movie?"

"Are you feeling better?" Jay asked, while they awkwardly stood in the kitchen.

"Yep," she said. "I'm fine."

"Really?" Mac walked into the kitchen and leaned on the refrigerator; his arms crossed in front of him.

"Yep. Um, if they're not going to pick a movie, why don't you pick it?" Casey took the bag of popcorn out from the microwave and put it in a bowl.

"Let's take a walk," Mac suggested. "You're really tense."

"Nope. I'm fine," Casey insisted.

"Come on." He set his hand on her arm, but she pulled away.

"No," she said. Bracing herself on the counter, she took deep, cleansing breaths. She knew she needed to stay in control of her emotions for at least the next two days, despite the fact that they wanted to spiral out of control.

"Are you sure?"

"Quit pushing!" She snapped. When she turned, she saw the look on their faces. They just stood there, jaw-dropped. "I need...." She bolted from the kitchen, outside toward the basketball court. She felt like she was suffocating and needed air.

Grateful they finally gave her space and didn't follow her, she breathed a sigh of relief. She needed the fresh air and the openness of the outside. She took her cell phone out and called her brother, Jack.

"Hey, Space Case!" He answered his phone.

"Hey Jumpin' Jack, I...." As soon as she heard his voice, she couldn't help but start crying.

"Casey? What's wrong?"

She fought to control her tears. "We had this horrible fire."

"Yeah, I figured you did. I saw it on the news. Were any of those guys who died from your station?"

"Yes."

He took a moment before he asked, "Casey, what happened?"

"Two of them were ours. One of was burned alive, and the other died of asphyxiation."

"Were you there?" he asked in understanding. He knew her so well that there was no need for her to tell him much in order for him to comprehend the reason for her call.

"Yeah."

"Case, talk to me."

"We just got back from their calling hours."

"And?" he pushed.

"I was okay at the first one. It was a closed-casket."

"But you lost it on the second one, huh?"

"As soon as I saw him, I started having flashbacks. They were even to the point that I could smell the smells and hear the sounds from that day. It was like I was right back there."

"Being in the military, this isn't something I'm a stranger to," he started. Casey knew he, of all people, would understand. "It's something you never get used to either. This is one of the reasons why I didn't want you to become a firefighter, but it's in your heart to want to help others. I knew when you started on the ambulance company you would be headed into things you would never forget. I also knew the things you would be doing would help save lives. I understood that the danger would be high, but the reward would outweigh the danger. In all honesty, it's basically the same things I deal with all the time. I've buried friends. I've carried their bodies back to the extrication point. These are men I trusted with my life. I couldn't leave them, even if they weren't there. My heart breaks for you. I know the position you are in now. I also know beyond a shadow of a doubt that you are going to be able to handle this. You *will* get through it."

She rolled her eyes. "I'm glad one of us thinks so."

"You are stronger than you think. Get through the funerals, and then you can go home and cry it out."

"Is that what you do?"

"Despite what the world thinks, yes, real men *do* cry. Casey, I can't hug you right now, but you know I'm there in spirit."

She wiped the tears off her face. She couldn't help the smile on her face through her tears. "You're amazing."

"Why?"

"Because, even though you are anywhere from ten to thousands of miles away, you still know what I need just by talking to me."

He chuckled. "I'm only a couple hundred miles away right now."

"Right *now*."

"You are a very strong woman, Case. What you went through, what you are going to be going through, is going to test you, but you *will* pass. Given time, you will pass this test just as well as you have passed the other tests in your life."

"Thanks, Jack."

"I have known you all your life. While I might not be there right beside you, you have to know I'm with you in spirit."

She nodded. "I do."

"Then trust that I know you better than yourself. I know what you are made of. I *know* you can do this."

She smiled again. "Thanks."

"Work through it. Journal, scream into a pillow, go running, talk to someone who can give you a hug. I know with your job that last one seems like a virtual impossibility, but it *is* possible. There were times I pulled one of the other guys aside and we took a walk. We would talk about what happened, and there were times we even cried together. I won't do that with just anyone, but there are some who I trust enough to do that."

"There are a few guys here I trust like that."

"Then go grab one of them and cry."

"I can't until tomorrow night."

"Why not?"

"Because I'm still on shift and tomorrow is the funeral. I have to hold it until –"

"Casey, if you're calling me while you're on duty, then I know you need help. If you're on shift, and you're taking time out to call me, then you need to go find one of those guys and talk to them."

"What do you –?"

"I *know* you," he cut her off. "Yes, we keep in contact, but not when we're on duty unless there's an emergency."

Casey nodded in understanding. There was nothing she could say, he was right.

"Now, I love you," he continued.

"I love you too."

"Then go find one of those guys you trust and cry for a little bit."

"I will."

"Call me tomorrow if you want to."

"Thanks, Jack."

"I'm here for ya, babe."

"Thanks. I know."

"Go to work."

"I will. Bye," she said, and they hung up.

Chapter 8

Fallen Brothers

After Casey went back in, she took a jog instead of talking to someone. She needed to clear her mind. She noticed a couple other guys took off for a run as well, so she knew it would not be a problem. The funerals affected every one of the firefighters, even the new ones.

Since it was a quiet night, Casey ran for an hour that night. She had a lot swirling around in her brain, and she needed to get her head back under control. When she got back, she took a shower before heading to her bed to lie down.

Kim came into the room an hour later. "Hi, Casey."

"Hey, Kim. What's up?"

She sat down on the side of her bed as she admitted, "Today was tough."

"I'll bet."

"Um what are you going to do about…I mean with how tough today was, how are you''-- going to be able to handle tomorrow?"

Casey thought through how to word it for a moment before she said, "In a job like this, weakness is not something you want to show, especially as a female. I did temporarily lose it tonight. That's not something I'm going to be able to change – what's done is done. Having said that, I would hope those guys out there still respect me, knowing the way I have been before it occurred, as well as since the accident itself.

"They do. We were talking about it while you were gone," Kim admitted.

"You were…what did they say?" Casey's heart raced as a nervous panic churned deep from within her stomach. She hoped what happened tonight was not going to negate everything she worked for over the last few months.

"A couple of the guys shared their stories in detail. Some even cried a little." She shook her head. "It sounded horrific."

"You have *no* idea."

"They're concerned about you…not that you're mentally unstable or anything like that. It's just because you haven't vocalized what's inside of you. You haven't shared your feelings. And the fact that you just about passed out tonight, LT's worried about what tomorrow is going to do to you."

"I'll be fine. I'll deal with everything after it's over. I'll have a day and half to work through it before we have to be back on shift again."

"Casey! Babe!" Jesse came in and sat down on the side of the bed opposite Kim. He rested his hand on Casey ankle as he asked, "How ya doin', sis?"

Casey smiled as Kim glanced from Casey to Jesse in confusion. "I thought you said –"

"We're not," Casey smirked, cutting Kim off. "Some of the guys jokingly call us twins because we *do* look so much alike."

"The fact that we're the same age doesn't help matters," he added.

She shook her head in amazement. "Incredible."

"So, what brings you to the bedroom so early?" Casey glanced at her watch, which told her it was only ten o'clock.

"You," he said bluntly.

"Excuse me?" She asked, taken aback.

"I think we need to talk."

"Jesse, I.…" her voice faded as she shook her head.

"Nothing personal, Richter, but would you please leave us alone?" He asked her.

Casey crossed her arms in front of her in irritation, as Kim closed the door behind her on her way out. "So, did you draw the short straw and have to come after the fallen pup?" Casey snapped.

"Don't be like that," Jesse said. "You know we're all close here."

"Yeah."

"And, as a family, we're all worried about our sister. Now, before you object, know it wasn't a lottery in an evil or bad way – I won."

Casey narrowed her eyes at him. Sitting up, she waited for him to go on as he crossed his legs in front of him.

"Mac and Tommy fought over who would talk to you first, while LT and Vinnie argued over whether or not to talk to you at all. Then Campo, Nelson, Hanson, and Kendall pulled for all of us to just sit you down and talk to you together, while Katz, Weston, and I were just plain concerned because of what we saw at the funeral. Poor Donaldson sat there, forced to watch it all go on for over an hour or so." He nervously rubbed his hands together. "Casey, we love you. We have all sat down and talked it out. Some of us have even cried. We watched you stuff your feelings this week. Whenever anyone started to see a glimpse of you dealing with them, you stopped, took a breath, and plowed through leaving your feelings in the dust. Working this job, there will be more bad times that you are going to have to work through. There will be good times as well. You need to trust us, though."

"I do!" She looked at him, startled he would think otherwise. "How can you say I don't?"

"Because you won't trust us with your feelings."

The words hung in the air for a moment while she debated what he said, versus what her response should be. After another moment, she decided the best way to word it was, "If I do, then you will think I'm weak."

"Do you think Tommy's weak?"

"Oh, heavens no! He is a very strong guy!"

"He was crying tonight."

"Really?" Her eyes widened in surprise. Tommy was well liked and admired, but also known for keeping his feelings to himself.

"Do you think Vinnie is weak?"

"No way! He's got that Italian vigor behind him."

"What about Katz or Campo?"

"Jesse." She shook her head. She knew the direction Jesse was headed.

"Those guys were crying too…even Weston. And you can bet that Marshall was crying under that tent, knowing it was *his* partner that was burning alive right next to him, and there was absolutely *nothing* he could do about it."

His words struck her heart. She felt the same way.

"Casey," he rested his hand on her ankle, "Despite what it looks like, we all have a heart here."

"I know, but I'm a woman."

"And being a woman, there are times where we may need *you* to be the one to start the emotional conversations – mainly so we don't drown in the emotions of everything ourselves. We admire you and the work you do. I might not have been there, but I saw all of you when you came back on that day. You were all in shock. There are times when I still see that look on your face. And even though you were all hurting, you still got up the next morning and faced that beast head-on, and helped us defeat it. That takes a lot of guts in my book."

She nervously fiddled with her sock. "Thanks."

"You are strong, but you're only human. We may be guys, but we're the same in that arena," Jesse said. Casey looked up to see tears forming in his eyes as he continued, "Johnny and I came in together as rookies. We were together from the beginning. Jack was young, but he had a strong heart."

"He did," she agreed.

"Those were two very brave men, and you can bet they gave their all. Jack could always make us smile when he joked around, even if we were at the point of anger. And Johnny? He never gave any less than one hundred percent in everything he did. That man had so much heart and compassion for people, it was incredible sometimes to just sit down and talk with him. His insight into everyone was dead-on."

Casey wiped the few tears that escaped her eyes as she remembered her comrades.

"The way they went was unfair," Jesse declared.

Casey sniffed, wiping her nose with a tissue. "It was."

"Look at me, Case." He rested his hand on hers to stop her from playing with her sock. She looked up at him as he said, "Johnny was a best friend to everyone on this crew. They told me he had a look of peace on his face, which I think is very appropriate for him."

"He had that same look on his face at the…he looked today exactly the same as he did on that day."

"I understand that, but you know he's in a better place, right?"

Casey nodded as she wiped her tears away with her shirt sleeve.

"Jack always knew how to lighten the mood. The way he went was a way no man should *ever* have to go, especially him. He brought laughter to the world."

Casey shook her head.

"Vinnie told us you were looking at both of their bodies on scene. What were you thinking when you looked at them?"

"Honestly?"

"If you want, this conversation is top secret."

She nodded. "I do."

"Then trust me, as your brother."

She took a moment before she responded, "Heaven and Hell."

"Um, could you clear that up? What do you mean?"

"Remember the nightmare I had in the hospital?"

"Yeah, Weston, Campo, and Mac told us about it when you were unconscious, and we were changing shifts, so to speak."

"Well, in the dream, the people down there looked a lot like Jack did on that day. I also know Jack wasn't a Christian."

"He wasn't." Jesse shook his head. "Johnny was though."

"I know. And Johnny had a look of peace on his face." She took a deep breath before she explained, "It was a perfect picture of Heaven and Hell. Jesse, you have to understand that Jack was hardly recognizable." Casey felt as if she was on an emotional rollercoaster, as the battle to control her feelings raged inside her.

"I heard that."

"In seeing his photo beside his casket, I was still able to keep things in perspective, mainly because I didn't have to actually see his face. But when I saw Johnny...." her voice faded as she shook her head.

"What did you feel?" Jesse asked.

"It wasn't what I felt." She closed her eyes and shuddered as the events slowly crept back through her mind.

"What do you mean?"

"It was like I was right back there on the side of that mountain." She struggled for a few moments on how to explain it. "Seeing Johnny lying there with the same look on his face as he did on that day, sent me right back to when I was kneeling between them, looking at them. I saw Johnny lying there, in his peaceful state, knowing he was, at that moment, sitting with God up in Heaven. I saw Jack with his flesh still smoldering…his body, clothes, and skin were burnt off in places. You have to understand." She crossed her arms, holding herself. "The smell was horrific! The sound of the fire still danced around us, taunting us. As it slowly crawled away, it relished in the fact that it had captured two of us. We were trapped! We were at the mercy of the beast!" she cried harder as she tried to get him to understand. "We were –"

He cut her off by pulling her toward him. She was such a mess that she melted into his arms. He moved up to the top of her bed and held her as she cried for at least ten to fifteen minutes. She could not stop no matter how hard she tried. All of the emotion she bottled over the last several days erupted with a flow of emotions that refused to stop.

"Shhh, it's okay. You are alive. You're okay," Jesse said. It took Casey several long minutes before she heard him. "It's okay, Casey. You're okay."

She looked up at him not sure what to say. There was so much inside of her, she didn't know where to begin.

He moved back away from her and tucked some of her hair behind her ear. Looking deep into her eyes, he said, "You are okay.

You're strong. You *will* make it and you *will* continue to stand beside us in this battle. You can't let it win."

"I know."

"You're still going to have moments, but tomorrow I want you to concentrate on pride. I want you to be proud of what those two brave men took on and faced every day they came to work. I want you to have a sense of pride as you represent this engine company. I want you to be proud of Jack and Johnny and their bravery. I want you feel that sense of pride we all feel when we beat the ugly beast we call fire. I want you to know you belong to a family. I want you to know your brothers may have moved on, but we have a new brother and sister in their place. I want you to take all of that, and face tomorrow with that strength I know you have in you."

She wiped the tears off her face. "I will."

"We're all going to lose it sometime over these next few days, rest assured. We won't think you're weak if we see you lose it too. You're human, same as us."

"Thanks." Casey smiled. The release of emotions allowed Casey to gain control over her body once again.

"Now," he took her hands into his. "We still need the remainder of our family in order to have our family movie night activity."

"You guys haven't watched the movie yet?"

"No. I told you we've been talking." He stood. "So, grab your pillow and let's go."

Casey picked up her pillow and headed in to the main room with Jesse. As soon as they walked in, no one said a word. No one needed to. They could tell by their faces that the conversation was heavy. Now was not the time. It was a rough day, and everyone just needed to relax. They needed to watch a movie, while snacking on popcorn and soda…as a family. It was a family whose face had drastically shifted over the last few days, but Casey had faith that they would be stronger in the end.

Thankfully, that night *was* a relaxing one with only a few ambulance calls. The next morning after the next shift got there, Casey's shift was released. She went home and took a shower before changing into her dress uniform for the funeral. She returned to the station by ten o'clock to help, as the others from her shift slowly filtered back in by ten-thirty.

They took off the hoses and neatly stacked them in the back of the garage, so they could replace them after the funeral. They ran black banners along the sides and back of the engines. They also placed a black flag of mourning just below the American flag and their engine company's flag, which waved from the antennas of the trucks.

When they finished, the firefighters loaded into the two decorated trucks and headed toward the funeral home. The station closed for the day, leaving the other companies in the area to cover their territory until after the funeral. 'B' shift was set to begin their shift at six o'clock that night in order to give everyone some time of mourning.

There were several other companies represented by members of the shifts not on duty at the time. Overall, there were over two hundred people in attendance.

Due to the size, they were going to have the memorial part of the service at the gravesites. Those from the station would walk behind their fallen comrades the half mile to the graveyard from the funeral home, right behind their families.

When they arrived to the funeral home, there were cars lined up and down the streets. People were everywhere. Vinnie, Campo, Nelson, Tommy, Mac, and Casey carried Johnny's casket, while LT, Hanson, Kendall, Katz, Weston, and Jessie carried Jack's casket. They slid them onto the backs of the engines where the hoses were located on an average day, with their caskets draped by an American flag.

Afterward, those from the station lined up behind their families. Chief Adam Blazedale drove the vehicle with Jack's body, and Assistant Chief Sam Fredrickson drove the vehicle with Johnny's body. After the firefighters from the station, the friends and extended families of Jack and Johnny followed behind them. Then the remaining firefighters of the other stations walked behind them. As they walked, there was a small crew of firefighters who played bagpipes and snare drums walking between the families and the firefighters.

The mood was solemn but proud. Casey continued to run Jesse's words through her mind the entire time. While she did tear-up, she did not cry. She *was* proud to be in this engine company. She was proud to have the privilege of working beside those two great men. She would never forget their smiles and laughter, which blended well with their tenderness, compassion, and zest for life.

Both Jack and Johnny added a perspective on life that not only assisted in the formation of the crew in general, but also spoke deeply to Casey. The biggest thing they showed Casey was a visual difference between the choices of Heaven and Hell. Unfortunately, it cost them their lives. This was not going to be a gift she would dismiss without heavily weighing the decision she faced.

Chapter 9

Jumpin' Jack Carter

It took an adjustment period of a couple weeks before the crew bonded with its new members. They also had some trouble finding ways to work closely together due to the differences between some of the new partners. The adjustment process took a little more time, but they soon found themselves able to function well as teams.

After a while, the rookies even fit in. They relaxed with the others on shift a little more as the days went by. Jay and Jeff became quite a pair. On the basketball court, they were unstoppable. Casey was sure their height had something to do with that. While they bonded from the beginning, Kim and Brennon started a bit rocky. Since then, their relationship formed into a big brother/little sister relationship. She had become the official little sister of the shift, while Jay was the official little brother.

Also, during that time, Casey and her brother had several long conversations. He helped her by using stories from his military experience. He listened to what she was feeling without interrupting, allowing her to download. It helped her because with her feelings out, she was able to face her shift and focus on what she needed to do for the day.

While they worked hard, everyone excitedly anticipated the camping trip coming up in a few days, that is, except for Casey. She was not sure if she was going. While the rest and relaxation it would provide was something as a group that they needed, the fact that all the families and significant others were going to be there and she would be alone still weighed heavily on her mind.

"You know, Carter." Mac scanned the sign-up sheet while he ate his lunch. "I don't see *your* name on here anywhere."

"Really?" Scott took it from him. He quickly scanned through the list of names. "What's up with that, Carter?" He looked at her, almost hurt.

She shrugged. "I don't know if I'm going or not."

"How can you *not* go?" Jesse asked, upset. "*Everyone's* going."

"I know, but…never mind." She shook her head. "You won't understand."

"I think *I* do," Tommy said, knowingly.

"Care to explain?" LT asked Tommy.

Casey narrowed her eyes at Tommy, almost daring him to tell.

"I don't know if I can." He shook his head. He and Casey talked about when they were partners before the brushfire, so of course he knew the reason she was hesitant in going.

"What? Keeping secrets?" Will frowned. "And here, I thought we were closer than that."

"We are, but…." Casey started, but shook her head.

Jeff rested his crossed arms on the table. "What's going on, Carter?"

"Well, you guys have all your families and/or significant others, while I…," her voice trailed off.

"…Am going to be lonely?" Mac finished.

Casey nodded, ashamed and embarrassed.

"The only time you're going to officially be alone will be when we go to bed," Brennon explained. "We're together the rest of the time hiking, playing games, talking, swimming, or just plain relaxing. You need to go just as bad as the rest of us."

Casey debated it in her head. "I know, but –"

"No buts," Mac cut her off, as he snatched the paper back from Scott. He glanced through the list and said, "We need three two liters of soda and three bags of chips. You won't even have to cook."

"Fine." She rolled her eyes. "If I go, will you guys back off?"

"Please…and thank you." Will nodded, pleased.

"Go ahead," she agreed.

"Now, if you sign up, you need to come. We're counting on that stuff," Mac said, signing her name.

"I'll come. Geez! You guys are relentless!"

"No, we just want you to go," Jay pointed out.

"It wouldn't be the same without you," Rob added.

She shook her head, smiling. "I'm going already!"

*   *   *

Over the next couple of days, Casey got her tent out of storage and set it up in the middle of her living room to air out. It was a small, two-person pup-tent tent. She also laid her sleeping bag out to air as well.

Just as she was about to load up the rest of her belongings on the day of the picnic, her cell phone rang.

"Hello?"

"Hey, Space Case!" Jack said in a light-hearted mood.

"What's up, Jumpin' Jack?" Casey smiled. They had their nicknames for each other since they were young, but they were the only ones allowed to use them.

"Well, I was wondering what you were doing this weekend?"

"Oh, are you serious?" Casey sulked.

"What?"

"The picnic for the station is this weekend. This is one of those weekends off for you, isn't it?"

"I always enjoy camping with you," he said, walking through her front door on his cell phone.

"Jack!" She squealed in excitement. She dropped her phone and ran over, jumping into his arms. He spun her around in a hug and kissed her cheek. "I'm so glad you're here!" She said with tears in her eyes as he set her down.

Jack was about six-foot-three and had green eyes. His dark brown hair was well trimmed, and he was always clean-shaven. Being in the military had left him fit over the years, even for a forty-year-old.

"So, we're going camping?" he asked.

"If you want to." Casey grinned. "I'm so excited you're here." She hugged him again. "Here, let me get you a sleeping bag." She ran into her bedroom and pulled out her spare sleeping bag from the closet. "You have clothes, right?"

"Yes." He laughed. "You're funny!"

"I'm just so excited! I can't believe you're here. I've wanted to see you for weeks."

He hugged her and kissed her head. "Love ya, Space Case."

"I love you too, Jumpin' Jack."

After a couple more minutes of loading Casey's jeep, they headed to the station for directions. Casey neglected to pick them up when she was on shift the day before.

"Well, how are you this morning, Carter?" Chief asked when Casey walked into the station with Jack.

"Great! Chief, this is my brother, Jack Carter," Casey introduced them. "Jack, this is my Fire Chief, Adam Blazedale."

Chief shook his hand. "Nice to meet you."

"It's a pleasure to meet some of the people taking care of my little sister." He smiled.

"She's a treat! A great cook too," Chief bragged.

"You don't have to tell me twice," Jack squeezed her shoulders.

"Thanks." she blushed. After a moment, she asked, "Um, are there any more maps to the campsite?"

"Sure. Just a second." Chief took off for his office. He was back in a matter of minutes with the map.

Zoey whistled, as she and Bobbi Jo walked through the garage. "Well, *hel-lo!*"

"Hi guys." Casey cringed. She felt bad for Jack. She knew what was coming. Zoey and Bobbi Jo had a horrible reputation for almost throwing themselves at any cute guy who had the unfortunate circumstance to cross their path.

"And you are?" Zoey asked, as she and Bobbi Jo gave Jack the once-over from head to toe on their way over to them.

"Jack Carter." He shook Zoey's hand.

"Carter, as in…?" Bobbi Jo questioned Casey, as she took her turn to shake Jack's hand.

"As in my brother," Casey clarified.

"Well then," Bobbi Jo grinned even bigger, "it is *my pleasure* to meet you."

"We, uh, need to go. We're headed out to the campsite," Casey said, shoving Jack toward the door.

"We'll see you tomorrow then." Zoey winked at Jack as they left.

"*What* was *that*?" Jack laughed when they were outside.

"They are a couple of barracudas. Keep your distance."

"I'll try my best! Trust me!" He laughed again. "I don't like girls who are *that* forward."

"I'll do my best to run interference for you. I'm sorry." Casey's face flushed in anger at her fellow firefighter's behavior.

"Why? You didn't do it." He rested his arm over her shoulders while they walked to the car.

"No, but they're part of my station."

"Don't worry about it. Here, let me see that." He took the map from her. "Um, this is about an hour and a half away. What if we go out to breakfast first?"

"What if we drive-through fast food and eat on the way out? I want a decent spot for the tent."

"It's a pup-tent," he razzed her. "How much room do you need?"

"There's a small porch for it. I also have a small gas grill and table I want to set up. Besides, we're going to be there for a couple of days. I don't want to be stuck on an anthill or something," she said, as they got into her Jeep.

"Let's go." He started the Jeep. He was going to drive, which was fine by Casey. She tended to get lost when heading into the mountains. Her sense of direction was slightly skewed, despite Jack's best efforts to train her when she was younger.

It took a couple hours to get to the campsite. By the time they got there, most of Casey's shift was already there, along with their families or girlfriends. Kim was there with her family, no boyfriend.

"Carter! About time!" Mac smiled when he saw her go to the back of her Jeep to retrieve her belongings.

"Yeah, did ya get lost?" Will teased. He stopped, and his smile faded when he caught sight of Jack getting out of the jeep. Stunned expressions flashed across several of the firefighter's faces.

"Looks like I took a couple people by surprise," Jack said, noticing the sudden mood shift. "What do you say if we mess with them a bit?"

"What do you have in mind?" Casey asked.

"Unless they specifically ask, don't volunteer that I'm your brother. I want to see what *they* volunteer."

Casey shrugged, pulling out a few bags. "Works for me."

"Need a hand?" Mac walked over to the Jeep.

"Sure." Casey handed him a bag of groceries along with Jack's sleeping bag. She carried half the cooler and her sleeping bag, while Jack carried the other half, along with their tent.

When they put everything down, Mac turned to Jack and put his hand out. "Bryan MacIntyre. I'm her partner."

"Jonathon," Jack shook his hand. Jack's formal name was Jonathon, but his nickname was Jack. He had gone by Jack since he was a little boy.

"Nice to meet you," Mac said. "Um…pick a spot," he gestured toward the campground. "There is room over by us. My brother and I are over there." Mac pointed to where there was another two-person tent. His brother was with Marty and Tommy. They kept an eye on Jack and Casey while they worked on the fire.

Jack nodded in approval. "Sounds good."

Casey and Jack made quick work of the tent, sleeping bags, and pillows. Then they returned to the car for their gym bags of clothes.

"They're curious," Jack whispered to Casey on their way back.

"What do you mean?"

"Well, that one and those two, along with the three over there have been watching us since we got here…mainly me." He nodded toward Mac, who stood with Tommy, Mac's brother, and Marty at the fire pit. Then he nodded toward Jeff and Jay at the basketball court. Finally, he nodded toward Jesse, who was over in the woods getting firewood, but keeping an eye on them as well.

Casey smiled in amusement. "That's funny."

"Casey, I'm so glad you're here." Kim walked up and gave her a hug. "And you are?" She asked, as she put her hand out to shake Jack's hand.

"Jonathon."

"I'm Kim Richter. I work with her at the station."

"You're a firefighter too?" He asked Kim, slightly surprised.

"Yeah, why?"

"You just look so…I'm sorry," he stammered. "You look so young."

"She's a rookie," Casey explained. "She's only been at the station for a couple months."

"Ahh," he nodded in understanding. "I see."

"Sooo, do you have a last name?" Kim pushed.

"Yep," he said, and ushered Casey away from Kim, leaving her there jaw-dropped.

"You're bad!" Casey glanced back at her. Kim turned and headed over toward the fire where she talked with the guys.

"This is *very* funny," Jack said, scanning the group at the campsite.

"What is?" Casey asked.

"You're open with them, aren't you?"

"Yeah, why?"

"Because they *expect* you to tell them who I am. They don't want to assume, but they're surprised that you *might* have a boyfriend and them not know."

"You think so?" Casey took another look around before she and Jack ducked into their tent.

"I *know* so," he said. "And they sent Kim to find out what she could."

"Hey, Carter, are you going to cook for us here too?" Jay yelled from the basketball court. "I'm hungry!"

Casey poked her head out of the tent and said, "Sorry guys, you're on your own. I was told I wouldn't have to cook."

"By *whom*?" LT shot from one of the lawn chairs.

"I *believe* that is why I was assigned soda and chips."

Jay shook his head in disappointment."Aww, man!"

Casey smirked as she ducked back into the tent. "So, what do you think we should do first?"

"I think we should help set up camp. Maybe see if we can find some more rocks to build up a wall for that fire. Then maybe we'll take a dunk in the lake afterwards to cool down."

Casey nodded as they headed out of the tent. "Sounds like a plan."

Casey and Jack walked to the fire pit with armfuls of dry rocks they gathered from the woods. Jack said not to get them from near the lake, because the wet ones would explode when exposed to the heat of the fire.

Mac furrowed his brow. "What's that for?"

She huffed. "You call yourself a fireman, and you have that skimpy wall for a fire?"

"Good point," he conceded. He and his identical twin brother helped Casey with the rocks, while Marty and Tommy took them from Jack.

"So, is Sally here?" Casey asked Tommy while they stacked the rocks around the circle to make a higher wall.

"Yeah, she's swimming with Kara." He gestured toward the lake where Jesse's girlfriend was swimming with her.

She nodded. "Cool."

"So, um, I know it'll seem blunt, but I thought you were coming alone? Wasn't that your concern?" Tommy probed.

"Yeah." Casey glanced up at Jack, who smiled down at her.

He gestured for Casey to finish. "Then?"

"I didn't come alone." She shrugged as she stood up. Jack casually draped his arm over her shoulders.

"Casey," Jesse came over with piles of wood in his arms, "level with us. We're your brothers, here."

Casey smiled as she hugged Jack. "Guys, this is Jonathon."

"Jonathon...*what*?" Mac crossed his arms in front of him, getting impatient with their game.

"Lieutenant Colonel Jonathon 'Jack' Carter, at your service." Jack put his hand out to him.

Mac stood there, stunned for a moment before he reluctantly shook his hand.

"I'm Tommy McCormick. I used to be her partner." Tommy shook his hand as he studied him trying to figure out if Jack was who he thought.

"Lieutenant Colonel? As in the military?" Jesse brushed his hands off on his shorts to shake Jack's hand.

"Yes, sir. The United States Air Force, to be exact," Jack clarified.

"Jesse McFadden."

"I'm sorry, did you say Carter?" Mac made sure he heard what he thought he heard.

"Yes, sir," Jack said.

"You know," Jesse rubbed his chin in thought for a moment before he said, "I'm known around the station as her brother, but I think, and this is just a guess, mind you, but I think you are her *real* brother, aren't you?"

"Yes, sir." Jack nodded with a grin.

"Jack." Mac snapped his fingers as he remembered. "In the hospital, you said you had a brother named Jack who was five years older than you."

"Right," Casey said.

"But you said your name was Jonathon," Mac said, still confused.

"Jack is a nickname for Jonathon," Jack explained.

"True." He nodded, as he unsuccessfully attempted to connect the dots in his head.

"Don't hurt yourself thinking about it." Casey crossed her arms. "It's all good."

"Okay, so, I *think* I have it," Mac started, "You are her brother, Jack?"

"Yes," Jack said.

"And *when* did you come around? Last I knew, you were somewhere in Abu Dhabi."

"Not this week," Jack said, sitting on a log resting near the fire pit.

Mac crossed his arms. "You get my point, though, right?"

"Yeah, I got it." Jack shrugged. "And, I got in this morning."

"As I was loading the car, he came and surprised me," Casey added.

Mac stood there, still trying to fit some pieces of the puzzle together. "Well, that makes sense."

"Well, ya got some height on ya, brother. How about a game of hoops?" Jesse asked. "Maybe we can beat Campo and Donaldson."

Jack looked around the campground. "Who are Campo and Donaldson?"

Jesse pointed out the two still playing on the basketball court. "That's Campo, and that's Donaldson."

"They're good, eh?"

"Good? They're unstoppable!" Jesse baited Jack.

"Well then, brother, let's go show them what the Carter family is made of," Jack said, with a look of determination on his face.

"Go show them exactly *why* I call you Jumpin' Jack," Casey said, as she squeezed his hand before he left with Jesse for the basketball court.

After they took off, Mac pulled Casey aside for a walk. "What's up?" Casey asked, as they walked toward the tree line.

"Is that really your brother?"

"Oh, yeah! That's Jack Carter in the flesh." Casey glanced back at Jack, before she turned back toward the direction they were walking.

"You *really* had no idea he was coming?"

She stopped. Brows drawn together, she asked, "Why is this bothering you?"

He put his hands on his hips. Looking up at the sky for a moment, he turned back to her and asked, "You didn't lie to me about coming alone, did you?"

"Oh! Heavens no! I really didn't know he was coming until he walked through my door this morning. Please don't think I lied to you."

"I just…." he shook his head. "It seems weird."

"He pops in and out whenever he can," she shrugged. "I'm guess I'm just used to it."

"What if you weren't there?"

"He would have called my cell phone and probably met me up here. What's your problem, Mac?" She wasn't sure what was going through his mind, but she knew there was something.

"I don't know," he shook his head. "I guess with meeting your real family when we have been your family for so long it was just a bit much."

"Consider it an extension. I'm not upset that you brought your brother. I don't get it."

"Casey, I…." He looked up at the sky and sighed.

"Mac? What is it?" she rested her hands on his shoulders as she searched his eyes for answers. "What's going on?"

He shoved his hands into his pockets. "Never mind."

"Mac, we're partners. I *know* when something is bugging you. You can't hide it from me."

"If we weren't partners, would you still know that?"

"Of course! We're close. We're as close as Tommy and I are."

He took her hand and pulled her down the path.

"Where are we going?"

"For a hike. Are you okay with that?"

"Yeah, that's fine. It's just that you're acting a little weird. What's wrong?"

"There's a ridge up here I want you to see."

"Okay." She shrugged. It took her a moment to catch up to him enough that he wasn't dragging her. When she did, they walked side by side down the path, still holding hands.

When they arrived, what she saw took her breath away. "Oh, Mac!" She stared at it in awe. "I had no idea something this beautiful was so close."

Looking down at her, he quietly said, "I did,"

Soaking in the view, she was amazed by the natural beauty around her. "This is absolutely stunning!"

"What angle would you take the shot from?" he asked a few minutes later out of curiosity.

"This one is perfect. I would take one from this side and one from right here." Casey made a rectangle with her fingers so he could look through.

"Beautiful." He nodded in approval. "Here." He sat down on a rock, patting the seat next to him.

Casey sat down beside him. "Mac, what's wrong?"

"Nothing."

"There is something rolling around in that thick skull of yours, and it's big. What is it?"

"How do you know?"

"Because, ever since we got here, and you saw Jack, you have had a different look on your face. It's kind of like when you're on a fire scene and you're trying to stay alert, because something is amiss."

He shook his head, smiling. "That's exactly how I feel."

"Why?"

"Because I'm in love with my partner, and knowing her older brother is right there watching every move I make has me on edge," he said, and waited for her reaction.

"I love you too. And, just because Jack is here, doesn't mean you need to be on edge. He's only looking out for me."

"I know, but he's a big guy," he pointed out.

"Then don't mess up," she jested.

He looked out over the valley for several minutes, before he asked, "On the day of the accident, you wanted to accept Christ as your Savior. You haven't asked since then. Is that still something you want to do?"

Watching an eagle soar and land in its nest on the side of the mountain, she said, "I do."

"Why?"

"I don't want to die without Him. I want to know that when I die, I can run into His arms."

"What about now?"

"What do you mean?"

"Well, you're talking about when you die, but what about now? What would make you want Him now?"

"I don't know," she said. "I don't completely understand it all, but I know somehow, for some reason, He felt I deserved Him. He felt I was worth giving His life for me. We work together all the time, and there is not a single one of you guys I wouldn't give my life for, to make sure we all get out of a fire scene alive. But this Jesus? He went above and beyond the call to duty. He willingly gave *everything*. He was tormented, tortured, and even disgraced for me. I don't know why, but I know that Man loves me for some reason. He thought I was valuable. He fought for me. I want to do that for Him in return. I don't know how, but I'm sure He'll teach me."

"Well said." He nodded in approval. "Is that something you want to take care of soon?"

"Actually," she looked around, "there's no one else here, and we are in this incredibly majestic setting, created by God Himself. Why not now?"

"Well, okay. If you remember, there were two sections of verses I read to you – one in Matthew and one in John. The one in Matthew said, '*Ask, and it will be given to you; seek, and you will find; knock, and it will be opened to you. For everyone who asks, receives, and he who seeks finds, and to him who knocks, it will be opened.*' All you have to do is ask and He will give you everything you need. If you just ask Him to take control of your life, He will lead you. He has a plan for you – one that will fulfill you beyond your wildest dreams! Look at this view. What do you see?"

Casey scanned the valley and saw another eagle soaring over the trees. "Freedom," she said in a sigh.

"If you remember, the verse in John said, '*And you shall know the truth, and the truth shall make you free.*' Jesus *is* the truth. With His life, He set you free. He is all-powerful. He is all mighty. He is all knowing. He is the Alpha and the Omega, the Beginning and the End, the First and the Last. He is the One who is, who was, and who is to come…the Almighty One. Is this the One you are choosing to follow?"

She smiled as tears filled her eyes, and she felt tingles all through her body. "Yes."

"Then," he reached out with his hands and she took them. "Repeat after me," he started, "Lord Jesus…"

"Lord Jesus," she said with her eyes closed.

"I give You everything I am."

"I give You everything I am."

"I give You everything I am not."

"I give You everything I am not," she said, smiling in understanding.

"Because You already know it."

"Because You already know it."

"I'm giving my life back to You once and for all, and I'll never take it back again."

"I'm giving my life back to You once and for all, and I'll never take it back again." she repeated. As she did, she felt more tingles through her body.

"Forgive me."

"Forgive me."

"Heal me."

"Heal me."

"Fill me."

"Fill me."

"In Jesus's name."

"In Jesus's name."

"I thank You, Lord God for a Spirit of Grace…a Spirit of Fire."."

"I thank You, Lord God for a Spirit of Grace…a Spirit of Fire." The tears overflowed her eyes, flowing in a steady stream down her cheeks.

"By the Blood of Jesus, I thank You for everything You are."

"By the Blood of Jesus, I thank You for everything You are."

"And I ask You for Your guidance and protection all the days of my life."

"And I ask You for Your guidance and protection all the days of my life."

"I ask You to allow Your plan to come to fruition in my life."

"I ask You to allow Your plan to come to fruition in my life."

"In Jesus's precious name I pray…Amen."

"In Jesus's precious name I pray…Amen," she sighed, soaking in the presence of God.

"Oh, Jesus," Mac kept Casey's hands in his, "I thank You for the decision this precious daughter of Yours has made. I ask, by the blood of Jesus, that You go in and heal her mind…heal her soul…heal all those little pieces of her shattered heart. Let her feel Your forgiveness. Let her feel Your presence. Let her feel Your Spirit soar within her. Let her feel *You*, Lord. Let her *know* You are with her, and will *never* leave her. Let her know that she is a daughter of The King." He took a moment to reflect before he continued, "Father, this is absolutely beautiful. What a wonderful place for her to start her new life with You. She is a new creation in You. Let her feel just how much You value her. Let her know You created this just for her. Let her feel Your strong arms around her. Let her feel safe. In Jesus's precious name I pray, Amen."

Casey smiled as she looked up at him. "Thank you."

"It was my pleasure. How do you feel?"

"Wonderful. I finally feel peace." She looked out over the valley and sighed, "What a beautiful place to do this. I'm glad I waited."

He smiled, pleased. "I'm glad I was able to walk through this with you."

They both quietly looked out over the valley deep in their own thoughts. Casey prayed in her head to God about everything that happened over the last couple of months. She felt like she had a clean slate in her mind, and could face whatever challenges lay ahead of her. She had an energy and vigor in her that replaced the heaviness she felt since the brushfire.

They walked the half-mile back to camp and made a beeline for the lake where Jack, Jesse, Jay, and Jeff were sitting in the water, cooling down after their game. Casey ran and jumped in right in front of them, splashing the water over all four of them. This sent the six of them into an instant water fight. Jack picked Casey up and threw her into the air about five feet. She splashed into the water, landing on her back. As she sunk under the water, the coolness of the lake instantly surrounded her, refreshing her body and soul. She stayed under for a few moments to enjoy the energizing effect the water had on her before she went back to the surface.

She cheered as she came up. "That was awesome!"

"Glad you think so!" Jay tackled Casey, sending her back under again. As soon as they came back up, she dove for his middle, sending him back under again.

"Whoa, little one." Jack wrapped his arm around her waist, holding her slightly out of the water.

"Let me go." She laughed, kicking her legs to wiggle free.

"Not until it cools down a bit. It's getting a bit too feisty for my taste."

Mac floated on his back in the water near them, as Jesse and Jeff continued to battle in out in the water near them.

"Ugh! I just want to play!" Casey grinned. "I have so much life in me right now."

Mac smiled up at her knowingly. "Gee, I wonder why."

She smiled back at him, knowing it came from God.

Chapter 10

Let the Games Begin

That night in the tent, Casey explained to Jack what happened with Mac on the ridge. While he said he understood, he also said it was not for him.

"Relax," Jack tried to encourage her while she sat, biting her finger nails out of nervousness, "I'll be fine."

"How can you say that? This is your eternal life we're talking about here. You're not guaranteed another tomorrow. Jack and Johnny taught me that."

"I can tell you're passionate about this, but it's not for me."

"You didn't see Jack's body. You didn't smell the flesh the way I did in that dream. It's real, Jack! It really is! How can you sit there, knowing everything you've gone through even in your own life and say it's not real?"

"I don't know that I believe this Lord God Almighty thing. I mean, how can there be One person in charge of billions of people? I can't wrap my brain around it. I also don't know if I believe this Jesus guy was real either. If I'm good, I'm sure I'll go to Heaven…if there even *is* a Heaven."

Casey knew Jack well enough to know she could not convince him, but she knew who might have the words he needed to hear. She got up.

He grabbed her arm. "Where are you going?"

"I need Mac."

"No, you don't."

"Yes, I do."

"Casey, you don't *need anyone*."

She stopped. Studying his body language for a moment, she suspiciously asked, "What are you trying *not* to tell me?" His behavior told her something was going on with him, but it was not until that moment that she understood.

He shook his head. "Casey."

"Jack, I *know* you! You are protective of me, but today you are more so. It's like you've been on edge, making sure I'm set in case...." She gulped. She didn't want to know the answer, as she asked the question. "What's going on?"

"In doing what I do, I've been exposed to some things that have dangerous side effects."

Her stomach lurched. "Please don't tell me...."

"I only have a couple months left."

"*What*?" Casey dropped to her knees. A trail of tears streamed down her face. "Jack...no."

"Casey, I love you. You know that."

"You're the *only* family I have."

"No. I know you have a family here. I needed to see it for myself. I needed to know you were going to be okay. These guys will look out for you. They're going to be your family now."

She shook her head, distraught.

"Casey, get a grip for me." He grabbed her arms. "We've been together since the beginning. You'll always be my Space Case. Look at it this way. I'm going to be with Mom and Dad. We'll be waiting for you."

"No!" She desperately pleaded, "You have to be with *me*."

Shaking his head, he explained, "That's what I just said."

"Mom and Dad, as far as I know, weren't Christians. If you die and you are not a Christian then I *won't* see you when I die. I'm going to be in Heaven with God, but you won't. Please let me go get Mac so he can explain it to you?"

"They're sleeping."

"Please?" she begged.

"If it'll make you feel better," he finally relented.

"Thank you! I'll be right back." She grabbed his head and kissed it before bolting from the tent.

She knew it was around three in the morning, but she also knew Jack needed to hear what Mac had to say. "Mac?" Casey lightly knocked on his tent door. She didn't hear anything, so she tried again a little louder. "Mac?"

She heard shuffling around in the tent, before she saw the zipper unzip. "Casey?" It was his twin brother, Ryan.

"Is Mac awake?"

"Not really." He rubbed his eyes. "He sleeps like a rock."

"Can I try? Please? I really need him right now."

"What's wrong? Are you crying?"

"Yes. Please?"

"Yeah, go ahead." He moved aside, so she slipped by him into the tent. "If you can wake him, more power to you."

"Mac?" Casey gently shook him. When he didn't move, she shook him harder. "Mac, please?"

"Mac, Casey's crying." Ryan threw his pillow at him. "Wake up, man."

"Why you…!" Mac sat upright, less than six inches from Casey's face, as Ryan turned on the camp light in their tent. "Casey?" He stared at her in wide-eyed surprise. He touched her face to make sure she was real. "Are you crying?"

"Jack needs you," she pleaded.

"What happened? Is he hurt?"

"He's dying, Mac. He needs Jesus. He doesn't know Him. Please come help me. He only has a couple of months."

"Is he still in your…hey, Jack," Mac said, as Jack suddenly appeared in the doorway of the tent.

"Come on in, bro." Ryan shifted so there was room. "The more, the merrier."

Jack slipped in and sat down on the bottom half of Ryan's sleeping bag. Meanwhile, Casey adjusted herself to a more comfortable position on the bottom half of Mac's sleeping bag.

"What's going on?" Mac asked, his head clearing from the fog of waking from a deep sleep. He got a good look at Casey. "Casey, you look horrible! I haven't seen you this upset since…." It suddenly registered in his sleepy brain what Casey told him. He turned to Jack and asked, "Did she say you were dying?"

"I am," he admitted. "That's why I've been so alert this weekend. I need to know you guys are going to take care of my little sister. I have always been there to protect her. I was the one responsible for her, but I am not going to be around after a couple of months. I need to know, for my own peace of mind, she is going to be okay."

"She is now," Mac said.

"She told me what happened on the ridge," Jack explained. "And, she's scared because I don't know if I want to trust this God of yours. Trust, for both of us is hard."

"But especially for you, since you've pretty much had to raise her as your own," Mac finished Jack's thought. Jack didn't say anything. He just stared at Mac, letting him know he struck a chord. "Yes, your aunt and uncle physically raised you guys for five of those years," Mac continued, "but I know she relies on you more. You are very important to her. You're the only dad figure she's known since she was eight. You had a lot put on your shoulders for a thirteen-year-old. You did a tremendous job taking care of her emotionally, as well as financially. She told me how, after bootcamp in the military, that she moved in with you on the base when she was only thirteen. You did a wonderful job raising her. You fought for her, protected her, and gave her your all. But, what about you? Who protects you? Who looks out for you? Who takes care of you?"

Jack blankly stared at him. He never thought about things from that perspective.

Casey took comfort by his facial expression. She could tell things were sinking in.

Jack glanced at Casey, looking back to Mac. "I-I don't…."

Mac rested his hand on her knee. "Casey, we love you, but can I talk man-to-man, *alone*, with Jack?"

"Yeah." She gave Jack a hug before she left the tent. She sat on a log near the fire that was still smoldering. Ryan joined her a moment later.

"Want some company?" he asked, as he sat down. "Things are going to go deep in there."

"Yeah." She wiped the tears away. She felt more at ease knowing Mac was talking to Jack. She prayed it would be enough.

"Casey, I may have just met you today, but I've known about you for a couple months now. Mac told me what happened today, and I'm proud to have you as a sister in Christ. What if we pray for your brother right now, that he will choose to join our family?"

"I would like that," she agreed.

Ryan offered her his hand, so she took it. "Father," he started, "I thank You for the confidence of knowing You are in control. I thank You for the confidence of knowing Your timing is perfect. I praise You for Casey's decision this afternoon, and ask that You now be with Mac as he talks to Jack about You in this moment. This may be new to him, and may take a little bit to penetrate his spirit, but I know You are stronger than anything in this world. I know Your Spirit can penetrate even the hardest of hearts. While his heart may not be hard, his life has been. He needs to rest in You. He has taken care and protected Casey, as well as this country. He now needs *You* as his Protector and Caregiver. Most importantly, he needs You as his Father. I demand, by the blood of Jesus, that the pride that has a hold on him releases. I pray against the powers that are trying to keep him down. I pray for an awakening of his heart and soul to what is going on around him. He is used to battles, being in the military…now I pray he sees the spiritual battle that is trying to encompass him. I pray he sees it for what it is, and makes the right decision. I pray he makes the choice to follow You for the remainder of his days here on Earth, and retires into Your arms when his race is won. I thank You, Father. In Jesus's name we pray…Amen."

*   *   *

"Wake up, Casey." Jack jostled her.

"I'm…give me a minute. Wow. I slept hard." Her eyes fluttered open. "You're wide awake. Did you and Mac have a good conversation?"

"Yeah."

"Are you going to be okay?"

He grinned."I am now."

"Good," she said, relieved.

"It was weird. While we were talking, I began to see and feel this fight going on around me."

Casey took Jack's hand into hers and gave it a squeeze. "You're going to be fine."

"I know," he said confidently. "When I die, I now know I'll be in Heaven with God, waiting for you to get there. And until then, I'll fight for Him and His Kingdom, along with my country."

"No, you're going to be fine. I prayed for it."

"Case, I've accepted my fate."

"You can't give up." She sat up in her sleeping bag. "I need you."

"Casey, let God decide. I'm not going to complain either way."

Casey didn't want to ruin the time she had with him, so she decided it wasn't worth the fight.

"Come on, let's go get something to eat. I'm hungry."

She nodded as she got up. "Go ahead. I'll be out in a minute."

"Hurry up. You slept in, and your crew is beginning to wonder about you," he pointed out. "Getting kind of lazy in your old age, eh?"

"Shut up!" She laughed, throwing her pillow at him. He ducked out of the tent just in time to miss getting hit with it.

* * *

"She's alive," Brennon remarked from where he sat at the table.

She squinted at the sunlight, protecting her eyes as they adjusted to the stark difference in brightness.

Jack held up his plate of food. "Hungry?"

"Yeah." She sat down next to him on a log and grabbed a chip off his plate. "What time is it?"

"Eleven-forty-five. Are you okay?" Jack asked.

She waved him off. "I'm fine."

"Then, go get something to eat." He playfully added, "While you're at it, grab a soda to wake up."

"Now *that* sounds like a plan," she said, getting up from her spot, making a beeline for the table.

As she headed over, she noticed that Captain Lance Hartley from 'B' shift was at the grill cooking burgers with LT. Then she looked over at the basketball court and saw Jay, Jeff, and Jesse playing Christian Hawke, Ted Kelley, and Allen Getz, also from 'B' shift.

Her heart picked up speed when she saw Zoey Patterson and Bobbi Jo Martin from 'B' shift come out of the lake, walking toward their blanket. They walked to where Paul Sharpe and Pete Van den Bergh were, and pulled a soda from their cooler. It was as if there was a shift change and she missed it!

"Hey, sweet thing!" Matt Miller smiled at Casey as he grabbed a handful of chips from the other side of the table from her. "Haven't seen you yet today. Where've you been hidin'?" Matt was a six-foot-two, athletic, thirty-seven-year-old southern boy. His smile and attitude instantly brightened up any room he walked into. He had short, light brown, highlighted hair, and light blue eyes.

"Hitting on her already, are ya, bro?" Matt's partner, Dale Mansfield, shook his head as he sat at the table. Dale was a six-foot-one, thirty-four-year-old, African American. He was one of the biggest guys at the station. While he might have seemed intimidating to those who didn't know him, on the inside he was a big teddy bear at heart. He kept his black, curly hair very short, and had sparkling, brown eyes, with a mischievous smile continuously on his face.

"No, just lookin' out for my stomach." Matt winked at Dale. He turned back to Casey, and said, "I hear you're cookin' dinner."

"Now, where did you hear that?" she asked. "It's not me. I have to work in the morning. I'm leaving tonight."

"Shame." Matt pouted. "After hearin' Hawke brag about your cooking, I was *really* hoping to get a taste."

"Hey, Morgan!" Dale called out to a drop-dead gorgeous guy who got out of his car. Casey had never seen him before.

She watched him, stunned. "*Who* is *that*?"

"*That* is our rookie, Hunter Morgan," Dale said. "He just started this last week, you know since Tucker retired. His retirement party, by the way, is next Friday. You coming?"

She nodded, not talking her eyes off Hunter. "Actually,   I probably can since 'C' shift is on."

Hunter Morgan looked to be about thirty-six or thirty-seven years old. He was six-foot-three, and had short, light brown hair that was slightly feathered on the sides and in the back, and the top was parted on the side. He also had amazing bluish-gray eyes. His tanned body, told how enjoyed his time off at the pool. Casey was sure Zoey and Bobbi Jo were already drooling over him. Unfortunately for them, it was against regulations to have relations with someone on your own shift.

"Hunter, man, come get some lunch!" Dale waved him over.

"*He's* a *rookie*?" Casey asked, making sure she heard them right.

"He's a transfer from outta Chicago," Matt explained.

"I see," she picked up a plate and absentmindedly filled it. She caught herself periodically staring at him while he unloaded his vehicle and dropped his stuff off in an area for his tent. She realized she was staring at him when he walked over to the table, and quickly turned her attention back to lunch.

He stuck his hand out to Casey. "Hunter Morgan."

She set her plate down to shake his hand. "Hi.   I'm   Casey Carter, from 'A' shift."

"This is *the* Casey Carter…as in the one that Hawke's been braggin' about," Matt hinted to Hunter.

"Oh! As in the famous cook of Engine Company Fifteen?" He smiled. Casey felt bad for Zoey and Bobbi Jo. Knowing them the way she did, and seeing how gorgeous Hunter was, she knew *she* would have a hard time concentrating at work with him, let alone those two.

"Yeah, we're trying to con her into cooking our dinner t'night."

"It looks to me like Hartley and LT have it all under control," Casey pointed out.

"I'll tell you what," Matt said, thinking. You could almost see as the wheels turned in his head.

"Uh oh." Casey smiled. "Do I *want* to know?"

Noticing the guys clustering around Casey, Jack walked over. "Hey, getting a little lonely over there. I thought you were coming back."

"I got side-tracked." She nodded toward the guys. "Um, Jack Carter, this is Matt Miller, Dale Mansfield, and Hunter Morgan from 'B' shift. Guys, this is my brother, Jack Carter."

"Heard about you." Matt smiled, as Jack shook everyone's hand. "Zoey and Bobbi Jo were –"

"Yeah, I know." Casey rolled her eyes. "I'm keeping my eye out for them."

"Wasn't there a deal in the works?" Hunter pressed. "I'm curious to see how good a cook she is for myself. Hawke can't stop talking about her."

"Hey, Jack! Jay and Jeff are ready for a rematch," Jesse called from the basketball court.

"Come over for a sec," Matt called to them.

In a matter of minutes, the firefighters from both shifts were standing around the table, while Hartley and LT listened from the grill where they were cooking. Matt put one foot up on the bench, and leaned on his knee while he said, "I have a challenge for 'A' shift from 'B' shift."

Casey narrowed her eyes, crossing her arms."What's the prize?"

"You."

Her jaw dropped. "*What*?"

"If Hartley and LT agree, we get you for a month, where *you* cook for *us* if we win," Matt challenged. Cheers echoed from the 'B' shift crew.

"Yes! Decent food!" Christian did a fist pump. "No offense to Patterson or Martin, but…*yes*!"

"Wait! This is my partner we're talking about," Mac objected as his heart sunk.

"Wait! She's *our* cook! We do all the chores just so she *can* cook!" Jesse shouted over the yelling.

"Whoa!" Casey put her hands up. "Hold on! This is *me* we're talking about! Don't *I* get a say in this?"

Hartley put his fingers to his lips and let out a loud whistle. Everyone turned toward him and LT. "What does 'A' shift want if they win?" Hartley asked. "Mainly Carter, I think, since she seems to have the most at stake here."

"We have a lot at stake too," Vinnie protested. "This is *our* health! And who are we going to have to put up with from 'B' shift if we have to trade out Carter?"

"You'll get me." Dale stood. He was the strongest, so it seemed like a fair deal. "And, when I do, *I want* leftovers." He glared at Matt.

"And you'll do the heaviest work around the station when you're on shift?" Vinnie challenged.

"I will," he agreed.

"Okay," Vinnie conceded.

"What if *we* win?" Scott asked. "What do *we* get?"

"What do you want?" Hartley asked. "It's obvious what we want."

As 'A' shift went off to the side in a huddle, LT walked over. "All right, gang, there are two ways to look at this. We could ask for something that would benefit us, or something that will humiliate them for coming up with this lame-brained idea in the first place." He shook his head with a sigh. Then he added, "Sorry, Case."

"Well, we'll just have to win. I don't want to leave my shift, even if it *is* only for a month." Casey crossed her arms, visibly upset at the prospect.

"And I don't want to lose my partner," Mac added.

"Not to mention that our food will suck for a month." Jesse cringed.

"Is your stomach all you think about?" Will rolled his eyes.

"Hey!" He grinned. "A happy Jesse makes a happy 'A' shift."

"Focus here, guys," Jack said within the huddle. "This is my sister we're talking about."

"Carter, what do you think?" LT asked her.

"They have to clean the station top to bottom, and I mean white-glove clean, to be inspected by Jack." She nodded toward him, as a grin slowly formed on Jack's face. "He's military. It will have to be spotless."

"All the rigs are to be spotless and restocked too," LT added. "And I say that Jack and Chief are the two who do the inspecting."

"I say it's a consensus," Brennon interjected, "between LT, Chief, Jack, and Captain Hartley."

"*That* sounds like a plan," LT agreed. "Carter, do you agree?"

"You guys had better not lose!" She glared at her shift mates.

"We won't." Jesse shook his head. "Our stomachs depend on it!"

"Okay, Jesse you're the captain," LT told him. Jesse nodded in response. LT turned toward 'B' shift. "If we win, you guys have to scrub the station top to bottom, making it spotless."

"That's easy." Matt waved him off. "I thought you could come up with something better than that."

LT went on, "Making all the rigs white glove clean and restocked. And the inspectors for this are Air Force Lieutenant Colonel Jack Carter, Captain Hartley, Chief Blazedale, and me."

"Wait a minute!" Christian objected. "Why would Lieutenant Colonel Carter over there have anything to do with this?"

"Because I'm competing too. I have the most at stake," Jack dared them as he stood, his arms crossed.

"How do you figure?" Zoey challenged.

"It's *my* sister," he said sternly.

She shut her mouth and nodded in agreement.

"Deal?" LT looked at Hartley.

"If we win, Carter starts on Monday," Hartley clarified. LT agreed, so he looked over at his shift. They nodded, so he shook LT's hand. "Sir, we have an agreement."

Cheers instantly erupted as Chief Blazedale pulled up. In seeing everyone clustered around the tables, he came over and asked, "What's going on?"

"We have a challenge between these two shifts," Hartley explained.

"Oh yeah? What would it be that has them *this* excited?"

LT and Hartley explained the stakes. Afterward, Chief, LT, and Hartley made a list of competitions. They were going to be the judges as well.

The first one was a tug-of-war. On 'A' shift side, there was Will, Mac, Jeff, Kim, Rob, Jack, and Casey. On the other side, they had Hunter, Dale, Matt, Bobbi Jo, Zoey, Christian, and Paul.

Bobbi Jo Martin was a thirty-three-year-old, five-foot-seven, redheaded, green-eyed, spitfire! She might look tame, but she had an Irish temper that often got her in trouble!

Zoey Patterson, on the other hand, reminded Casey of the women from the movie about the Amazon. She was a five-foot-nine, muscular, dark-brown haired, brown-eyed, thirty-seven-year-old. Some of the guys on Casey's shift were actually afraid of *both* of those women.

Christian Hawke was the opposite of those two. He was a sweetheart. He was thirty-six-years-old, and was six-foot-five, black-haired, and had dark brown-eyes.

Lastly, not yet described on the team, but certainly not least, was Paul Sharpe. He was Captain Hartley's partner, and was a very intelligent man. He may have been six-foot, forty-five years old, and had the gray hair to match his age, but his knowledge and wisdom would beat anyone at the station, outside of Chief, without any trouble. He was an odd choice, Casey thought, due to his age and his weight. He usually played Santa Claus at the Christmas party. And, Casey had heard he didn't need the padding either. His brown eyes even twinkled when he laughed!

His partner, Captain Lance Hartley, on the other hand, was a six-foot-one, dark-brown haired, blue eyed, forty-year-old. They looked quite the opposite of each other. What Paul had in weight, Captain Hartley had in brawn.

To make it even more challenging, they were tugging the rope in the lake. Captain Hartley hammered two stakes in the water as boundaries to get the bodies across. The first team to get the lead body from the other team over their boundary marker would win.

'C' shift brought one of the ambulances and the ladder trucks up for safety purposes, so LT grabbed a two-inch thick rope from one of the rigs. They tied Casey's blue bandana in the middle as the center marker so they would have something with which to judge. The bandana would be about four feet from the lead person on either side.

Kim was first in the lineup, followed by Casey, then Mac, Will, Robbie, and Jack, with Jeff as their anchor. They lined up by height. 'B' shift's lineup was Bobbi Jo, followed by Zoey, then Paul, Hunter, Christian, and Matt, with Dale as their anchor.

"Teams ready?" Chief asked, standing in the lake with his hand on the bandana. The water was up to Casey's knees.

"Yeah!" Everyone yelled at once.

"Go!" he shouted and let go of the rope.

Casey immediately felt a yank, but everyone on her team had their feet anchored deep into the sand so they held their ground. Their strategy was to do their best to hold them until the other team tired themselves out and then start tugging.

This went on for ten agonizing minutes before Casey's hands got rope burn.

"We need to pull," she said over her shoulder to Mac. "My hands are starting to burn."

"I agree. Ready gang?" Mac shouted.

"For what?" Zoey looked at them, wide-eyed.

"This!" he shouted.

At the same time, the entire team yanked with everything they had. The men from the shift still on the shore from 'A' shift, along their families, let out shouts of joy as Casey's team pulled the other side a good four feet.

Casey's team quickly scrambled to grab the extra rope without moving their feet. Kim reached down first, and then re-wrapped her hand, as the rest of the team passed the rope back while 'B' shift recovered.

"Carter!" Christian shouted to his team, and they commenced pulling again.

"Carter!" Jeff yelled, reminding them what they were playing for as they did their best to hold on and not give them any more rope.

"I can't…." Kim screamed before she fell forward into the lake. She quickly scrambled to get back up and grab the rope.

"Ahhh!" Casey screamed as the three feet of rope slipped through her hands, burning them. "Get up, Kim! We're losing ground!" she shouted. She was able to get her footing and grab the rope, but not before her team slid forward about another foot, making the teams even again.

"You okay, Casey?" Jeff called, from the back.

"Just pull! I'm mad now!" she shouted back. The team decided to take the offense instead of the defense.

The cheering intensified. The teams were evenly matched. Without warning, Casey's side gained ground, pulling the other team toward them about a foot and a half.

"One..." Dale shouted from the back of his row, "...two...three!" he said and walked backwards, as his team members turned toward him and pulled along with him.

"Now!" Mac shouted, and everyone jerked on the rope at once. The entire 'B' shift team, with the exception of Dale, fell backward, so Casey's team pulled the rope toward them as the other team scrambled to get back in position.

As 'A' shift got the bandana over their boundary marker, the roar from the shore got louder and louder. A couple more of the 'B' shift teammates got up and grabbed the rope in an attempt to get it back as 'A' shift got the bandana two feet beyond their boundary.

"Pull!" Jack shouted. "We're almost there! Pull!"

"Not a chance!" Hunter jumped up. He, Dale, Matt, Zoey, and Paul pulled on the rope as Bobbi Jo and Christian came up out of the water.

"Pull for the pride of 'A' shift!" Jeff yelled.

The 'B' shift teammates looked up at 'A' shift in surprise, as with one more yank, Zoey tumbled across their boundary pole.

"Yeah! Yes! We did it!" were heard yelled among the teammates of 'A' shift. The remainder of the 'A' shift cheered as they ran into the water toward their teammates. They excitedly hugged each other, while 'B' shift picked themselves up out of the water.

After a moment, Captain Hartley whistled. As everyone turned their attention toward him, he said, "Not so fast."

"There are still two more competitions. The stakes are high, folks," LT smiled, proud of his team. "The score currently stands at 'A' shift – 1; 'B' shift – 0."

"The next on the list is a basketball game," Captain Hartley explained. "We need two players from 'A' shift, and two from 'B' shift."

"Who's playing?" Jesse whispered as their team congregated in a small huddle.

"Jack and Jesse beat us yesterday," Jeff said in a low voice to the team. "They are better than us, let them play."

"I agree," Jay concurred.

"Jack?" Jesse asked him.

"Sounds good," he nodded.

The others on the team quietly agreed, as Chief announced, "First we are going to set up an obstacle course." The 'C' shift ladder engine crews stood behind Chief with their engines behind them, side-by-side. Chief looked over his shoulder toward the engines before he looked at back to the people in front of him. He had a devilish grin on his face as he added, "We're gonna do this Engine Fifteen style."

The crewmembers from 'A' and 'B' set up an intricate obstacle course while Captain Hartley, LT, and Chief gave instructions. The first obstacle was a set of poles set up to about six feet apart with a wall of netting stretched over it that the runners would have to climb. The next obstacle would use the two ladder trucks driven-in by 'C' shift. The teams had to, one-by-one, climb the one-hundred-foot ladders and touch the American flag at the top. There would be one team assigned to each rig. The third obstacle was a rope swing over the lake. The team members were to swing out to where there was a stake marked in the lake and then back. The fourth and final obstacle was putting on a SCOTT Pack (which weighed about forty pounds), and running from the lake to the finish line a quarter-mile away, which was actually the starting point. Both team members had to get across the finish line to win.

When the obstacle course was set up, they made their way over to the basketball court to watch the basketball game. The teams who played were Jesse and Jack verses Allen and Hunter. It was a brutal game. At one point, someone made a comment that it looked more like a hockey game than a basketball game because the players fouled on each other so much. The two who fouled the worst were Hunter and Jack. Knowing Jack the way Casey did, she figured Hunter must have made some comment about Casey that set him off, because under normal circumstances Jack played fair.

Just as the time ran out, Hunter fouled Jack. It sent Jack to the free-throw line, leaving the game with a score of 80-81 (Hunter and Allen were currently ahead.)

Jack dribbled the ball a couple times before he sent it into the air. The ball swished through net. The cheers that erupted at a now tie game were almost deafening.

As Hunter rebounded the ball and tossed it to Jack, he said something in his ear. Jack shot him a nasty look. Mac and Casey looked at each other, wide-eyed, before they turned back to the court.

Jack stood at the line, dribbled the ball and lined it up. He shook his head before he dribbled again, lined it up again, and shot. The ball bounced off one side of the hoop and then the other. The ball hit the back rim of the hoop before it bounced off into the court.

LT and Captain Hartley looked over at Chief and shrugged. They were not sure what to do with a tie. "We are going to add ten seconds overtime," Chief decidedly announced. He didn't want the game to end in a tie. He flipped a coin. Allen called heads while Jesse called tails. Unfortunately, it was heads so it was Hunter and Allen's choice. They took possession of the ball.

Jesse tossed the ball to Allen, who took three aggressive steps forward before he spun around, took two steps back, and shot just outside of the key. In the meantime, Jesse ran down the key thinking Allen was going to do a lay-up. He realized too late that Allen faked him out.

As the ball slipped through the net, Jack grabbed the rebound and tossed it over Hunter's head to Jesse. Jesse ran around Allen and took the ball to the other end of the court. As Jack flew past him with Hunter on his heels, Jesse side passed the ball to Jack who did a lay-up and scored two points.

"Time!" Chief called. "Great game! 'B' team won it by one point. That means the teams are tied to one point apiece."

Casey gave Jack and Jesse a high-five in congratulations of a job well done when they walked off the court. 'A' shift knew it was a tight match and congratulated Jack and Jesse on a good game.

"Stay away from Hunter," Jack warned.

Casey's eyes widened, as her jaw dropped. Jack grabbed her arm and ushered her over to the cooler to get some water, with Jesse on their heels.

"What's going on?" Casey demanded from Jack, getting her arm back.

"Hunter's a jerk!" Jesse shook his head. He glared at Hunter before he looked back at her. "He was making comments about you the entire time. I'm surprised Jack didn't flatten him out."

"One more comment outside of the games and I will," Jack said as he sucked down his water, glaring at Hunter. When Hunter caught sight of him, he smiled and winked. Jack swore under his breath.

"Jack!" Casey scolded him. "We're Christians now. We're not supposed to swear. Besides, we're on different shifts," Casey tried to set his mind at ease, "so he won't be near me."

"Either way, stay as far away from him as possible."

After a fifteen-minute break, giving the two teams who played a chance to rest, Chief called everyone over to the starting line of the obstacle course. There was only to be two from each shift running. Both teams had to face a lot of pressure due to the tie, so the two shifts had to choose carefully. When they were in the huddle, 'A' shift looked up to see Hunter Morgan and Matt Miller from 'B' shift walk up to the starting line.

"Casey and me," Jack said firmly when he saw the other team.

"What about…?" Jesse started, but Jack cut him off.

"Casey and me. Trust me. We're both ticked off enough. And when we get mad, we're unstoppable. Not to mention the fact that it's *her* who is on the line in these games."

"I agree with him," Mac said. "Both are tough competitors. They'll do us proud."

"I agree too." Tommy glanced at the pair from 'B' shift. "When she gets mad, she's tough to beat."

"All right." Jesse nodded. "Let's do it, 'A' shift!" he shouted.

Everyone put their hands in the middle of the huddle and shouted, "Let's go!"

Casey and Jack jogged over to the starting line, at the same time Chief walked toward the starting line to begin the obstacle course.

"Is this fair?" Hunter scoffed. "She's a girl."

Casey scowled. "How *dare* you!"

Hunter looked at Casey in wide-eyed surprise for a moment, before a sly smile came across his face. "Nice."

"*Watch it!*" Jack snapped at him.

"Okay, folks, this is how it's going to work," Chief started as the crowd hushed. "First, you'll climb up one side and down the other of this net wall. When you're done, you will run over to the ladder trucks, put on a harness, and then climb the entire one-hundred feet, touching the American flag at the top, before climbing down. After that, you'll run down to the lake and swing out, making sure to go past the markers that are there before moving on to the last leg of the race. In the last leg, you'll both put on a SCOTT Pack, and run as fast as you can the quarter-mile back here to the finish line, which is also the starting line. Any questions?"

"Will there be someone at the ladder truck to help Jack with his harness, so he has it on safely, and can give him some quick safety instructions while I climb?" Casey asked.

"I think that's fair," Chief agreed.

"I'll do it." Jesse raised his hand. Chief nodded, so Jesse moved to where the trucks were located in between the net walls and the lake.

"Any more questions?" Chief asked.

"Nope." Hunter shook his head. Then he looked at Casey out of the corner of his eye as he added, "If you're sure it's okay she runs, that is."

"Stuff it, Hunter!" Matt shook his head in irritation. Then, to lighten the mood he added, "We want what she cooks us to be good."

Jack put his hand out to Casey. "Let's do this, Case."

Casey gave his hand a squeeze before she returned it to her own leg. "Consider it done."

"On your marks," Chief started, and the runners got into position, as the crowd talked in anticipated excitement. "Get set," he said, and the roar of the crowd got loud. "Go!" he shouted.

The teams ran to the net and swiftly climbed it. When Jack and Casey got to the top, Jack dropped down. He had Casey drop into his arms to save time, before they turned and headed toward the trucks as fast as they could.

Both teams got to the truck at the same time. While Jesse helped Jack with his harness, Casey slipped into hers and climbed the ladder at the same time as Hunter. Casey ignored him. She concentrated on the flag at the top of the ladder, climbing as fast as she could.

When she got to the top, she tapped the flag before she headed down. She had to use caution on the way down so she didn't slip on the rungs of the ladder. When she reached the bottom of the ladder, Jack took off at the exact same time as Matt.

"Looking good." Hunter winked at Casey as they took their harnesses off.

"Shut up!" she growled. She was angry with Hunter. If his comments were that rude to her face, she couldn't imagine what he said on the court! While he might have been gorgeous on the outside, to Casey he was ugly on the inside. She reprimanded herself for only seeing his looks in the beginning.

Jack and Matt came down, neck-and-neck. When Jack got to the ground, he grabbed Casey's wrist. They ran down to the lake, with Jesse on their heels. Matt took his harness off at the truck before coming down to the lake, while Hunter ran for the rope.

Casey pulled the rope back and ran, swinging out over the lake. She more than cleared the marker. While she was out, Jesse helped Jack with his harness. By the time Casey got back to the shore, Matt was out in the middle of the lake. Jack came in just after Matt came back to the shore.

When Jack got back, Jesse helped Jack with his pack before they could run for the finish line. In that time, Hunter and Matt took off for the finish line a few steps ahead of them.

"Go! Go!" Jesse shouted as he shoved them toward the finish line.

"Case!" Jack put his hand out while they ran.

"We got this!" Casey grabbed his hand. They pushed as hard they could, running hand-and-hand across the finish line…at the exact same time Matt and Hunter crossed. It was a tie.

Casey went to her knees. She wiggled out of the SCOTT Pack, while Jack hung his hands on the netting in an attempt to catch his breath. Hunter held onto the finish line pole, while Matt took his pack off before he dropped to the ground behind Casey.

"Well, folks, after conferring with the other judges, I hate to tell you, but the decision was a tie." Chief shook his head. "We have to come up with a tie breaker."

"Another run?" Vinnie suggested.

Chief shook his head as he watched the four runners. "I   don't know. We may have made it tougher than we should have."

"Come here, Case," Jack said, as he took his pack off before helping her up. He tightly hugged her to him as he kissed her head. "Good run, sis."

"I know…good job…I…wow," Casey stammered, doing her best to catch her breath.

After a moment, Casey and Jack helped Matt up off the ground and shook his hand, before the three of them headed over to Hunter. The four of them shook hands in congratulations for a great race.

"What's the tie breaker?" Christian asked.

"We didn't think you guys would be so close," Chief admitted. He looked over at LT and Hartley, who both shook their heads.

"Another tug-of-war?" LT suggested. "Using all members of the shifts on each side?"

"You guys will have an extra man," Hartley objected.

"Looking at Mansfield are you really going to object to Jack being on our team? If nothing else, it makes it fair," LT pointed out.

"Good point," Hartley agreed. "I'll concede."

"Then we are in agreement?" Chief asked the two shift leaders. They nodded, so Chief smiled and said, "Then, let's head down to the lake."

"Can we see who wins before we take the trucks back?" Ken Kirby from 'C' shift asked. He and his partner, Jason Richards drove one truck, while Brett Thomas and his partner, Kyle 'KC' Cross, drove the other one.

"Get the trucks ready to go while we set up, and you guys can watch the game before you have to take them back," he agreed.

While Chief, LT, and Hartley set up the tug-of-war, the 'C' shift members pulled the ladders down and got the trucks ready to go. The rest of the crews rested and talked about the last race run while they waited. It was a tough race but ended appropriately in a tie. Both teams were tough competitors. Casey thought the use of tug-of-war between all members was a suitable tiebreaker. This made all team members equally responsible for the win or loss.

When they set up the tug-of-war this time, they wanted to make it a little more challenging. The water was up to Casey's waist. This would make it more difficult for the shorter members of the shifts. For example, Kimmy was only five-foot-seven, so the water hit just below her chest. While she would be able to grip the rope, her arm dragged the water more than anyone else's on their team. The good news for 'A' shift was that Bobbi Jo on 'B' shift was having the same trouble.

"Let's do this," Jesse encouraged.

The lineup for 'A' shift went: Kim, Casey, Jesse, Mac, Vinnie, Tommy, Marty, Will, Brennon, Jay, Robbie, Jack, and Jeff, with Scott as their anchor. Once again, they lined up according to height.

The other team lineup went: Bobbi Jo, Zoey, Ted, Paul, Johnny, Hunter, Allen, Christian, Pete, Matt, Carl, and Craig, with Dale as their anchor. It seemed to Casey that they lined up according to height, but with strength toward the back of their line.

"Now, before this starts," Chief said, standing in the middle of the two teams as he held the rope in place. LT stood in the water to watch 'B' shift's team, while Hartley watched 'A' shift. The family and friends lined the shoreline watching with anticipation. "I want you all to know that I am proud of what you guys have done today. You have given your all. Neither shift should feel *any* amount of shame for losing this. You all have made Engine Company Fifteen proud today."

The teams on both sides nodded in acknowledgement of Chief's words before they glared at the other team. In this competition, neither team wanted to lose.

"On your marks…get set…go!" Chief shouted, and let go of rope before he took several steps back.

The sound from the shore was an instant rush to both teams. The deafening cheers for both sides were equal.

"Pull! Pull!" Jesse shouted. "Take the offense, team!"

"Give it your all!" Zoey yelled.

"Don't leave anything behind!" Casey encouraged.

The strain of the event went on for over twenty minutes before Kimmy groaned, "I don't know how much longer I can hold on."

"Give it everything you have, Kimmy," Casey pushed. "Don't give them the satisfaction of calling you a wimp."

"I am *not* a wimp," she growled as she yanked harder.

"I don't think this is fair," Hunter said loud enough for everyone to hear. "We have Bobbi Jo and Zoey over here, while they just have little Kimmy and Casey."

"How *dare* you!" Casey scowled at Hunter. What he said set off both Casey *and* Kimmy. What made them angrier was that Bobbi Jo and Zoey thought it was funny and started laughing.

That's when it dawned on Casey how they could win. "That's it!"

"What's it?" Jesse asked as he continued to pull on the rope behind Casey.

"Make them laugh, Jess! Come on, you're good at it," she said over her shoulder.

"I'm too mad," he growled, irritated.

"Jesse, when they laughed, they slipped."

"That's true," he stopped pulling for a split second when it hit him. Unfortunately, when Jesse momentarily stopped pulling the rope, it slipped for the other team.

"Jesse!" Casey screeched as the rope slid through her hands. "Ahhh!" she screamed as she felt it burn her hands again. "Ahhh, geez! This hurts!"

"Quit your bellyaching and pull!" Brennon barked.

"Jesse's the one who stopped," Casey grumbled. She grabbed the rope to pull once again.

"Ya know, Carter, maybe it won't be so bad sending you to 'B' for a bit, I know we could use the peace and quiet," Jesse said, as an attempt to make the other team laugh.

"Why you…!" Casey started, but the other team laughed. When they did, the rope slipped and Casey's team pulled the slack.

Will felt the rope slip in their favor and caught on to what was going on. "All that whining is getting old. I know I could use the peace and quiet."

"Why are you being so…?" Jack started, but he saw that when the other team laughed, the rope slipped in their favor once again. "Now you know why I make my visits brief," Jack attempted to add to the laughter.

Hunter studied Jack for a moment before he figured out what was going on. Casey's team got about five feet of their rope, leaving the bandana a foot over their boarder pole before he figured it out. That left only three more feet until Bobbi Jo crossed the pole line.

"Quit laughing!" Bobbi Jo yelled at her teammates, as she struggled to keep the distance between the two teams. "We're losing rope."

"That's the point." Jesse winked at her with a smile. "Now!" he shouted. Casey's team yanked on the rope at the same time, pulling it another two feet toward them.

"Oh no you don't! Pull!" Hunter shouted. "Pull! Pull!" he continued. With each time he shouted, they, as a group, pulled together. They got a couple inches of rope each time.

With only four more feet between Hunter's team winning and Casey's team losing, Jesse yelled, "Come on! We can't let them win."

After a several minute standoff, Dale let out a war cry and walked backwards. This time their team didn't turn around. They continued to walk backwards, pulling on the rope with Dale.

As much as they tried, Casey's team could not combat the strength from the other team. Kimmy even put her feet up on their pole to brace herself, only to have the pole fold and fall into the water as she crossed it. As soon as she did, Casey tumbled forward. She was able to push Kim out of the way, as Jesse and the rest of the guys fell like dominos, shoving their entire team under the water.

It took a few moments until Casey was able to kick free and get to the surface. As soon as she did, Kimmy grabbed her so she wouldn't go under again. "Thanks!" Casey said, out of breath.

Kimmy released her, and they rested in the water, watching as the shore clear for both sides, as both teams were welcomed with shouts of joy.

Kimmy looked over at Casey nervously. "We lost."

"I know. Don't worry, it'll go by fast…I hope." Casey glanced over at 'B' shift, who cheered for joy while they congratulated each other.

"Casey!" Jack called out as he searched through the ocean of people.

"Over here." She stood up and waved her hand so he could see her.

He made his way over the mountain of people and hugged her. "I'm sorry. We tried."

"We did good. Don't worry. I'll be fine," she said.

He took a step back and brushed her wet hair off her face. "You need to stay away from Hunter. He's no good."

"I will," she promised.

"You know I am very proud of you."

"Thank you." She grinned. "I'm proud of you too."

"You did good, kid." He hugged her again. "You did good."

Chapter 11

A Shift Change

It was a long month, as Casey knew it would be. While she enjoyed getting to know the 'B' shift team members, she missed the personalities from her shift.

"Well, one more night," Hunter said, as he sat down on one of the chairs at the table.

Casey was cooking dinner, as the others from the shift did their chores, worked out in the weight room, or played basketball on the court at the back of the station.

"Yep," Casey said, stirring the pot. "I like you guys, but I can't wait to go back."

He leaned back in his chair. "I gotta tell ya, you impress me."

"Excuse me?" she said, taken aback. It wasn't what he said that bothered her, but the way he looked at her.

"You handle yourself superbly on a fire scene. You are an awesome cook. You blend in with our crew magnificently. And you were even amazing in the challenge itself…not to mention that you were a good sport about losing in the first place."

"Was that supposed to be a compliment?" She glanced at him before she turned back toward the chicken cacciatore she was cooking.

"It was." He nodded. He sat there for a few minutes in silence before he asked, "Why don't you trust me?"

"What do you mean?"

"Well, to a degree you have to trust all of us on a fire scene. However, when we're not on scene, you avoid me like the plague."

"You're being paranoid." While Casey laughed at him, she knew an element of what he said was true. She did avoid him, but he persistently found her wherever she went.

"No, really. I've watched you. I can't get Zoey and Bobbi Jo to leave me alone, but you won't come near me. Why not? Are you a lesbian? If you are, I respect that, but…."

Casey burst out laughing at his arrogance. "No. I'm straight."

"Well, you don't have a boyfriend. You don't go hog-wild over the nicer-looking guys on the shift, and this is a shift you *can* date from. Why not? What's the problem?"

"Why is it so important to you?"

He shrugged. "Inquiring minds want to know."

"Curiosity killed the cat," she mentioned, not looking at him.

He studied her for another minute before he sat up and looked at her as though a thought struck him. "What did he do to you?"

The question struck her at the core. She stared at him like a deer caught in the headlights for a moment, before quickly turning back to her sauce. Flustered, she clumsily picked up the spoon back, stirring the sauce again in an attempt to gain composure. After a minute of the question hanging in the air, she cleared her throat and asked, "Who?"

"Whoever hurt you so badly." He got up from his chair. Leaning on the refrigerator near the stove where Casey was working, he crossed his arms deep in thought. He realized by her reaction that he struck a chord. While it was originally a guess, her body language told him all he needed to know. "You've been hurt badly. I can see that. What happened?"

"It's not…." Casey sighed, flustered. She wouldn't look at him. He was dancing around her core, and she did not like it when anyone went that deep into her soul…especially him.

"What happened, Casey?" He set his hand on her shoulder. As soon as he touched her, she jumped back in wide-eyed surprise. "Whoa!" He put his hands up in surrender. "I'm not going to hurt you. But, Casey, who did it?"

"Did what?" She felt trapped, as he took another step toward her, blocking the exit. She nervously glanced from him, to the sauce she was cooking, and back again.

"Who attacked you?" he pressed.

She felt herself go pale as she stared at him. He seemed to know exactly where to hit.

"Case, you're pale," he said, realizing he went too far. "Can I get you to sit down?"

She shook her head. "I…no."

"Case, work with me here. You're pale, but you're cooking. I need you to sit for a few, but I don't want to touch you and send you further into a tailspin. Will you please sit down?"

Her heart raced as she stood her ground. "No."

"Casey, now." He rested his hand on her shoulder to turn her toward the table.

She gasped and jumped, backing away from him. The spoon she used to stir the sauce flipped onto the ground, and the sauce splashed on the floor and cupboard as it bounced. Casey held onto the counter to brace herself and clear her head. Her heart felt like it was going to pound out of her chest.

"Okay. Okay." He put his hands in the air in front of him for Casey to see he wasn't going to touch her again. "I'm going to sit back over here at the table while you work on dinner. I'm not going to say anything. In return, I want you to breathe and calm yourself down. Deal?"

Casey nodded. As soon as he sat down on the chair, she finally let the breath of air out she had been holding. Her heart rapidly beat within her chest. She took a couple deep cleansing breaths in an attempt to calm herself down. After another minute, she moved back over to the stove, keeping a close eye on Hunter. She needed to be sure where he was at all times. When he stood too close, she felt trapped. With him at the table, that gave her the space she needed to do her work.

Casey picked up the spoon and washed it off, before wiping the cupboards and floor where the sauce splattered. She then went back to cooking again, a lot more focused.

Neither Hunter, nor Casey, said a word for over fifteen minutes, until Christian and Ted walked into the kitchen. Pete and Carl closely followed them. They played basketball on the court behind the station, and knew it was almost time for dinner, so they came in to take their showers.

They were almost all the way through the kitchen, when Pete suddenly stopped short of the doorway. The other three turned to see why he stopped when he spun toward Casey and Hunter.

While Casey was cooking like she normally did at that time, and Hunter was leisurely flipping through a magazine, there was a heavy feeling in the room. He suspiciously looked from Casey to Hunter in order to figure out who the feelings were coming from. "What's wrong?" he asked.

Hunter shook his head, not looking up from the magazine. "Nothing."

Pete rested his eyes on Casey for a minute. Over the last month, they had several talks. He felt he knew her well enough by that point to know when something was not right. While the other guys stood at the end of the table, watching what was going on around them, Pete walked over to where Casey was cooking.

"Your eyes look like you're scared," Pete said quietly so only she could hear. She nervously turned her attention back to dinner. "Look at me," he said.

Stirring the pot of noodles, she simply said, "No."

"Leave her alone, Van den Bergh," Hunter said, continuing to flip through the magazine. "She needs space."

"Why?" Pete pressed.

"If you don't leave, I'll purposely burn dinner," Casey jokingly threatened. She didn't look up from her cooking. She prayed that in joking around with Pete, he would get the hint and leave her alone.

Pete glared at Hunter as he asked, "What did you do, Morgan?"

"Nothing," he said innocently. "Why?"

Christian looked from Casey to Hunter. When he looked back at Casey, he saw the look on her face. "Morgan, what did you say to her?"

"Why are you guys accusing me? I didn't do anything!" Hunter protested.

Casey shook her head. "He didn't."

"Are you sure?" Pete set his hand on her back. Casey jumped when he touched her. Pete stared at her for a moment, before he turned and glared at Hunter. "If he didn't do anything," Pete turned back toward Casey, "then tell me what happened, because this doesn't look good."

"*He didn't do anything*!" she snapped. "We were just talking and he struck a chord. Now, will you guys just back off and let me...." Casey got cut off by the fire alarm. "Great!" She sighed, tossing the spoon into the sink out of frustration. She quickly shut everything off on the stove.

There was a mad dash for the engine bays, as they heard dispatch state it was a house fire. Casey got in her seat next to Matt, with Hunter on her other side. Allen drove, while Captain Hartley sat in the front passenger's seat of the rig.

The ambulance crews were Bobbi Jo and Johnny, with Pete and Carl for the other ambulance. Everyone else was in the other engine.

When they arrived on scene, it was a multi-million-dollar house. Casey sighed as she shook her head – it was going to be a bear! A house of that size had so many rooms it was nearly impossible to search every room for survivors with any decent amount of speed.

Captain got on the radio. "Hartley to dispatch."

"Go ahead."

"Can you send Engine Seventeen for back-up?"

"Copy, sending Engine Company Seventeen," she confirmed.

Matt, Casey, Allen, and Hunter set the supply and relay hoses up, and Paul was the engineer. When they finished, Hunter and Allen were the first team in with the attack lines. Christian and Ted were behind them. Then Zoey and Craig followed Matt and Casey into the smoke-filled mansion.

As they entered the doorway, Paul shouted, "Incoming," and charged the lines. Casey heard the other engines pull up, just as their group penetrated the belly of the house.

"You guys head down that way, while we go this way," Christian shouted over the roar of the fire. Everyone had to shout in order to be heard.

Christian, Ted, Zoey, and Craig headed in one direction, while Allen, Hunter, Matt, and Casey headed in the opposite direction. They divided in order to cover more ground.

"These look like bedrooms," Hunter said from the front of the line. "Why don't you two take this one, and we'll take that one? We don't go on to another set of rooms without the other team. These houses are a maze."

"Sounds good," Matt agreed. They dragged their hose into the bedroom with them for two reasons. Not only was it for the water, but it was also for a way out. The smoke in the room was so thick that worst-case scenario they could follow their hose back to the front door to get out if needed.

"Hello?" Casey called out. "Anyone in here?" No one answered. They checked the closet and under the bed before they headed back out to the hallway.

"We got one!" Hunter walked out of the room with an unconscious woman over his shoulder.

"Get her outta here!" Matt yelled at him. "We'll keep looking!"

"Be careful," Hunter warned, before he and Allen took off down the hall and out the front door.

Matt and Casey continued down the hall to the next room. There were five bedrooms located off that hallway.

When Matt and Casey checked the next room, and saw it was clear, they moved on to the fourth bedroom. Casey looked under the bed, while Matt searched the master bathroom…when a sudden burst of flames shot through the floor! They dove toward the ground, covering their heads.

"Something blew in the basement!" Matt shouted into the radio. "The room we're in, just had a hole blown through the floor!"

Casey crawled to the hose and practically lay down on it to keep it under control, knowing what opening the line would do. She opened the line into the hole created by the blast, while Matt scrambled over to help her.

"Get outta there!" Hartley shouted into the radio.

"We would…if we could," Matt said, looking around the room where they were located. It was the master bedroom. Matt and Casey were in the doorway of the master bathroom, which was on the opposite side of the room from the bedroom door. The gaping hole was slowly swallowing the floor space between them inch by inch.

"Can you get to the door?" Hartley asked.

"No," Matt responded.

"Can you get to a window?" Hartley pressed.

"There's a bathroom in here. We're gonna shut the hose down and…oh, no way!" Matt looked at the bathroom window in horror, and then looked at the bedroom window as well, with the same look of shock on his face. The house had bars on the windows. "We're locked in! There are…."

"…Bars on the windows," Captain Hartley finished, as he looked at the windows along the front of the house. "Keep the hose on it. We're sending a team in there after you. If you can get around it to the door, do so!"

"Yes, sir," Matt responded.

Matt and Casey shoved the nozzle end of the hose down into the hole with a lot of extra slack. The hose flailed wildly in every direction, soaking the basement. Then they crawled over to the edge of the hole. When they peeked over the edge, Casey gasped at what she saw.

"Capt'n!" Matt shouted, as he looked down into the basement, wide-eyed. "Clear this place! It's a meth lab!"

With unmistakable alarm in his voice, Hartley responded, "Copy that."

Casey and Matt worked together to crawl over to the bed just under the window in the bedroom. They broke the glass out, so the others could see in which room they were located.

The firefighters outside used the Jaws of Life to pry the bars apart far enough for their comrades to get through. Meanwhile, while the fire continued consume room with a ferocious attitude.

Casey tapped Matt on his shoulder and pointed to where the fire had caught the bedspread on the bed they were on. A second later, Hunter reached through the bars and pulled Casey through. As soon as she was out, Allen yanked Matt through the bars of the first-floor window.

The four of them got to the middle of the lawn before the house suddenly took-off. Everything in the basement ignited, setting off an explosion that sent the four firefighters flying into the air about ten feet, while the others dove for the ground. Casey, and the three with her, landed on the sidewalk. The glass, wood, and debris rained down around them.

"Was everyone clear?" Captain yelled out.

"Engine Seventeen's are clear," Lieutenant Callaway from Engine Seventeen shouted back from near his engine.

"We're fine, and have Carter and Miller with us," Allen confirmed.

Bobbi Jo and Johnny ran over to the four on the sidewalk. "Are any of you guys hurt?" Bobbi Jo crouched down in front of Casey.

Casey shook her head. The other three confirmed that they were fine as well. Casey and the others took their masks off for a moment, while the other teams continued to douse the house.

"Wow." Matt shook his head in amazement at the fireball in front of him.

"Thanks," Casey said to Hunter and Allen.

"Yeah, another minute and we would've been shish kabobs." Matt loosely crossed his arms, resting them on his knees, while his helmet dangled from his fingers.

"Can we check you guys out?" Johnny asked. "You guys caught some air on that one, and we want to make sure you're okay."

Casey stood. "No, I'm fine. Thank you, though."

"Yep, ready for battle." Matt stood back up, and together they helped Hunter and Allen off the ground.

The crew of four headed over to another set of attack lines. "Ready?" Casey asked Matt, with her hand on the nozzle.

"Yep. Go ahead." He nodded, holding tightly so they wouldn't lose control of the hose line.

A charged line holds approximately ninety to a hundred pounds per square inch (PSI) of pressure. If a fire hose got loose, the nozzle would whip around out of control and could cause serious damage or injury.

At the same time Hunter opened their nozzle, Casey opened theirs. They took a step back due to the pressure, before moving toward the house. The firefighters hammered the house, giving everything they had to save it. They did their best, but it still took over two hours before they were able to contain it. The partially intact shell of the house was charred and whatever was left of the inside had major smoke damage. Large pieces of the roof had caved in or blown out when the house exploded, and there was not a single window left in the place.

When it was over, the firefighters were exhausted. After they cleaned up the scene, they slowly dragged themselves into the vehicles.

"Good job, Carter," Matt said, sliding into the vehicle beside her.

Leaning back in her seat with her eyes closed, she mumbled, "You too."

While Allen drove, Captain Hartley called in to dispatch to let them know they were off scene. The ride was a silent one, as people were lost in their own thoughts. The firefighters were drained and the house was destroyed, but there was one rescue and no fatalities, so to them it was bittersweet.

When they returned to the station, Zoey, Casey, and Bobbi Jo flipped for the use of the shower first. Zoey won, with Bobbi Jo second. Casey and Bobbi Jo helped clean the rigs while Zoey jumped into shower.

When they were about halfway through, Zoey came down in a clean uniform. Instead of her getting dirty again, she helped by getting food and drinks ready for when the others were finished.

After Bobbi Jo, it was Casey's turn in the shower. When she was on her way through kitchen, Zoey looked up from stirring the spaghetti together with the chicken cacciatore sauce and asked, "Is there anything else I need to add to this?"

"No. There is a salad and garlic bread in the fridge. Just pop the garlic bread in the oven on three-fifty for ten minutes," Casey said, walking through to the shower.

Casey let the water run down all over her for a few minutes as she stood in the warm shower. She wanted more than anything to soak in a hot bathtub at that moment, but that wasn't going to happen.

She quickly took her shower, dried off, and got dressed. She decided to blow her hair dry since she knew she would be going to bed soon. She didn't like going to bed with wet hair.

Zoey knocked on the door. "Carter?"

"Come on in," Casey called out as she brushed her dry hair.

"Dinner's been on the table for about fifteen minutes now. The others have already started eating. You coming?"

"Yeah, give me a few. Don't worry, go ahead and eat. I'll clean up the kitchen when I'm done in here."

"Sounds good," she said, and left.

Casey brushed her teeth and wet her face down to cool off, before folding her clothes. Afterward, she headed out of the bathroom, setting her dirty clothes in a bag on her bed, before heading to the kitchen. By the time she got there, it was around midnight.

"About time," Christian said, when Casey walked into the kitchen.

Matt stared at her in wide-eyed surprise. "You,   uh,   look different with your hair down."

"Yeah." Allen stood up to give her his seat. "Here, sit down and eat."

"No, that's okay. I'm just going to clean up and go to bed. I'm tired," she said, and went over to the kitchen to clean up what she could until everyone finished eating.

Zoey got up to lend her a hand. "Here, let me help you."

"That's okay, Zoey," Casey said, appreciatively. "Thanks anyway, but this is my job."

"We're all tired," she insisted, as she filled the sink to wash the dishes.

When the others finished eating, they also pitched in to clean up the kitchen. They had the kitchen completely cleaned in about twenty minutes. They even had the dishes dried and put away in the cupboards.

"Thanks, guys," Casey said, as she hung the last of the towels to dry on the handle of the oven.

"No problem. Thanks for cooking for us for the last month," Hunter said. "You are an awesome cook!"

"I agree." Pete put the last glass into the cupboard. "If we could keep you, and still have Mansfield back, we would do it in a heartbeat."

"I'm afraid that as much as I like you guys, I miss my crew too much," she admitted.

"Trust me. I'm sure they miss you too." Matt hopped on the counter. "Mansfield is a horrible cook." Everyone burst out in laughter.

"The rest of us could use some cooking lessons," Ted pointed out. "I am afraid there's not a single chef on this shift."

"Yeah," Zoey agreed, as she crossed her arms, "eating can be hazardous to your health on this shift."

"Ya know," Hartley jokingly stroked his chin as if he were deep in thought, "we should have had you give Patterson and Martin some lessons while you were here."

"Hindsight's twenty-twenty, my friend." Paul put his hand on Hartley's shoulder. "We should have started that a month ago."

"Hey!" Bobbi Jo crossed her arms in offense. "We're not *that* bad!"

"You're not *that good*, either," Craig said in a chuckle. She reached over and smacked his arm.

"On that lovely note, I'm going to bed. I'm tired," Casey said, cracking her back as she stretched.

"Sounds like a plan. It's brutal in here anyway." Bobbi Jo glanced at Craig.

"Aww, don't be like that," Craig said. "You know we're only playing."

"Yeah, I know." Bobbi Jo smirked. "If you weren't, we'd spit in your food before we served it next time."

"Wow! You guys are vicious!" Casey's eyes widened.

She waved her off. "No, we're just messing around."

Casey shook her head and smiled, as she headed out of the kitchen to the bedding area. She liked the firefighters on 'B' shift, but she missed her crew.

"Hey, Carter," Hunter called after her, stopping her in the hallway.

"What's up?" she asked.

"Earlier in the kitchen –"

She put her hand up to stop him. "I don't want to go into that right now."

He awkwardly put his hands in his pockets, as they stood in the hall. "You did a good job tonight," he finally said. They started walking toward the bedding area for those on the rigs.

"Thanks."

"So, um, why *don't* you like me?" he asked.

Casey turned her bed down. "Who said I don't like you?"

"You don't talk to me that much." He leaned against the partition, folding his arms. "And when you do, it's as if you're looking for a way out of it."

Casey shook her head. His persistence was wearing on her.

"Come on, I'm a big boy," he said. "I can take it. Why don't you like me?"

Casey looked at him a moment, before she walked over to him. "On the day of the picnic, I don't know what you said to him, but you ticked off my brother."

He stood up so he wasn't more than a foot away from her. He looked down at her and said, "It was in the spirit of the game."

Casey didn't back down. She wanted this clarified so he would leave her alone. "You have to understand that my brother is a Lieutenant Colonel in the United States Air Force. He has worked with people of all races, creeds, colors, and sizes. He understands people just by looking at them. What he saw in you, he didn't like. He told me not to trust you and I trust his instincts."

"He's only your brother. Why does he have such a hold on you?"

"It's a long story. And one that I don't want to get into with you right now. I'm tired."

"I'm not that bad of a guy. On that day I was, because I was purposely trying to ruffle his feathers. I saw he was protective of you, and I used it against him. Why though?"

"Because he's the only family I have."

"Where are your parents?"

Casey looked at him as the tears brimmed her eyes. She blinked until they went away. She did not want to give him the satisfaction of seeing her cry.

"Your parents are dead, aren't they?" he asked, feeling for her.

She did not take her eyes off his as she nodded.

"For how long?"

"They died when I was eight."

"Wow!" His heart broke. "I'm so sorry, Casey."

"Look, I'm tired. I need to go to bed. I just pray that we don't have another fire tonight."

"It's okay." He put his hands up. "I surrender. I can take a hint."

"Thanks," she said, relieved he wasn't going to push the issue.

When she went to walk toward the bed, he said, "You intrigue me."

"What?" She turned toward him, stunned, as a couple of the other guys came into the room.

"I said that you intrigue me," he said again.

"Yeah," Allen snickered, walking over to his bed, "she has that effect on people."

"Why?" Casey ignored Allen's comment.

"These guys are going to bed. If you want to talk, let's go take a walk," Hunter suggested.

Casey was curious as to what he had to say, so they headed down to the garage, away from everyone else. "What did you mean when you said that I intrigue you?" Casey asked, as she sat down on the back of the engine.

Hunter sat down beside her, as he explained, "You're an enigma, a puzzle, a mystery. There are so many different facets to you. The more I see, the more I want to know. The more I find out, the more there *is* to know."

"That was deep."

"I'm as multifaceted as you are." He winked with a smile. "I'm just as deep too."

"Just as deep, or just good at shoveling it?" She smirked.

He laughed. "You're good!"

"Did I ever tell you that I work with mostly men at my job?"

"I had heard something along those lines." He said with a smile. He appreciated her sense of humor.

"And with that, comes experience in learning how to read men," she said, with a look of seriousness on her face.

When he noticed that Casey wasn't laughing, he nervously cleared his throat before he asked, "So, um, what do you see in me?"

"I see someone who's trying too hard. I see a guy who is used to getting what he wants by using his looks. He is used to girls throwing themselves at him, and is surprised or *intrigued* when there is one who doesn't. You know your job well, and look out for those who are on scene with you, which attests to your sense of responsibility. However, you do have a slight lack of confidence when it comes to relationships, which is why you haven't been able to keep one."

"What are you talking about?"

"How long has your longest relationship lasted?"

"I don't know." He shrugged. "Maybe three years?"

"Were you ever married or engaged?"

"No. Why?"

"You don't have confidence in your relationships."

"What do you mean by that?"

"You don't know if they like you for your looks, or for you at your core. You want a woman to love you for you, not for a trophy. You probably have a good relationship with your family, particularly with your mother," she offered.

"How do you know?" He looked at her, not sure what to think. What she said was dead on. It surprised him how accurate she was in describing him.

"Well, you're intuitive when it comes to people, which attests to your sensitive side. And while you can hang with the guys, you go deeper in conversations than the average guy does. Guys who are closer to their fathers tend to skim the surface in conversations, while those who are close to their mothers tend to go below the surface.”

“Wow!” He shook his head in amazement. “You’re dead on.”

“Any more questions?”

“Yeah. You know so much about me, and can I ask some about you?”

“Sure.” She shrugged. “Why not?”

“What happened to your parents?”

Casey looked at him, stunned. “You dive right in with the tough questions first, don’t you?”

“Just the obvious ones.”

“They were going on a business trip for my dad’s company when their plane went down.”

“What business was he in?”

“He was a stuntman.”

“Really? That’s cool!”

“Yeah. They went to Africa to work on a movie set, where he was going to be a stunt double, when their plane crashed. They were on a charter plane at the time.”

“Wow! I’m sorry.” He shook his head. “Bad break.”

“My aunt and uncle took us in. They already had four other children, so we were more than painfully aware that we were a burden, but they did it anyway. Then, when Jack graduated high school, he went right into the Air Force. As soon as he was out of basic training, and landed on a base, he talked to my aunt and uncle, and they agreed to sign over custody of me to him. I was thirteen when I moved in with him.”

"Wow! Really?"

"It was some of the better times of my life. I had my own room. I had freedom when he went on assignments. I was responsible though. I knew what Jack was going through just to take care of me, and I didn't want to mess that up. I didn't want to disappoint him either."

"Impressive."

Casey smiled in remembrance. "I would watch cooking shows every day. That was where I learned how to cook. He was one of the best fed guys in his squad."

"I'll bet," Hunter said in a chuckle.

"Well, after I graduated high school, I went to college for photography. I became a professional photographer. Photographing landscapes was my specialty."

"I never would have guessed," he said, pleasantly surprised. "If you were a photographer, how did you get from there to becoming a firefighter/paramedic?"

"Long story. Better leave that one for another night." She nervously fidgeted with the string of her hooded sweatshirt. "It's already been a long day."

"Okay. One more question, though?"

"Go for it."

"What did *who* do to you, that has you so jumpy when it comes to men?"

"Man," she shook her head, as she nervously chuckled, "what's with you and the big questions?"

"Just curious as to what I'm dealing with here."

Her heart skipped a beat. "What do you mean by that?"

"Well, I don't want you jumping every time I touch you."

"Why would you be touching me at all?"

"Such paranoia!" He laughed. When he settled, he said, "Look, let's be realistic, there's an obvious attraction between us."

"Such arrogance!" Casey stood up, offended.

"No. Just honest."

Casey crossed her arms. "I don't trust you."

"But…are you attracted to me?" He looked up at her with a smile of satisfaction.

She looked over at him. She was not one hundred percent sure as to the answer for that question, so she shrugged him off. "I'm attracted to a variety of men, but I don't trust them. That's why I don't have any type of romantic relationship right now."

"Why don't you trust men?" He stood up so he was about a foot away from her, as he looked down at her.

He was too close. She turned away from him. "It's a long story."

"Let's take it one step at a time. Who did it?" He reached up and turned her back toward him.

She couldn't look away. This was the second time he danced around her core today. *Could Jack have been wrong about him? Should she trust him?* She responded, "I don't know what his name was."

He studied her for a moment before his face softened. "You *were* attacked, weren't you?"

"Yes."

"What happened?"

Casey kept her eyes locked on his, as she took a step away from him. She didn't want to get into this with anyone, *especially* not *him*!

"Don't pull away now," he pleaded. "We're making progress."

She took another step back. "No."

He stayed where he was, not wanting to scare her again. He liked Casey a lot. She captivated him. He forced himself to keep in mind his mission, but he was struggling inside. He saw her heart, and wanted more than anything to help free her from that which was holding her heart prisoner. He wanted to be her hero. "Talk to me," he pleaded.

She adamantly shook her head. "No. Not about this."

"Why not?"

"It's too much." She took another step back. "Please don't push the issue."

"Okay," he relented. "I'm not going to ask any more about it right now. Can I give you a hug though? You look like you need it."

"No." She tightened her arms around her body in protection.

"Okay." He put his hands in the air in surrender. "I respect you too much to push anymore."

"Thank you," Casey said, eyes toward Heaven as she breathed out a sigh. She longed to get back to her shift, and was relieved it was the last night with this crew. Those on her shift respected her and knew she was not open about her past. They gave her space when it came to personal issues.

"I'm going…." He pointed toward the door. "I'm going to head on up to bed," he finished. When he had his hand on the doorknob, he asked, "Are you coming?"

"In a little bit."

He shook his head in frustration as he went through the door, leaving her in the garage by herself.

After a few minutes, she sighed, stuffing her hands in her pockets, walking toward the door to go inside the station from the bays. She walked up the stairs, quietly slipping into the bedroom area. She heard several of the guys snoring as she lay down in her bed.

"Night, Casey," Hunter whispered from the bedding area next to hers.

"Night, Hunter," she responded and drifted off to sleep.

Chapter 12

Jack, Signing-Off

Casey headed into the bathroom the next morning at seven to start her day. She excitedly folded her bedding, but made sure to take her sheet set with her to wash. She then bagged her blanket and pillow, before stuffing them into her cubby for storage until her next shift, which would be the day after tomorrow.

"You were a delight to have on the shift," Captain Hartley said, walking up to Casey. He shook her hand as she stopped at the doorway of the conference room to be released. "Thanks for being such a good sport about the whole thing."

"It was no problem." She politely smiled. "It was nice to get to know the people on another shift. I do miss my crew though, and am excited to get back."

He chuckled. "I'll bet. Each shift is like a family."

At the shift change, the two shifts would meet in the conference room where on one of the walls were photos of those fallen heroes through the years. This reminded everyone not to take their job lightly. Once the entire incoming shift was present, Chief released the outgoing shift to go home.

After 'C' shift arrived, Casey and her crew were released. She went out to her royal blue Jeep Wrangler, with a black hard top, to find Mac standing next to his other vehicle. It was a Ford F150, two-toned maroon and silver truck, with a special ordered bench seat and custom interior.

"Mac!" Casey smiled. "What are you doing here?"

"I got a call from Jack."

"What?" She glanced down at her cell phone, which had no messages. "Why did he call you?"

"Because he wanted me here to talk with you."

Not taking her eyes off Mac, she crossed her arms and demanded, "What happened? Talk to me...*now*!"

"He's in the hospital."

"Why didn't he call *me*?"

"Because I needed to do some legwork to take you out to him. He wanted me and Jesse to come with you."

"Why?" She shook her head. What Mac told her was not making sense. Jack did his business a certain way, and that was not his style.

"Did you tell her yet?" Jesse asked, as he pulled up on his red and black Ducati Superbike.

Mac leaned against his truck. "I started to, but she's not being too cooperative."

"So, when do we leave?" he asked.

"When do we *what*?" She looked from Jesse to Mac in stunned confusion.

"Chief has us covered for the next week," Mac explained. "We have to take you to Jack. He took a turn for the worst last night."

"What?" Her heart raced in panic. "When?"

"About seven o'clock," Mac said.

"Why didn't you start with that?" She looked cross at Mac. "I need to call him."

"You can't." Mac shook his head. "He doesn't have his phone."

"What? Why not?"

"They won't let him use it in the hospital, so he had to turn it off."

"He's in…." What they said finally registered in Casey's mind. All color drained from her face, as she slowly looked from Jesse to Mac.

"I'm going to park this thing." Jesse parked his motorcycle. He tightly covered it with a tarp and bungee cords, before he took his gym bag over to Mac's truck. "So, whose vehicle are we taking?"

"Mine. The gas tank is filled and it's all ready for the trip," Mac said. Glanced at Casey in concern, he rubbed the back of his neck. Not sure what state she would pull through this in, he prayed for strength for everyone involved. His worry climbed, though, as she went from confused to shock, while she stood there with tears in her eyes. She was visibly struggling.

"Sounds good," Jesse said. "Let's head over to Casey's and get her packed. Sooner rather than later, so she can sit down…preferably before she passes out." Jesse ushered Casey to the passenger side door of Mac's truck.

As they were on their way to Casey's home, she looked over to Mac, and said, "I don't understand. I prayed for him to be healed. God's supposed to hear my prayer and answer it, right?"

"Right, but wrong," he corrected her. Mulling around in his head how to word what the answer to her next question was going to be, he prayed for clarity. He needed to make it simple as possible with her current mental state.

"How can it be wrong?" she asked.

"There are three answers to any request – 'yes', 'no,' and 'wait.' We don't know what His answer will be, but rest assured that He *will* answer it," Mac explained.

"But I prayed for him to be healed. I know God heard it."

"Casey, just relax." Mac set his hand on her knee. "It's going to be a long ride."

She looked at his hand for a moment, before she grasped it with hers. Then she looked over at Jesse, who sat beside her in the front bench seat of Mac's truck, and asked, "He's going to be okay, right?"

"Just rest, Case," he said, as he took his hand, drawing her head toward his shoulder to relax.

When they got to her house, she changed from her uniform into jeans and a t-shirt. While she was in the bedroom, she packed a gym bag before returning to the living room.

Mac didn't say a word as he took her bag. He tossed it into the back of the truck with the other bags, while Casey and Jesse got in the front. When Mac got into the driver's seat, they took off for the base.

*   *   *

Casey had Mac and Jesse stop to get visitor badges before they headed to the entrance gate. "This is wild," Jesse looked down at his pass as they walked to the truck.

"Never been on a base before?" Casey looked at him surprised.

"Have to say this is a first."

When they pulled up to the checkpoint, the Airman asked for their ID. Casey handed hers and Jesse's to Mac, who passed it onto the soldier at the gate. He glanced through them for a moment before he looked into the truck, "Casey?"

Casey leaned forward to get better look at him. A smile formed on her face as she said, "Hey, Matthews!"

"Long time, no see. How are you doing?" he asked.

"Good. You?"

"Good. Haven't seen Jack in a while either. Where's he been lately?"

"He's here in the hospital. That's why we're here."

"Gotcha. Well, everything looks good," he said, handing Mac back their IDs. "Give my best to Jack, and tell him I hope he recovers quickly."

"Thank you, sir." She nodded politely, before Mac pulled through the checkpoint.

"Where to?" Mac asked.

Casey gave him directions to the house. As they drove through the base, they saw military personnel working on drills and airplanes taking off. There was even an obstacle course being utilized at the time.

"Now *that's* an obstacle course!" Jesse remarked as they stopped and watched for a moment. "How many bases have you lived on?"

"I don't know. Probably *lived on* five, but every time they transferred him, I had a key to the house. I have been to more than I can count. He has been on this base for about four years now. That's a record for him."

"Good grief!"

Casey sighed. "That's military life."

"I like the planes," Mac said, as he leaned out the window to watch a jet take off.

"They're my favorite too," Casey said. "That sound means home to me."

They drove the couple more minutes to the house. "That's tiny," Jesse remarked, looking at the house when they got out of the truck.

"He's a single guy. It's only a two bedroom. He doesn't need much," Casey said, taking her keys from her pocket. She grabbed her gym bag from the back of Mac's truck. Mac and Jesse followed suit as they followed her into the house.

She had a feeling of home rush over her when she walked through the door. It might have been a different house, but the contents reminded Casey of growing up with Jack. It was still home to her, regardless of where it was, or what the shell of the house looked like. He always decorated it the same.

"Wow," Jesse whistled, as he looked at the photos on the wall. "It's not a matter of *Jack* going all over the world – it's *you*!" The pictures he looked at were pictures Casey took of herself in the various countries she had been in, in her travels as a photographer.

"He's just as well-travelled, if not more so, only he wasn't allowed to take pictures where he went. Well, none that would be allowed to be on a wall anyway," Casey pointed out.

He nodded in understanding. "Good point."

"So, where's the hospital?" Mac came in from locking the truck, and set his bag down on the floor. "Wow! Nice!" He smiled as he looked around. "You decorated in here, didn't you?"

"Well, not specifically in here, but I did the decorations. He always puts things back the same way in each house. As a matter of fact...." Casey went over and opened one of the bedroom doors. "This is his." Then she opened the door across the hall. "*This* is mine."

Jesse and Mac walked into her room with her. There was a twin-sized bed, a dresser, and a desk in the room itself. The decorations were the same from when Casey grew up, minus the posters and schoolbooks. The photos and trophies still adorned the room, along with some of her stuffed animals. Jack also put some of her photos on the wall that she took as a photographer. She could even smell the potpourri in the hurricane vase on her desk that he would refresh on a regular basis.

"Awww! You were cute." Mac smirked, looking at the family photos on the wall.

Casey playfully shoved him. "Shut up."

"No, really, you were. Look at this one. Adorable," he said, pointing to a picture of when she was six and Jack was eleven.

"That's the last real family photo taken," Casey remarked when she saw her parents in the picture as well. "We were on a set in France when that was taken."

"Cool!" Jesse came over and looked at it before moving on to other pictures. "Wow!" He whistled as he picked up the photo from her Senior Prom.

"What now?" Casey nervously tucked her hair behind her ear. She didn't normally let people get as close to her as she had let Mac and Jesse. She felt vulnerable and awkward with them in her room.

"You were beautiful," he remarked.

She raised an eyebrow at him. "*Were*?"

"Well, you are now too, but I, uh…." He cleared his throat, handing the photo to Mac so he could look at it. "Never mind. I'm shutting up now."

Casey chuckled. "Good idea."

"Nice," Mac said, handing the photo back to Jesse. "Who's the guy?"

"That was Todd Peters. He was captain of the football team, a starter on the basketball team, pitcher on the baseball team – your typical jock," she said.

"Popular too?" Jesse questioned.

"I wouldn't say that." She shook her head. "He was a military brat like me, so we bonded that way."

They looked around the house for a few more minutes before they went over to the hospital. The planes mesmerized Mac while they drove through the base. He enjoyed every minute of it!

Casey got Jack's room number, and the directions to it before they quickly ascended the stairs. Casey was done wasting time waiting for an elevator. She wanted to see Jack.

Mac and Jesse had not prepared Casey anywhere near well enough. When she walked in and saw his condition, her heart sank to her stomach.

"Hey, Space Case," Jack said, with a forced smile.

She knew he was glad to see her, but he looked immensely weak. "Oh, Jack!" Casey covered her mouth in shock. This wasn't the strong Jack she was used to seeing. It sickened her how frail he looked.

He shook his head. "You missed your cue."

"I'm sorry, but...." She shook her head unable to finish. She could not control the tears this time as they flowed freely down her cheeks. "You look awful."

"Thanks, I love you too."

There were tubes and wires hooked up all over him. They monitored him, while pumping vital fluids and medicines into his body. He looked so fragile. His body almost seemed void of any color except for the unmistakable yellowish tinge of jaundice. There was a vast difference from when she saw him last, even though it was only a month ago.

"Guess we're not playing hoop anytime soon, eh?" Jesse smirked, as he made his way to the other side of the bed.

He shook his head. "Afraid not."

Mac went behind Casey and nudged her forward. She took a step, but stopped. This man was her tower and strength. He was the only family she had. He looked so weak, so frail...so not Jack!

Mac gave up after another minute and pulled her with him to the side of the bed with his arm around her waist. "There, that's better." He smiled.

Jack reached up and took her hand into his. "Let's try this again…hey, Space Case," he said with a tender smile.

"Hey Jumpin' Jack," she squeaked out, tears slowly rolling down her cheeks. All she could do was stare at him. She had seen enough horrific things in her life to know that death was imminent for him, and that it wasn't too far away. She wanted to memorize him, but she was having a hard time seeing through the tears.

"Thanks for bringing her, guys," he said to Jesse and Mac. Turning back to Casey, he coaxed, "Come on, I need to see that beautiful smile."

"Why didn't you call?" she asked, as Mac got a chair and set her down in it. Casey didn't let go of Jack's hand or stop looking at him. She decided she would hold on to him as long as she could. She knew once he was gone, she would be alone.

"Because I knew what mental state you would be in if I told you the shape I was in," he said. "I also wanted you to have back-up when you found out."

"It's a good thing too. She's been in shock since we told her," Mac pointed out. "Nice house, by the way."

"You like it?" he asked.

Mac grinned, as another jet flew over the hospital. "I like the planes more."

"Yeah," Jack said in a sigh. "I love that sound too."

"One of my favorite sounds. It always reminds me of home," Casey said. She tried, but couldn't wipe the tears away fast enough as they continued in a steady stream.

"I'm sorry, Casey." Jack shook his head. "I tried to make life for you as good as I could."

"You did! If you didn't get me out of that house…thank you for everything you've done for me," she said, standing, giving him a gentle hug. As soon as he wrapped his arms around her, she lost any amount of control she had over her feelings. The tears poured in an uncontrollable stream. She knew he was close. "Thank you!"

He held her tighter in response to her sobbing. "You know I would do it again in a heartbeat."

"Please don't leave me," she begged.

"I did the best I could. They said I should have died several years ago. They're surprised I've made it this long," he said, reminding her of the words he told her in the tent.

She let him go and sat down on the side of the bed. She didn't know what to say. She was terrified of losing him. She couldn't imagine life without her Jumpin' Jack in it, and she didn't want to! She looked toward the heavens for help from God for strength.

"What's going through that beautiful brain of yours?" he asked as he tucked her hair behind her ear.

She didn't know what else to do. In desperation, she stood up and took his hand into hers, closing her eyes. "Daddy," she cried, "I bring before You a man of strength, a man of integrity, and a man of honor. Please, I beg You not to take him from me yet! I ask that You remove the cancer that has eaten away at him. I ask that You give him a couple more years, at least, with me. This man has given his all for me. I ask that in return You give him the gift of a couple more years. I treasure this man as much as You do. I know he can be a man of strength for Your Kingdom. Please, Father! Please don't take my brother!"

He reached his arms around her and held her as tight as he could. He kissed her head, as he said, "He heard you, but I don't want to fight this anymore."

"You have to!"

"They have to give me morphine for the pain." He nodded toward the morphine drip. Knowing what all he had gone through in his life, for him to take medicine meant that the pain was probably close to unbearable. "I've held on for you. Please don't ask me to stay. I want to live in peace with our Father. You can bet, though," he wiped the tears off her face with his thumbs, "that I'll be getting a room ready for you up there. I will *always* look out for you."

She fought to get her sobbing under control for his sake. "You always have."

"Then know that I've done my best. I've fought for you, my country, and have even won a few battles for Christ as well while I was at it. I love you, Casey."

"I love you too, Jack," she said, resting her head on his chest. She listened to his staggered breaths as his heart rate slowed.

He reached his arms around her and held her as tight as he could. He kissed her head. "I love you," he quietly cried.

"I love you too. Thank you for everything you have done for me. Please, go be at peace with our Daddy. You're free."

She heard the rhythm of his heart monitor lag as his breathing faltered. She felt desperate as she cried, "I love you, my Jumpin' Jack!"

"I love you too…Space Case," he whispered, and he was gone.

Within seconds, a nurse came into the room, closely followed by a tall gentleman in uniform. The nurse turned off the monitors and pumps, before she covered his body. "I'm very sorry for your loss," she said and left the room.

"My name is Captain Michaels. I'm the Casualty Assistance Representative for Special Operations. Your brother has been working with me over the last several months," the man explained.

"The nurse turned off the monitors and pumps because Lieutenant Colonel Carter had a living will. She called me to be on standby, knowing his time was short."

Casey nodded in understanding.

"There are going to be some things you will have to sign for at my office. He's already made arrangements in several areas. There are companies coming to clean and pack the house within the next couple of days. He wanted me to tell you all of this when he was gone." She wiped the few tears that escaped her eyes as Captain Michaels continued, "He didn't want you to have to worry about anything. The belongings from the house are getting shipped to this storage facility." He pulled some paperwork from his clipboard. "Here are the keys and the information on the storage garage." He handed the paperwork to Casey, who passed it to Jesse. "He paid for six months, so you won't have to do anything right away."

Jesse shook his head in amazement. "He *was* thinking about things. He was an amazing man."

"He knows how fast they clear the houses out," the Captain explained. "They need to clear them so new people can take them over. There is also a letter for you from him in the paperwork."

Casey shook her head, beside herself.

"I called Doctor Ellis when he was going. He should be up here in a minute or two to talk to you," he explained. "There is also information on his life insurance we need to discuss." He handed that to Jesse as well. "I'll be contacting you tomorrow to discuss the arrangements Lieutenant Colonel Carter has already made for his funeral. Here is my card with my number on it in case you need to contact me before then. You have my sympathies. He was a man of honor."

As Captain Michaels left the room, Casey brushed away the continuous flow of tears that refused to stop, while she continued to hold Jack's lifeless hand in hers. "He's finally at peace. Good bye, my Jumpin' Jack. I love you."

"He loved you too." Jessie bent down, gave her a hug, and kissed her head. "He was a good man."

Casey stood up straight and tucked his hand back under the covers, while Mac rested an arm around her.

"He was a strong man," Mac said, "who loved you with all of his heart."

Casey couldn't say anything. She saw the form of her brother, but knew he was no longer under the sheet. His body was there, but it was just a shell. His heart and soul were in Heaven. As the memories of Jack flooded her mind, her heart shattered into a million pieces. She turned in Mac, who wrapped his arms around her. Her tears continued to flow.

Jesse scanned the stack, while Mac held Casey. "There is a five-hundred-thousand-dollar life insurance policy, the storage information, details about the funeral and gravesite, and a letter," he said, and looked up at Casey for her reaction.

"Read it," Casey stared at Jack's covered body in front of her, periodically wiping her tears. If she couldn't see his face or hear his voice, she wanted to listen to his words.

"'*Hey, Space Case,*'" he started, as tears filled his eyes, "'*If you're reading this, then I'm in Heaven with our Daddy, and our Brother, Jesus. Kind of nice to know that we have more family out there, eh?*'" Jesse read aloud, and then looked up at Casey. He shook his head. "I can't do this. I'm sorry."

"Please, Jesse?" She didn't take her eyes of Jack's covered body. "I need to hear from him."

His heart broke for her. As much as he knew it would kill him to read it, he looked back down and read the letter as clear as he could, while he struggled to keep his emotions under control. "'*Once again, I've taken care of business. Everything is set, so you won't have to do anything. Just know that big brother is still looking out for you, even from Heaven.*'" Jesse smiled for a moment before he continued, "'*There is one piece of unfinished business, though. This is something you will have to take care of on your own. Over the years, I have kept track of her. Angelina Maria Montoya is living in Boise, Idaho with her family. The little angel's family contacted me about three years ago and wanted to keep in touch. Now, I know you wanted it to be a closed....*' Casey, what's going on?" Jesse looked up, stunned by what he read.

"Keep reading," Mac said, still holding Casey.

"You knew, didn't you?" Jesse's jaw dropped.

"Yes. Just keep reading," Mac insisted. "I don't know how long we have before the doctor comes in, and I want that read first."

"You know what is in this?"

"Yes. Now please read," Mac said calmly, as he had one arm around her. He brought his other hand up and rested it on her shoulder.

"All right," he sighed before he looked back down and read again, "'*Now, I know you wanted it to be a closed adoption, but the family felt for you and wanted you to get an idea of the life she was living so you wouldn't worry. The photos of her are in a box on my dresser marked with your name on it. There are also a couple letters, including one with the information you will need to contact them. Casey, for your own peace of mind, please contact them. I know it tore you up inside, because I went through it with you. I also know the reason you did it was an honorable one. Well, that was the last loose end I had to tie up, so now it's time to go. Just know that I will always love you. I'm sorry I could not hold on any longer, but it literally hurts. Taking care of you while you grew up was the biggest and best privilege and honor of my life! You were a wonderful kid and I could not be prouder of you.*'" As he read the letter, Casey's sobbing became uncontrollable. Jesse felt for her. He brushed his tears out of the way before they had a chance to fall as he continued to read, "'*No one could ask for a better sister. We made a great team! Not to mention the fact that we almost kicked 'B' shift's behinds!*'" Jesse had to chuckle at that one before he went on, "'*Mac,*'" Jesse read, and then looked up at Mac, in surprise. "Did you know you were in this?"

"Just read," Mac said. He leaned down and kissed Casey's head as he held her tighter. "I don't know how much longer I can hold her here."

Jesse nodded in understanding. He looked down and continued to read. "'*Mac, I can never thank you enough for leading me to the Father and to Jesus. They have been my source of strength and courage to help me push through and finish my race. Please take care of Casey for me. I would consider it an honor if you and the guys from 'A' shift would continue to look after her.*'" Jesse shook his head. Reading Jack's heart to Casey was harder than he thought it would be. "No problem, man," Jesse said, looking toward Jack's covered body. "Consider it done." Then he looked back down and read more of the letter, "'*You guys are all the family she has now. Help her to know more of her heavenly Christian family, so she knows she is not alone. As far as what you asked me in the tent, you have my blessing...just don't hurt her, or I'll come back from the grave and personally kick your behind!*'" Jesse read. Then he looked up at Mac, confused, and asked, "What did he mean by that?"

"That's between us." Mac hugged Casey. "Just read."

"All right," Jesse said in a sigh. Then he looked back down and finished the letter, "'*Jesse, keep her smiling. You are her brother now,*'" Jess shook his head as a couple tears came down onto his cheeks. He looked up at Mac and asked, "How did he know I would be here?"

"He wanted you here. Please read." Mac glanced at the door before he looked back at Jesse and reminded him, "The doctor will be here any second.

"'*Jesse, keep her smiling. You are her brother now. Make sure she's safe, and look after her for me, will you?*'" He looked toward Jack's body again, and said, "No problem." Then he looked back down, "'*Casey, I love you, but I have to be signing off. You will always be my Space Case and I will always be your Jumpin' Jack. Never forget me, or what our family stands for.'"*

Casey sniffed as she wiped her eyes. "I won't."

"'Make God, Jesus, and me proud! With all my love, Lieutenant Colonel Jonathon 'Jack' Carter,'" Jesse finished. "Wow!" He shook his head, "That was –"

"Jack," Casey smiled as she looked down at him.

Chapter 13

Picking Up the Pieces

The funeral was one of the most difficult things Casey ever had to do in her life. Innumerable military personnel attended. There was a twenty-one-gun salute, and some of Jack's friends flew their planes overhead in honor of him in the missing man formation. Casey thought it was an appropriately powerful and patriotic way for Jack to leave this planet.

Even though the chaplain asked her to, Casey was too much of a mess to speak at his funeral. Mac and Jesse flanked either side of her the entire time. Casey was sure she wouldn't have made it if they weren't there.

As the funeral closed, two Colonels in their dress blues lifted the flag off his coffin and proceeded to fold it in military fashion. When they finished, they saluted his casket before they took the flag to Casey.

"He was a man of honor," the one holding the flag said as he knelt in front of her with the flag between his hands. "We were proud to serve with him." Then he continued, "On behalf of the President of the United States, the United States Air Force, and a grateful Nation, please accept this flag as a symbol of our appreciation for your loved one's honorable and faithful service."

Casey nodded as she accepted the flag from the Colonel, and both saluted. While Casey knew he was in a better place, the pain inside her cut deep. Having to bury not only another family member, but also her brother, her strength, her caregiver, and her best friend, was killing her on the inside!

As people left, many of them put a white rose on his casket, before coming over and saying words of condolence. While Casey appreciated the sentiment, she was lost in the thoughts and memories of her brother. She felt numb as she clutched the flag to her chest.

When the last attendee walked away, the chaplain came over to Casey and knelt in front of her. He took her hands into his as he said, "He was a brave man. I knew many men who he, himself, had a hand in saving or rescuing over the years. He will *never* be forgotten."

"Thank you," she said. She wiped her face for what seemed like the hundredth time that day.

"He was also a Christian, which makes a service like this a privilege. I know at least three people he had a hand in leading to Christ over the last few weeks, not to mention the strong witness he was to those in the hospital. For the last four years, since he has been on this base, I have watched him. He was a happy, strong man, but he was sick. It wasn't until this last month, that I saw true joy and happiness in him, even though he was at his worst, health wise. When I asked him what happened, he replied that he had a new Daddy in God, and a new Brother in Jesus. He was relieved to be able to be at peace inside. It was an honor to serve with him, and to finally meet you. Thank you for sharing him with your country. May God bless you," he said, and then stood up. He left the trio sitting there with the funeral director and a couple other men, who calmly stood a little way back as they waited for them to leave.

"Are you ready?" Mac asked.

Casey's mood was listless and absent since Jack died. As she walked over to Jack's casket, she hugged the American flag close to her heart. She leaned down and kissed his casket, and whispered, "Rest in peace, my beloved brother. I love you with all my heart. Thank you."

She picked up a couple of the roses and took them with her as she walked back to Mac and Jesse. The funeral director said a few more words of condolence to Casey before they left the national cemetery. Casey didn't hear them though. She felt sick to her stomach and dizzy. She felt like she was in a fog, and prayed that this was some terrible mistake or a nightmare.

She didn't remember packing her bag, nor packing the family photos from around the house. She didn't even remember the drive back to the house, where Jesse kept his arm around her until she ended up crying herself to sleep.

*   *   *

Over the next few days, Casey felt like she was in a daze. She knew she had to go to work, even though she didn't want to. She knew Chief and the other firefighters were counting on her to return.

On her first day back, Casey sat with Jesse in the meeting room. The two shifts were waiting for a couple stragglers to get there, when Chief came in with Pete Van den Bergh from 'B' shift.

"What are you doing here?" Jeff looked up at him, caught off-guard.

"I'm changing shifts. I wanted Carter's cooking," he joked.

Casey only half-heartedly smiled. She was not in the mood for playing around today.

"What's up?" Vinnie asked Chief. He took a quick inventory of who was in the room before he asked, "Where's Mac?"

At the mention of Mac's name, Casey scanned the room in alarm. Jesse did the same thing before they both looked at each other, then up at Chief for an explanation.

"Don't worry, he's fine. He just transferred to 'B' shift. And, in return, you guys get Van den Bergh," Chief explained.

Casey looked up at Chief feeling sick to her stomach. "But…he was my partner." This was the last thing she needed to hear today.

"I know. He's in the office waiting for you. Don't worry. Go in and talk to him. We'll be in here when you're done."

"Chief, I…." Panic churned within her. "I really…."

"Go. I have to talk to these guys while you're gone."

Casey turned to Jesse; terror written all over her.

"Sir," Jesse pleaded, "She really has had a –"

"I'm fully aware of what's been going on," Chief cut him off. "Do you trust me?"

"Yes, sir," he said.

"Then trust me." Chief gently smiled.

"Yes, Chief," he said in a sigh. He looked over at Casey and nodded for her to leave.

Casey anxiously looked from Chief, to Jesse, and back to Chief again.

"Go ahead," Chief encouraged her. "I need to talk to these guys."

"Yes, sir." Casey stood. She had no idea what would make Mac change shifts. *He was her partner! How could he do this to her with everything else she went through this week?*

"Morning, Carter!" The receptionist, Margo, looked up at her and smiled when she walked around the corner to her desk.

"Morning," she politely responded.

"Go on in, Mac's waiting."

Casey looked toward the office door. She could see Mac in one of the chairs, praying, as the door was slightly ajar.

She said a quick word of payer to the Lord for strength. Then she took a deep breath before she pushing the office door open. "Mac, what's going on?" she asked, closing the door behind her. "Why are you changing shifts?"

"Have a seat." He gestured to the chair across from him. The chairs were turned so they faced each other.

Casey's heart raced as she sat down. "What is it?" she asked.

He took both of her hands into his. "Chief and I had a serious conversation after we got back from Jack's funeral."

"I can see that. He doesn't normally shift people around for no reason."

"Oh, there's a reason." He nervously wiped his sweaty hands on his jeans before grabbing her hands again. Then he took a deep, cleansing breath. "You see," he said, "there's this rule, and in order to get around it I had to change shifts."

She furrowed her brow. "I don't understand."

"Wow! This is harder than I thought it would be." His leg started bouncing, as he bit his bottom lip.

"Mac, if you tell my something's happened to you, I'll...." A sense of panic now overwhelmed her.

"It has, but not what you think." He reached up and brushed the tear that escaped down her cheek. "There's no need to cry. You remember when Jesse read Jack's letter in the hospital?"

"Of course."

"Do you remember what it said?"

"Every word."

He looked down for a moment to think, before he looked back up at her. "When Leah died, something deep inside me died with her. She was my love."

Casey struggled to follow his train of thought. "Mac,   you're not making sense."

"I love you, but be quiet for a minute…please?"

She nodded. She knew whatever he was about to tell her was hard for him. She prayed he would be able to get what was on his mind out soon, though. With Jack's passing this week, she was apprehensive as to what Mac was trying to tell her.

"When Leah died, something deep inside me died with her. It wasn't until recently that it was awakened again. It took Ryan telling me for me to see it."

"What does Ryan have to do with you changing shifts?"

"Work with me here, please?" he sighed in frustration.

She nodded as she held her lips tightly together to remind herself to be quiet.

"You see, Ryan and I talked about it that Friday night at the campout when we were in the tent. And then, when I woke up to find you sitting there less than a couple inches away from me, I thought it was a dream, a product of our conversation."

Casey bit her lip to stop herself from asking him what in the world a dream would have to do with his conversation with Ryan, but she respected his request and kept silent.

"Then when Jack came to the tent, after our deep conversation regarding Christ, we had another deep conversation…regarding you."

Casey raised an eyebrow at him. He smiled and went on with his thoughts. "This brought me to my dilemma. It took me this last month of not seeing you because of the contest, to realize just how much I needed you in my life. And with Jack's death, on the heels of Marshall and Callan's deaths, not to mention you almost blowing up with Miller, to realize just how much I love you," he said in one breath before he studied Casey for her reaction.

He could tell by the look on her face she was stunned and confused. He sighed as he prayed for the right words. He decided that with everything swirling around her that he would have to be blunt. He took a deep breath and looked at her beautiful green eyes, as he said, "In Jack's letter he gave me his blessing to ask if I could court you."

Casey stared at him in wide-eyed shock as her heart skipped several beats.

"Due to the regulations here at the station, we're not allowed to date someone on our shift. So, in order to ask you, I had to change shifts," he explained.

Casey's jaw dropped.

He smiled as he reached up and closed her mouth. "You are my best friend. I trust you with my life every day we are here at work. There have been multiple times where we've even gone out with just the two of us as friends. I trust you completely, and I'm pretty sure you trust me. So, Casey Ann Carter, will you allow me the privilege of courting you, with the later intent of possible marriage sometime in the future?"

Casey's jaw dropped in shock again.

He laughed as he closed her mouth again. "Chief is aware of what we're talking about in here and supports it. Pete isn't exactly sure why he was asked to transfer shifts, but he didn't have a problem with it, since, and this is his theory, he gets paid either way. Now, if you say no I will understand, since I know your past. And if you do, that's okay. I'll be on a different shift so I'll be okay."

"Mac, I...." Casey shook her head, still in shock. This was the man she trusted her heart and life to for over four months.

Mac anxiously waited for her answer.

She nervously cleared her throat before she said, "This is not what I was expecting."

"It may not be, but what's your answer?"

There were so many thoughts and feeling swirling around, she wasn't sure where to start in order to sort them out.

"Casey, I love you. I meant it when we were at the mountain and I said I was *in love* with you. There is a world of difference between those two statements. In either one, I would give my life for you. However, when I say that I'm *in love* with you, to me that means I can't imagine my life without you in it. You know my past. You know how hard it is for me to even consider love again."

"Yes," she decidedly responded in answer to his original question.

He thought she was agreeing to the statement he made and said, "Then you know how hard it is for me to ask you."

"Yes," she said again, a little more forcefully as she looked directly into his eyes. This was the man she could not imagine her life without. In his statements, he was right. They should be together.

"Then, will you?"

Casey laughed, as a smile lit her face. "I *said* yes!"

"You mean…I thought you were saying –"

Casey cut him off by grabbing his face and kissing him. It took a second to register what she did before he reached up, rested his hands on the sides of her face, and joined her in the kiss.

"I take it she said yes," Chief leaned on the doorway with his arms crossed. He had been standing there for a minute to see if they were going to stop.

Mac grinned, as he stared at her, less than a few inches from her face. "Yes."

"Good. Because I didn't want to have to change my men around just for her to say no. Congratulations, guys."

"Thanks!" Casey grinned. She still had her hands on Mac's face.

"Now, I *do* believe you still have a shift to work. Think you can do it with a clear head?" Chief asked.

"This is probably the clearest my head has been in days."

"What did you tell the guys?" Mac asked out of curiosity.

"That for personal reasons, you and Pete were trading slots." He shrugged. "Unless you volunteer it, they don't need to know any more." Chief watched them for a moment before he sighed, "Go ahead and hang out for a bit. If there's a call though, she has to go. She's on the rig today, so no need to worry about ambulance calls."

Mac stood up. "Thanks, Chief," he said, shaking his hand.

With that, they left for the meeting room. The other firefighters from 'A' shift were still sitting in there, and they looked upset. The few conversations that had been going on abruptly stopped when the pair walked into the room.

"Hey, guys," Mac said, as he leaned against the table with Casey right beside him. They were not touching because they wanted to respect the firehouse rules.

"What's going on, Mac?" Jesse asked angrily. He didn't have a smile on his face, so everyone *knew* he was upset.

"I changed shifts," he started.

"We got that," Marty snapped.

"There was a good reason, though," Casey added.

"There had *better* be!" Jeff growled. "We're a family, and you broke it up."

The firefighters were beyond upset. They were almost angry with Mac. Casey nudged him to explain, because she knew they needed to know what was going on before they got angrier.

"Well," he crossed his arms in front of him. Casey shifted so she was sitting on the table beside him. "You see, there's this rule."

Casey rolled her eyes with a smile. "Oh, don't go there again."

"We're *not* in a joking mood. Spill it, Mac!" Will said sternly.

"Well, there's this rule where we can't date anyone on our shift, right?" Mac asked.

A smile slowly formed on Jesse's face. "Mac?"

"And, well, Jesse, since you're on this shift, I had to change," he said, and winked at Jesse, who burst out in laughter. The joke was lost on the others in the room.

"Is that what Jack meant?" Jesse asked.

"Yep!"

"You dog!" He went over and gave Casey a huge hug, before he shook hands with Mac and gave him a hug of congratulations.

"Wait a minute." Pete put his hand up. "Are you trying to tell me what I *think* you're telling me?"

"That you changed shifts, so I can court my best friend…yes." Mac grinned.

"Well, then I'd say it was worth it. Congrats, man," Pete said, and walked over and shook their hands.

"Are you two…?" Will started, stunned. He shook his head, and then looked up at them again, "You changed shifts, *leaving us*, just so you could date *her*?"

"Not date…court," Mac corrected.

"What's the difference?" Scott crossed his arms, leaning against the wall.

"Courting is with the intent to marry," Mac explained. "Dating is just dating."

Scott had a blank look on his face for a moment, as he watched the others get up to congratulate them. When it registered what he said, and what it meant, he quickly congratulated them as well, giving each a hug. Afterward, everyone slowly dispersed to do their chores.

When the last person left, Mac stood in front of her and took her hands into his. "So, how are you feeling?"

"It's a little weird," she admitted.

"Weird?"

"Foreign weird…not strange weird."

"You? Imagine what it's like for me. I haven't had anyone that I have even been remotely interested in since Leah died when I was twenty-three."

"Which makes me feel even more honored." She kissed his cheek. "Thank you."

"That's gonna take a little getting used to." He blushed.

"Oh," she winked. "I don't think it'll take *that* long."

"I'll sacrifice." He shrugged, smiling, as he draped his arms around her waist.

"So, does your family know?"

"Kind of." He nodded. "Ryan knows I was going to ask you, but that's it."

Rob poked his head into the room, and said, "Just a gentle reminder that you have drills here in about thirty minutes. Might wanna get the lead out on your chores."

"I'll be there in a minute," Casey acknowledged. After he left, she turned back to Mac, who met her with a kiss. His lips were soft, and his touch was tender as he rested his hands on her waist.

"I *am* in love with you," he grinned as he pulled away.

"And, I'm in love with you too," she said, feeling a thrill of excitement run through her. It was a feeling she hadn't had for a long time.

"Can you imagine what Jack's thinking right now as he's looking down at us?" Mac asked.

"Yeah. He's probably happy we took a chance on love."

"That too," Casey said. "But, he would probably say that it's about time"

Chapter 14

Blindsided

Over the next several months, Mac and Casey's relationship got stronger than it was already. It got to the point that they could even finish each other's sentences. They knew what the other was thinking half the time before the other person knew it. It was a risk to say yes to him, but it ended up being one of the best decisions of Casey's life! Casey was pleased that she got along with his family too. Over the holidays, she was able to get to know them on a deeper level while they celebrated together.

Also, during that time, Mac helped Casey work through Jack's death. Despite her loss, she continued to work her regular shifts at the station. Being a firefighter/paramedic could be an emotionally hard profession, but when one added the death of a close family member to the emotional load, it made it that much harder to focus and do the job with proficiency.

Casey and Mac did a lot of work regarding Jack's death by praying and talking. There were times Casey would drive down to the cemetery by herself and talk to Jack as well. She usually did it on the days Mac was on shift, so she wouldn't take time away from their limited schedule together. In her conversations at Jack's gravesite, she would imagine it was Jesus, Jack, God, and her sitting around talking as a family.

It was during one of these conversations that her cell phone rang. When she looked down, she saw it was the station's phone number. "Hey, sweetheart," she answered the phone, thinking Mac was calling her the way he usually did when he was on shift.

"Carter," it was Chief, "can you come down to the station?"

"Sorry, Chief, I thought you were Mac. Yeah, I'll be there in about…twenty minutes?"

"Sounds good. Thanks," he said and hung up.

"Well, I hate to do this, but duty calls." Casey lovingly touched the gravestone with Jack's name carved into it. "I'll see you later, Jack."

Casey didn't waste time getting to the station. Something in Chief's voice had a feeling of urgency. When she got there, she noticed there were more vehicles than normal in the parking lot. She saw Jesse's motorcycle out of the corner of her eye when she was about to walk into the station. It caught her by surprise. She did a double take as things began to line up in her head. As she looked at the other vehicles, she realized they belonged to firefighters from all the shifts. She got a sick feeling in her stomach, as the adrenaline coursed through her body. She was sure something bad happened, but she was not sure of the extent.

She ran into the station and demanded from Margo, "Where's Chief?"

"He's in the meeting room, dear." Margo's face was streaked from crying. When she saw Casey, she burst into tears again.

Casey's eyes got wide, as she bolted for the meeting room. She flung the door open to see there was standing room only. The members of all the shifts were present, and looked over at her as she opened the door. The room was completely silent otherwise.

"Carter," Chief looked up with tears in his eyes, "come on in."

She couldn't believe it when she saw several firefighters crying as well. She frantically searched the room for Mac and Jesse. She didn't have to look too hard for Jesse, before he stood up from the end seat he was sitting in, and came over and got Casey. He sat her down in his chair with his hands braced on her shoulders while he stood behind her.

Chief took a moment before he continued, "While I know this is something we had to go through not more than eight months ago, I have the confidence that we will come through it stronger than ever."

Panic churned so strongly inside Casey, that she thought she was going to throw up. "Chief?" She stood up. Jesse held her arms so she couldn't go anywhere. "Chief, where's Mac?" Casey nervously asked. She did not see Mac *or* his partner Carl Warner in the room. "Where's Warner?"

"Carter," Chief shook his head. Barely able to get the words out, he said, "I'm sorry."

She gulped. "He's in the hospital, right?"

He shook his head.

"No," she whispered. Her eyes locked on Chief, she said, "This can't be! No, *he wouldn't do this to me*!"

Just then, Ryan and the rest of Mac's family walked through the door. Casey took one look at them and shook her head again, as the words and events around her clicked in her brain. Jesse tightened his grip on her arms when he felt her want to move.

She looked back at Chief. "Chief…no," she shook her head. "Please…no. No! This isn't real. He wouldn't do this to me!"

"It was an accident," Chief apologized. "I'm truly sorry, Casey. I really am. Our hearts are breaking for you."

"No," she whispered. Jesse tried to lower her to her seat, but she refused. As she stood there slowly shaking her head, she desperately tried to line any thought in her head she could, but they were scattered at best. When she turned to Ryan, he hung his head. "No." She shook her head again.

She moved to run, but Jesse still had a hold of one of her arms and spun her around, facing him. "Don't." He shook his head. "Let us, as your family, help you through this."

She stared at him as the tears of realization flowed down her cheeks. The longer she stared at him, the faster the stream flowed.

Jesse watched his friend's world come crashing around her. He felt her body shaking under his hands.

Ryan walked over and put his hand on her shoulder. He turned her into him, wrapping his arms around her in a hug.

"Please don't say it's true! I can't handle this again!" Casey shouted as she sobbed uncontrollably. Her body shook with the intense emotions that flooded her system.

"I'm so sorry, Casey," he tried to hold her.

Casey backed away from him. Looking around the room, she desperately searched their faces for answers. "No," she whispered.

Jesse took a step toward her, but she bolted for the door, only to be caught around the waist by Hunter. He used his other arm to hold her arms down as she kicked and screamed.

"Let me go! Let me go!" she screamed.

Jesse walked over to Casey. When he did, she stopped screaming and stared at him, wide-eyed, pale, and motionless. While Hunter did set her down, he didn't let go of the grip he had on her. He knew if she ran, they would have trouble catching her again.

"Chief called us all in here, because he knew what this was going to do to you," Jesse calmly explained. "Now, please pull yourself together. We're not going anywhere...and neither are you."

Casey looked over at Mac's mother who was sobbing in her husband's arms. This seemed like a horrible nightmare to her. As Casey watched Mac's mom, she felt disorientated and disconnected from a world that was doing its best to swallow her.

"Casey?" Chief rested his hands on her shoulders, standing in front of her. "Casey, look at me."

She couldn't. All she could see at that moment was Mac's parents, as she was lost in her own thoughts Mac. He was so tenderhearted, so affectionate, so open. Here was a man who was devoted and loyal to God. He gave everything he was for everyone else. He was a strong witness for God. He gave everything for every person in that firehouse. He loved and respected her…and she loved him with everything she had in her. However, in one swift motion God snatched Mac away from her, much the same as he ripped Jack from her.

"I hate him!" Casey growled at Chief.

He looked at her, wide-eyed. "Who?"

"God!" As soon as she said that, Mac's family turned and looked at her, stunned. His mother gasped. "God did this! He took away my brother, my anchor! And now, just when I worked through that loss, he took away the only man I was ever in love with! How *dare* He!"

Ryan stared at her, appalled. "Casey, you can't mean that!"

"I dare you to say otherwise!" She snapped. She reached her max. "It's true! He took my parents when I was eight. He took my brother several months ago. He was my lifeline! And now, when I'm finally getting *some* semblance of peace about it, He took Mac away. I loved that man, and he loved me in return. And *this* is supposed to be my *loving* Father?" She turned to Mac's dad, and asked, "Would you do this to one of your own children?"

His dad shook his head in shock at the scene unfolding in front of him.

Casey turned back to Ryan, and demanded, "Then how can you say God loves me? How could He do this to one of His own children?"

"You need to calm down," Chief said, trying to get her to focus.

"No!" she shouted, and just about everyone in the room jumped.

Hunter tightened his grip on her, afraid of what she was going to do.

"No! *I will not* calm down!" She struggled to get free from Hunter, as Chief took a couple steps back. "Let me go!" she demanded.

"No," Hunter calmly said, as he lifted her off the ground while she struggled to get free.

"Let me go!" Casey repeatedly screamed, fighting to get out of Hunter's arms. "Let me go!"

"No," Hunter said again.

Jesse tried to get to Casey to calm her down, but she screamed and thrashed about so wildly to free herself from Hunter that he couldn't get to her. "Casey!" He slapped her face.

"I —" She stared at Jesse in shock for a moment. She didn't move a muscle, until she saw Ryan out of the corner of her eye. When she did, the anger rushed back into her like a tsunami as she saw Mac in him. Her strength dwindling, she still fought Hunter with everything she had. "Let-me-go!" she screamed.

After several minutes, Jesse fought his way past her fierce kicking and shrill screams. He firmly held her face as he yelled, "Casey! Stop!"

"Let me go!" she shouted.

"No!" Hunter insisted.

"I'm —" Casey shook her head. Her body felt like it was disconnected from her mind. Despite her body slowing down, she continued to fight, even though she was losing the battle.

"We love you, Casey, but you're losing it," Jesse calmly said, once she finally stopped screaming. Her breathing was heavy from the fight.

Casey looked at Jesse, hoping he would understand what was going on inside of her. "Jesse…" she breathed heavily, "Jesse, h-he…." Her eyes rolled into the back of her head, as her body went limp. Exhausted from struggling for over forty-five minutes to get free from Hunter, she couldn't move anymore.

When he felt her give up the fight, Hunter lowered her to the ground. Ryan ran over with Jesse to see if she was okay. Casey looked up at him, barely able to get her eyes open. "Mac?" she asked, weakly.

"No." He shook his head. "He's in Heaven with his loving Father."

The tears rolled down her cheeks as she looked at Ryan in a daze. "No, my Daddy wouldn't do this to me."

"Casey," Jesse pleaded as his shattered into a million pieces for her. "Come on, we don't want to have to take you to the hospital."

"This is mean. Why would He do this to me, Jess?" she asked.

Hunter kept his arms around Casey's waist. He moved his other arm behind him to brace himself as he readjusted to a better position on the ground.

"Why would He take Mac away too? I can't handle another funeral right now." She turned her head toward his parents, "I'm sorry, I can't."

"We understand," his dad said, feeling full of compassion for her. While his heart was already broken at the loss of his son, seeing the display before him, knowing her past, his heart broke all over again.

"Jesse?" She closed her eyes, and opened them again as she saw sparkles in front of her.

"Yeah?"

"I...." she shook her head. "Help," she whispered and passed out in Hunter's arms.

*　　*　　*

"I'm glad we were able to schedule a little camping trip," Mac nudged Casey, as they sat on a log in front of the fire. His brother, mom, and dad sat across from them on another log.

The way the schedule worked, they took off as soon as Mac was off work on 'B' shift. They would have one overnight before Casey had to return to work by eight the next morning.

"I agree. It's been great getting to know you better," his dad, Scott, said, tossing another log on the fire.

Casey was able to join Mac and his family a couple of times over the last few months for dinners. Outside of the dinners and holidays, she wasn't able to spend much quality time with them. An overnight trip allotted for much closer companionship within the group.

"I know. Thank you for inviting me," Casey said.

Ryan pulled a bag of marshmallows from the camping box. "Anyone want s'mores?"

"Yum!" Casey jumped up and grabbed the skewers to roast the marshmallows, while Mac got the graham crackers.

"Ghost stories?" Mac suggested, while the marshmallows roasted over the open flame.

Ryan rolled his eyes. "Aren't we a little old for that?"

Mac winked with a mischievous smile. "Never too old for a good story."

His dad chuckled, shaking his head. "One of these days you boys will grow up."

"Never." Mac shook his head. He wrapped his free arm around Casey and gave her a squeeze. "What would be the fun in that?"

"Go ahead," his mom said. "As the official storyteller of the family, it's your right."

"Okay, let me see." Mac thought for a moment.

"Don't think too hard, now. We don't want to cause any brain damage," Ryan teased.

Mac stuck his tongue out at Ryan, before he said, "All right, I have one." He waited a moment to set the tone. The fire crackled, letting the light flicker and dance off the trees around them. The smell of the wood mixed with the marshmallow scent. To add the pine smell, Mac's mom, Maggie, threw in some pinecones and needles.

As the silence encompassed the group, Mac went into his storytelling voice, "These woods have been here a long time. They are filled with a history long forgotten. As a matter of fact, here, in this very spot, used to live a pioneer family. The mother and father trekked through the States, bringing with them the hopes and dreams of a better future for their children. Many of their friends had gone before them, sharing with them the many opportunities the West provided. The family held off for a bit, waiting to see how the other families fared in their journey. It was hard, but the families were tough. They relied on God and each other, and survived many a harsh season."

As he told the story, those who listened put themselves in the pioneer family's position.

"The pioneers of old were admired for their strength and fortitude. This young family's journey began from Virginia one March morning. The mother and father discussed it long and hard, until they finally concluded nothing ventured, nothing gained.

"They loaded up the wagon, and with their four children in tow, heading off on their adventure. Their oldest, Charlie, was about seventeen. A strapping young man, filled with much promise of a good future. He was strong. He learned his father's trade as a carpenter, working in the workshop since he was seven.

"Then there was Claire. She was a beautiful, fifteen-year-old young lady. She had many men who wanted to court her, but none were up to her father's standards. He wanted only the best for his daughter. His main requirement wasn't money – it was love. He wanted to know the man who would take his daughter as his wife, would love her and treat her the way she was supposed to be treated.

"Christopher was next. Coming third in line at ten-years-old, he survived where some of his other siblings had not. You see, the mother, Christine, had miscarried five times before having Christopher. Her husband, Clark, stood by her each and every day. He knew she had the strength to care for the two older children, even after the loss of the others. If the good Lord only provided them with two, he would be more than content. However, God granted them with two more. Christopher was a very talented young man. The pictures he drew were spectacular and admired by many. The chalk drawings he created almost looked like a photograph. The insight God gave him, the way he guided young Christopher's hands with his drawings, was a miracle to say the least.

"Young Carissa was last, but certainly not least. Carissa was eight at the time they pulled away from their home in Virginia. She enjoyed things that most young girls did not. She loved to hunt. That little girl was a crack shot! She, however, did not stop there. She not only shot the animals, but she cooked and cleaned them as well. She was a wonderful cook. Her mother taught both Claire and Carissa the secrets of cooking.

"Christine, the mother, was a wonderful cook, and she learned it from her mother, before passing the secrets down to her daughters. Her daughters were going to know how to take care of their man. She prided herself on how well behaved her children were, and how well rounded and talented they were.

"Christine didn't want to leave their gorgeous home in Virginia, but her other friends had already left for the West, and now it was their turn. Keeping in close contact, Clark learned from his friend's mistakes. They were not going to make the same ones. He kept a journal, compiling within it the stops. He also included what the others had run into during their trek. He noted what areas to avoid, what to take with them, and how to speak to the Native Americans they would undoubtedly run across. The family left with five other families, knowing there was safety in numbers.

"The trail was long and hard. There were multiple narrow escapes and close calls with illness and weather. The rains slowed them down quite a bit, making an otherwise dangerous trail, treacherous at best.

"After their long journey, they finally made it just before the first snow. They arrived one September afternoon, much to the joy of their friends. Together, the group of friends worked on building their home, making sure the new family was settled before the first snowfall. They also built them a barn, and stocked it with enough food, wood, and hay to make it through the winter. These ten families had made it through several seasons already, and had the experience to know what was needed.

"It was a rough winter, but the family struggled through. That spring, just like their friends did the years prior, they planted crops. As a group, the families harvested together to ensure each family's harvest did not suffer.

"Then it happened. It was a winter storm like they had never seen before. The families got snowed into their homes. The husband and wife struggled to keep their children calm. There was no way to make a fire, because the wood was outside, and they couldn't open the door.

"At first, the children thought it was fun, but Clark and Christine knew they were in trouble. With hushed voices, they discussed their options. They ate what they could get, but the food storage was about twenty feet from the home in the barn. They only had to get twenty feet to survive the storm. It was so close, yet so far away.

"The snow continued to fall through several days. At first, the snow covered the door, and then it slowly crept up past the windows, rapidly closing in on the chimney. If the snow buried the house, they would not be able to survive.

"The children began coughing, sniffling, and sneezing around day two. They continued to get worse with each passing day.

"'Why would God do this to us?' Christine cried one night as she listened to her children coughing in the loft upstairs. 'We have been good.'

"'I know we have,' Clark hugged her.

"'I just want to see my children grow up and have children of their own,' she said, before she began coughing.

"'I know. That is what any parent wants.'

"That's when it happened. There was a strange silence that hung in the air for a few moments, before the children began to cough again. Clark and Christine knew who was who by their cough.

"'There are only three,' Christine's voice trembled in fear. 'Why don't we hear Claire's cough?'

"'We will check her in the morning. Maybe her cough finally broke. Let's not disturb them.'

"'I'm so cold. I wonder if the children will be okay.'

"'Honey, they have had the cough for over a week. Maybe it has run its course.'

"'Mommy, I'm hungry,' Carissa called, before breaking out in another coughing fit.

"'There is nothing to give them. There hasn't been for two days,' Christine whispered, as the tears fell down her cheeks, dropping onto Clark's pajamas.

"'God will help us one way or another,' Clark said confidently.

"Christine cried herself to sleep. The next morning, the house creaked with an eerie silence. The roof moaned under the weight of the snow that steadily fell outside. The windows were crystallized. The air hung heavy, but the silence was not broken.

"Claire was first, followed by Charlie, then Christopher, and with Carissa being the youngest, she held on the longest, passing around three in the morning. Christine and Clark passed a couple hours later, as they lay in their beds, starving and frozen."

Maggie gasped, "How morbid!"

"They say the ghosts of the family still move around in this territory, oblivious to the fact that they are no more. Sometimes, you can hear the coughing at night. Sometimes, you can smell a deer cooking on the fire. Sometimes, you can hear Clark and Charlie in the workshop, with their saws, hammers, and chisels. Sometimes you can see a chalk drawing on a tree, and wonder where it came from. The family was taken by God that night, but they refused to give up and leave."

Casey shuddered. "Creepy, Mac."

"I know," he smiled, "But you never know. It could be true."

"History is all around us," Ryan said in understanding. "When you really think about it, it gives you a greater appreciation for those who have gone before us."

"Yes, the pioneers made many mistakes," Scott pointed out. "Just like their history is recorded, so is the history in the Bible recorded for us to learn. Sometimes people think that a couple-thousand-year-old Book doesn't pertain to them, but it does. It's not just a Book of history. It's a Book of redemption."

"Amen," Mac said. "And, I, for one, am a very happy camper to know what is contained within those sixty-six books."

"Me too," Ryan agreed.

"It's still kind of new to me. I'm working with it, but I still struggle. With God taking Jack, along with my parents at a young age, it's –"

"It's understandable," Maggie cut her off, giving her an out.

"So, um, do you have a lot of those stories?" Casey asked Mac, hoping to change the subject.

"Yep," Mac said.

"I keep trying to get him to write them down," Ryan pointed out. "With all of the stories he has told over the years, he should have been a writer, and not a firefighter."

"I love my work," Mac defended himself. "Yes, it's dangerous, but I get to help people by doing what I love. I wouldn't trade what I do for anything. It's been incredible to be able to bring someone back through resuscitation, or pull someone from a burning building after facing certain death. God has shown me many miracles, along with a lot of tragedy, over the years. Through it all, though, I have had the confidence of knowing He was with me every step of the way. I know He led me to safety on more than once occasion."

"Me too," Casey agreed.

"Yeah, the warehouse fire comes to mind." Mac glanced over his shoulder at her, as she leaned behind him to get the graham crackers and chocolate for her s'more.

"Exactly. Along with the fire where we lost Callan and Marshall," she agreed.

"Not to mention the fire where you and Matt almost bit it," Mac added.

"I feel really bad for your guardian Angel." Ryan chuckled. "Does he ever get a break?"

"Sometimes I wonder," Casey said in a sigh.

"Don't worry," Mac squeezed Casey's shoulders, "He promised to never leave you."

"And He won't take you until it's your time," his dad pointed out.

*   *   *

"Thank you for taking me to the football game tonight," Casey said, as they sat in the bed of Mac's truck on a hill that overlooked the valley. He backed his truck so they could look out from inside the truck bed. He had blankets in the back to make it a little more comfortable for them.

"I'm glad we get at least one night off together," she sighed. "I wish it could be more."

"Sorry, babe, our lives are busy."

"At least we can spend every third day together."

"Yeah, but it's a sacrifice we're willing to make."

"Firefighters by day…"

"…Couple by night," Mac finished. He looked at Casey for a moment before he tickled her.

She giggled and wiggled. "Mercy!" She laughed.

"If I must."

"You must!" She laughed. "Please!"

As soon as he stopped, she turned and tickled him. At first, he resisted as he laughed, until he grabbed her and pulled her toward him in a kiss.

*   *   *

"Casey," Mac tucked her hair behind her ear, "I know you're upset, but you have to know you did everything you could."

"I know, but it doesn't make it any easier," she shook her head. Mac came down to the station after she called him. She had a rough call, where they responded to a teenage boy who collapsed during a football game. By the time Pete and Casey got to the stadium, the boy was not breathing, and there was no heartbeat. They did their best to bring him back, but it was too late.

"In our job, we face a lot of loss. We're not in control. Thankfully, we know the One who is in control. The Father knows that boy's family is suffering, and is in a state of confusion."

"He was their star receiver."

"Who got hit one too many times," Mac finished her thought.

"Pete said there was nothing we could do, but there had to be. I don't understand why God would take such a promising young man."

"We may never know either." Mac shook his head. "God has a plan. He knows what's going to happen before we do."

"I just don't understand *why* though."

"Case, in Isaiah 55, verses 8 and 9, it says, '*For my thoughts are not your thoughts, neither are your ways my ways, saith the Lord. For as the heavens are higher than the earth, so are my ways higher than your ways, and my thoughts than your thoughts.*' We may never know why that young life was taken, but God does."

"I don't understand why…."

"We never know when our time is up, but God does. I hold that sacred, and close to my heart."

Casey shook her head. Talking about death for her was hard. As constant as it was in her life, it didn't make it any easier for her.

"There may be a day where I may not come home from a call," Mac pointed out. "There may be a day where *you* may not."

"Mac, I don't want to talk about this. It hurts too much," she said, as a tear slid down her cheek.

"Casey, it is a fact we may someday have to face. Not that I plan to go any time soon, mind you, I just found you and don't want to be apart from you."

She wiped the tears off her face as she looked down. "I don't either."

He rested his hand under her chin, turning her toward him. "You are my love. I cherish your heart."

Her bottom lip trembled. "I know."

"You're going to be my wife someday. I thank God every day I get to see you and be with you."

"I love you too. That's why the thought of you not being with me breaks my heart. I've never had someone love me the way you do."

"I would give my life for you."

"I don't want you to. I want you to live a long, happy, and healthy life."

"I love you so much. I look forward to seeing your smile when I walk into the room." He sighed, shaking his head. "It lights up my soul. You look at me like I am the only person in your life."

"You are. You're my love. When you look at me, my heart skips a beat." She smiled as he eyes lit up.

Mac looked deeply into her eyes. "There it is."

"What?"

"That gorgeous smile. That's what I look forward to seeing whenever we're apart."

Casey hugged him. She held him for several minutes, not wanting to let him go.

* * *

When she woke up, there were tears running down her cheeks onto the pillow. The thought of Mac's words, even his face, was still fresh in her mind. The scent of his cologne filled her lungs. She loved his smile and heart the most. His love for her seemed never-ending.

It took Casey a moment to realize she was upstairs in one of the bedding areas of the station. In the dim light, she could see Jesse and Tommy both asleep in chairs next the bed. She felt someone's arm around her, and turned to see Hunter holding her.

She gently lifted Hunter's arm off, before silently slipping out of the bed, doing her best not to wake anyone up. Her head pounded when she moved. She held onto the wall to stop from passing out as she made her way across the room. It had been a long time since she had a headache this rough.

She kept one hand on her head, as she looked at the red digital lighted clock on the wall. It said 21:13, which meant it was 9:13 at night. With the exception of Casey and the sleeping trio, the bedding area was deserted. She struggled to remember what happened, that she would not only find herself on a shift with Hunter, but also in the same bed as him…and Tommy and Jesse not have a problem with it. Where was Mac in all of…suddenly it hit her like a ton of bricks. She dropped to her knees, grabbing her head in pain. "Mac!" she cried. "No!"

"Casey?" Hunter felt the bed around him, and then suddenly sat up in alarm. "Case!"

"I'm…shhhhh!" she cringed in pain.

"Casey?" Jesse got up out of his chair. He knelt on the floor in front of her, and lifted her head by her wrists since she would not let her head go.

Tommy sleepily looked around the room. "Wh-what happened?"

"Mac," she whimpered. Casey's body shook, as she swallowed the vomit that wanted to come up.

"Come on, let's get you back to bed," Jesse said, gently lifting her off the ground.

As soon as she was in standing position, she bolted for the trashcan. Clutching it, the vomit seemed never-ending, like it wanted to choke her out.

Tommy held her hair for her, while Jesse held the trashcan to make sure she got it in there.

"It's okay," Jesse said, soothingly rubbed her back. "It's going to be okay."

She threw up several more times before she dropped to the floor. She wanted to brush her teeth, but at that point she was too weak to move anywhere on her own.

"Casey?" Jesse moved her hair away from her face.

She moaned in pain.

"We need to get you back to bed. You're shaking." Tommy said as he attempted to get her off the ground, but she closed her eyes, resting her head on him. "Okay," he relented, "maybe we'll wait."

"I need to brush my teeth," she groaned.

"You can't even keep your eyes open." Jesse cocked his head to the side. "How do you expect to stand up to brush your teeth?"

"I'll get it," Hunter said, and left the room. He came back a couple minutes later with a toothbrush, a small tube of toothpaste, and Chief.

"How's she doing?" Chief knelt in front of her, in concern. "Can you open your eyes and look at me?"

She slightly opened her eyes, but she couldn't hold them open, and they slowly closed once again.

He shook his head. "She's still not in there."

"She said his name." Hunter crouched next to Chief. "That's what woke me up."

"Teeth," she mumbled.

"You wake up and you can brush your teeth," Hunter said, setting the toothbrush and toothpaste in her hand.

As much as she wanted to, Casey couldn't move. All she could do was lie back on Tommy. She clasped her fingers around the toothbrush and tube of toothpaste.

"Get her back to bed." Chief stood. "I think some more sleep, and she'll be thinking a little more clearly," he decidedly said before he left.

As Hunter scooped her up in his arms, Casey tightened her fingers around the toothpaste and toothbrush. He laid her down on the bed, covering her with the covers. "I need to go get something to eat."

"Go ahead. We'll eat in shifts," Jesse said. "Tommy, you can eat next. I'll stay."

"Sounds good," Tommy agreed as Hunter walked out of the room.

"She's gonna be okay, right?" Jesse looked up at Tommy when they were alone.

"She's strong," he said confidently. "Give her time."

* * *

Chief let Casey have the next week off. When she went home, all she did was watch television, curled up on the couch. Everything reminded her of Mac. On the day of the funeral, she went into the station to help adorn the truck with the banners of mourning, and help stack the hoses in the back of the engine bays to make room for Mac's casket.

Despite the objections of her fellow firefighters, Casey knew there was no way she could attend his funeral. There were too many funerals this year for her to handle this one. Instead, she went to Jack's grave and talked to him. She confessed to him what she was feeling, and what happened to Mac.

As she sat there, she felt a hand rest on her shoulder, and jumped. When she looked up, she saw a man standing in the sunlight. She tried to shade her eyes to see him, but his head was in direct line with the sun.

She squinted up at him. "Can I help you?"

"Are you Casey?"

She hesitated in answering him for a moment, before she responded, "Why?"

He crouched down beside her in the grass. When she was finally able to focus on him, she noticed he was wearing his BDUs (Battle Dress Uniform) and jacket. The name on his jacket said 'Col. O'Donnell.' He was about six-foot-one, and had medium brown hair that was mixed with about forty-percent gray. He had brown eyes, and looked to be in his late forties.

"Who are you? And what do you want with Casey?" She asked.

He put his hand out for her to shake. "I'm Colonel Ethan O'Donnell."

She looked at his hand for a moment, before she lowered her hand from shielding her eyes and shook it. "What do you want with Casey?" She asked again.

"Are you her?"

"Why?"

He sighed in frustration. "Look, I've seen you down here a lot. And while you're not the only one I've seen, you are the only one young enough to be Casey, at least the way Jack described her anyway."

"Who were you to him?"

"I was his C.O. – Commanding Officer."

"I know what 'C.O.' means. However, I have never heard your name before."

"You *are* Casey, aren't you?" He smiled in satisfaction. He spoke as if he was telling her and not asking her.

"What do you want with her?"

He sighed again, shaking his head. "He *said* you would be stubborn."

She gave him a cross look. What right did this man have to say something like that to her? She had never seen him before in her life, nor had she even *heard* of him.

"Look, I need to know if you're Casey or not. I have something for you, but it's taken me a while to track you down…if indeed you are her."

"If you're military intelligence, then you really stink at your job. Look at the date. He died eight months ago," she said, gesturing to the date of his death etched into the cross. Along with the death date, there was his full name, rank, and date of birth. Inscribed below read, *"Jumping Jack, a true heart for others."*

"No, I don't stink at my job." He smiled at that one. "I know he died eight months ago, but I was overseas on an assignment. I, unfortunately, missed his funeral, or I would have caught her there. I just got back a couple days ago."

"If you are who you say you are, then Jack would have told you what Casey did, and you could have tracked her through her job."

"That's true." He smiled at the game she played with him. He decided to play along. "But the way Jack described her, she didn't seem to fit anyone down there…until today when I saw you."

She looked at him wide-eyed for a moment before she crossed her arms. "I was there, but it doesn't mean that I am Casey."

"All right," he said in a sigh, shaking his head. "Jack said you were tall, thin, and were beautiful. He said you had medium to long wavy brown hair, and the Carter trademark of green eyes. He said you were a thinker and very smart. He also said you didn't take crap from anyone and to watch out," he smiled as her face softened. "He said you were an excellent photographer, but admirably chose to change careers to firefighter/paramedic, so you could help other people. He was very proud of you, and loved you with all his heart. He said he raised you from the time you were eight years old after your parents died. He said from the time he was eighteen, he raised his, then thirteen-year-old sister, completely by himself."

Casey sat there…not amused. Anyone who knew their family knew what he told her.

"He said he called you Space Case because there were times, especially when you were tired, where you didn't always make sense. He said you got silly and made him laugh so hard that he started calling you Space Case. He would get an instant smile on his face when he talked about you, because it would remind him of the fun times you guys had together."

Okay, not everyone knew that, but she wanted to know what else he knew.

"He said you were an excellent judge of character. He said he often joked that you should have joined the police force, because you could tell if someone is lying just by looking at them. Am I getting warm yet?"

"That sounds a lot like her, but you haven't told me anything yet that would incline me to tell you know where she is."

"He said you would probably say something like that." He chuckled. "Okay, how about this? When you were in high school, you went to prom with Todd Peters."

Casey raised an eyebrow at *that* one. It surprised her.

"You guys were living on an Air Force Base in Texas at the time, and he was an Air Force brat too."

She shrugged in an attempt to play it off. "If you were in his house at all, you could have found that out."

He shook his head as if he were upset or frustrated. "All right, if you're going to make me tell you, I will. He said to only use it as a last resort."

"Use what?"

"About five years ago he had to take an emergency leave-of-absence. I know, because as I said, I was his Commanding Officer. When he asked for it, he confided in me the reason for the leave-of-absence, which is why I pushed it through as fast as I could, so he could get to you in Columbia," he said. Then he looked at her with a knowing look on his face.

"Which is what?" Her heart raced, but she kept her face as steady as she could, so he would not think he had her yet. The fact that he knew Jack went to Columbia, and that it was five years ago, made her nervous.

He hung his head and shook it, before he looked up at her and asked, "*Are you Casey?*"

"Which is *what*?" Casey insisted. She wanted to know *exactly* what he knew.

He looked steadily into her eyes for a very long minute before he said, "Angelina."

He saw the look of shock on her face, as it flushed red before it immediately shifted to pale. "You are Casey. I can tell by your reaction. And since you are, then I feel safe enough to tell you that the reason for his leave-of-absence was because you were attacked and raped in Columbia. About two months after the attack, you found out you were pregnant. You gave the baby up for adoption, but it was a closed adoption. A couple years ago, Angelina's parents contacted Jack to look for you. He stayed in contact with them, with the idea of telling you when he thought you would be able to handle it. She is a beautiful little girl. She has tan skin, dark, black, wavy hair, and your green eyes."

Casey felt like she was going to throw up as he described Angelina.

"Still think I stink at my job?"

Casey sat there completely speechless.

"So, as I was saying, in looking at the girls in the department, none of them looked the way Jack described you, until today when you were there. And since you were the one I saw here, I thought it was pretty safe to assume you were Casey." Then he added with a smirk, "Not to mention the fact that you look just like him."

Casey quietly sat there in shock, as she attempted to collect her thoughts. How could he know so much about her when she never saw him before? While she didn't know the names of the guys in Jack's squad, mainly for her protection, she thought she should have seen him at least once on the bases where she lived.

"Do me a favor and breathe…please?" He sat down on the ground in front of her with his legs crossed. He leaned back on his hands as he pointed out, "You haven't breathed since I said her name."

Casey shook her head in disbelief. "I just…."

He sat up as he put his hands together on his lap in front of him. "I didn't say it to make you pass out. You didn't leave me any choice, though." He looked at her for a second before he said, "I tried to avoid mentioning Angelina, but you didn't give me any other option. He said you were smart, and like him didn't trust anyone. Look," he set his hand on her arm. She jumped so he quickly pulled it back. "I'm sorry."

She looked at him apprehensively. He was a complete stranger to her, who was telling her an awful lot about herself. In looking around, she saw that there was nowhere for her to run. There was no one else around to help her either. With his information and his rank as Colonel, she finally decided that she may be able to trust him…at least until she found out what he wanted from her.

"Look, there are some things I need to give you. I just needed to know that you were you. And, now that I do, here you go." He handed her a plain brown box. The lid was taped shut with Jack's signature at the seal points in black permanent marker. She had seen his signature enough to know it was his. She was convinced that if it wasn't his signature, it was an excellent forgery.

"What's in this?" she asked, accepting the box.

"I don't know. It's personal." He shrugged. "In our job you do as you are told, and you don't ask questions. Now, I was his C.O., and as his C.O., he trusted me. That was the *only* reason I got custody of the box along with the assignment. I had the utmost respect for Jack. In fact, there was an instance where he saved my life by dragging my butt out of a jungle to the helicopter that was waiting for us at the extrication point. I thought sure I was a goner when the enemy attacked us. They shot me in three different areas, but Jack refused to leave me. He carried me on his back the entire way."

"Wow!"

"I know as a firefighter there are times you have to carry people out of burning buildings. You lay your life on the line for other people every day you are at work. You put their lives ahead of yours. You see, our jobs aren't too much different…with the exceptions that ours can occur anywhere in the world, last up to months at a time, often we have bullets flying at us instead of walking into flames."

"*And*, if you ever told me what happened on *your* field it could get *both* of us killed," Casey finished in all seriousness.

"Good point," he nodded with a smile. "Casey, Jack was a good and honorable man – on and off the field. He never wanted you to feel as if you were alone in the world."

Casey looked at him in confusion. She wasn't sure where he was going with that statement.

He laughed for a couple moments, before he shook his head and said, "Yeah, he was right, you *are* very animated. You're good, but there is quite a lot I have been able to read about you just by your face." He stopped for a moment to compose himself before he continued, "Jack wanted you to know that as much as he loved your photos, he wanted you to stay a firefighter. He knows that in being a photographer you work and travel alone. He wanted you to have a family like you have at the station. He also wanted you to be protected, and he said you were very well protected there. He knows you live alone, so he wanted you to work with people. His concern was that you might pull into yourself again like you did when your parents died." He looked her and asked, "Did you really not say anything at all, not even one word for two whole years after they died?"

"Yeah. They took me to counseling, but it didn't work because I wouldn't talk. The counselor finally told my aunt and uncle that I would talk when I was ready. She said that, in essence, it was a control thing. Not in a bad way, though. She said I was trying to find some kind of control in my life since it erupted into chaos after my parents died."

"That makes sense." He nodded in understanding. "You know he was proud of the job you do and just wanted you to be happy."

"I am. Well, I *was*." She glanced toward the cross that was Jack's gravestone.

"What happened?"

"I was being courted by a guy from work –"

"Mac?"

"How did you know?" she looked up at him, wide-eyed.

"I told you." He smiled. "Well, actually, I *can't* tell you, it might get us both killed."

She took a deep breath to keep her emotions under control as she nodded.

"He was at a fire scene about four days ago," Colonel O'Donnell went on. He looked up and saw Casey going paler by the second. "They were called out to a warehouse fire. He went in with the first three teams. While they were trying to find the fire that set the alarm off, he and his partner separated from the other crews, which I understand is nothing abnormal."

Casey nodded. When an alarm goes off and they don't know where the fire is, they split up to locate it.

"Anyway, they went into an office area. His partner went one way and he went the other. When he opened the office door of the manager, there was a back draft that ended in an explosion when he opened the door. When it blew, Mac was killed instantly while his partner, even though severely injured, will recover in time."

"How did you know?" She stared at him in astonishment. It took her a couple days to get the exact details of the accident and she was in the department.

He sighed as he said, "Casey, Casey, Casey, there's not a lot I *don't* know, or at least can't find out if given enough time."

Casey nodded in understanding. She knew Jack had the same pull, and he was only a Lieutenant Colonel. A Colonel would have a lot more than he would.

"So, how are you doing with his death?"

She shook her head as tears came to her eyes.

He reached his hand out, but stopped and asked, "May I? You just look like you need physical contact. I'm not comfortable enough to offer a hug, but I can offer a hand."

Casey nodded, so he took her hand into his.

"Know this…I will be keeping tabs on you. You will even hear from me from time to time. It's not to scare you. It's just to look out for you as one of our own. The guys on this squad swore an oath to Jack about two months before he died, that we would look out for you. You won't always know we're there, but have the comfort of knowing that wherever you go in this world, someone is looking out for you." He gently squeezed her hand.

She smiled weakly. "Thanks."

"We're doing it because we care, which brings me to another point. You are in a bad place right now. I think whatever is in that box may help you. How about if we open it together?"

Casey looked down at the box and lovingly rubbed her fingers over his signature. She didn't want to cut the tape on his name.

"We can cut it on one side, leaving his signature on the other one," he read her thoughts. Casey agreed, so he pulled out an all-purpose tool and sliced the tape on one side.

She took a deep breath before she opened the box. She did not expect what was inside. On the top, was her corsage from her Senior Prom. Jack had dried it out and carefully placed it on the top. Casey set it aside before she looked back down right into Jack's face. There was a photo of him just after he graduated basic training. She shook her head as she ran her fingers over his very young face when she pulled it out.

"Why?" She looked up at Colonel O'Donnell.

"One never knows."

"Are there any more of you guys sick?"

"No, just him."

"Why?"

He sighed as he looked down for a moment. He struggled whether or not to tell her. "I'm going to trust you."

Casey felt she needed to know, so she nodded.

He took a deep breath, before he said, "I'll try to stay as general as possible, so you can't be implicated in anything."

Casey nodded in understanding.

"He was on a mission in Kazakhstan, when he and his partner found themselves face to face with a mysterious substance. After they blew up what was left in the lab, along with the lab itself, they brought a sample back with them. Measures were taken to limit the exposure, but it occurred as soon as they touched it. When they got back, they passed off the substance, and were immediately directed to medical to get blood work done and a physical. Their exposure left them with only three years maximum to live. That was seven years ago. Now," he held his hand up to stop Casey when she went to open her mouth, "just so you don't think it was a fluke or that the doctors were wrong, his partner died two and half years later."

Casey looked up at him, dumbfounded.

"Jack went above and beyond in that one. He fought to stay here for you. He knew you needed him. He knew it would kill you inside when he died. About four months before he died, he got more and more tired. While he still went on missions, I kept them light – low-risk. I didn't want him to push himself, knowing he had already pushed himself for several years." He stopped for a moment to reflect before he continued, "A couple of months before he died, he went back to the doctor and the doctor confirmed his worst fears. He went home and immediately contacted the squad. We met in secret of course. We are undercover officers. We couldn't very well meet in public." Casey nodded as he went on, "When we met, he told us what the doctor said, and made us swear on everything we hold dear to look after and take care of you to the best of our abilities. Of course, we did it in a heartbeat. Over the years, we had come to know and love you as our family member, even though you didn't know any of us." He paused, knowing what was coming next. "He only went on a couple more missions before he finally ended up in the hospital the week before he died. And the rest, you know."

"Yeah." She glanced at the cross, before looking back at Colonel O'Donnell.

"I hope that helps you."

She nodded. "It does."

"Good. Now, what else is in there?"

She turned her attention back to the box. She wiped the tears off her face, as she pulled out three books of journals that were on the top of the stack. As she scanned them, she realized they were Jack's personal journals. He started them the day after their parents died. She set them aside to read later. She needed to read them when she was by herself.

The next items were several photos of her, which were tied together with a white ribbon. In them, she was doing various activities throughout the world. Some were taken when she was a photographer. Some were even taken when she was on a fire scene. On the backs of each of photo was a two-by-two-inch, black and white picture of a man. Each man was labeled by his first and last name – no ranks. Some of them were even of O'Donnell himself.

Colonel O'Donnell took them and scanned through them. Then he looked up at her, and explained, "These are for your reference only, so you know who is looking out for you. Don't show them to anyone else, okay? That could get you into a lot of trouble, possibly even killed."

"Could Jack have gotten in trouble for doing this?"

"No. He already put it past me. He said he trusted you with his life."

Casey nodded as she glanced back down at the box. While Colonel O'Donnell tied the ribbon back around the photos, Casey pulled out the last item. It was his dog tags.

"Yeah, okay, I knew those were in there. I had a new set made for him so he could put this set in. These," he held them up, "were with him on every single mission he went on. The set on him when he died, were the new ones I gave him about two weeks before he passed." He showed her where one of the tags had her name scratched on it. "He did this so he could take you everywhere he went, to remind him as to why he did what he did. He said it was ultimately to protect you. Oh! Speaking of which, here," he said, and reached into his back pocket, pulling out a savings account book.

"What's this?"

"He would stash away the remainder of the money he had each month into this account. It was for you."

She opened it to find the opening date to be the first month he was in the service, when he was in still in basic training. Around the last day of every month, there was a deposit. On some months, it was earlier in the month, but it was every month regardless. When she got to the last month, she just about had a heart attack!

Colonel burst out in laughter as she stared at the amount in wide-eyed shock with her jaw dropped. "Breathe!" He was laughing so hard he had tears in his eyes. After a moment, he composed himself enough to add, "He gave that to me the day he put the dog tags in. He said I was the only person he trusted it to."

"I don't know what to say."

"Your brother loved you and only wanted the best for you." He rested his hand on her ankle. "And knowing what I do of you, I fully understand. While you might have had a rough start, you turned it around and turned out to be a strong, confident, wonderful woman. This, from what he said, is still not as much as he wanted to give you, but it was the best he could do."

"This is...." She looked down at it and then back up at him. "This is *a lot* of money!"

"You were worth more than that to him," he said confidently.

"This is an incredible amount of money!" She tried to get him to understand the amount in the account. She could not imagine how much he did without, just to turn around and give it to her. He gave her so much of his life. She didn't feel she deserved it.

"That may be a lot of money, but you gave more than that to him."

Stunned, she shook her head.

Once again, he burst out in laughter. "This is going to be a long conversation, if you don't stop that." He held his stomach as he wiped the tears out of his eyes. "I have to calm down every time you do."

"How can you say that?" She shook her head. "That man gave his life for me! He has taken care of me since I was eight years old. We might have been living at my aunt and uncle's house for five years before we moved out, but he was the one who truly took care of me. He gave me his all, which is hard to do in a military family."

"That's true," he admitted. "But you gave him the chance to know Christ as his personal Savior." Casey looked at him with a blank look on her face, as he went on, "Look, I'm a Christian too, so I can tell you by experience that I know the value of knowing Jesus."

Casey narrowed her eyes as she said, "I *hate* Him!"

"*What*?" He looked at her in shock.

"That Man took away my parents. He let that man attack and rape me – resulting in me having to give up the one child I will probably *ever* have! That Man took my brother away! I was willing to move on even though *all* those things happened, until He took

Mac away too. When He did that, He ultimately ripped away every last shred of love I had in my life!"

He shook his head, stunned by her words. "Casey."

"Tell me different! Tell me I'm wrong!" she challenged.

"You are so wrong it's not even funny!"

She was furious. "If you think I'm wrong, then tell my *why*."

"Oh, Casey," he said, his heart broken for her. "God loves you. Jesus loves you. The Holy Spirit even loves you. They wouldn't do this to you. They are trying to help you through it."

"How can you say that?"

"What happened to your parents was an accident. No one, not even the pilot was in control of that situation."

"I thought *God* was in control of *everything*."

"He is, *but* He also gave us this thing called free will. While the concept of it is good, the outcome is unpredictable. God, however, has the capacity to understand and compensate for this. What Satan usually uses for evil, God can use for good."

"So, what's the good that came out of my parent's death?"

"I can't answer that. I *can* say that there was a wonderful couple who couldn't have children of their own, who now have a beautiful baby girl thanks to you. What Satan used for evil, God used for good. Yes, you still have to deal with the pain, but ultimately you chose to give her a life instead of having an abortion, which attests to your character. Giving that child up for adoption turned into good, because at the end of the day you gave her not only a shot at life, but a wonderful life at that. As for Jack, God let him hold on until he was able to go to that camp-out with you to find Him. In his last seven years God gave him an opportunity to line things up for you, to be there for you when you were attacked, to stand up for you when you graduated college, to be there to receive that call from you from when you saved your first life, had your first fire, and to set aside more money for you, therefore setting you up for the rest of your life. He loves you, Casey – Jesus really does! While that account may have monetary value…what Jesus did for you is worth ohhh so much more than that."

"What about Mac?"

"What *about* Mac? That man was a strong man for Christ! His life held so much value in the Kingdom, it wasn't even funny! He sent Satan screaming and yelling many times by bringing more and more to the saving knowledge of Jesus."

"But, why did he have to die? How is God going to use *this* for good?"

"Again, that may be something we may never know. Maybe more will come to Christ through it. Only God knows the answer to that. Know this: Jack's up there with Mac right now, and they're looking down here in deep concern. They love you and are probably scared for you right now."

"I know," Casey admitted. "They're probably ashamed of me."

"How *dare* you!" he snapped, almost angry. Casey's jaw dropped, as he said, "Those men love you! They love God too! Do *not* disrespect their concern for you!"

Casey realized she had never thought of it that way. She didn't mean to disrespect them in any way. She closed her mouth, listening to what the Colonel was telling her.

"Do *not* disrespect God, the Almighty, that way either! You, in the statements you have made over the last couple of days, have disrespected and dishonored God, Jesus, the Holy Spirit, Jack, *and* Mac."

"Why would you…how can you say that?"

"Because you took something all those Men held in high regard, held dear to their hearts, and trashed it just because you were hurt.

That's selfish! Those men are the most selfless men I have ever known. God even gave you the gift of having these men in your life, and you –"

"I get it," Casey cut him off.

He crossed his arms. "Then what are you going to do about it?"

Casey's heart was breaking at its core. What he said not only hit home, but also sunk in deep, as it slowly filled in the cracks of her shattered heart. As it did, the love that *all* of these Men – God, Jesus, the Holy Spirit, Jack, and Mac – had all poured into her life, slowly molded her heart back into a solid, true, strong heart of love, as it spilled over in the tears that cascaded down her cheeks.

"That's it," the Colonel said with a knowing smile. It was almost as if he could see the healing as it occurred right in front of him. "Keep going," he encouraged. "Let Him work."

Colonel O'Donnell watched as God worked in her heart. He then set both of his hands on either side of her head as he quietly prayed, "Mighty Father, God, Almighty One, Prince of Peace, Lord of all, You are more than our minds can conceive. The concept of You would blow our minds if we tried hard enough to understand. You are the Heart-Healer and the True Judge of our hearts and souls. I ask you to heal Your daughter's heart right now. I ask You to not judge her heart, but understand, and mold it back into the love You created her to have, but that the world corrupted. I ask You to show her just how much You love her." Casey felt tingles wash over her body, as in her mind she saw her heart overflow and spill over into her body in restoration. The Colonel continued, "You placed strong, honorable Men into her life for a reason. I ask You to let her see the strength that was poured into her, even before she knew she had it. I demand that whatever evil creature has been trying to sink his hideous claws into you, be immediately released!" he prayed.

Casey's body shook as she sat on the ground, soaking in the Holy Spirit.

"I demand that this woman be set free. What is free in Christ is free indeed!" he declared with strength and authority in his voice. "I pray for her angels of protection to wield their fiery swords and win the battles that have ensued around her. I pray for strength and honor among them. I pray that she will feel amazingly refreshed, revived, and have an indescribable amount of understanding of the actions that have arisen against her and surrounded her. I pray for her the gift of discernment to understand what is You and what is Satan. I pray for knowledge and insight, as well as for awareness and a deep appreciation for the battles that cultivate around us every day. I pray for things that are unseen, to be seen. I pray for things that were previously unclear, to be unmistakably obvious. And I pray for her heart that had previously been shattered, to become whole. Show her Your strength. Give her Your power. Shower her with Your love and Your Spirit. She is Yours, Lord. Lay claim to this heart once again! Take her hand and show her the plan You have for her life. Give her purpose and direction. Give her strength to go above and beyond the call to duty You have enlisted her for. Continue to protect those angels who look after her every day. Thank You, Father. Praise Your name. You are the Holy One! You are the Mighty One! You are the *Only* One!" he said, before he spoke in a language Casey did not understand.

As he prayed, her body felt faint. She felt dizzy. She shook her head to clear it, but it didn't work. The longer he prayed, the more her body shook, until she passed out.

After several minutes, the Colonel got up and stacked everything back into the box, including the account book. He placed her right hand on top of the box so she would be able to find it. Then, the Colonel took his military jacket off and laid it over Casey. As he left her, she laid there shivering and soaking in the blissful peace that engulfed every fiber of her being.

Chapter 15

Overload

It took Casey several minutes before she could focus and sit up. When she did, Colonel O'Donnell's coat slipped down onto her lap. She glanced over at Jack's box, which was under her hand, before turning back to the Colonel's coat. She decided by the evidence that was right in front of her, that it was not a dream. Casey cautiously opened the box to find the savings account book, along the remaining contents of the box still intact.

Casey sighed as she looked around to find the cemetery practically empty. She glanced at her watch to see that it was four-thirty in the afternoon. Realizing that she arrived at eleven-thirty that morning, she panicked. There was no telling how long she was unconscious!

She checked her phone and saw that it had no messages. It had been silent since the day Mac died. Her last incoming call was from Chief asking her to come down to the station on the day of his death.

Her heart broke, and she got sinking feeling in her stomach. Mac was dead. Jack was dead. Family wise she was alone, but she had many friends from the station. She questioned whether or not she trusted them. While she rationalized in her head that she trusted them with her life on duty, she questioned if that was only reason they like her. She wondered whether they liked her because of her skills, or if they liked her as a person.

Before the feelings swallowed her, she gathered what was with her and walked out of the graveyard. She glanced at the other gravestones while she walked, and reminded herself that she was not the only one hurting. She knew each gravestone was a life, and it represented a family in mourning.

Her Jeep was parked at the end of the row. She was almost there when she saw it. With the box and jacket in hand, she crouched down in front of a gravestone. She felt the color drain from her face as she stared at the name etched on the cross – Colonel Ethan O'Donnell.

The date marked on the cross of his death was three weeks ago. A sudden urge to run filled her, as she panicked inside. Terrified, she wanted to get into her Jeep and lock the doors, but she couldn't move. All she could do was sit there and stare at a man's gravesite, who she had just talked to that day!

"Are you okay, Miss?" An Airman walked up to her in his uniform. He had been making his way down the road when he saw her. "You don't look so good."

She gulped, almost afraid of the answer to the question before she asked it. "Are you real?"

"Yes." He laughed. He crouched next to her, as he commented, "You, however, look very pale. Is there someone I can call for you?"

"Yes."

"Who? Just name it."

"Colonel Ethan O'Donnell, Peterson Air Force Base." She knew if the Colonel was real, and was really Jack's CO, then he would be stationed at the same base as Jack.

"Just a moment." He stood up, and got on his radio. "Porter to Quinton."

"Go ahead," the voice on the other end of the radio said.

"I'm doing rounds at the cemetery," he started. As soon as he said that, Casey noticed the 'MP' on the sleeve of his uniform. He was Military Police. "There's a young lady here who needs to contact someone at the base."

"What's the name?"

"Colonel Ethan O'Donnell."

"Colonel Ethan O'Donnell," he confirmed.

"Affirmative."

"Copy. Stand by."

"Standing by," he said. Then he crouched down next to her to explain, "He needs to look him up."

Casey nodded. She nervously glanced from the gravestone, back to him, as he nonchalantly scanned the rest of the cemetery.

"Quinton to Porter."

"Go ahead," Porter picked up his radio.

"Is this an emergency?"

He looked at the radio, confused for a moment, before he explained, "She looks like she needs some medical attention. When I asked her if I could contact someone, she gave me that name."

"Stand by," Quinton responded.

"Copy. Standing by."

A few moments later, his cell phone rang. He looked down at it, and asked, "What is he doing?" Then he answered his phone, "Quinton, what's going on?" He had a look of surprise on his face as he said, "Oh really? Um, I'll see what I can do. Thank you," he said, and hung up. He rested his arms on his knees as he explained, "There's a little problem. Is there someone else I can contact for you?"

"Is he alive?"

He looked at her suspiciously before he asked, "How do you know Colonel O'Donnell?"

She showed him the jacket. He checked it out, before handing it back to her. He shook his head as he said, "I'm sorry, ma'am."

She knew the MP was not going to leave her alone, so she called Jesse's cell phone. He said he would be there in several minutes, and that he would bring someone to drive her vehicle back to the station for her.

"I have some friends coming to get me," she said as she put her phone back in her pocket.

"Mind explaining something to me?"

"What?"

"Why would you ask for a Colonel, who's grave you're sitting in front of?" He nodded toward the gravestone.

She looked at the gravestone and then back up at him not sure what to say.

"Why would you ask for Colonel O'Donnell, if you're sitting right in front of his grave?" he asked after a moment when she didn't answer.

"It's a very long story," she sighed.

"Look, your friends are coming. Why don't you tell me a story while we wait? I'm not going anywhere until you have someone here with you. With the way you look, you could pass out and no one would be here."

"I did pass out. That's the problem."

He sat cross-legged on the ground next to her. "What do you mean?"

"I don't think you'll understand. Heck! I don't understand!"

"Try me."

"Was Colonel O'Donnell special ops? Was that why your partner called you instead of telling you over the radio?"

He narrowed his eyes at her as he asked, "How do you know Colonel O'Donnell?"

"I had a visit from him. He was my brother's Commanding Officer."

"And who *exactly* is your brother?"

"Lieutenant Colonel Jonathon 'Jack' Carter."

"Do you have any ID on you?"

"Yes." Now it was Casey's turn to look at *him* suspiciously.

"Can I see it?"

"Why?"

"Just to run it. Don't worry. You're not under arrest for anything. You haven't done anything to get arrested, at least that I'm aware of."

Casey handed him her driver's license, so he used his cell phone to call Quinton back. He ran both her name and Jack's name before he hung up. "You're clear. Sorry for your loss in Lieutenant Colonel Carter." He gave her the license back.

"Thanks."

"So, you had a conversation with Colonel O'Donnell where he told you he was special ops?"

"He didn't need to."

"What do you mean?"

"My brother was special ops. If the Colonel was his C.O., then he was special ops too."

Porter nodded in satisfaction. He thought for a moment before he asked, "If you're sitting here in front of the Colonel's grave, why would you ask for him?"

"I needed to know if he was dead or alive."

He shook his head. "I don't understand."

"I needed to know if he was dead or alive. I needed to talk to him, but I saw this grave marker, and…here I am," she said.

"I see." He nodded, satisfied. "Your friend, does he have a motorcycle?" He asked as he looked toward the entrance of the cemetery.

"Yep." She looked up to see Jesse come in, with Hunter on the back of the bike behind him.

"Casey? What's up?" Jesse asked as they pulled up to where Casey sat with the MP. "You look pale."

Hunter got off the bike, while Jesse turned off the bike. Hunter went over and knelt in front of Casey. He put both of his hands on either side of her face, and looked into her eyes. "What happened?" he asked, taking her wrist to check her pulse.

"I passed out at Jack's grave," she admitted.

"I found her here, and wouldn't leave until she called someone to come help her," Porter explained.

Jesse knelt down on the other side of her. "Thanks.   We appreciate that."

"Kind of high, but she should be moveable to her Jeep anyway," Hunter said, letting her wrist go.

Porter picked up the box and jacket, while Hunter and Jesse helped Casey to the passenger's side of the Jeep. "These are hers," Porter said, handing the box and jacket to Jesse, as Hunter went around to the driver's side.

"Thanks for your help," Jesse said to Porter, as he gave the jacket and box to Casey.

When the doors were closed, Hunter put his hand out to Casey and said, "Keys, please? Nothing personal, but you don't look well enough to drive."

Casey pulled the car keys out of her pocket and handed them to Hunter. As he started the Jeep, she glanced back at the gravestone.

"Want to tell me what happened?" Hunter asked, as he quickly glanced at her, before turning back to the road. Jesse followed them on his motorcycle back to the station.

"I don't know if I can," she said in a sigh. "I'm not even sure if *I* believe it." She opened the box on her lap for a moment before she closed it again. While she saw the undeniable evidence of the box and jacket in front of her, she struggled to make sense of what happened.

"What's that? And who is…O'Donnell?" He questioned, glancing, at the jacket and the box before he looked back toward the road again.

"I don't know if…I don't know." She shook her head, lost in thought.

"Casey? Are you feeling okay? I know you've eaten, because you ate breakfast at the station this morning." Casey didn't say anything, so he went on, "Today was a tough day for you, I'll admit that. Do you want to go to his grave?"

"No!" She looked at him in wide-eyed horror as her heart raced. She knew with everything else that had gone on that day, going to Mac's grave could prove disastrous!

"Breathe, Case!" Alarm written all over him. He felt her wrist for her pulse, as he glanced from his watch to the road.

The emotions of everything that happened surrounding her bubbled up and virtually exploded inside of her. The idea that Mac's funeral was today and the idea that she had a conversation with a man who died three weeks ago while sitting by her brother's grave overwhelmed her. Having the knowledge that the box in front of her contained access to so much money that her loving brother gave to her…was all a part of her reality.

"Slow down your heart rate and breathing or I'm pulling over and we're calling the ambulance to meet us," Hunter warned. "We're almost there, but I need you to calm down."

Casey felt like she was having an anxiety attack, as she stared at the jacket and the box on her lap. Her head felt like it was spinning out of control, while her heart rate continued to soar.

She knew everyone would be at the station. Could she handle that? On top of this entire day, could she handle seeing everyone there? She closed her eyes as she struggled to slow her breathing.

"This is your last warning," Hunter threatened. "We're five minutes away from the station. Slow it down before you pass out on me."

Casey remembered the prayer Colonel O'Donnell prayed while she was on the ground. She went through it word-for-word. When she got to the part where he said, 'Continue to protect those angels who look after her every day,' she gasped as her eyes popped open. "He was an angel! I wonder if the others are angels too?"

"What?" Hunter asked, as they turned down the road where the station was located. He saw her head fall to the side as she slipped into unconsciousness. He shook his head out of frustration, before calling Chief on his cell phone. He very briefly, but quickly explained what was going on, and asked for the ambulance to be standing by.

As soon as they pulled in, Tommy, Chief, Will, Robbie, and Jeff met them at the Jeep. Tommy flung the Jeep door open, and turned her face toward him. "Look at me, Casey. Open your eyes."

"Just get her to the ambulance," Will said as Jesse pulled up next to the Jeep.

Hunter shut the Jeep off. He ran around to the other side as Jeff and Tommy reached in and pulled her out. Jeff carried her to the awaiting ambulance. The crew for the run was Tommy and Hunter in back with Casey, and Jesse insisted on driving – he did not give them an option.

Chapter 16

Reality

"Hey, Carter," Jesse poked his head into the kitchen where she was cooking.

"Yeah?"

"Turn that off and come out to the bays. We take a day one photo of all of the probies."

"Okay." she shrugged. She shut everything down and went out into the bay. The door of the firehouse opened up into the bay for Engine One, and the garage door to the outside was open. She heard indistinct conversations from around the bays, but she didn't see anyone except Jesse and LT.

"Come on out here," LT called to her.

She went out the engine bay door into the sunlight.

"Right about here," LT positioned her right in front of the engine. "We like to get them on day one, so the firefighters remember it. Then we take one every other year after that so they can see the difference."

"I see," she said.

LT took a step back as Jesse got the camera lined up.

"Um, that's on record, not photo," Casey pointed out as she saw the red flashing light.

Suddenly she felt a cascade of ice-cold water dump all over her. She looked up to see Mac and Marty Nelson on the roof with buckets of water.

"Welcome to Engine Fifteen, probie!" Mac winked at her. As the rest of the guys came around from behind the engine. They were all laughing…Casey included.

A couple of months after she got to the station, Jesse and Scott Kendall came into the kitchen where she was cooking dinner. "Shhh," Jesse put his finger in front of his lips.

Casey shook her head, laughing. Those two were famous for their practical jokes. She was happy to know she wasn't the one getting pranked this time.

Scott and Jesse took one of the bench seats, pulling all of the screws out of one side. Jesse dropped the screws into his pocket before they slipped back out of the kitchen to go restock the ambulances, which is what they were supposed to be doing in the first place.

At dinnertime, as Casey sat where she normally did, Scott sat on the secure end of the bench and waited for the others to sit down as well. He snickered, but covered his mouth as the other firefighters came in for dinner.

As soon as Brennon and Vinnie sat down, and Will was about to sit, the bench collapsed. Scott slid down the bench, knocking Will into Brennon and Vinnie. They laughed about that one for days.

*   *   *

"Let's go! Drills!" Rob yelled to the firefighters from the bottom of the stairs. "Let's get the lead out!"

The firefighters ran downstairs to get into their turnout gear. As soon as Jesse, Marty, Mac, Will, Tommy, and Casey put their feet into their boots, they cringed.

"What in the world?" Casey looked down into her boots to see them full of shaving cream.

She looked toward Rob, to see Scott and Rob give each other a high-five.

*   *   *

Casey decided to take matters into her own hands. After surviving numerous practical jokes, she determined it was time to play some of her own. Since she had the kitchen to herself while the others did their chores, Casey took the time to grab the bag of sugar, the syrup, and plastic wrap before she headed down the hall toward the bathroom and bedding areas.

"What are you doing, Carter?" Mac asked as he walked down the hall from the sleeping area.

"Having a little fun of my own. Is the men's bathroom empty?"

"Yeah. What are you going to do…and can I help?"

"Sure!" She smiled, relieved he was going to go along with it.

Together they went into the men's bathroom. While Casey put the plastic wrap over the urinals, Mac put the syrup on the toilet seats. The stalls in the men's bathroom were dimly lit at best.

When they were through, they headed into the bedding area. "Okay, who do we get?" She asked, holding up the bag of sugar.

"What are you going to do with that?" He asked, unsure of how to respond.

"It goes in between their sheets. They will never get it out until they wash their sheets."

"Well, go ahead and do McFadden, since he doesn't sleep a whole lot anyway," Mac said, thinking.

"What about Katz for retaliation of the shaving cream incident?"

He looked at her in surprise. "How rough do you want your drills?"

"Good point. What about…?"

"Hanson." Mac nodded decisively.

She went over and put sugar at the bottom of their two beds, before she looked at the others. "Vinnie?"

"I'm trying not to get you killed here," Mac said. "I would leave it with those two."

She shrugged. "Okay."

Throughout the night, the guys found their booby-traps. There were howls of laughter, mixed in with the cursing of those who found the traps. Since Casey proved to be a formidable opponent, she wasn't singled out quite so much, knowing she could get them back just as bad.

*   *   *

Casey woke up with a smile on her face. For once, her dreams were good dreams. Lately, that was a rare thing for her. Unfortunately for Casey, she was in the hospital. and would remain for the next few days, so Dr. Benton could keep a close eye on her. He had her on a moderate sedative throughout that time, finally releasing her four days after she arrived. The doctor recommended a counselor, and sent her home with a mild sedative. She decided not to use it, because she didn't like to take medicine if she didn't have to.

The day she was released, Jesse gave her a ride to the station to get her Jeep. He offered to follow her home, but she insisted on going home by herself.

Home. It seemed like forever since she was there. It almost seemed foreign. The first thing she did was take a long hot bath. As she basked in the warmth of the water, she enjoyed the tranquility and peace. She left the lights off in the bathroom, so as the lavender candles dimly lit the room, they harmoniously united with chamomile scent of the soap bubbles to grant her the serenity she needed.

After her bath, she checked on the savings account. The easiest way for her to have access to the account was to convert it to a high-interest-yielding checking account. She added the five hundred thousand dollars from the insurance policy, to make the amount in the account over two million dollars. She decided to let it sit until she figured out what to do with the money. In the meantime, she headed down to the station to talk to Chief.

He sat down at his desk, as she sat down in the chair across from him. "How are you feeling, Carter?" he asked.

She shrugged. "A little fuzzy-headed, but okay."

He looked at her for a moment before he asked, "Feeling a little lonely?"

"Actually, yeah," she confessed. "My brother left me a lot of money, and I took care of that today, but the financial freedom came at a valuable price. I would trade the money I got for Jack and Mac in a heartbeat. They were worth more to me than any amount of money." She sighed. "Isn't there a fine balance between being financially secure and being alone?"

"I wouldn't trade places with you right now for anything," he admitted. "What you have gone through over the last year, no one should *ever* have to go through. I'm sorry."

"Level with me. Is my job still safe?"

"Oh! Heavens, yes! Of course it is!"

She looked down for a moment in thought.

"What's going on in there?" He asked in concern.

"I'm just thinking. Would I be able to take a little time off?"

"Well, you get four weeks of vacation time a year. Do you need some of it?"

"Actually, I think I do. I need to recoup, so to speak. I need to make some assessments and figure out what direction I want to go in."

"What do you mean?"

"I'm at a cross road in my life. Everything I have known and loved is now gone. I need to figure out where I'm going to go next. I *do* want to stay at the station, that I know for sure. I just wish I could be sure what to do with the rest of my life."

"I understand," he said. "I'll tell you what. If you can wait about two weeks, it'll help me in finding someone to cover you. Then you can take the next two weeks. Check back with me in the middle of week two, and we'll see where you are to reevaluate if you need more time."

"Really?" She was surprised by his generosity. "Thank you, sir." She smiled in relief.

"Carter, you're a good firefighter and paramedic. I would be a fool to turn you away. You have had an awful time lately. You lost your brother and your lover both in the same year. Not to mention the fact that you don't have any relatives near here, at least that I'm aware of."

"I'm not close to any of them anyway."

"Then, from what I can tell we're your family. We understand your need for time off. If you want to come in sometimes while you're off, we would appreciate seeing your smiling face, but we'll understand if you don't."

"Thank you, Chief." She felt grateful and sad at the same time. She felt so alone. It was a feeling she had never had before, and she wasn't quite sure what to do about it.

"You have a lot of work to do, and I don't envy you. If you need a sounding board, I'll be here. If I'm not, there will be someone on shift I'm sure you can talk to."

She nodded in appreciation. "Thank you."

"Know you do have a family here and we love you."

"I do." She shook his hand before she left the office.

When she got out to her Jeep, Jesse ran out of the station. "Carter!"

"Hey, Jess, what's up?"

"You tell me. You come here and don't even come in to say hi?"

She looked down, as she shoved her hands into her pockets. She didn't want to hurt any of them, she just needed some time.

"Casey?" He put his hands on her shoulders and stooped down to look her directly in the eyes. "This is your brother, here. What's going on?"

"I feel so alone. I need to...." She looked up at the sky in an attempt to keep her emotions under control. "Jesse, I've lost my brother and my lover in less than a year. I need to figure out what direction to go in my life."

"Are you leaving the company?"

"No. Chief and I talked, and he asked for two weeks before I take some vacation time. I need to assess my life. I need to figure out where to go from here."

"What do you mean? You work here."

"What am I going to do outside of the station? I need to do something with my life."

"Casey, you have a life and family here. Let us help you through this."

"I'm alone right now. I need to find myself. I need to find my purpose. I need to find God again."

After a moment, he sighed. "I understand. Do me a favor, though?"

"What?"

"Keep me on speed dial. Wherever you are, if you need me just call. I don't care if it's the middle of the night."

"I wouldn't do that."

"I'm telling you to."

"What about Kara?"

"What *about* Kara?"

"Won't she get mad?"

"She and I aren't dating anymore. We haven't been for a couple weeks now."

"What?" she asked, stunned. "Why? What happened? Why didn't you tell me?"

"Because you were going through a lot. You didn't need that too. As far as what happened, she cheated on me."

"Oh Jesse! You didn't deserve that! I'm so sorry!"

"Don't worry about me, I'm fine. I'm worried about you travelling alone to wherever you're going. I'm also worried about you because of what has been going on lately."

"Jess, I need to do this by myself. Please understand that."

"I understand that, but it's dangerous. What are you going to do if something happens like it did at the cemetery?"

She thought for a moment, before she said, "There's a trip I need to take to Boise, Idaho. You can come with me if you want to."

"When are you going?"

"When can you take about a week off?"

"Well, it will technically only be two shifts off. Let me talk to Chief and I will get back to you."

"Okay. Then depending on when we leave, will depend on what I do for the rest of the time."

He grabbed her wrist, pulling her back into the station with him. He sat her down in the reception area, and left to talk to Chief.

By the time he came out an hour later, Casey read just about everything she could get her hands on in the reception area, and ran through a myriad of thoughts about what to do during her time off. She knew she needed to take care of the unfinished business Jack left for her. He took care of her all her life. The least she could do was follow through with his last request.

"Thanks, sir," Jesse said. He came out, shaking Chief's hand.

"Take care of her, huh? I want you two both back in one piece."

"Thanks." Jesse nodded before he sat down in the seat across from Casey. "Okay, here's the plan. I have my shift to work today, and am off in the morning. We can do something on our days off so you're not alone for the next two weeks. Then when you take your two weeks off, we can go to Idaho. Chief said he would feel more comfortable if I was with you anyway. You were worrying him."

"Thanks, Chief," Casey said over Jesse's shoulder. He smiled and nodded before he went back into his office. "So, how did you do that? 'B' shift is missing Mac, and we're both gone from 'A.' How is Chief going to cover all of that?"

"He pulled some strings. We're also getting a new guy on 'B' shift in about a week. Look, we need to worry about you, not them."

She sighed. "All right."

"So, what are you going to do for the rest of the day?"

"Well, what if we plan a little camping trip for the first couple of days of our vacation? I think we need a little 'happy' bonding time as a shift."

"Do we get to join too?" Hunter walked through the door.

"What are you doing here?" She looked up at him in surprise.

"I had to bring some paperwork in to Chief for my 401K."

"Oh."

"So, is that open to all the shifts?"

"If you want." She shrugged. "It won't be for a couple of weeks, but I guess we can open it to all shifts."

"Sounds good," he said. "Same place up in the mountains?"

"Yeah."

"I can make sign-up sheets," Margo volunteered.

"Thank you." Casey grinned. "That would be great!"

"This isn't anything official by any means," Jesse clarified. "It's just been a rough year, and I think it's needed."

"Totally understand." Margo waved him off. "I'll put them on the table upstairs with the announcement. In two weeks you said?"

"Yes. Please?" Casey nodded.

"Consider it done."

"Thank you."

"Okay, see you in a couple weeks," Hunter said before he headed into the office with Chief.

"Are you going to be okay for the rest of the day?" Jesse asked.

"Jess," she rolled her eyes, "I'm a big girl."

"Who has had a horrid week and an even worse year. Look, I'm going to need your cooperation if this is going to work."

She smiled. "I'll be fine."

"Okay. You want to do lunch and a movie tomorrow?"

"Sounds good." Casey went to leave, but stopped and gave Jesse a hug. "Thanks Jess."

"No prob, sis." He kissed her head as he hugged her. "Be careful, okay?"

"Will do!" She smiled, and then left the station.

*   *   *

Later that evening, Casey was watching a movie, when there was a knock on her door. The clock said it was nine-fifteen. She went over and slowly moved the curtains back just enough to see who it was. She didn't recognize the man at the door, so she paused the movie and sat down under the window. As her heart raced, her hearing was heightened. Her mind reeled with questions, when she had a sudden thought of the photos on the back of the pictures. She bolted for her room and pulled the stack out the box. She whipped the ribbon off and quickly flipped through them. She heard another knock on the door. When she got to the fourth picture, she flipped it over to find the picture of the man at her door.

She went to the window and cracked it open about an inch. "Can I help you?" she asked.

"Casey, I'm Mark English." He looked at the window. "Jack sent me."

She turned on the porch light, and asked him to step back off the front porch before she cracked the door open. "What can I do for you? And why are you here so late?" She had her foot braced behind the door to stop him from pushing it open, and her hand on the dead bolt, ready to lock it in a moment's notice.

He looked down and sighed before he looked back up at her, "You're not making this easy, are you?"

"Making *what* easy?"

319

"May I come in? It isn't good for me to be out in the open. Look, I could have just broken in if I wanted to, but I didn't want to scare you."

She debated in her head for a moment before she asked him to go to the side of the house. There were shadows over there, but it was still out in the open.

While he went to the side of the house, she grabbed a large metal flashlight before she went outside. She closed and locked the front door behind her, sliding her keys into her pocket. Then she positioned the flashlight in a way that it could be used as a weapon if needed. Mark was a muscular guy; some people might even use the term 'ripped.' He looked to be about six foot tall. He had short blonde hair, dark brown eyes, and was about thirty-eight-years old.

When she walked around the corner of the house, he was leaning against the wall with his arms crossed, one foot braced on the wall. His eyes continuously darted around, as he kept an eye on any movement in the area. "Very good," he nodded in approval.

"What?"

"You passed the first test. You didn't open the door. You, I assume, checked the photos to see who I was since you disappeared. You also barely moved the curtain when you checked to see who was at the door. The only reason I noticed is because of what I do."

"Which is?" she questioned.

"You know full well what I do. I was part of your brother's unit."

"Was?"

He impatiently sighed. "He's been gone for over eight months."

Casey tested him, "Did O'Donnell send you to talk to me."

"O'Donnell's dead too. He died on an assignment about four weeks ago."

"How did you know where to find me?"

He gave her a look she had come to know all too well with her brother. "All right," she smiled. "I get it. What are you doing here, though? As you said, this isn't a good place to meet me."

"It's late, because I needed to know for sure you were alone. I've been following you all day, but this is the first time I've felt comfortable enough to approach you."

"What's up?"

"I know where you're about to go, and I'm asking you not to do it."

"What do you mean?"

"Don't go to Boise."

Her heart skipped a beat, as she stared at him wide-eyed.

"Casey, we know what you're doing half the time before you do. We've kept an eye on you for years. Now, I know Jack asked you to contact them, but for your own peace of mind I am asking you not to go."

"Why not?"

"Because you've had a hard year. Didn't your visit to the hospital show you that?"

"Jack asked me to do it. It was in his letter. That makes it a dying wish. Are you telling me that if he asked you to do something you wouldn't do it?"

"I would give my life for that man if he wasn't already gone. That's why I'm here. I swore to protect you, and I am doing just that. The other guys and I are worried about you going on this trip."

"I'm not going alone."

"We're aware of that."

"How?"

"We have our ways. We have also checked him out. Mr. McFadden has no record, and he has a true and loyal heart. He is not the reason for our concern."

"Then what is?"

"Your mental health. We're afraid it will throw you back to five years ago." He saw the color drain from her face. "Don't worry, Casey. We know. Jack told us everything so we knew what we were looking out for."

"Then you know he asked me to do it."

"I'm pretty sure he didn't mean for you to do it on the coattails of your lover's death!" Mark snapped.

Colonel O'Donnell suddenly appeared from behind the house. "Geez, Colonel! You've got to cut that out!" Mark smirked.

The Colonel smiled as he strolled over to where they were located.

"Um," she stared at him, as she went even paler than she already was, "You're-you're supposed to be...."

"I know," he said. "And in a way, I am."

She looked from him, to Mark, and back again. "You can see him, right?" she asked Mark.

"Of course," Mark responded.

"I saw Jack die before my very eyes. I know he's dead, right?" she asked.

"Yes," Colonel O'Donnell said.

She gulped before she point-blank asked Colonel O'Donnell, "Are you dead?"

He nodded. "In a way."

"Sir, you'd better explain yourself before I pass out again! I just got out of the hospital after passing out in front of my brother's grave, and almost passed out again in front of *your* gravesite! Explain *exactly* what 'in a way' means!" she demanded as her heart raced. Then she turned to Mark and asked, "Are you dead too?"

Mark nodded. "In a way."

"Someone had better start explaining!" she snapped, as her body shook with adrenaline.

"Can we go inside?" The Colonel glanced around the area. "We're still exposed out here."

She shook her head as she crossed her arms. "Not until you tell me what's going on."

He rested his hand on her arm. "Casey."

When he did, she felt tingles emit from his hand. She looked down at it, and then back up at him. "What's going on?" she demanded.

"Casey, this is really a bad place. Can we please go inside?" the Colonel asked.

She adamantly shook her head. "There's too much going on for me to just let you two into my house. I need to know what's going on first."

He sighed with his head down, before he looked back up at her, "The code name for our unit is 'A.N.G.E.L.'. There is Angel1, Angel2, etc. – Jack was Angel2."

"There are only four of us left," Mark added.

"Casey, can we please go in?" The Colonel nervously looked around. "There are too many ears around out here."

"Okay, give me a minute, and then go to the back, sliding glass doors. You'll have to hop the fence to do it."

"Thanks," he said, relieved.

When Casey went in the front door, she locked it behind her. Then she went through the house to open the sliding glass doors. When she did, the Colonel and Mark walked in with two other guys close behind them. "Um," Casey looked from Colonel to the other guys.

"They're fine," the Colonel said.

The two guys she didn't know, took the two chairs on either end of the couch, while the Colonel and Mark each took a seat on the couch.

"What's going on?" Casey asked, as she leaned on the doorway of her kitchen with her arms crossed.

The Colonel gestured toward them. "This is what's left of the squad."

Casey pulled a chair from the table and sat down across from Mark and the Colonel.

"You've already met Captain Mark English." The Colonel nodded toward Mark. "This is Major Derek Cruise." He nodded toward the man in the chair to his right.

Derek Cruise looked to be about thirty-nine-years-old. He was about five-foot-eleven and had blue eyes. His short, dark brown hair was mixed with gray. As he sat there, Casey noticed that he was fit, but not nearly as muscular at Mark.

He nodded toward the man on the left. "And this is Major Keith Mariano."

Keith Mariano was about thirty-seven years old. He had dark brown hair, brown eyes, a natural slight tan, and was about six-foot-two.

"Guys, as you all know, this is Casey Carter, Jack's sister," Colonel continued. The men nodded as they sat in their seats, on edge.

"What's going on, Colonel? You're dead, but you're not. Mark over there is in the same position. Are you two dead?" She asked Derek and Keith. They nodded, so she turned to the Colonel and demanded, "*Explain*!"

"In doing what we do, we need to not exist."

"That was cryptic. Mind clearing it up a bit?" she snapped. "I'm not in the mood for games."

He sighed, as he shook his head with a smile on his face. "You're amusing. I give you that."

"Colonel," she warned.

He looked up at her and said, "We aren't here. This never happened."

"Fine! Just explain!"

"We do work for the government, specifically special ops in the Air Force."

"Tell me something I *don't* know." She crossed her arms in a huff.

"We're not allowed to exist in order to do what we do. We go in and out of the law all the time. We go into places that no one should ever see. We are exposed to things that if the average person saw it, it would give them nightmares. If we told you exactly what we did, it could literally put your life in danger."

"Fine. I get the cloak-and-dagger action. Now, explain why I shouldn't go to Boise."

"Because it could pose a danger to you and to her," Mark said.

"Why?"

"Right now, she's protected, and we're watching you, so you're protected."

She narrowed her eyes at him. "From *what*?"

"There are powers out there that our governments won't acknowledge, but they do exist. These powers mostly want money and information, and will do anything to get it."

"Okay, you're beginning to make sense. Now, what does this have to do with me?"

"First off, you're sitting on over two million dollars," Keith said, intertwining in hands in front of him, as he rested his elbows on his knees. "That's the first problem."

"The second," Derek sat forward and looked intently at her, "is who your brother was."

"So, how am I to know who to trust?" she asked.

"Don't tell anyone about the money," Derek, said. "The only thing they need to know is that Jack left you some money. Tomorrow when the banks open, take all but two-hundred fifty thousand, and spread the rest out in different banks in the same increments until there is under two-hundred-and-fifty-thousand. Then put the remainder in a checking account. That way it's not all in one place."

"That's smart," she agreed.

"With it spread out, it will lower your value to them," Derek added.

"Now, as far as your trip to Boise, please don't go. If you want to contact them by letter or phone, go ahead," Mark suggested. "They know you're out there. If you go, they could follow you, and that will paint a target on that little girl. We know you. You wouldn't forgive yourself if anything happened to her."

She nodded. "That's true."

"Now, as far as your camping trip in a couple of weeks, that's fine. Just be careful," Keith added. "There will be one of us around you at all times. So, if you see us don't freak out."

"Why am I suddenly under guard?" she asked. "Was there a threat?"

"In a way, yes," the Colonel said. "There's something stirring up, and the information you have could put you in danger."

"What information is that?" she asked.

"It's in the stuff from the house in the storage shed."

"How do I know I can trust *you*?" she challenged.

Surprised, he asked, "Haven't we proven by now what we know?"

"You said there are other powers that have the same access, right? How do I know you're not telling me to move the money just so you can kidnap me in the morning? How do I know you're not going to break into the storage shed while I'm gone, and take whatever it is you guys are after?"

"As far as your second question, it's safer in the storage shed right now," Mark explained.

"As far as the first question, if I was going to take the money I could have posed as Jack and emptied the account before you even knew about it. I had the passbook, his signature, and the exact amount." The Colonel shrugged. "Jack put that money in there for you, not for us. We're just trying to protect you…and it."

She put her chin on her hand, deep in thought. "Why am I just now finding out about this?"

"Those photos should have told you that we've been watching you for years."

"While your discretion is appreciated, it's misguided here," Derek pointed out. "We're on your side. We've been protecting you for years. We just wanted you to be aware of it, so you wouldn't be paranoid if you caught sight of us."

"If you guys have been protecting me, what happened in Columbia?" She asked the Colonel.

"That was Marcos's assignment," he said somberly.

"Okay. And *who* is *that*?" she asked.

"Marcos was Jack's partner. He was weak from being sick, but he still wanted to pull his weight," Keith explained. "Columbia was his last assignment. He died while he was down there." Wide-eyed, she gulped, as he continued, "When you were attacked, he was dying in his hotel room. When you called Jack, we knew something happened to him. His job was to protect you, and if something happened to you, then something had to have happened to him."

"We scrambled after we got your call," Derek continued. "We had to get Jack cleared for his leave-of-absence, and get our behinds down there to find out what happened. While Jack went to you, the rest of us looked for Marcos and found him dead in his room."

"So," she put her hand up for him to stop, "if I'm following you right, you're telling me that everywhere I ever went in the world one of you guys was following me?"

"Yes," the Colonel said. "We would trade out so one person was watching you at all times, while the rest of us were on assignments."

"So, in doing that, you probably saved me from getting hurt, with the exception of Columbia."

"Yes," Mark said.

"When did this start?" she asked.

"From the day Jack first became an A.N.G.E.L.," Mark explained. "Jack was the only one with immediate family, so we took turns keeping track of you. That way his mind was at rest when he was in the field."

"That makes sense," she said. Then she looked at the Colonel and said, "That brings me to the question of, if you knew what I looked like, then what took you so long to get the box to me?"

He cringed. "Part of that was timing."

"Why didn't you just level with me at the cemetery?" she asked.

"Because we were being watched."

"The MP?"

"Yes."

"I talked to the MP."

"What did you tell him?"

"That I needed to talk to you. He called into the base to contact you, but Quinton said you were dead. He wanted to know how I knew you, and I told him while we talked."

"Everything is still in your box, right?" the Colonel asked.

"Yes."

"You're sure?"

"Yes."

"He saw the coat, right?"

"Yeah." She narrowed her eyes at him. "Why?"

"I wanted him to. I wanted him to know we were looking out for you."

"Why?"

"Because he'll pass the word."

She shook her head. "I don't get it."

"You're not going to understand everything. Just trust us."

"Can I?"

"Yes," he said, confidently.

"What's the code word?" She crossed her arms as she sat back in her seat. She and Jack had a code they used in emails. For example, any conversation with the word 'stilts' meant that he was working hard in a tough place. Any conversation with the word 'waves' meant that things were good and he was safe. If the conversation had the word 'shell' in it, it meant to stay on your toes there is trouble around. If it had the word 'dolphin' in it, it meant to go ahead and relax and have fun. If it had the word 'koala', it meant that she was in trouble, and the word 'tiger' meant that he was in trouble. The word 'strategy' meant to trust the person saying it, while the word 'snickers' meant not to trust them, and so on. They set it up after she was attacked in Columbia, because Jack realized she was a target, and that they and their communications were being monitored.

"The koala bear at the zoo likes to play games." The Colonel looked her square in the eyes. "He enjoys the shell game in particular, mainly due to the strategy involved,"

She sat up in her chair, studying him for a moment, before she asked, "What about the tiger?"

"He's playing with the dolphins in the waves."

She looked at him for a couple tense minutes before she finally agreed, "All right."

"All right, what?" the Colonel tested her.

"All right, I'll trust you. If you knew the code words, then Jack trusted you enough to not only give them to you but their meaning too. He could have purposely messed them up and I would have known, but you used them all correctly."

The Colonel smiled in approval. "He trained you very well."

"If you need to contact me, and don't want to do it face to face, then text me with a code."

"I am Angel1, Jack was Angel2, Mark is Angel3, Derek is Angel4, and Keith is Angel5. I'm telling you this, because if you get contact from any of us, those are our individual IDs," the Colonel explained. "You are going to be Angel7."

"Going to assume Marcos was Angel6?"

"Yes."

"Gotcha," she said, as they all stood up.

She walked them back to the sliding-glass door. After they left, she let out a sigh of relief. She knew she would have to be more on her toes from this point forward. As she went back to the living room, her cell phone got a text from Jesse. He said 'good night,' and confirmed their lunch for eleven the next morning. She told him she would be late, because she had to take care of some business.

Chapter 17

Duel Mindset

The next morning, she ended up going to eight different banks, separating the money among them. She felt better with the money spread around, and was grateful to the A.N.G.E.L.s for suggesting it.

After that, she met with Jesse for lunch, and then they went to a movie. He dropped her off at her house around five that night before he went home.

Once again, around nine-thirty Casey got a knock on her door. "Really?" She sighed as she got up off the couch. When she pulled the curtain back, she saw Mark standing there. She slightly opened the window, and told him to go to the back.

When she opened the sliding glass door, she said, "This is getting to be a really bad habit."

"Just checking in with you," he said, sitting on the couch.

She sat in the chair near the end of the couch where he was sitting. "I'm fine. You guys don't have to hold my hand."

"The Colonel said he had a rather disturbing conversation with you at Jack's grave the other day," Mark said.

"You can't be serious! Do you guys tell each other everything?"

"When it's something as important as your relationship with God, then yes."

"Are you a Christian?"

"Yes. I found Jesus through the Colonel about ten years ago in the field. We were in Cuba at the time. We were being held prisoner in a rebel camp when I just about lost it. They tortured both of us, but got nothing. We were there for about two weeks when the Colonel sat in the shed, singing. I was furious. How could he be singing in the middle of that? He said he had a peace within him. I wanted that peace. I wanted to feel free, even though I was being held captive. Well, long story short, I accepted Jesus as my Savior in that little shed in the middle of the forest in Cuba, and haven't steered from Him since. God is a God of love, Casey."

"I don't know. While I appreciate your concern, I'm angry with Him."

"How can you be?"

She looked at him, furious. "He took everything from me!"

"He gave everything *for* you!" Mark shot back. "Jesus gave His life for you. He sacrificed just so you could be with Him in Heaven. Isn't that what you told Jack?"

"I did," she admitted. "But that was before He took Jack and Mac away."

"Casey," he rested his hand on her knee, "you're being tested. God has something really big in store for you, or He wouldn't be taking you through this test. You *are* strong. You have a tremendous heart. God loves you and knows what you are made of."

"Then He might want to check the owner's manual on me. In case you missed it, I was in the hospital, remember?"

Mark sighed, shaking his head. "I've watched you for years. I have seen you grow up and turn into this amazingly beautiful woman. You purposely go into fires to help other people. Do you understand how much courage that takes?"

"Yes."

"Think about it this way: the fires you go into are nothing compared to the fires of Hell. Jesus went down there for three days, only to come back out with –"

"I know the story," she cut him off.

"Do you understand why though?"

"Yes. I fought to trust Him for a long time. That's the part that infuriates me. I trusted Him, only to have Him rip away any security I had in this world."

"Maybe He wants you to rely solely on Him. Maybe He wants you to feel your security is in Him, and not in people. Maybe, just maybe, He wants you to fully trust Him."

"I do." She sighed. "Well, I did."

"Casey, God loves you. He really does. He wants you to trust Him again."

"How can I? I don't feel comfortable trusting anyone right now. If I get close to them, are they going to die?"

Stunned, he asked, "Where did that come from?"

"My parents? Jack? Mac? I loved all of them, and they died."

"You don't seriously think you did that, do you?"

"Sometimes I wonder," she admitted.

"Casey, maybe Mac was with you to show you something. God may yet give you another man to share your life with."

"Why? So, He can take that person away too?"

"You're reading this all wrong. Mac's time was done. Jack's time was done."

"Well, I'm kind of tired of people being done when they get close to me. Am I a curse or something?"

"No. Definitely not! Casey, you're not in a good mind set right now. Your mind is clouded, and it's going in the wrong direction."

"The only direction I can go in, is what I can see."

"Not true." He shook his head. "Look, imagine this table is a map of your life. We can look down and see where you start and where you finish, right?"

"Right." She nodded, as she imagined the map in front of her.

"Okay, so you're walking down this path in a maze of twists and turns. There are many paths you can take. You often don't know which one to choose, but you have to make a choice. In making that choice, are you going listen to someone who has a bird's eye view of the map, or someone who is walking in the maze with you?"

"I would think the person looking down would have a better idea of the safer route."

"Then why aren't you asking Him which direction to take? You've gone to your Chief. You've gone to Jesse. You've even gone to Jack, who, by the way, can't even answer you. You have yet to go to the One who is looking down at the map, to tell you which route is the safest. You need to ask God. He's trying to guide you in the safest direction, but you're too angry to listen."

"Why should I trust someone who took everything away?"

"Maybe He took it away, because there is something better on the horizon."

"Maybe," she said, deep in thought.

"I can come back on the nights you're off, if you want me to. My shift for watching you starts at eight for now."

"You can," she agreed, as they stood up. "I appreciate the extra ear to listen."

*   *   *

Over the next two weeks, Jesse and Casey had some long talks when they were on and off shift. They were often joking around or talking when they were at the station, or going out to lunch when they were off work.

Her talks with Mark on the evenings she was off were of a different nature. While Jesse helped her by reminding her of Jack and Mac, Mark helped her remember Jesus, God, and the Holy Spirit. She had a feeling of peace when she talked to Mark. They shared many stories, thoughts, and ideas. Casey found herself looking forward to getting a knock on her sliding glass doors at around nine-thirty the nights she was home. Often when he left, she had to reprimand herself for enjoying his company so much when Mac just died a month ago. Casey didn't know what to do with her feelings.

About a week and a half after they started talking, Casey finally got on her knees in prayer. She poured out her heart to God. She yelled, got angry, frustrated, and even sobbed. She broke at her core. She didn't want to disrespect Mac's memory, but she also wasn't sure what to do about Mark. She was also confused on whether to trust God again or not.

*　　*　　*

The day of the campout finally came. Casey was excited, as she met the others at the station that morning.

"So, you guys headed out?" Hunter came out with his partner, Allen, when they saw the crowd gathered.

"Yep. You guys coming out tomorrow?" Casey asked.

"Yeah. We'll probably be out there around eleven or twelve."

"Would you guys mind bringing some hamburger for burgers?" she asked. "We'll get the condiments and buns."

"We can do that," Allen said. "We'll grab hot dogs for the kids, too."

"Can you bring some potato salad?" Jesse asked, as he went around to the passenger side door, while the other members and their families pulled out of the parking lot for the mountain.

"Yeah." Allen chuckled. "We'll get you some potato salad."

"Great!" He grinned. "Thanks!"

"All right, have a safe trip, and we'll see you guys tomorrow." Hunter waved, and they turned to go back inside.

"Guess we're stopping by the store for hot dog and hamburger buns." Casey started the Jeep.

"That, along with ketchup, mustard, mayo, and relish," Jesse said.

"Yep." She nodded, deep in the thought regarding the events of the last two weeks. After a couple minutes of driving to the store in silence, Casey said, "Um, I don't know if you want to talk to Chief or not, but I'm not going to Boise. I changed my mind."

"Why?"

"I don't want to see her. I'll write them or contact them by phone, but it will hurt too much to see her," she said, as they pulled into the parking lot.

"Casey, we had an agreement to go to Boise, but now you don't want to go. What's going on? Did something happen?"

She shut the Jeep off. Debating on how to explain it to him, she finally said, "I have a lot going on in my head right now."

"I know. Part of it is taking care of the *one thing* Jack asked you to take care of. What was that, eight or nine months ago?"

"Yeah, something like that."

"You also have that storage shed to clean out."

"I know."

"Casey," he rested his hand on her shoulder, "I think you need to get away from here. I don't care where we go. We just need to go. If it's not Boise, then pick somewhere else. You've had too much go on over the last year, and you need a break. Frankly, I just need a vacation."

"All right," she agreed. "You're right about that. We both *do* need a vacation. What if we talk about where we're going over the next couple of days?"

"Sounds good." With a smile, he added, "Right now, we need to go shopping and get our behinds to the camp site for some fun!"

"Let's go," she agreed, and they got out of the Jeep for the store.

*   *   *

When they got to the mountain, Casey set her pup tent up next Tommy and Sally's (they had gotten married a couple months ago), with Jesse and Jay sharing a tent on the other side of her. She felt safe tucked in between them.

Casey enjoyed a relaxing day of sitting in the shallow water, looking around at all the families. Some were swimming, some were hiking, some were playing basketball, some were playing volleyball in the sand pit, and some were just standing or sitting around talking. It was very serene.

As she looked around, she caught sight of someone in the trees across the lake from her. She stared at the movement for several minutes, wondering if she in fact did see someone. The more she looked in that direction, the more it looked like a bunch of trees and bushes.

She dried off with her towel, keeping an eye on where everyone else was through the campground. The main person she was concerned with was Jesse, since he seemed to be keeping the closest tabs on her. Jesse was in the middle of a basketball game, so she knew she could slip away.

She changed into jeans, a t-shirt, and her hiking boots, before she grabbed her camera, so she could get some scenic shots while she was out. She nonchalantly walked around, periodically taking photos, as she kept an eye on where she saw the movement. When she got to the basketball court, Jesse nodded toward her. She smiled back, but continued to walk around after she took a couple of photos.

It took her a good ten minutes until she got to the tree line of the woods. She made her way around to the other side of the lake in the shadows of the trees, giving her eyes a chance to adjust to the movements around her.

She glanced at the campsite one more time. Then, she ducked in. Walking about ten yards, she stopped and allowed her eyes to adjust to the tree coverage.

She reached into her pocket and pulled out her pocketknife. She flipped the blade out, bracing it in her hand in case she needed it for defense. She found a spot right along the shoreline and tucked her camera into the nook of a rock where she would remember. Then, she went back into the woods again.

In the dark thickness of the woods, the more she looked, the less she saw. Everything seemed to blend in the shadows. When she got to the spot where she saw the figure, she looked toward the lake and sized up where she sat in the lake, compared to where she stood.

It took her a couple more minutes before she got to the exact spot. When she did, she saw several boot prints. They were the same size boots, so she guessed there was only one person. When she saw the prints and knew she did, in fact, see someone. Her heart raced, as her body was instantly on edge. She heard every sound and saw every movement around her.

She crouched in the bushes to look for any sign of movement. It took her a moment before she saw movement about fifteen feet to her left. She stared at it without moving a muscle. It was a slight shift in the bushes, but she was sure she saw it.

She tightened her fist around the knife as she slightly raised it. She kept her eyes steady on the movement, not even looking away for a second. She sat there for several more minutes before she slowly got up. She stayed in a crouched position, moving from tree to tree, keeping an eye on where she saw the movement.

As she stood, her back to a tree, she suddenly saw a set of hands come around. One wrapped around her body holding her arms down, while the other one went over her mouth.

She screamed as loud as she could! A few birds in the trees took off, but the muffled scream could only be heard inside a twenty-foot range.

"Quiet!" the man said in a low tone.

She froze. The fact that the situation was real, scared her worse than if it was her imagination!

"I'm going to let you go, and you're not going to make a sound, right?" the man said up next to her ear. She didn't move or say a word. "Casey, it's Mark. I need you to not freak out or scream again. Do you understand?"

She let out a sigh of relief as she nodded.

"Good. I feel you relaxing. On the count of three. One…two…three," he said and let her go.

Casey took several steps forward while she sucked in a big breath of air. Then she spun around and hissed, "What are you doing here?"

He came around the tree and rested his foot on it, while he stuffed his hands in his pockets. He was decked out from head to toe in camouflage. Even his face was painted.

He smiled as he said, "Just doin' my job, ma'am."

"Well, you are terrible at it!" she snapped. "I saw you!"

"Yes…and no," he clarified. "You *thought* you saw movement, only because I wanted you to know I was here."

She rolled her eyes. "Yeah, right."

"Did you know I was in the store with you earlier?"

She looked at him in wide-eyed surprise for a moment before she slowly shook her head.

"Did you know I was with you in all of the banks a couple of weeks ago?"

She narrowed her eyes at him as she put her hands on her hips. "Have you been following me?"

"Yes."

"Why?"

"Because I'm doing my job. I thought the Colonel made that clear."

"So, one of you guys will shadow me at *all* times?"

"Yes."

"To what extent?"

"To the extent that we will know what you're doing even before you do." He shrugged. "That's part of our job description."

"So, I don't get *any* freedom?"

"Don't look at it like that."

"How am I *supposed* to look at it?"

"Just look at us as your guardian angels."

"That brings me to another question."

"What's that?"

"If you guys are supposed to be dead, then why are the dates on Jack's, O'Donnell's, and *your* grave so recent? Why weren't they earlier?"

Mark smiled as he shook his head. "You don't miss a thing, do you?"

Crossing her arms, she impatiently tapped her foot.

"All right." He sighed. "Jack's is the actual date of his death. I supposedly died on an assignment about six months ago. And, as for the Colonel, he was in the listed ranks up until a month and a half ago."

"Huh?"

"Everyone else has been dead, according to the government, for over fifteen to twenty years, which I'm sure you found out when you went to our graves last week." he challenged her.

Her jaw dropped. She went to the gravesites at about six o'clock one morning last week to check out the dates of death on their gravestones. It took her over two hours to find them all. She did notice that Marcos's was about five years ago on the date of the attack.

"As we physically die, the dates on our gravestones get changed, just as you saw on Marcos and Jack's graves."

"Then why is yours six months ago, and the Colonel's only six weeks ago?"

"Because they think we died on assignments."

"Why?"

"The other two of us are going to die on their next assignments."

"Isn't that going A.W.O.L.?" she asked suspiciously.

"It's safer for all of us that way. We can operate in the shadows better if no one knows we're alive."

"What if someone gets sick or injured?"

"Oh, Casey," he chuckled. "Getting fake IDs for the hospital is a piece of cake. We have a stack of those, along with the myriad of passports we used for previous missions. We will be fine."

"Why are you guys doing this now?"

"Because the threat has gotten hotter. We're doing it for our safety."

"Does the government know you're doing it?"

"In a way," he said. Then he smiled in amusement, as he asked, "Any more questions?"

"Nope."

"Good. Then go play like a dolphin in the waves knowing I've got your back." He used the code.

"Thanks." She smiled and gave him a hug.

"What's that for?" he asked in surprise. He hugged her again before he let her go.

"For taking care of me." She shrugged. "You've been a great help to me over the last couple of weeks." She cocked her head to the side as asked, "When was the last time someone hugged you?"

"For real?" He questioned. He left his hands on her waist while she rested hers on his shoulders.

"Yeah."

"When I left for basic training. It was from my mom," he admitted. He had a look of hurt in his eyes. "After that, to everyone I was dead."

"Oh, Mark!" Her heart broke for him. "I'm so sorry."

"That's why we look after you so closely. We don't have any family. Jack was the only one who had someone he had to take care of. To us, you were like our little sister. You represented family to us. That's why we knew something big happened to Marcos when you were attacked. We would give our lives to protect you."

"The stakes are raised, eh?" She said in understanding, taking a step back. Then she looked up at him and asked, "Was the money only from Jack? That seems like an awful lot of money from just one person. I don't think the military paid him *that* well."

"No. We all added to it," he conceded.

"Well, there are eight different accounts our money has been spread through. When you guys need it, let me know."

"*Our* money?"

"We're a family, right?" She smiled. She felt less alone knowing that she was part of a family again with the A.N.G.E.L.s. She would do anything to help them.

He smiled as he hugged her again. "Trust is hard for all of us, huh?"

"Yep. I have a feeling we're going to need each other more and more in these upcoming days. Now that I know who my guardian angels are, it helps me to know I can help them."

He looked at her as he touched her face. "Your skin is so soft."

She stared at him in shock. She felt something stir deep inside her. How could she already have feelings for a guy she just met two weeks ago?

"I watched you over the years, and admire the woman you've turned out to be."

"Thank you." She couldn't look away from his dark, chocolate brown eyes. The various colors of green, black, and brown face paint covered his face, as his eyes looked deep within her soul. She often longed to see them, along with his brilliant smile each day she was off work.

Neither of them moved for a couple of moments before he hugged her again. "This feels good."

"I know."

"You have to go. They'll be looking for you soon."

"I know." She took a half-step away. Truth be told, she didn't want him to leave. "Thank you."

He looked into her eyes for a moment, before she watched him disappear into the woods. Then she absentmindedly went to look for her camera, daydreaming about Mark.

When she found the rock, she pulled her camera out and headed for camp, feeling more relaxed knowing he was looking out for her. She felt safe. She didn't feel alone anymore knowing the A.N.G.E.L.s were watching her. It was a nice feeling to be a part of a family she never knew she had. Were her feelings for Mark just that though? Could she be reading more into this than there was between them?

"Casey!" Jesse called, interrupting her thoughts. "Where have you been?" He looked concerned.

"I was taking a hike while shooting photos." She shrugged as she walked over to him on the basketball court. "It's a beautiful day."

"We're going to take a hike here in a bit. Interested?" Will asked.

"Sure," she said. "We should eat and fill our water bottles first."

"Good idea," Jesse agreed.

After lunch, they took the trail that headed out to the mountain ridge where Casey accepted the Lord as her Savior. Casey fought the flashbacks of Mac, as she scrambled down the ledge with the others.

"How are you doing?" Jesse quietly asked her as they sat down on the rock.

"Doing okay," she said, staring out at the canyon before her.

"I can see it."

"See what?"

"The memories going through your head."

"Are you two going to whisper the whole time?" Brennon scowled. "It's like you guys have a secret. Want to share?"

"Just talking." Jesse shrugged. He sat back and crossed his arms.

"Well, you two have been 'just talking' a lot lately," he pointed out.

Jesse huffed. "Jealous?"

"They're close. Get a grip, Hanson." Kim rolled her eyes.

"What's *your* problem?" he snapped at her.

"I'm just tired of you complaining about it. No one else seems to have a problem with it."

"They do too," he said. "They just don't say anything."

"Why would anyone have a problem with us being close?" Casey asked.

"Probably because we just buried your fiancé about a month ago, and you're already joined at the hip with him."

"Hanson!" Jesse snapped, almost in a yell.

Casey looked at him, appalled.

"How *dare* you!" Jesse growled.

"It's true. I dare you to say different," Brennon challenged. "Where one is, the other one is not far behind."

"Jeff and Jay are like that, but you don't accuse them of anything inappropriate," Casey pointed out.

"Hold up!" Jeff put his hands up to stop the conversation. "Jay and I *are not* gay!"

"We know that." Casey rolled her eyes, as Kim and Sally giggled. "The point is, Jesse and I are not in any way, shape, or form, romantically involved either."

"Jack made me her brother on his deathbed," Jesse explained. "We're close because of that."

"And Kara's affair had nothing to do with how close you two are, huh?" Brennon challenged.

Jesse looked like he wanted to punch Brennon. He probably would have if they were not separated by six other people and on the ridge of a mountain.

"She said it was because you were either spending time at the station or with her," Brennon said.

Jesse glared at him. "How would *you* know?"

Brennon stood in front of Jesse with his arms crossed. "*Who* do you think she had the affair with?"

Jeff and Jay immediately jumped on Jesse, who went to lunge at Brennon. There was a momentary struggle to control Jesse, before Will got up and pulled Brennon up the path to a safer spot. Kim followed them up, and together they both forced Brennon back to camp.

It wasn't until they were out of sight, that Jeff asked Casey, "Is it clear?"

She stood up and looked over the ledge. Brennon was nowhere in sight, so she nodded.

"Good." Jeff looked back down at Jesse. "We're going to let you go, and you're going to go back over there and sit on the rock so we can talk. Got it?"

Jesse didn't move. You could see the anger in his eyes. Every muscle in his body was tense.

"Jess?" Jay asked after another minute of silence.

Tommy and Sally stayed beside Casey. They hadn't breathed since Brennon's confession.

"I will *never* forgive him for that!" Jesse seethed.

"Let's talk about this, okay?" Jeff tried to calm him down. "We're going to get up, and you're going to go over and sit by Casey. Can you do that for us?"

Jess looked at Tommy, Sally, and Casey, before he turned back to Jeff and Jay and nodded. Jeff and Jay got off him, and Jesse slowly sat up.

"Jess?" Casey asked. "Can I come down?"

He nodded, so she went over to him and gave him a hug. When she hugged him, she felt the anger inside of him. Jesse and Kara were dating for almost two years before it happened.

"Come on over to the rock, okay?" Casey coaxed.

He shook his head.

"Please? We're too close to the ledge here. I'm pretty sure if Jeff and Jay didn't jump on you, that you and Brennon would have gone over the side."

Jesse stared at Casey for several tense moments before he said, "I loved her."

"I know," she nodded in understanding, "just as much as I loved Mac. That's another bond we share."

He sighed before he turned to the others, and asked, "Why would one of my brothers do this to me?"

"She did it too," Sally point out. She was furious with Kara. They had been best friends for over five years.

"But he had an option of saying no, and he *obviously* doesn't regret it." Jesse got off the ground. A combination of hurt, shock, confusion, and fury churned inside him. "Why would he do that to me?"

"Jealousy is an ugly beast," Tommy said, as he and Sally came down off the rock. "He has liked Casey since she came to the station. He was beside himself when she and Mac started courting. Then, watching the two of you bonding more and more over the last several months, becoming closer than you already were, you could see the jealousy raging inside him. I wouldn't be surprised if he got together with Kara and they planned it."

"But, we have a brother/sister relationship. Why couldn't Kara see that? I would do anything for my family."

"We know that. Brennon can be pretty persuasive though," Jeff said. "I know he planted that seed in my head too."

"About us?" Casey asked, stunned.

"Yep. There were several of us keeping an eye on you two. He was trying to get something on either one of you, to get one of you guys either fired or transferred," Jay added.

"Why would he do that?" Casey asked.

"Probably because he wanted you for himself." He shrugged. "He put it by us as the rule was being broken. Out of fairness, it was our duty to make sure the rule still held."

Casey whistled in astonishment. "Wow."

"We need to get back and figure this thing out." Jeff reminded them, "We have to go to bed sometime here in the next couple of hours, and I would rather not do it with all that rage stirring around."

"Do you think you two can have a civil conversation?" Jay asked Jesse.

"I doubt it." He shook his head. "Maybe I'll just go home."

"You can't!" Jay and Casey objected at the same time.

"You've got my house!" Jay referred to the tent.

"And you came in with me," Casey pointed out.

"Besides the fact that we'd miss your smiling face," Sally added. "Come on, stay?"

He looked at them for a moment, before he finally relented, "All right."

"We have to talk to Brennon. Think you can stay here with Casey while we do? I think we need some referees before you two get together again," Jeff said.

"Yeah," he agreed.

After they left down the path, Jesse went over and sat down on the rock. He closed his eyes as he crossed his arms. Then he stretched his legs out in front of him and took a deep breath.

"Want some company?" Casey asked.

"Yeah, come here." He patted the seat next to him. When   she sat down next him, he said, "I love you like a sister."

"I know."

"While I do love you, it's not the same love I had for Kara."

"I know. I feel the same way."

"There's nothing I wouldn't do for you."

"Same here."

They sat in silence for several minutes as they stared out at the view in front of them. Casey saw the eagle fly by while they sat. It landed in a nest on the mountain across from them, which was nestled into the side of a ledge, and fed its babies. Casey sighed before she asked, "Jesse, are you a Christian?"

"Not yet. I'm getting there, though."

"What does that mean?"

"I'm close," he admitted. "But with everything that has happened, I'm struggling. There are times where I know I need to, because you are never guaranteed a tomorrow. Then I get angry when I see what you're going through, knowing you're a Christian. You were right. Why would a God of love do that to you?"

"Jess?"

"What?"

"I'm struggling," she admitted.

"Me too, Case. Me too," he said, and they looked back out at the mountains again.

*   *   *

It took the others a couple of hours before they came back to get Jesse and Casey. In the meantime, they got to watch a spectacular sunset. They didn't say anything, as their own thoughts clouded their minds. As the sun went down behind the mountain, to Casey it was as if God was saying 'let it go, tomorrow is a new day.'

She struggled with her anger toward God. In the grand scheme of things, she knew she could not live without Him. In the immediate time, though, she fought within herself as to how she could trust a God…a Father…who would take away every love she had in her life.

What the Colonel said at Jack's grave struck deep within her. She did not want to disrespect God, Jesus, Mac, or Jack. She was

352

angry and hurting though. In seeing Jesse's reaction, and feeling the rage, she did not want that in her life anymore. She longed for the peace she had even up to a month ago. She wanted her Father back.

She took the time while they watched the sun slowly crawl beyond the mountains to ask God for forgiveness for her anger and hatred. She asked him to replace the anxiety with peace. She asked for her life of confidence in Him back.

* * *

When they got back to camp, Jeff, Tommy, Sally, Kim, Jay, Jesse, and Brennon went into Tommy and Sally's tent to talk. As soon as Brennon saw Jesse, the yelling started and Casey left the campfire.

It put her too much on edge to hear people yell, so she just went to her tent, changed, and lay down, lost in her own thoughts. It took over three hours before it calmed down in the tent next to hers enough for her to fall asleep.

* * *

The zipper on her tent slowly opened, waking her up. It had to be about three or four in the morning.

She slowly reached into her pocket and pulled her knife out as a foot came into her tent. Her heart raced, but she did not dare move. As long as the person did not know she was aware of them, she had the upper hand.

"Case?" She heard Mark's voice as he poked his head in.

"My word! This is daring!" she whispered in shock.

"Come outside," he said, before ducking back out of the tent.

Casey scrambled out of her sleeping bag. She cautiously climbed out of her tent, looking in every direction. She didn't zip it back up, because she wanted to be able to slip back in without unzipping it.

He grabbed her wrist and pulled her to the tree line, his eyes continuously darting in every direction. He took her there, so he could see what was going on at camp without anyone seeing them.

"What's going on?" she whispered.

He didn't say anything. He just grabbed her face and kissed her. She reached up and rested her hands on his wrists as she joined him in the kiss. The passion, electricity, and excitement behind the kiss made her not want to stop.

Several minutes later, Mark took a step back. He looked at her with a lot of intensity, as he rested his hands on her face. "I'm sorry. I just couldn't hold it in any longer."

"Where did…? That was…wow," Casey stammered, as she rested against the tree to catch her breath.

He took a step forward, bending so he was eye level to her, as he said in a low voice, "I have had feelings for you for years, but you were untouchable. You were my assignment. You are not supposed to get emotionally close to your assignments. But as we got closer over the last couple of weeks, and then you hugged me today…." He sighed. "Feeling you so close to me…I'm sorry. We don't have to mention this again, if you don't –"

She cut him off by kissing him again. He ran his hands tightly down her sides to her waist, as he strongly returned the kiss. "Is this…possible?" Casey asked in between kisses.

"If we're careful…yes….There will be times…when you won't see me…maybe for weeks at a time….You think…you can handle that?" he asked in between kisses as well.

"Yes," she said…and the kiss exploded!

She wrapped her arms tightly around his neck, as he pulled her closer to him. Their bodies tingled. Their thoughts were lost in each other's kisses.

"Wow!" Casey said as she breathed heavily. She leaned against the tree to catch her breath.

He looked up at her and admitted, "I've waited for so long. Jack and I even talked about it."

"What did he say?"

"He said if circumstances were different, he would whole-heartedly approve. The problem was that you weren't to know we existed."

"And now that I do?"

He looked at her and very seriously asked, "Can you lead two different lives?"

COMING SOON:

Book 2 of the Holy Flame Trilogy:
EXTRICATION

Unbeknownst to Casey, things had gotten 'hot' around her. The Angels have now stepped in where Jack and Mac could no longer be. They were now providing safety and security for her on a twenty-four-hour basis. But, did she find something more than just security within their ranks?

Isaiah 41:10:

[10] So do not fear, for I am with you; do not be dismayed, for I am your God. I will strengthen you and help you; I will uphold you with my righteous right hand.

To learn more about C.J. Peterson, you can find her online at:
http://cjpetersonwrites.com/

'While the stories are fiction, the journey is real!'

Books in the Holy Flame Trilogy.

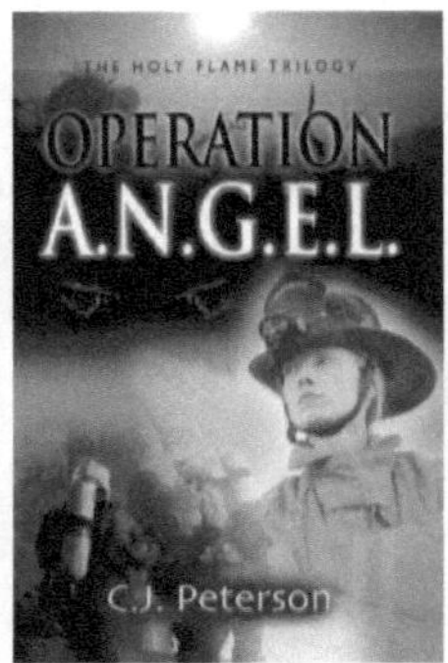

See what the other A.N.G.E.L.s have been assigned -

Books in the Grace Restored Series

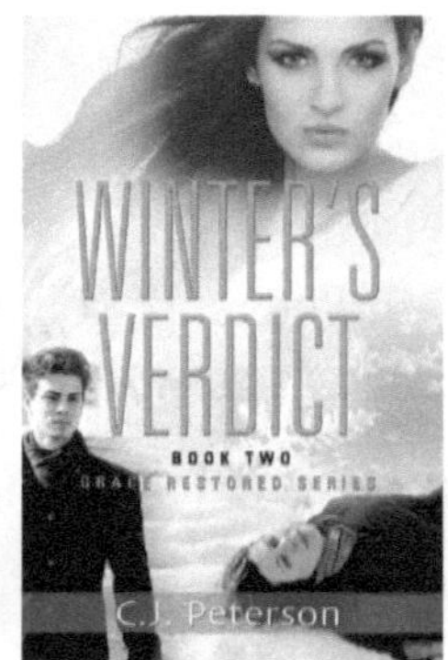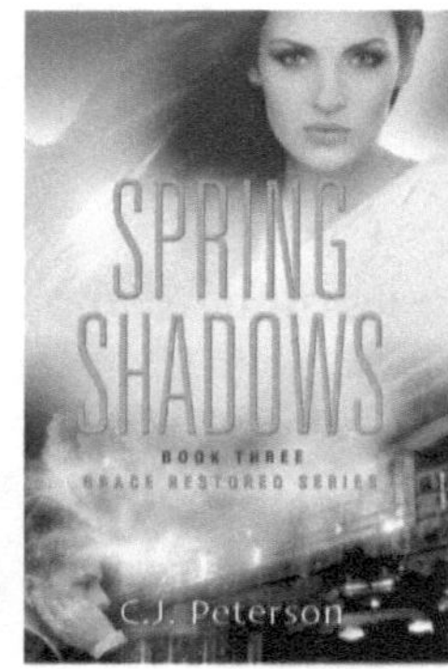

C.J. Peterson

The next generation is taking over. In the Award-Winning Divine Legacy Series.

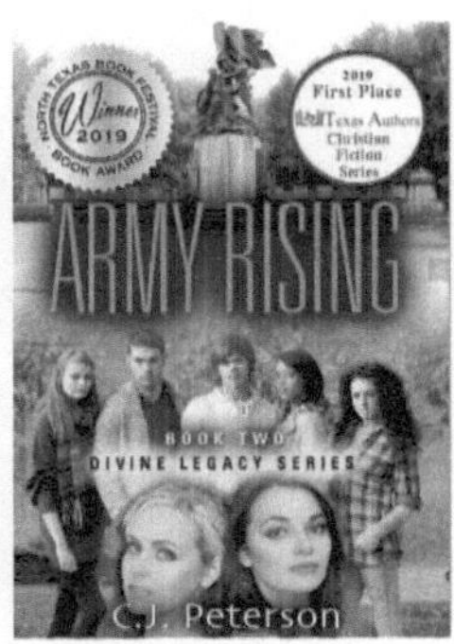